NEW STORIES
FROM THE SOUTH

The Year's Best, 2009

NEW STORIES
FROM THE SOUTH

The Year's Best, 2009

Selected from U.S. magazines
by MADISON SMARTT BELL with
KATHY PORIES

with an introduction by Madison Smartt Bell

Algonquin Books of Chapel Hill

Published by
ALGONQUIN BOOKS OF CHAPEL HILL
Post Office Box 2225
Chapel Hill, North Carolina 27515-2225

a division of
WORKMAN PUBLISHING
225 Varick Street
New York, New York 10014

CONTENTS

Madison Smartt Bell

INTRODUCTION
Down in the Flood

I made my first trip to New Orleans in the late seventies, and stayed a week or ten days or so, but much as I loved it I didn't get back there for a couple of decades and then just for one night, though I managed to visit many of the same places I had been the first time. My gig was in the Garden District and when it was done I walked back through the long summer twilight along Tchoupitoulas Street, toting a sawed-off Strat on one shoulder and a Pignose amp in the opposite hand, stopping at a bar or so along the way and feeling, never mind the dripping, suffocating heat, as footloose and fancy-free as I had when I was twenty. In one of the high-rise hotels near the Superdome I dropped my gear and then went on, my step lighter now with the load off of me, to stroll the Quarter, get the prix fixe menu at Tujagues, where my father used to eat back in World War II, himself in his teens and a trainee in the Navy V-12 program at Tulane. After supper I climbed to the top of the levee to look at the river and eavesdrop on pockets of old black folk congregated there, in hope of hearing a snatch or two of Creole. I noticed again, as most people do, how far the level of the water was above the level of the street.

That was 2002 and I next got back in 2007, for a one-night tour stop again, and a long walk through the post-Katrina world. They were running tour busses to rubberneck the wreckage of the Ninth Ward, which seemed an especially New Orleans thing to do. War stories aplenty—I remember best the one told by the dark and lovely barmaid Désirée, who'd spent the storm trapped in one of the high-rises, no power, no plumbing; she and her two small children had survived for days on a couple of inches of water caught on the floor of the concrete balcony. . . . I had supper that night, at Tujagues again, with a former student who'd been planning to move to New Orleans just *before* the storm, and afterward decided to come anyway; she was working for a grassroots outfit with a long history of helping underserved communities organize to do better for themselves. In these two young women, native and newcomer, I felt I'd touched a couple of essential elements the city would use to rebuild itself, perhaps in a new image, but containing a good many shards of the old one.

Let's try to say it some other way.

Lee Smith, in her preface to the 2001 edition of this anthology, announced, "We are going to have to seriously overhaul our image of the South, and of Southerners, for this millennium," and then went on to do it excellently well herself, with a series of hilarious anecdotes that leave you thinking, rather seriously, when the echo of laughter has faded. How the economy of the South has changed! And how the population has changed! To the traditional black and white recipe (ever a tricky and volatile mixture) have been added new shades and strains, from Asia and Central and South America and just about everywhere else on the shrinking globe. How then do we retain some special Southern culture, with its literature?

The white Old South, haunted by the Confederacy and the KKK, has pretty well gone up in smoke by this time, in the year of our Lord 2009—just a few wisps and fumes remain. The black Old South, perhaps always more durable, which persisted not only below the Mason-Dixon Line but in the black communities of Chicago and New York and Boston, must surely have been suddenly, radically altered by the astounding events of this election season. The Southern quality of those communities has always meant, to me at least, that every black American writer is also necessarily a Southern writer—unless her forebears arrived here sometime after 1864. The exception that shatters that rule is President Barack Obama, who contains a dash of everything in his genetic composition, who comes from everywhere and nowhere at the same time. Obama embodies a certain kind of contemporary American rootlessness, though one might just as well say his roots are everywhere.

Rootedness used to be the core quality of Southern culture, holding fast to the plantation (big house or quarters), to the scratch farm or small town. That isn't altogether gone, but it has drifted into polarity with the nomadic quality of so many new Southerners' lives. We educate most of our writers now, scattering them into craft schools all over the nation. They marry outlanders and settle in compromise locations, where one day they'll wake up to realize their children aren't safe out of their sight, because there's no longer any way to recognize a stranger.

What the Southern experience used to be has already passed. Whatever it is now, this too shall pass. . . . Wendell Berry (from "Fly Away, Breath"): "the ancient silence filling the dark river valley on that night, uninterrupted in his imagination by the noise of engines, the great quiet into which they have all gone."

Let's try again. New Orleans was and maybe still is a quintessentially Southern city because it's unlike anywhere else in the South. It's the first international city of the region, and along with its hoary traditions and lineages, it has always accommodated hordes of transients, and has been the repair of pirates, indeed. Its delta is a filter that trapped a good deal of everything that drifted down the Mississippi and a lot of what tried to thrust its way up. An upside of Katrina (okay, it was a mighty thin slice of goodness) was getting to hear, in the national media, all those marvelously rich and various New Orleans voices. The flood flushed out into the open so much of what we are, as Southerners, as Americans, as citizens of or wanderers through the world.

I was struck while reading these stories (and by the way I was only able to shoehorn in about a third of the really good ones) by how many seemed to reflect Katrina in some way. I included them all, but I won't spoil them by telling you which ones they are. The connection is subtle in each one of them—an achievement, since Katrina, the subject just as well as the storm herself, has a way of swallowing everything else up.

The hurricane tore New Orleans to shreds and left it to put itself back together in a whole new way . . . but maybe something like that has happened all over the South, with no need for a material hurricane. Against the great longing for home we all share is the fact that so many of us are unhoused and uprooted by our own choice (maybe unreflecting choice)—that we have cast ourselves upon the wind. . . . That tension, then, becomes a germ of the stories we now have to tell.

Katherine Karlin

MUSCLE MEMORY
(from *One Story*)

I f Destiny had three wishes to make, the third would be that she could learn to weld. The first two which involved her father coming back to life and things returning to the way they used to be, would never come true, but learning to weld was a possibility. She just had to get off her ass and decide to do it.

Her father had been a welder, up to a couple of years ago when he died. Drowned. But once upon a time he used to come home from work earlier than the other daddies, the bill of his cap still turned backward, his skin smelling of hot metal and acetylene, his forearms covered with white scars like splattered paint. At night he would sit in the kitchen with his buddies from the shipyard and play dominoes, slapping tiles on the table and talking trash. As she did her homework in the rear room she could hear their voices bubbling with music. Her mother, who was a nurse at Charity, didn't have the energy or the spirit to invite her friends to the house. It was all she could do to come home and soothe her feet in a salt bath.

Destiny was eighteen. She and her mother lived in a house without neighbors. Occasionally a masterless dog would trot down the street, clicking its paws on the pavement, and turn his curious face to their house as he passed. Their view—once crowded with houses, churches, bars, and a corner store where the little kids bought Slim Jims after school—now let them see straight to where the levee used to be, and in the daytime they could watch ice chests and laundry baskets bobbing in the canal like buoys.

Destiny worked in a tool crib at the same shipyard that once employed her father, across the river in Jefferson Parish. She spent the day in a cage, signing out boxes of hex nuts and fittings of galvanized steel. Whenever a new boy would start work on the ship, a tacker or a pipefitter's helper, he would come to the crib asking for a skyhook or a left-handed screwdriver or an automatic crescent wrench. It was her job to break them in, to tell the rookie that his coworkers were just messing with him, that there was no such thing as a skyhook, and after she eased his embarrassment, she watched from her cage as the boy went back up the elevator and onto the ship. The tool crib was, for most of the day, a lonely place, and the pay was the lowest in the yard. She had to learn a skill.

"What you want to do is you want to talk to Augustine Beaudry. That's what you want to do," said Shelton Binns. He was a pipefitter, about thirty, with a face as smooth as a Frenchman's. When he leaned across her counter she could smell his cologne. "He's taught about half the welders up there."

"For real?"

"I got no reason to lie. See what you gotta do is on your lunch break go on up to the ship and ask him to teach you. You're not going to learn anything stuck down here."

Even though she had been working in the yard for four months, she had never gone up to the ship. It was ten blocks long, docked in its berth, elephant-colored, its skins glaring with sunlight and filling her field of vision. Upriver floated two more crafts just like it. The shipbuilding business was good.

The ship frightened her a little, only because it was so large, and because she watched so many men (and some women too) disappear into its depths every day: one second, at shift change, the yard was full of people, chatting and laughing—country people, Cajuns who came up from Houma and old-timers who were staying with family all the way in Picayune or Biloxi, and, more recently, Mexicans, with their dusty ball caps and their *mira-mira* talk, who lived in makeshift trailer parks over in Plaquemines Parish and who climbed into the crane cabs or steered the forklifts up and down the docks (Shelton Binns said he wasn't prejudiced, but he wondered if it was such a good idea for the Mexicans to be running the cranes and the forklifts, as they had different safety standards down there; it was a whole different system). Then the next second all this jabber was silent, and only Destiny and a couple of expeditors were left on dry land. The sudden depopulation spooked her. It was as if they had all died until quitting time. But she knew Shelton was right, and she had to go up to the ship. No fairy godmother was about to show up in the tool crib and teach her to weld.

The elevator was a little red cage with a plywood floor, operated by a one-armed coonass named Guilfoyle. His gums were black and his teeth were yellow against his blotched white skin. He clanged the door shut behind her and pulled on the lever with his one arm and they started up with a jolt, running so close to the hot surface of the ship she could have poked her finger through the mesh and touched it.

Guilfoyle had a stack of egg cartons at his feet.

"Hard-boiled egg?" he snarled.

Destiny shook her head.

"Twenty-five cents. Five for one dollar."

"No, thank you."

He kicked a hatbox next to the eggs. "Praline?" He said it the coonass way. *Pwa-ween.* He was really country. "Fifty cents each. No exceptions!"

"No, thank you."

As they reached the main deck Destiny felt as if they were peeking over the walls of a hidden city. Workers darted around. Hoses streamed across the deck, grinders planed their wheels this way and that, throwing off cascades of orange sparks. Propane bottles in canvas slings dangled from overhead hoists. The hot white glow of the welders (Destiny knew to shield her eyes) burned off to the side. Men shouted warnings to each other: Watch your back! Boom on the right! Women, tackers, looking tough with their caps turned back and their kerchiefs knotted around their necks, dropped the stubs of welding rods from their clamps onto the floor and ground out the embers with their steel-toed boots.

"Here we is," Guilfoyle said. He slid open the door and Destiny stepped out. All around her: noise, heat, and the cheerful sound of people at work. Destiny looked for a familiar face, like Shelton's, but finding none, opted for a group of men who had spread their bandanas on the floor of the deck for an improvised picnic.

"Hey," she said.

The men looked up, not scary. They were peeling hard-boiled eggs and wiping the little triangles of shell and skin on their kerchiefs. "Hey."

"You know where I can find Augustine Beaudry?"

One of the men made a face. "Now that's a shame. What's a beautiful young girl like you looking for a beat-up old piece of shit like that for?"

"I need to ask him to teach me to weld."

"I see." The man speaking rubbed his chin. "What you want to do is climb down to the ballast tank."

"The what?"

"Come over here." He stood up and turned her fore. "See that hole in the deck? Climb down that ladder. That's what you call the ballast tank. You'll find Augustine Beaudry right down there."

She thanked him and as she walked away she knew their eyes were on her. Her old boyfriend used to say, Baby, when you walk it's like your hips are the Atlantic and the Pacific fighting it out between them. She was tall, and even in her work clothes she looked good. The tackers cut their eyes at her as she passed.

"Good luck," one of the men shouted.

She descended to the ballast tank on an iron ladder. The tank was cramped, but at least ten workers were down there, grinding and burning. An enormous exhaust fan sat at the end sucking fumes into a large duct. Everything sounded louder here, and she had to watch her footing, taking care not to get tangled in the ropes and hoses.

"You know where I can find Augustine Beaudry?"

"That's him right there."

Augustine was a hard-looking man, with a permanent frown and nasty shave bumps and a mustache with gray in it. His welding mask was pushed back on his head and he held a fresh rod in his clamp. "Well?" he said.

"You Augustine Beaudry? They told me you could teach me to weld."

"That's what they told you?"

"Yes."

"You want to be a tacker?"

"No sir. I want to be a full-fledged welder."

"Oh, I see. A *full-fledged* welder." A couple of men standing by him, small and hunched, started to cackle. "And what do I get out of this?"

"Excuse me?"

"I understand what you get. But what do I get? You want to take my time, my expertise, probably my welding gear, too. But here you come without so much as an egg, and you could have gotten that in the elevator."

"You want an egg?"

More cackling. Augustine rubbed his forehead with his knuckle. "Come back when you're serious."

That evening, as she helped with her mother's footbath, Destiny asked who had taught her father how to weld.

"I don't think anyone taught him. He picked it up. He was gifted in that regard."

Destiny knew her father was gifted, but she was always suspicious when people told her they just "picked up" a skill, like French or playing the guitar, almost as though they were ashamed of the hard work that went into it.

"Well, where did he pick it up? Was he at the shipyard already?"

"Oh, no. It was something he learned as a boy. Over at his cousins's, if I'm not mistaken. Baby, what's wrong? You want to learn to weld?"

"Some of those welders make twenty-five dollars an hour," Destiny said. "I'm only making nine." She squeezed a washcloth so the water ran down her mother's damaged legs. "You could start thinking about retiring."

"Well, I don't want you to do it on my account. I remember your father waking up in the middle of the night feeling like someone threw sand in his eyes."

Destiny knew all about that, but it seemed like a small price to pay. While her mother dried off, Destiny sat down to read a magazine, and as she landed on the sofa she heard the crackle of paper. She reached between the pillows and pulled out an unwrapped Snickers bar. Her mother always discouraged candy in the house. She wondered how long ago it had been lost, and from whose pocket.

When Destiny returned to the ballast tank she opened her hand to reveal a large brown egg. Augustine took it from her without thanks and turned away.

"Hey," she said. "You wanted an egg. Now you got it."

"Like I said, back when you're serious."

The third day she bought a praline from the coonass, who with his one arm fished it out of the hatbox at his feet. It was in a baggie sealed with an electrician's tie-wrap.

"Here." She presented the praline to Augustine.

He grunted and took it from her.

"You gonna teach me now?"

He tore open the bag and popped the praline in his mouth. "You're gonna have to try harder than this, girl."

She had a mind to ask him to spit out the praline into her hand, if he wasn't going to keep his end of the bargain. But she turned and climbed out of the ballast tank.

"I'm not surprised he's acting ornery," Shelton said, when she told him her troubles. "You know who he is, don't you?"

"You mean besides being Augustine Beaudry?"

"I mean he is *the* Augustine Beaudry. From the Scorchers?"

"The what?"

"Oh, man. You're so young you don't even remember. You ever hear a song called 'Hell and High Water'?"

"Sure. My father used to listen to that."

"Now see, he had good taste. Well Augustine Beaudry, that's the man who used to sing it."

"What?" She turned toward the glare of the ship and blinked. "What's he doing in there? They play that song on the oldies radio all the time."

"Well, you know. They didn't pay royalties back then. A group would go into the studio and get five, six thousand dollars for cutting a record. That was considered good money."

"Man." She could see why he was a little cranky. All that money being made off his song and he wasn't seeing a dime.

On the way home she stopped at an old record shop on Magazine Street. "Do you have anything by the Scorchers?" The boy she asked had a sunken chest and a scraggly beard. He struck a pose, one hand on his waist and the other on his chin. The he put his finger in the air and said, "'Hell and High Water'!"

"Yeah, that's it."

"If we do," he said, leading her down one of the long aisles, "it'd be over here." He flipped through some old LPs in a bin. "Here it is."

The cover featured five men in tuxedoes against a lilac background. She studied their faces. The second from the left might have been Augustine, although his face was rounder. But the one all the way on the right—that was him. He was smiling, so he was hard to recognize. And he was thirty years younger, of course. "How much?"

The boy removed the disc from its cover and balanced it on his fingertips, checking for warps and scratches. "Three dollars."

At home, Destiny set up her father's old hi-fi to listen to the record. "Ma, do you remember the Scorchers?"

"'Hell and High Water.' Of course I do. Time was your daddy and I used to hear them play over at the Maple Leaf. 'Hell and High Water' was what put them on the map, but I always preferred another song they did, called 'I'll Take Fire.'" Splashing her feet, she sang. "*Some men drown from lonesomeness, some men burn up with desire. Baby I know how I will die—between fire and water, I'll take fire.*"

"That's a spooky song."

"Reminds me of those old blues they used to do."

Destiny looked for the track on the record and lowered the needle into the groove. The song had a kind of hollow sound to it, as though it had been recorded at the bottom of a tin can. She tried to connect the high, yearning tenor voice coming out of the speakers with the grumpy old man in the hole. When the song was over she went to pee, and when she flushed she heard a clatter in the tank. She lifted the lid and found two cans of stewed tomatoes bobbing alongside the float.

The next day she put the record album in a plastic Safeway bag and hung it from her wrist as she lowered herself into the ballast tank.

"What do you have for me?" Augustine said.

She pulled the record from the bag and handed him a pen. "I was hoping to get your autograph."

He took the record from her and turned it over, looked at the back cover, then turned it back to the front. "Where in hell did you get this?"

"Magazine Street." She didn't tell him it cost her three dollars.

"You like 'Hell and High Water,' I suppose."

"S'all right. But what I really like is 'I'll Take Fire.'"

He stared at her hard. "So you like a good ballad, then?"

"I guess."

He took the pen from her and scribbled his name. "I told them that should have been the A-side. They wanted to go with something more upbeat." He gave her the pen and the record. "You're the girl they call Density."

"Destiny," she corrected.

"So you're looking to be a welder?"

"Yes sir."

"It's a very, very honorable occupation," he said. "You take something that isn't there and turn it into steel."

"I know."

"You got a welding hood or do you expect me to supply that too?"

"No, I got a hood. My daddy's."

"Won't your daddy be needing it?"

"He's gone."

"I see. Bring your hood and gloves tomorrow and we'll see what we can do."

The hood was right where her father had left it, hooked on a nail in the garage, just inches over the water mark. Mildew grew over the walls like ivy. She buried her face in its plastic hollow and smelled the ash. There weren't any scorch marks on the inside of the hood—it was curved like an eggshell, made to hold her face. She looked for any stubborn remains: whiskers, dandruff, streaks of salt from his sweat, anything that attested to his having been alive. But the hood was clean. She might have known; he did not often leave a mess behind.

It was two weeks before they found Destiny's father, washed up beneath a bridge by St. Claude Avenue. At least they believed it was him. His body was bloated and purple, his shirt buttons popped and his clothes in shreds, his skin filleted and peeling in thick wrinkled layers like a soggy roll of toilet paper. An inspector laid him out in the animal shelter they were using as a morgue and suggested they check dental records for a positive identification, but their dentist had run off to somewhere in Arkansas and left his records behind in a filing cabinet that had by now floated into the sea.

The corpse's fingers were so swollen they had engulfed his wedding ring the way a tree will grow around a chain-link fence. The inspector offered to cut his finger off.

"That's all right," her mother had said. "I know who it is."

For a long time Destiny thought her mother might be wrong. After all, the corpse did not smell like her father. It smelled like wet garbage, rotting apple cores, and spoiled corn and vomit. Her father had the hot, dry smell of burning metal, an aroma she so closely identified with him she figured he was born with it. It took her weeks to comprehend that a man's smell will die with him. Now she knew.

Destiny ratcheted the headband of her father's welding hood tight around her head. With a sharp nod she dropped the mask and she saw nothing. She lifted it and the moldy garage was still around her. Sharp nod: nothing. Lifted the mask, everything was the same. Looking for his gloves, she opened the drawer of his old Kennedy tool chest and found rows of Peppermint Patties, shining like silver dollars. They fit perfectly in the drawer, three deep and five across, as if they were in a display case. She removed one of them, upsetting the pattern, unwrapped it and popped the candy in her mouth. The peppermint oil burned her tongue.

At her first lesson, Augustine set up two pieces of scrap metal in a vise so that the seam between them was narrow and long. He straightened the lead, whipping it like a cowboy's lasso, and pulled a fresh rod from his quiver. Inspecting the clamp, Destiny saw there were different grooves she could fit the rod into, so it would be angled up, angled down, straight ahead, or at a perfect ninety. She tried different positions and settled on angling the rod up.

"Finished playing?" Augustine said.

"I'm all right."

"All right then. Pretend like you're going to strike an arc but don't make contact."

She pawed at the air with her welding rod.

"What you want to do is stroke the surface of the metal lightly. Stay in one spot too long and that rod'll freeze up on you. Too fast and you won't get a spark. But once you nod down that hood you won't be able to see a thing. You'll be alone in the darkness.

So get a sense now of where that metal is and how far you got to reach it. Clear?"

"Yes."

"All right then, let's go." They dropped their masks by nodding sharply. Everything around her went black. She could hear voices and the buzz of a grinder, but they seemed distant, on the other side of an ocean. The smell of her father's hood reassured her. She poked the welding rod towards the metal and a shock zapped her arm. The rod was jammed.

"Froze it! Lift your mask," Augustine said.

She lifted her mask and released her clamp. The rod was sticking to the metal like an arrow in flesh.

One of the little hunched men said, "Whoo, whoo! Indian attack!"

Augustine twisted the rod loose. He threw it on the ground. "I told you, you gotta keep that tip moving." He produced a fresh rod.

Destiny tried the different grooves. Pointing up, pointing down, pointing straight ahead. "What way do I put it in?"

"That's what I asked her last night," one of the little men jeered.

Augustine scowled. "It don't matter a goddamn which way you put it in there. Just quit messing around and get to work."

She slid the rod in a groove, pantomimed striking the arc a couple of times, and snapped her mask shut. She reached into the darkness. Zap. Her arm buzzed. Froze again. This went on for a good fifteen minutes as Destiny ruined one perfectly good rod after another. Then Augustine said, "That's enough for today."

"I didn't even strike an arc yet."

"It's your first day. What the hell did you expect?" He sat on a twelve-inch duct and motioned for her to sit by him. Then he pulled an egg from his breast pocket and peeled it.

"So what kind of music you listen to, mostly? Hip-hop?" he asked.

"Mostly, I guess."

"Any old school?"

"Well, you know. What my parents liked. Earth, Wind and Fire."

Augustine stared hard into the distance. "What about the music from around here?"

"You mean like the Nevilles? All right."

"You young people shouldn't forget. You're the only ones who can remember."

"All right."

"Do you know who Screamin' Jay Hawkins is?"

She shook her head. Augustine pulled apart the white of the egg and sucked the yolk out of its socket.

"I want you to find out." As he talked he showed his yellow-coated tongue and Destiny had to look away. "You come back tomorrow and we'll continue your lesson."

It meant going out of her way to Xavier and using the library computer. She found a website about Screamin' Jay Hawkins and scrolled through it quickly. It was weird and ancient stuff. That night she shook off the moldiness by listening to her favorite DJ, Yolanda, send out her late-night love dedications on Q93. Yolanda used to end every show by saying, "To all my boys offshore to-night, Yolanda sends you a big wet kiss. Mmmwwaah." Nowadays she said, "To all of you on land and at sea, wherever you are, Yolanda misses you and sends you a big wet kiss." It made Destiny both happy and sad to think of all the people who were listening at the same time.

The next day she said, "That was one strange brother."

"Who is that?" Augustine asked.

"Screamin' Jay Hawkins. Big hit: 'I Put a Spell on You.' Which he used to perform from an *actual* coffin."

"He did, too." Augustine chuckled. "I caught him with a lady in a quilted Eterna-Rest 5000 more than once."

"Oh, no, he did not."

Augustine's eyes were shining and she could see he was pleased. As she tried to strike an arc he spoke to her gently through the darkness. "Don't try too hard," he said. "If you try too hard you defeat your own purpose. Just stroke it like you're tickling a baby's belly."

Destiny zapped a couple of more times and sighed deeply as Augustine twisted the fresh rods off the metal. But he was not impatient. The third time, a small red light glowed, and it illuminated the seam, the rod, even the vise, and a fragile, concave, silver pool of flux spread beneath her hand. Then the surface of the pool trembled and cracked and the light snuffed out.

"I *had* it," she said, lifting her visor. "I had it for a second."

Augustine bent down to inspect the seam. "You did, too. Look at that there."

A slender silver bridge slung like a canopy between the two edges of metal. It was sloppy. But it was welding. Destiny put her hand to her hood, but Augustine said, "That's enough for today. Tomorrow I want you to tell me about Fats Domino."

An hour later, when Shelton came by the tool crib to chat, the phone on the wall rang. "Supplies and expedition," she said.

"Density."

"Destiny," she corrected.

"Who's that you're talking to?" Augustine's voice was thick and gruff on the line.

Destiny squinted and looked out the window. "How you know I'm talking to somebody?"

"You better watch yourself."

She hung up. "Fool."

"Augustine Beaudry?" Shelton asked.

"How does he know what I'm doing?"

Shelton shook his head. "Augustine's one pack of Camels short of a carton. It's like the water picked him up and set him down someplace else."

That afternoon her mother went to Algiers to talk to people from the government. Destiny took a look around her room while she was gone. Everything was in order: the framed pictures on the vanity of Destiny and her father and grandparents, her mother's hairbrush, a Bible, a physician's desk reference. The floorboards turned up at the corners and squeaked when she stepped on them.

She was sneaking around on her own mother. She didn't like doing it, but she snuck anyway. She opened the closet. On the right side, her mother's scrubs, pink sets and green sets and one printed with Shrek characters, for the occasional pediatric rotation. On the left side, dresses for church and luncheons. Destiny put her hands between the dress section and the scrubs section and parted them. Behind the clothing she found tins stacked from floor to ceiling, Hawaiian pineapple, cocktail franks, barley soup, mandarin oranges, corned beef hash, smoked oysters. Also jars of Zaratrain mustard and clam juice. No two foods that would actually make a meal together.

Destiny went out for a walk. She wanted to hurt somebody. On Prieur Street she saw a dead frog splayed on the sidewalk. She kicked it like a football. At the home of the Landrys, whose daughter was two years older than Destiny, a fish skeleton was washed against the front door. The block smelled of rotting cabbage and wet plaster. Then she smelled something like burning rubber and went towards it, across Caffin Avenue, past an abandoned FEMA trailer with its door slung open and, inside, a tricycle with plastic streamers hanging from its handlebars, past a house twisted off its axis, past a single Air Jordan on the curb, a few busted pallets, and a dog carcass that shimmered with maggots. When she saw where the smell was coming from she was surprised to find a live person, a man of about fifty in a purple velour tracksuit, arms crossed, watching a greasy oil drum fire. She stood beside him and helped him watch.

"What are you burning?" she asked after a while.

"All of it."

Once Destiny learned to strike an arc, she guessed it was only a question of weeks until she would be a welder. She had run long distance in high school, and she knew what it meant to persevere, to practice every day until she mastered the task. But welding had a different learning curve. Every day the went up in the elevator and down into the ballast tank, and every day she buried herself in the dark and worked on whatever old chunks of metal Augustine had scrounged up for her, and then one of two things would happen: the red glow of her arc would sputter and extinguish, and she would raise her hood to find a trickle of flux like birdshit sucked into the seam, or the glow would deepen and rage out of control, and instead of joining two pieces of metal she would drive them farther apart, their jagged edges gaping like the red gates of hell. She was willing to try again, but instead of scavenging new scrap metal Augustine preferred to sit her down and deliver his sermon for the day on Ernie K-Doe or Professor Longhair. She had no time to improve.

If she had a good day Augustine would share the egg she had bought for him, cracking it open and handing her half the egg white.

"What do you think it means," Destiny asked, trying to sound casual, "if people hide food all around the house?"

Augustine chewed his yolk, bunching up his lips as he chewed. "You hiding food?"

"Not me. I'm talking hypotheticals."

"Hypotheticals," he repeated. He swallowed his yolk so she could hear it. "Usually it means somebody's been acquainted with hunger. Hypothetically speaking."

Destiny watched the little men lower buckets of water into the ballast tank.

"There's a lot of people around here," Augustine said, "doing things they didn't used to do."

Every day she looked up the old-timers he assigned. She understood what he was trying to do, to connect her to her roots and give her a sense of belonging to something big. But listening to that musty music did not make her feel connected. It made her feel alone. Destiny wanted to hear what other people were hearing. Living people.

"How's your welding coming?" her mother asked as Destiny sponged her legs.

Destiny shrugged. "I thought after this many weeks I'd get the hang of it. Be better at it, anyway. It's like I'm not improving."

"Oh, it just seems that way."

Destiny felt desperation rising in her throat. She wanted to ask, what will happen to us if I can't learn a real skill?

Her mother ran her fingers over Destiny's scalp in a way that made her feel five years old and coddled.

"It just seems like you're not improving, but you are," her mother said. "It was the same way when I had to learn how to take blood. I used to stick and stick and stick. Lord, I bruised those patients black and blue with all my clumsiness. Then, lo and behold, one day I just did it. Simplest thing in the world, like I'd been doing it all my life. It just takes time to burn a new habit into your muscle memory is all."

Destiny knew her mother was trying to be encouraging, but she also knew that welding would never be the simplest thing in the world. As she trickled water over her mother's knees a boom rattled the windows. They looked at each other.

"Sounds like the Hayes house," her mother said. The house across the street.

Destiny's mother stepped out of the footbath and hurried to the front room. Her arches were so high and regal she left wet prints like questions marks on the floor. Destiny followed.

The Hayes house had collapsed. The walls and windows were gone. The gutter of the roof rested on the ground, and through the rising smoke Destiny could see white four-foot letters painted on the shingles. "Two Alive."

One day Augustine asked her, "You go to dances, proms and such?"

"Proms? I graduated from high school last year." She tried not to sound exasperated. She still needed him to teach her to weld.

"You go to clubs? Where do you go to hear music?"

"Clubs sometimes. Parties." Destiny drew a fresh rod from a box to show him she was concentrating on her work. "Most of my friends aren't here anymore."

"I bet you could get me a gig."

"A gig?"

"Someplace where young people are."

Destiny dropped her mask. Instead of arguing she struck an arc and focused on welding.

When Shelton came to visit her that afternoon he turned her wrist and inspected the soft underside of her forearm. "You're getting scars. Looking like a welder."

Destiny withdrew her arm to her side of the cage.

"Don't hide it, girl. You're supposed to be proud of your battle scars."

He thought she was hiding because she was ashamed of her scars. She was hiding because she still wasn't a welder. The scars lied.

The phone rang and she said, "What?"

"Who sang 'Wish Someone Would Care'?" Augustine asked.

"Irma Thomas."

"What was the B-side?"

Destiny sighed. "I don't know what the B-side was. Now go do your job and let me do mine."

When she hung up, Shelton said, "He always knows when I'm here."

"I better get back to work," she said. "I got a shipment of copper tubing to log in."

Augustine had a habit of asking Destiny a question just as she was about to drop her visor. He was like a boy needing attention. And he was getting worse with his pestering. Destiny was getting the idea he didn't want her to learn how to weld so much as keep him company.

"You remember to get me a gig?" he demanded.

"I never promised you that. You think I know people. I don't know anyone."

"Hell you don't. You're a pretty young girl. Pretty young girls know people."

"I don't." She used to. Now she had so few people in her life she was about to die of suffocation. She dropped her mask and Augustine knocked on it. "What is it?" She lifted the visor. "I gotta practice."

"I spend my valuable time here setting up your lessons every day I expect something in return."

What valuable time? She looked at the metal scraps in the vise—two round discs that a burner had cut from a pipe and left on the floor. Big deal.

"I already told you, I don't know anyone. I can't make something out of nothing."

"I bet you haven't even tried. People remember 'Hell and High Water.'"

"Then ask one of them." Her face grew hot.

"They don't owe me like you do." One of the little men cackled, so happy Destiny thought he was about to dance a jig.

"I don't owe you nothing, old man. And you know what else? There ain't nobody wants to listen to what you have to offer."

As soon as she said it she was sorry. She remembered the young hipster in the record store putting his finger in the air and saying "'Hell and High Water'!" Lots of people remembered. But Destiny was so annoyed she didn't want to admit it. Something drove her forward. "Your music is older than whaleshit, and anyone who ever liked it is dead."

Augustine's pupils constricted. "That's what you think."

She turned from him, lowered her visor and struck her arc. There it was, the low red glow, the silver pond like a sunken belly. She teased it out by making a figure eight with the tip of her rod and there, a second, interlinking pond, exactly the same size. Then another, and another, descending rings of silver. It was easy. She sealed off the bead with a final flourish, like a period to her sentence, and pulled away. When she lifted her mask Augustine and the little men were back at work, ignoring her. She drew her little triangular hammer from her belt and chipped away at the slag. Underneath was a perfect bead, not too fat and not too skinny. She spat on it and watched the saliva skitter across the hot surface, and picked up a stiff wire brush and shined the bead until the silver reflected reds and blues. It was beautiful. And it was hers. She knew in her arms that she could do it again. Anytime and anywhere.

Augustine saw her admiring her work. He came over to look at her bead.

"Feeling pretty good, are you?"

"Pretty good."

"Think you're some kind of welder?"

"It's looking that way."

"Hell." He stepped across the tank and picked a torch off the floor. With his thumb he opened the gas valve and lit the jet with a Bic lighter so a steady blue flame like a laser flowed from its mouth. Then, squinting, he aimed the torch at her beautiful silver bead. She watched it melt and disappear into the seam of the discs.

"There," he said, turning down the flame. "Try again."

The two of them looked at where her weld had been. She wasn't angry. But she knew to hang around him anymore was to sink fast. "You know what?" Destiny said. Her heart pounded. "I can't help you."

"*You* can't help *me*?" Augustine said, mimicking her. The little men around him started to laugh, and as she climbed up the ladder she could hear their voices echoing in the ballast tank. On the main deck she felt a salty wind blowing up from the Gulf. A gang of riggers scurried beneath an overhead crane swinging a sharp sheet of metal from fore to aft. She didn't mind the tackers giving her dirty looks. They were just tackers. She was a welder.

Three weeks later she took her examination. An inspector with an X-ray machine scanned her weld like a baby in its mother's belly, and, satisfied with its density, proclaimed her a welder.

"Pretty soon your handiwork will be going off to Eye-Rack or Eye-Ran," he said.

When she got home she taped her welding certificate to the refrigerator. Then she cleaned out her mother's closet, stacking up cans of food and packages of ramen noodles on the front step. She was still stacking them up when her mother came home from work. "We can bring these to the homeless shelter," she said.

"Oh, well," her mother said. She said it as if she were running late for church. *Oh, well.*

"I passed my welding test." Destiny sounded angry.

"I knew you would."

"I can buy you anything you want. Anything you're hungry for."

"That's just a little something in case of an emergency." Her mother picked up a box of spaghetti and rattled it, close to her ear. "It doesn't hurt to keep this around, does it?"

Destiny bent over and straightened a pile of boxes. "It takes up room."

Her mother sighed. "I just keep thinking. If we had been a little more prepared last time, we could have saved ourselves a whole ocean of trouble."

Destiny picked up a bag of elbow macaroni that had fallen out of a carton. When she was a little girl she used to listen to her father say, "Taking responsibility, Baby: that's the hardest thing to do." Now she knew that, in this one thing, at least, he was wrong. Taking responsibility was easy. Learn a trade, train your hands to do something they couldn't do before. The hard part was all the ruination that lay outside of your responsibility.

Destiny's family had brought what they thought they needed to the roof. It would be like a beach picnic—they would eat crackers and drink from a ninety-ounce bottle of orange soda and watch the water rise and fall with the tug of the moon. Sooner or later help would come. Only help didn't come. At night they tried to sleep on the pitched tar shingles and listened to the noises of the neighborhood shut down, one by one. A dog quit barking. A far-off car alarm went silent. And a long, angry back-and-forth between a mother and son stopped suddenly and deafeningly. As her father rolled up his pant legs on the third morning, getting ready to go look for food, he told jokes about catching fish in the floodwaters. And Destiny, her head pounding from thirst and sunstroke, rolled her eyes.

But she was not the same person now that she was on that roof—anyone could see that. Her shoulders were widening and straining against the seams of her T-shirt. When she crooked her arm her biceps were hard as billiard balls. Her throat burned and her mouth tasted of flux, and now and then her retinas lit up with a flash so white she could see the blood vessels of her own eyeballs. Not only that, she had a head crammed with voices, songs and singers that she hadn't even known a few weeks earlier, all kinds of jerky rhythms and crazy instruments.

Destiny's mother ran her finger around and around the ridge of a can of pears. "Baby, I *know* you can provide."

"What is the issue then, exactly?" Destiny glared at her mother.

"When I wake up at night it gives me some comfort, looking at these cans." Destiny's mother turned the pears over in her hand. Then she fit her finger into the metal ring at the top of the can, bent it back, and peeled the lid off. She fished a piece of fruit out and passed it over to Destiny.

The pear was a soft molten white, heavy with juice. Destiny hesitated for a moment, holding the fruit, and then she took a bite. The sweetness spread across her tongue and for a moment she felt like crying.

From somewhere, on the next street over, maybe, or the street after that, a radio played an accordion tune. Destiny couldn't imagine where the music could be coming from; what houses still stood on the block were abandoned, their doors swollen and busted from their frames. Across the street a turtle the size of a manhole cover crawled from the wreckage of the Hayes place back into the gutter.

"All right," she told her mother, the sweetness still in the back of her throat. "Maybe then you'll let me build you something to put them on. Just so they're not all over the floor. I can weld some brackets right to the wall, so you don't even have to get out of bed.

Destiny's mother smiled. She took another piece of fruit and slid it between her own lips, then carried the can back into the house.

The song in the distance was a Boozoo Chavis two-step, Destiny knew. Rounder Records. She strained to hear more as she picked up the supplies, once more, to return them to her mother. She had the bill of her ball cap turned to the back and her bandana around her neck and she pushed her sleeves back on her arms, admiring her scars. Propping the screen door open with her foot, she wrapped her hands around four cans of red beans and listened for the record to end and the next one to begin. She knew all the songs and the artists before the announcer named them, and she could sing all the words.

———————

Katherine Karlin's stories have appeared or are forthcoming in *One Story, ZYZZYVA,* the *North American Review, Alaska Quarterly Review,* and other journals, and in the 2007 Pushcart Prize collection. In the fall of 2009 she joins the faculty at Kansas State University.

I used to work in a shipyard outside of New Orleans, driving a forklift and delivering copper tubing, PVC pipe, and galvanized steel fittings to the ships under construction, and I spent my lunch breaks trying to learn how to weld. It was a humbling experience; with each day I showed no improvement. My co-workers assured me it was a knack you got all at once. Since then, I've read that this phenomenon—the sudden acquisition of a motor skill—is about the brain burning neural shortcuts: what we know as muscle memory.

Over the years I tried to write about a girl learning how to weld, and when I returned to it in the summer of 2007, I figured I had to move the piece away from New Orleans. To write about the city as I knew it— pre-Katrina—was to douse the story in nostalgia. That wasn't what I was going for. It occurred to me then to set it in post-Katrina New Orleans, significantly raising the stakes for Destiny's ambitions. I wrote about the people I used to know, imagining how they would turn their dignity and resourcefulness toward matters of survival. Hannah Tinti, the editor of One Story, *made wise editorial suggestions that strengthened the story, and I am grateful to her for bringing "Muscle Memory" to light. I never did learn to weld worth a damn.*

Kelly Cherry

BANGER FINDS OUT

(from *Commentary*)

B anger's father was not the man whose last name Banger bore. His father was a sweet tryst that lasted the baseball season, and he had left his mother even before she learned she was pregnant. He had been headed down to the coast, looking to strike it rich at the casinos, and Banger's mother would bet that he had not gotten to New Orleans before landing in jail. For about one-tenth of a second, if that long, she had considered an abortion, and then she never thought about it again.

Banger's mother, Plummy, despite her name with its suggestion of round vowels and luxe towels, was not a high-class woman; she was a low-down, walk-all-over-me-and-I'll-show-you-how-good-I-can-make-the-soles-of-your-feet-feel kind of a woman. Plummy tended bar at Moon Shots near the Redstone Arsenal in Huntsville, Alabama, and she lived with her twelve-year-old son—he had received his nickname when he was little and had let the screen door bang whenever he came in or went out—in a rickety rented two-story-with-wood-siding.

Huntsville, where Wernher von Braun and his team had settled after World War II, billed itself as Rocket City. At the municipal pool, heated to ninety degrees and cherished by seniors with arthritis, members of the founding families still gossiped in German. Plummy's own father, recruited in the early 1960s, had been an aeronautical engineer from Augsburg. Her mother was an Alabama girl. They had met on the front lines of the civil-rights campaign, her father the foreigner marching, he liked to say, for the first and last time in his life. When she was little, Plummy used to sit on her father's knee while he sang his own German translation of "Oh! Susanna. Oh, don't you cry for me. I come from Alabama with a *banjo* on my knee." Every time he came to the word *banjo* he hollered it in English and pretended she was a banjo that he was strumming.

Plummy's parents had been kind and cheerful. She was their only child, and they had played Go Fish and Old Maid with her and taken her trick-or-treating on Halloween and kept a photo album on the cover of which her mother had written, in Magic Marker and capital letters, STARRING OUR DAUGHTER. They had kissed her and hugged her and told her they loved her. When she had the measles they drew the shades down and brought her soup and ice cream and gave her a plush toy giraffe as tall as she was. They ooh'ed and ah'ed over the Valentine's Day card she made for them at school and the ashtray she made at camp, though neither of them smoked. They came to every graduation.

She could not understand how she had bungled her life after such a good start. It was not as if she disrespected herself; she respected herself just fine. She supposed she just lacked the will to succeed. She had done okay in school, but she didn't work at it. Instead of studying Latin declensions or solving quadratic equations she cheered for her favorites at football practice on weekday afternoons, sang in the school choir—she had a creamy alto voice—hung out with her friends at the Tastee-Freez on summer evenings, and somehow, when she started double-dating, was always the one in the back seat with a boy pleading with her not to stop. The music was stereo, the car was a souped-up convertible, *Saturday Night Fever* was a contagion of the time. The friend in front would go for a walk with the guy in front, wearing the guy's letter sweater, and, in short, Plummy was on the pill and didn't see a reason to stop and didn't want to. She had been easy, especially if alcohol was involved. Nobody joked about her or was mean to her—she was too well liked for that, by both the boys and the girls. She didn't get into trouble, because she was too smart for *that.* But, she supposed, a pattern was established, and it was a pattern in which she was the girl you could count on and would never have to pay back. The opposite of high maintenance, she was no maintenance at all.

After high school she worked in data entry, punching numbers on a keyboard. Her parents had wanted her to go to college but she told them she was tired of studying; they could have pointed out that she had never done much studying, but they didn't. She chewed her nails and painted them with punk flair, messily swabbing brown or blue or green and occasionally even plain old red polish in the center of each. Some days she felt trapped by her job. Other days she felt light and floating and free, something spacey and slightly loony and cosmically effervescent. When she felt like that, she was liable to go dancing.

In a roadhouse on Route 72 Plummy met Earl Fitts. He was a mechanic in the army. An old burn had puckered the skin at the outer corner of his left eye, making him look like he was smiling even when he wasn't. She kept thinking he was smiling at her. Two days later she woke up sober in Tupelo, married. There was a knock on the door of their motel room. A twin-set of MPs was standing on the rubber welcome mat. Hands cuffed behind his back, Earl kissed her on the cheek before they led him away, down the crumbling concrete portico. He seemed to be smiling, which made her think he liked being married, but she never saw him again. She was divorced and not yet twenty-one.

So, she thought, maybe her parents had had the right idea. She enrolled at the university in Florence—not Italy, as she would explain to the Pentagon types who flew in to consult at Redstone: Florence, *Alabama,* about sixty miles from Huntsville. But the pattern didn't change. That surprised her; she had kind of figured that if she majored in philosophy, she'd absorb some wisdom. Instead, she discovered that life was even more inexplicable than she'd already thought.

The only thing that changed was that she went off the pill because the doctor said her body needed a breather. That was when she met the gambler. At twenty-five, more or less nine months after he had "borrowed" her car to drive to the coast, her body took a deep breath and exhaled, and William, eventually to be known as Banger, appeared, weighing seven pounds two ounces. Plummy not having gotten around to dropping the Fitts, it became, perforce, her son's name.

After Plummy gave birth, she centered her life on her infant son. She was careful not to smother him, made sure to encourage him to try new things and make his own decisions. He reminded her of her father. She had loved her mother, too, but it was her father who never lost faith in her.

Her son was twelve now, smart and good-looking and mannerly and, lately, intrigued by his family history. He had recently taken to rummaging through the souvenirs and family stuff that Plummy had shoved into the upstairs storage closet when they first moved into the house, which had no proper attic. She had always meant to go through the boxes and figure out what was and wasn't worth saving, but there was never a time for this. Either she was exhausted from work, or it was the weekend and the weather was wonderful, the air seductive with the dreamy odors of lilac and lobelia, or the weather was stormy, tornadoes threatening to form, and she called Banger indoors and they played Scrabble or Monopoly. When she asked him what he was doing poking around in the closet, he said he was just curious.

That was true enough, he thought. He remembered his grandfather as a genial, funny man who had held him on his lap and pretended he was a banjo. He remembered a lean man with a weathered face and large hands who helped him build model airplanes and rockets, who had carried him on his shoulders, who had trolled the back of his ears for quarters that he never failed to find, who was a whiz at Lego and Tinkertoys.

And his father? Banger had asked his mother about him and was thrown into confusion when she explained that he was not the man whose last name they shared. His mother's having been married to a guy who'd gone AWOL; the way she referred to his father as the Rambling Gambler: there were things he wanted to know, and one or two other things he would just as soon not find out about until he was older. One of them was if his mother had been, Jesus, a little bit easy. So he'd gotten in the habit of asking about his grandfather instead of his father. It made his mother happy to talk about him, and besides, until he was six his grandfather had been like a father to him. Banger had admired him wildly. He wanted to *be* like his grandfather. He was no kin to Earl Fitts, and he felt no kinship with his jerk of a hit-and-run father. Honey, his mother said to him, if your father had known about you I'm sure he'd have come back, but I didn't know how to get in touch with him. He still thought his father was a jerk.

Plummy told him about the German immigrant who had developed top-secret guidance systems. "He could multiply a three-digit number by a three-digit number in his head," she said, seeming to hold each low-pitched word in her mouth for a moment, savoring it before moving on to the next. She nibbled at the cuticle on her thumb. "He could recite Schiller."

"What about Grandmother?" Banger asked. "Was she smart too?"

"She was smart in a different way," she said.

"What way?" He was a kid who liked to nail things down.

"She was smart enough to say she loved to listen to him recite Schiller."

"In German or English?"

"Oh," Plummy said, "she didn't care. She said it was all Greek to her."

"Mo-o-om." Banger hated it when his mother made him her straight man.

"Sorry," she said, ruffling his hair. He hated *that,* too, at least when she did it in front of his friends; he liked it when they were alone.

When he found the handful of old photos, scissored from an album with the black backing paper still attached, he thought about telling her. And then he thought maybe he'd better not. He'd been opening the taped-down boxes with his jackknife, shuffling the contents, reading old letters and documents. His grandfather's passport was in one of the boxes. Digging deeper, he'd found the photos at the bottom, underneath a stack of technical drawings. He felt his face heat up. He was breathing too fast and swallowing air and when he held the photos up to his face, he inhaled dust and suffered a coughing fit until his throat cleared.

He decided he should think it over before he did anything rash. He was afraid of how his mother might react. She'd be upset. Shit, she'd be heartsick.

But she needed to know, didn't she?

Maybe there was an explanation. He wanted it not to be true. And how *could* it be? He remembered his grandfather, the towers of play blocks in primary colors. Tears overran his eyes before he knew he was going to cry. He wiped them on his sleeve. Snot ran from his nose. He sucked it up.

With a child to support, Plummy had moved back to Huntsville and taken the best-paying job her philosophy major let her find. She started at Strangelove's, near the square, where the restrooms were for Misters and Missiles. Circling the pond in nearby Big Spring Park, cherry trees, given to the city by the Japanese to commemorate international reconciliation, showed a blush of modest self-consciousness in April.

To the east of the city, the Tennessee River Valley sputtered out in a handful of mountains blue as lakes. From the top of Monte Sano, you could see the city lights spread out below like a fireworks display without the booms and flares and hissing wicks. In Strangelove's, the lights had been dim, the room smoke-filled, the music sad or raunchy or both, and the men lonely.

The job at Moon Shots offered her a little more responsibility and a little more money. At Moon Shots, the lights were low, the room smoke-filled, the music sad or raunchy or both, and the men lonely, but the men were better dressed and often leaned briefcases against their barstools. Sometimes they sat in booths, ate steaks, and checked e-mail on their laptops.

By now she was expert at her work. From sloppy to mean, she could handle a drunk with one arm tied behind her back. It was possible she knew how to mix every drink ever invented, even the ones with stupid names, though only the guys' dates wanted these—or the guys thought they did. She also had to oversee the wait staff, settle disputes, keep her temper in check when a customer sent a drink back. She worked an eight-hour shift, but often enough wound up staying longer. She got so tired she felt like grabbing a drink herself, but she had quit when she found out she was pregnant with Banger and she was not going to start up again.

Banger still had not told his mother, and keeping the news to himself made blood go to his brain and knock crazily against his ears. Still, he was trying not to jump to conclusions, something his mother always warned him against. He was thinking things through, and now he had a question for Mr. Singer, his social-studies teacher. For several days he tried hanging back after school, but his best friend, Thurgood Marshall Taylor, wouldn't let him. "What are you waiting for?" Thurgood demanded. "We'll miss the bus." So Banger would follow him out to the parking lot where the yellow buses were lined up. Finally on a Tuesday he managed to escape from the cafeteria, saying he had to go to the bathroom, and found Mr. Singer eating a tuna-fish sandwich at his desk.

"This is my lunch break, Banger," he said. "Ask me in class."

The question popped out of Banger's mouth anyway. "If a boy is wearing a uniform like—like a Nazi uniform, does that mean he's a Nazi?"

Mr. Singer slowly put down his half-eaten sandwich. "You know a boy who wears a Nazi uniform?"

"It was in a movie," Banger said quickly.

"Well, didn't the movie explain it?"

"Not really."

"I guess not," Mr. Singer said, "or you wouldn't have come to me." He had a high, brainy-looking forehead and an open face, and he was tall and looked tall even seated.

"I know you know history and stuff."

Mr. Singer was silent. Banger waited.

"What movie?" Mr. Singer asked, taking another bite.

"I don't remember what it was called."

"You can't remember the name of the movie?"

Banger shrugged. "I just thought you might know the answer."

"This is important to you, Banger?" Mr. Singer stood up, brushing crumbs from his front.

Face chalky, forehead damp, Banger nodded that it was important. It seemed to him that Mr. Singer looked as if he really cared about what was on his mind. But he remembered hearing some kids saying that Mr. Singer was a Jew, and realized that probably the last thing he wanted to hear about was Banger's grandfather. "Forget it," Banger said, and ran out of the room.

Thurgood said Banger looked as white as a ghost, then exploded into laughter. "Man, you look just like you been given detention for the rest of the year!"

"Shut up," said Banger.

They got off at the same stop, Thurgood turning left, Banger right. In the distance he could see the Saturn rocket at the Marshall Space Center: Huntsville's main tourist attraction. It rose against the skyline on the other side of the cotton field that stretched past his house and a row of others like it. When he was in third grade and then again when he was in fifth, his class had taken field trips to clamber around the rocket.

He threw his backpack onto the couch and went into the kitchen; his mother was still at work. Pushing his hair out of his face, he stacked the dishes in the dishwasher and wrapped potatoes in tin-foil and pricked them with a fork, setting the oven at 350 degrees.

He did what he could to help out his mother, mowing or raking depending on the season, doing his homework properly so that he stayed on the honor roll, leaving the porch light on for her when he went to bed.

"God," she said to him once. "My whole life would have been different if I had met a man like you."

A boy of twelve lives intensely, every bone in his body desirous of movement, every nerve lit, every brain cell on high alert. He wants to know as many things as he can. Every fact he encounters is absorbed directly into his skin. How to fix a motor, how to tie knots, how to kick a field goal, how to ask out a girl, whether there really is a God or if He's just a story parents tell children, like Santa Claus. He wants to know when his voice will deepen, when his body will get taller, when he'll be able to shave. He wants to know if his ancestry is one of Nazis and roaming gamblers. And he has to be cool about it all. If someone asks him how he's feeling, he has to say okay, like that, okay, even when his heart is going ninety miles an hour in a thirty-mile-an-hour zone, even when he feels history is kicking him in the teeth.

He kept the secret to himself for a week. Every time somebody said something to him, he had trouble answering because all he could think was that he must not mention what was really on his mind. Holding the secret made him hunch forward, as if he were keeping it next to his chest; the principal's secretary asked if he was coming down with the flu. He couldn't look his mother in the eye, knowing what he knew that she did not.

Coming home one night, Plummy was surprised to see the upstairs lights on. She mounted the stairs and found her son rummaging in the storage closet. "What are you doing, Banger?"

"Nothing," he said.

"My foot," she said. "It's the middle of the night. You're supposed to be asleep. How do you think you're going to go to school tomorrow?"

"Mom," he said, turning to her, making himself look her in the face. "Look at these." He held out the photographs.

She went through them, peering at each one as if she were examining a hand of cards. "Your grandfather must have brought these over from Augsburg."

Banger took them back and pulled out the picture of the line of boys in their short-pants uniforms. "Isn't this Grandfather?" he asked, pointing at the kid on the left.

He had seen enough photographs of his grandfather as a young man to know that it was, but he wanted to soften the blow.

Plummy followed Banger's finger. The picture had been overexposed and her father's face was bleached by the sunlight to a small white cloud, but it was indeed a picture of him.

How hot it is in here, Plummy thought. Hot and dusty. There were cobwebs in the corners near the ceiling and a dead silverfish, dried to a flake, on the floor. The slightest movement churned up a small storm of dust motes around the lightbulb. Plummy stopped breathing. She felt the color leach from her face, as if she were a nineteenth-century heroine and had consumption and was dying.

"Why is he wearing a uniform?" Banger asked. "Was Granddad a Nazi?"

"Was he a—?" The words were too peculiar to form. What language was this? "You know better than that, Banger. Your grandfather was a good man."

"Then why is he wearing that uniform?"

She sat down on the floor, next to the deceased silverfish.

"Nazis killed Jews," Banger said. "America fought the Nazis. That was what World War II was all about."

"There were other reasons to fight, too. Pearl Harbor, for example."

"He was a Nazi."

"Maybe you had to wear a uniform if you were just German. Maybe these kids are something like the Boy Scouts. It could be something like that."

"Boy Scouts! Mom, he kept this a secret from you."

"If your grandfather had done anything wrong, he would never have held on to this picture. These boys must have been his friends."

"His friends?" Banger asked, and the implication of it hung in the musty air, making the closet all the more crowded. "If it wasn't wrong, why didn't he show it to us? Why didn't he tell us about his friends? Granddad was a Nazi." He was talking loudly, and his voice cracked. Plummy reached for his hand but he pulled away from her and stood up. "A Nazi," he said again.

"He wasn't! I would know it if he was."

"My grandfather was a fucking Nazi."

Plummy jumped up from the floor and slapped him. They stared at each other in shock. "Oh," she said, horrified. "I didn't mean it!"

Banger ran down the stairs. Plummy rushed after him. "I'm so sorry; but you have to understand, honey, I'm sure there's an explanation." She didn't even know what she meant by that. It was just words. The words had come out of her mouth, but they had nothing to do with her mind, which was numb.

Banger slammed his bedroom door in her face and yelled at her not to come in. She apologized again, through the door, but he wouldn't relent. Finally she retreated to her own bedroom, with its pale yellow walls and deep blue window sills. She chewed her nails to the quick. She never really fell asleep, not really.

Banger dragged himself out of bed in the morning and got on the school bus with Thurgood, but he kept yawning and rubbing his eyes. On the bus, Thurgood asked if he could borrow his home-work for English. Banger clicked open his three-ring notebook and handed over the page. During social studies, Thurgood tried to pass it back, but Banger's fingers seemed to be as sleep-deprived as his brain and he dropped it, watching helplessly as it parachuted to the floor. He leaned over to pick it up but Mr. Singer's right foot landed on it first. Mr. Singer was wearing Timberlands. A black suit and Timberlands. He had big feet, and his shoe pretty much took up the page.

He lifted his foot. "Perhaps you'd like to pick that up," he said.

Banger reached down.

Mr. Singer put his foot down again, just in time not to step on Banger's sleepy fingers. "On the other hand," he said, "maybe I'd better look at it." He glanced at Banger's book report. "Who was your intended recipient?"

"Nobody," Banger mumbled. It was just his crummy luck that Mr. Singer hadn't seen that *he* was the recipient.

"Nobody. 'Nobody' was a famous answer to a question in a famous book. Have you been reading *The Odyssey?*"

Banger shook his head. He didn't even know what *The Odyssey* was.

The bell rang and everyone started to get up.

"You will stay," Mr. Singer said.

Banger sat back down. He opened and shut the lid of his desk just to be doing something. He was careful not to look up when Thurgood left.

"I would not have expected this of you, Banger," said Mr. Singer.

"I'm sorry. I never did it before."

"'Nobody,' or 'No man,' is what Odysseus answers when the Cyclops asks him his name. Do you know who the Cyclops was?"

Banger shook his head. Mr. Singer had asked the question softly, and Banger heard no taunt or disappointment in it. Mr. Singer was seeming more and more like an okay kind of guy.

"The Cyclops was a one-eyed giant."

Banger was feeling faint and a bit sick to his stomach from lack of sleep, but he was also interested—a one-eyed giant was kind of cool. He had thought he was going to be punished, made to stay after school and clean blackboards or something. But it didn't look as if that was what was on Mr. Singer's mind.

"My boy," he said, "I am going to bring you some books to read. You can keep them over the summer." There were only eight more weeks before school let out.

"Thanks, Mr. Singer."

"You're welcome." He sat down in one of the classroom seats—even though, Banger noted, it couldn't have been easy for such a big person to jam himself into a kid's chair. He looked at Banger, and Banger wondered what he saw. "By the way," he said, "why do we call you Banger?"

Banger squirmed.

"I once studied in England," Mr. Singer said. "In England, a banger is a wiener. Now, about boys in Nazi uniforms. The other day you left the room before I could tell you this. Toward the end of World War II, the Nazis drafted young boys into the army. Kids, still in short pants. The boys had no choice."

"Really? No kidding? Like the Boy Scouts? Are you sure?"

His mother had been right! Sometimes he forgot she was older and knew more than he did.

"I wouldn't call them Boy Scouts, but yes, I'm sure. So who was the kid in the uniform?"

Banger hesitated before answering. "My Granddad."

"Ah. Well, he had no choice in the matter."

Banger reached a fist up into the air over his head, pulled it down, and shouted "Yes!" the way athletes did on television.

Mr. Singer unfolded himself from the school desk and stretched. "We need to put your mind to good use, Banger. Maybe you'd like to know more about World War II?"

Banger wanted to know more about everything. "Sure," he said.

Mr. Singer dismissed him, and he raced out in time to catch the bus.

His mother was clipping back the wisteria when he got home. "I'm sorry I slapped you," she said, resting the clippers on the ground.

"Yeah. I'm sorry I said the f-word." He let his backpack slide to the porch. "Mom, did you know *banger* means wiener in England?"

"No," she said. "I didn't know that."

"Bangers and mash. That's franks and mashed potatoes."

"Really," she said.

"Yeah, Mr. Singer told me."

"That's nice," Plummy said.

"Don't you see? It's like everybody has been calling me a wiener all my life."

"Oh, no. It's not, sweetie, because we're not in England. In Alabama, a banger is someone who lets a door bang."

In Alabama, a banger was someone who did something with girls he couldn't talk to his mother about. A really hot thirteen-year-old-girl would walk past and one of Banger's buddies would punch him on the shoulder and say, loudly and gleefully, "Hey, Banger!" He was beginning to feel the pressure of it. But now he said, "If this gets out, it'll kill me. I don't want to be Banger anymore."

"Okay. What do you want to be called? Bill? Billy?"

"Will."

"Will is a great name."

"Mom?"

"What, Will?

He was too excited about changing his name to tell her what Mr. Singer had said about the draft. "Aren't you late, Mom?"

Plummy had spent the afternoon in a daze of memories, trying to square them with the photograph. She was sure, as sure as she could be about anything, that her father had been kind and good. Not only to her and her mother, but to their friends and relatives, their neighbors, to dogs and cats and winter-starved birds. She had once watched him chase a fly out the front door rather than swat it. He had turned the chase into a dance, waltzing around the room and humming a melody by Strauss. As for politics, she remembered her father telling her how proud he was to live in Huntsville, a city that had integrated itself peacefully, even before the marches in Birmingham and Selma. Maybe not because this was the morally right, legally right, spiritually right thing to do but because it was a city whose economy depended on federal funding to keep its space program going. Still, Huntsville had done it.

But she could see now that he had lied when he said that the one and only time he had marched for anything was during the civil-rights movement.

All morning she had tried to make the two things fit. She would look at the photo and then drift into thought until she found herself looking again at her father in his short pants and armband and finally she got out the clippers and put on gardening gloves and went to work on the wisteria. And when Banger—Will—arrived home, she had been thinking that while her father had been a good person, she was not. Her father had never laid a hand on her, but she had slapped her son.

She put her wallet in the back pocket of her jeans and clutched her car keys. "I want you to get to bed early tonight," she said to Will, on her way out.

"Oh, and Mom?" he called after her, as she was turning the key in the ignition. "You were right!"

Right about what? When had she ever been right about anything? It had been right for her to have and keep Will, but that was about it. In the ladies' room at Moon Shots, she sat on the toilet in the handicapped stall, holding on to the safety rail; the seat was so high that she felt shaky, the floor as far away as another planet. But anyone coning in would be more likely to want the regular stall, and she was safe here for a while.

The stall smelled of antiseptic. Someone had gotten mad at the toilet-paper dispenser and taken off the whole side of it to get at the roll. Some of the paper had been left on the floor, and Plummy realized that she had stepped on it and that it was probably stuck to her shoe.

She remembered being her father's banjo. She remembered playing Crazy Eights and how he would wiggle his eyebrows like Groucho Marx while he studied his cards. For God's sake, he had walked with Martin Luther King, with Fred Shuttlesworth. A

German who was a better American than many Americans, if you asked her.

What could any child know about politics, she thought. What could her father have known? Dueling clubs in Heidelberg, fraternities, football, the scouts, street gangs, Hitler Youth—to a boy, they must all have been the same, with rules, insiders and outsiders, initiations, insignia, and secret codes. Boys were savages. Part of a parent's job was to civilize them. Her father had become the most civilized of men, considerate of all and gentle with his girls, as he called Plummy and her mother. He had come home one day with a bright new wedding band to replace the original, worn thin with the years. When Plummy drove home from Florence to confess to her parents that she was going to be a single mother, he had taken her shopping for maternity clothes. Her father! Her mother had been crying and hysterical, wailing that Plummy's life was over, that now she would never do anything with her college degree, she would just be a slave to motherhood. Her father said, "You're going to need things." At first, she had thought he was speaking philosophically, but then he said, "We must help you to get ready." He was starting to be old by then, and he was losing his hair and was not quite as tall as he had been when she was little. "Come," he said to his wife, with that trace of an accent that remained, more in the sound than the syntax. "We must take our daughter to the mall."

Plummy got off the toilet, peeled the toilet paper from the bottom of her shoe, and washed her hands again.

Out front, her boss said, "God, Plummy, what's wrong with you? First you're late and then you disappear into the Ladies so long I was beginning to think you died in there."

"I'm fine," she said, and started washing glasses.

The television over the bar was on, and everyone was staring at it. She looked up to see what they were watching. "It's Mir," her boss said. The space station was falling to earth, breaking up as it entered the atmosphere.

A guy at the bar motioned to her and said, "Jack straight up,

Bud chaser." She set it up. He was wearing a tie and seemed un-comfortable on his stool. "I hate endings," he said, jerking his head toward the TV.

In the department store, her father had talked to her about be-ginnings. He had put an arm around her shoulders. "I am glad you chose to have this baby," he said. "I want to say thank you."

"Thank you? For what?"

"For believing in the future," he had said. "It is important for life to go on and on."

She wondered now if he had been trying to tell her something, a confession of his own. It occurred to her that this might have been how he thought of her when she was born: as life going on and on, a sequel to the life he had had in Germany.

It wasn't until the following year that she had realized her father was dying. He wasn't especially old, and it didn't happen all at once. Parts of him were failing, breaking down. He grew hard of hear-ing. His hands grew arthritic. His hips gave him trouble when he walked. He could no longer make out print with his glasses and had to use a special machine to read. He developed high blood pressure. The aeronautical engineer was falling to earth. Like Mir.

It took six years, and for those six years he doted on his grand-son. For months after his grandfather died, Banger kicked chairs, punched pillows, slapped plates down on the table, taking his anger out on things that didn't know they weren't doing what he wanted them to do. When he had worn out his anger, he subsided into not caring. About anything. A year passed before he began to refer to the grandfather he had known, to remind Plummy of what his grandfather had said to him and done with him, to ask Plummy about his grandfather's life.

Plummy had begun to worry about the absence of an adult male figure in her son's life. She had a pretty face and was slender, with narrow wrists and ankles and a sense of style, but as a single parent those attributes were about as useful to her as a comb to a bald man. She figured no one who wasn't drunk was going to propose to her (who else did she meet, working in a bar?), and since she'd stopped drinking she didn't date drunks. So when he wanted to hear about his grandfather, she had been glad to tell him. She might have been a rotten failure when it came to providing a father for him, but she could tell him what a wonderful man his grandfather had been.

One of Plummy's courses in college had been a semester-long seminar in Evil. Like all the other students, she loved to say she'd gotten a good grade in Evil. They'd read the Book of Job, Freud, Nietzsche, Kierkegaard, Adorno, Benjamin, Sontag, and Wiesel. "And that was just in the first week," she would add, amused by the exaggeration. The "paradigm" for the course, as the professor put it, was the Holocaust. When she visited her parents and told them what she was learning in Evil, her father had said, "Good, good. It's always better to know the truth, even or especially when it is ugly. As even the English poet John Keats would have discovered if only he had lived a little longer."

Taking that class, she had concluded that there was no way of getting beyond good and evil. It was a trial just to tell the difference between them, and the more she thought about it, the less sure she became about everything she had learned. But evil, she came to think, was secondhand and unoriginal. It repeated itself, dragging its heavy body through murk, muck, and slime. It was redundant and strangulating. Goodness was singular, and always new. And it was expansive. It liberated.

That was her considered opinion.

When she got home that night, she revisited the storage closet. This time she was looking for a particular item. When she found it, she yanked on the string that switched off the overhead light bulb and carried it downstairs to give to her son. "I know nobody uses slide rules anymore," she said, "but this one belonged to your grandfather. It was made in Germany."

He ran his fingers over the grained leather case. Finally he asked, "Do you know how to work it?"

"I'm not sure anybody knows how to work one anymore."

"It's kind of neat anyway," Will said.

"Do you think I'm a good person, Will? In spite of—of the—of my behavior," she murmured, owning and disowning her past at the same time.

He could have taken the opportunity to ask about the boyfriends of yore. He could have, but he didn't. When the question was put the way she had put it, how could he say no? If she had slept with nine hundred ninety-nine men, she would still be his mother, kind and good. It was, after all, a simple question. "Yes," he said. "Naturally."

She had gotten that right.

When Will told her what it was she had been right about, Plummy at first felt relief. This was followed by anger that her father hadn't trusted her with the truth about his life. Now she tried to forgive him. Perhaps he'd been afraid. In the aftermath of World War II, people in America—people in Alabama—might not have tolerated his past. Maybe her father had worried about a *lynching,* for God's sake.

She began to wonder what she would have done if her father *had* been a Nazi. Could she have forgiven him, arguing that it was a horrid time, a horrid, torn place? Or would she have set her face against him, refusing the good because the bad was overwhelming? Or suppose it was her *son* who was a Nazi. How could she ever have loved him less, no matter what he did? But how, if he were a Nazi, could he be her son?

Aaron Singer telephoned to invite Plummy and her son to Passover seder at his house. "My wife and I thought Banger might find it interesting."

"Thank you for giving him that information about his grandfather, Mr. Singer."

"Aaron, please," he said. "The fact is, after 1938, German youth were required to serve in the Deutsches Jungvolk. As young as ten. A couple of years of that and they were drafted into the Hitler Youth. A few of them may have been Nazis, but what does it mean to be a Nazi when you're twelve? Not much, I think. Not much more than it means to be a robot. Does he have a friend he'd like to be there, too? At the seder?"

Plummy told him about Thurgood and that Banger wanted to be called Will now.

At the seder, Plummy and her son sat across from Thurgood and his parents while Aaron and Miriam Singer occupied the end seats. Plummy already knew the Taylors, of course. Everyone was on a first-name basis by the time they sat down at the table.

Will and Thurgood were making faces at the gefilte fish. "Will," she said.

Will was what Earl Fitts had not had, and what the Rambling Gambler had not had. But who could blame them? It was the flaw in Nietzsche's philosophy, or what people had made of his philosophy: if you weren't born with will, you had to will yourself to it, and you couldn't do that unless you already had will.

Aaron Singer explained the meaning of Passover, its relationship to the exodus from Egypt and to the transmission of Judaism, and called on Will and Thurgood, as the youngest there, to take turns reading the Four Questions. Why is this night different from all other nights? A copy of the Haggadah rested at every place. Why on this night do we eat unleavened bread? Aaron Singer explained that the three *matzot* symbolized the food of slavery and also of redemption, since the fleeing Israelites had no time to allow their bread to rise. On the seder platter there were bitter herbs, another remembrance of servitude, and *haroset,* mixture of chopped nuts and apples to resemble the mortar the slaves had used making bricks for Pharaoh.

"I learned about Pharaoh's slaves in Sunday school," Thurgood said.

Outside the perimeter of the light from the floor lamp, darkness waited without moving.

The hour grew late, and Will and Thurgood were granted permission to leave the table.

Plummy had worn a skirt and a short fitted jacket. She slung the jacket over the back of her chair. Decaf was poured into a mix of unmatched demi-tasse cups for the adults. Over her cup, she sneaked glances at her son sprawled on the living-room floor. In another year he would probably be taller than she was. A few short years and he'd be gone to college.

Deep into the evening, as the men unbuckled their belts and the women slipped off their heels, and everyone present had begun to think of the Singers' dining room as their own, while Miriam removed dishes and Aaron refilled glasses and the boys had fallen asleep in front of the television set, the talk, because of the occasion, was of history—Jewish and African-American and German—and community—Jewish and African-American and German—and good (that was a short subject) and evil, and before they knew it would happen, though when they later remembered the night they all thought they should have known it would happen, the Holocaust reared its ugly head. Voices were hushed, but there it was, the huge, ungainly centerpiece no one could see over. The paradigm, as Plummy's professor had said.

Wanting to turn away from it, wanting not to have to look it in the face, they substituted one atrocity for another, and another for another, veering into Darfur and Iraq, which were on everyone's mind. Miriam switched the conversation to the subject of anti-Semitism in the South. Aaron pointed out that in the South, at least in the nineteenth century and through much of the twentieth century, anti-Catholicism was a much bigger problem. The Taylors began to talk about racism in America, and Plummy—her bitten nails, splashed with silver-pink nail polish, wrapped around her water glass—blurted, loudly, "My father marched with Shuttlesworth!" The conversation halted.

How does one respond to a non-sequitur?

They recovered and rushed to ask when and where, and that rush spilled into the rush of leave-taking. When the heat of embarrassment had left her face—she and Will were back home by then, in their bedrooms—she asked herself if she had made that stupid, self-serving announcement because she was proud of her father, or because she was ashamed of his heritage, and she realized she would never know the answer.

A woman with a son takes on the mantle of his maleness at the same time that she becomes a servant to him. She knows what it is to be both the woman he loves and the boy he is.

Sometimes, when she is lying in bed after a hard shift, she hears him in his room. Surfing the web, maybe, or drawing cartoons, or pitching wads of paper over his shoulder into the basketball hoop/trashcan: these are the things she imagines him doing. She knows how graceful boys can be when they are being themselves. She wants him to become a happy man, without recesses of sadness, without anger or cynicism, true to himself and others. If this meant being left behind, she would watch over him like a lesser god from a half-forgotten religion, a local god, yes, of grove or natural spring, but present.

Kelly Cherry was born in Louisiana and grew up in upstate New York and Virginia. Her nineteen books and eight chapbooks of poetry, novels, stories, memoir, essays, and criticism include this year's *Girl in a Library: On Women Writers and the Writing Life* and *The Retreats of Thought: Poems.* Her short fiction has been represented in *The Best American Short Stories, The O. Henry Prize Stories, The Pushcart Prize,* and *New Stories from the South.* She lives in Virginia with her husband and two canine comedians.

I spent twenty-five years in Minnesota and Wisconsin, and when I returned to the South, every old house felt like home and every breath of wisteria was balm. I am now finishing a collection of stories about Southern women. It was almost as if these women, who are not based on anyone, were welcoming me back. The women are not connected in any way and live in different parts of the South, and their situations and challenges vary. I taught for a while as Visiting Eminent Scholar at the University of Alabama in Huntsville, a city with an unusual history, and I decided that's where Plummy needed to live. She became undismissably real to me and I wanted to see her through to a good place.

Stephen Marion

TOUCH TOUCH ME

(from *The Oxford American*)

Gerald said it was fun to drive by the jail on a Saturday night to see if any ladies had bailed out. He called it F-Blocking. Once he had driven Alexander County north to south and west to east and found it empty as ever, Gerald would say, We are liable to have to resort to F-Blocking.

Liable to, said a reporter, crinkling his can of beer.

Gerald was master of high jinks. It had been Gerald who re-arranged the letters on the dress-shop sign to read THIRTY-NINE KINDS OF TIGHT ASS. He had transformed this reporter into a re-porter. Last month, this reporter was a bagger, bagging with Ger-ald at Food City, until the help ad was clipped and he began to ask, Have you applied yet? Have you gone down there yet? Are you a newshound yet?

No no no no, said a reporter until Gerald with his own car forced him into the inky air of the newspaper office and this re-porter emerged assigned to the Connie Mack Tournament that weekend at the American Legion Field.

Remember, said Gerald, you don't say I. You say, A reporter. That is the first thing to learn about journalism. Everything else starts from that.

Gerald was up on journalism. He read the newspaper every day. He was up on all topics.

Look, said Gerald, waving the newspaper with Connie Mack inside. Lookahere.

But it may have been that summer with Gerald when a reporter chose his obesity. He may have selected a future of obscene fattitude, extraneous girth, additional gravity, because something was wrong, he was told later. Something was missing. But it did not seem so. But it may have been. A reporter, watching Gerald pop open the official brown bag of Food City, which his father had popped before him, may have made his choice, and not even known it. The man died at forty-eight, said Gerald. Died. People at Food City called Gerald Prince Gerald. He was manager apparent.

On the curb, between two empty patrol cars, stood a couple of girls. In F-Blocking, the idea was to find some who didn't have a ride, or, best of all, had a ride coming but if given the opportunity might choose a different ride. This, Gerald said, had produced memorable evenings in the past. This reporter could not see the girls very well in the dark. Gerald stopped, turned down the radio. They came up, one forwardly, the other cautiously. The forward one got hold of Gerald's door.

You all don't have a cigarette, do you? she said. She held her trembling hands against her chest as endearingly as a withdrawal baby.

Gerald kept a carton of cigarettes for F-Blocking. He was rendered open access to cartons of cigarettes through his Food City principality. In a few seconds, the girls were in the back seat smoking. Gerald went ahead and smoked, too, even though he didn't really smoke.

This looks kind of funny with the girls in the back and the boys in the front, Gerald said, slowing down. Switch with her, Marlin. By her it seemed he meant the one that talked, so a reporter opened his door but the cautious one had taken off running. She hadn't even waited for the car to stop. The forward one and Gerald went running after her. Gerald's cigarette bounced on the gravel. The tail of his sport coat flapped. It was a wide open field. This reporter felt big and empty as he ran, so absent everybody else ran through

him and sped away like rabbits. The forward girl caught her partner and they swung round and round until they both bent over
as if they were sick or very tired. Gerald had stopped way behind.
He was winded. He had the beginnings of a gut but he wore it
high enough that it seemed athletic and he was always very clean
as if just from a shower. A reporter had barely made it off the road.
Gerald watched them as if this were the best evening of the season.
He turned around and stage-whispered, Thing One and Thing
Two. At first, the cautious girl slung her arm wearily as if shaking
off a pesky insect, but the forward girl moved closer to her and
pulled a little the way a pony is straightened and finally they both
came back toward us. The cautious girl was trembling and the
trembles would grow into waves of shaking. Her teeth chattered
in the middle of summer.

Let's all tell our stories, said Gerald after we were back on the
road.

They ain't much to tell, said the girl in the seat next to him. But
she said it as if there were really very very much to be told. You
go, Penny.

I ain't going, said Penny.

I knowed she wouldn't, said the forward girl. She was not more
attractive than Penny, but more sparkly. This reporter deduced
that she was the kind of girl who wouldn't stay still. You all go.

Penny, said Gerald. Oh, Penny, when you came and you gave
what I'd taken. But I sent you away, oh Penny.

I think that is Mandy, said a reporter.

I don't know where to start, said the forward girl, as if she had
never received such a generous offer.

Her name is Anita, said Penny.

I could start there.

I'll start, said Gerald. My motto is, Quit the grinning and shed
the linen. He was looking in the rearview mirror, as if to gauge
Penny's reaction, but he said, You all know anybody with one
headlight?

They were quiet. This reporter noted the lack of backward looks.

The one headlight had come up very close, so close that its light picked up Penny's hair and showed her skin, so close it seemed to have heat. Gerald took off flying. Preacher Road had a long straight part through the flatwoods. The flatwoods flipped all around. Inside, a reporter felt bent over and trembling like Penny. The car went so fast his weightlessness made a reporter remember how little he knew Gerald. A bunch of nights tiding around Alexander County, some bag-popping, an invitation to sports journalism, was all. He was interested in history. But he seemed as if he needed something, some nutrient, that he was supposed to have gotten when he was a little child, but now he wasn't taking it from anybody.

Much better, said Gerald, slowing down.

The headlight was gone, but a reporter's heart still flew. He saw a black railroad trestle over water. Anita had helped herself to a beer. A reporter wished he could get drunk like a normal person. It would have helped in a case like this, but he had discovered that he could not. It was as if he had a race inside and nothing, especially not beer, could slow it down. He would drink of the beer and a picture appeared of his Mama and his Daddy, not a still picture but one in which they could be seen blinking and moving slightly, even scratching, though they stood posed as if in a still picture, and his Mama and Daddy, with whom he still resided, would not leave him to enter drunkenness. Gerald, with his Daddy dead at forty-eight and his Mama with whom he ate lunch every day, took hours to get drunk and many, many beers, but finally he would be drunk. A reporter never could reach it, and now with two F-Block girls and one headlight the race was even worse and his wish to get drunk even harder upon him.

Babe is catatonic, said Gerald. Don't get catatonic on us, Babe. Look at him.

Anita turned around and hung over the back of the seat.

Aw, she crooned.

I'm all right, said a reporter.

How come you call him Babe? Anita asked.

Look at what a Babe he is, said Gerald. Babe is a big journalist. He works for the paper.

Oh God, said Anita. He ain't going to put us in the paper, is he?

He might, said Gerald.

Oh God, said Anita. I'm jealous. Penny got the best one.

What paper? said Penny, dismissively.

The *Alexander County Plain Talk,* said Gerald.

That ain't no paper, said Penny.

Anyways, said Anita, settling back in her seat in the correct direction, I got one of them bad moles. They done told me and ever since they did I been scared half to death.

Anita! Penny called out as if water were carrying her away.

It's okay, said Anita.

It was quiet for a few seconds.

You ain't kidding, are you? said Gerald.

I wisht to hell I was.

What did they tell you?

I done told you what they told me.

I mean what else did they tell you?

That they didn't know how long I had. Not knowing how long I have is the worst part.

Can't they do nothing?

I don't know. I didn't go back. I ain't got no money.

Plus you were scared, said Gerald.

Gerald became quiet again the way he did when something interested him deeply. Anita opened another beer.

They got treatments and stuff, Gerald said finally.

I ain't got no treatment-and-stuff money, said Anita.

We could raise the money, said Gerald. We could do it at the store. We could put your picture on a jar and have everybody that came in give a dollar.

What store?

Or more than a dollar if they can, said Gerald. Food City.

You work at Food City?

We both do.

I thought Babe worked for the paper.

He has a day job.

I figured he did, said Penny.

You'll help us, won't you, Babe? Gerald said. Babe can sing. We could have a benefit with all proceeds going toward treatment.

Sing something, Babe, said Anita.

How great thou art, this reporter sang. How great thou art. He stretched out the last thou.

Damn, said Anita.

Babe can call a game, too, said Gerald. You ought to hear him call a game. We could have us a benefit ball game with Babe calling the plays.

I don't know nothing about sports, said Anita. She turned around again to look, longer this time, long enough for several lights to slide beneath the skin of her face and emerge from her hair, long enough to suggest that she and this reporter were of the same kind. Though she knew nothing of sport and this reporter could not forget anything of it, they were kin, kin enough, probably, for her to know The Fact, and she stared at him with a fondness discounted by kinship, and a reporter stared back asking with his eyes if she could really know his Fact, the one whose origin even he did not know, and he felt her answer, Yes, because her mole put them in the same family.

It seemed as if a reporter had been born knowing The Fact. It must have been told to him very early, by a heart doctor, or by his Mama in one of the times she tried to talk to him. It could have been taken out from under his Daddy's bed like a weapon. However he knew The Fact he knew best how to avoid it. From The Fact he turned. He backpedaled. Spun, head-faked. Knew not even that he knew The Fact. If all of life whirls round it, never touching it, is there even a Fact at all? Isn't the whirl it made the real part?

What are you going to do with your life, Babe? Anita said.

Get fat, a reporter replied.

She giggled. They came out at Jack's. The girls exited like long-distance travelers and went in Jack's bathroom.

Attaboy, said Jack. He meant the girls. He was standing at the counter watching a tiny television. Everybody loved Jack. He used to be a county judge.

We picked them up at the jail, said Gerald.

Ah shit? Jack said.

They bonded out, said Gerald.

Jack said, Ah shit, but it was because he had hit the wrong key on the cash register. He began to figure it upon a pad. Gerald gave him the money and handed the beer to a reporter. Attaboy, Jack said.

I should have waited to see if the girls need something, said Gerald.

Jack looked confused as if neither of his two phrases applied.

Ah shit, a reporter said.

A truck with one headlight was parked next to us in the gravel lot.

What the fuck do you think you are doing? said a man next to the truck.

What the fuck do you think *you* are doing? said Gerald.

The man pushed Gerald and Gerald pushed the man back and they started fighting. They were down in the gravels. Suddenly the girls were out and Anita was kicking fighters. She would wait a second and back up and try to aim for the right one and the man was getting kicked way more than Gerald. One of the kicks got him right in the face and he jerked back and quit. Anita ran back to the car on her tiptoes as if her feet were sore. She had lost one shoe. It had gone flying off her kicking foot, but not when she kicked. Instead, it had flown off backward in her windup. When Gerald and the man separated, the man was bleeding hard from his nose and mouth. You bunch of fucking bastards he hollered and blood splattered out. Jack had come out with his ball bat.

You fucked my teeth, said the man, trying to open his truck door. Fuck you fuckers.

Fuck yourself! Gerald hollered.

The man jumped back in his truck and tore out, throwing gravels all over the car. One stung a reporter in the lip. A squeal came out like a girl's. Gerald had his arms raised in a gesture of surrender toward Jack.

Attaboy? asked Gerald.

Ah shit, said Jack.

In the car, Gerald was breathing hard and had dirt all over his sport coat, which had one lapel turned up.

Did you see me fight? Gerald asked. I was fighting that guy. It was one hell of a fight. That fucker. Who was he?

I don't know, said Anita.

As he drove, Gerald and Anita started laughing hard. They would quit for a few seconds and then one would giggle and the other would start back up. Before long all were laughing so hard it hurt.

Babe is injured, said Anita. She was pointing to a reporter's lip.

How great thou art, he sang. How . . . great . . . thou . . . art.

In a break in the laughter, Anita hopped over and gave Gerald a big kiss.

What was that for? he asked, and she said, I don't know. I guess I put a big wet rag on everything.

No you didn't, said Gerald.

Ah shit, a reporter said.

Attaboy, said Gerald.

On a balmy night in August, a reporter announced, the group of four would go one on one against the world. The world and its fucker. With the fucker of one headlight they would grapple, and the outcome would remain unknown until the final seconds. Would it be the thrill of Attaboy? Or the agony of Ah shit?

Everybody howled, except for Penny, whose stomach seemed to be worse. Gerald pulled behind Food City, where the big trucks backed and idled. The store was closed but he had a key to the heavy back door. Inside in the dark, Gerald found the light switch and the lights popped and hummed. Penny was skinnier than expected and older. Skinny Penny, a reporter thought. Anita had large almond eyes with no rims around them. She was deathly skinny herself.

Are you hungry? Gerald asked a reporter.

I could eat, he said.

Get the box, said Gerald.

Gerald and a reporter kept a box of cakes and candies that had been discarded. The girls were amazed. It was a large box. A reporter lofted a double sweet roll with cherry.

That makes me sick to look at, said Penny, holding her stomach, which pooched out even though she was so skinny.

A reporter slid off the wrapper and began to eat. Penny looked as if she would puke. She and a reporter had not made friends the way Gerald and Anita had.

Strolling through each aisle of the store in its half-light, the girls looked at everything and the smells of the store were the same smells of daytime and childhood. Penny took a bottle of Pepto, and Anita selected a jumbo Slim Jim jerky. Gerald got some Carmex for a reporter's lip. It was a time of mirth.

What I remember the most about Daddy, Gerald said, was something he would say. He'd say he got into it with so and so, and he thought they were going to have to take it to the road. That meant he thought he was going to have to whip somebody's ass.

Gerald was standing still.

We took it to the road, didn't we? Anita said, chewing.

Gerald didn't say anything, but he had heard.

We took it to the road in memory of your dad.

In the back, he clicked open his boxcutter and sliced a cardboard mat for us to eat upon.

They said I write too much, a reporter said. They have to cut it back.

Gerald gave a look of amazement. Can't write too much, he said. He turned on a radio. It was much easier to hear than it was when the store was open.

Anita, said Gerald, where is your mole?

He asked it in a salesmanlike way. Anita swallowed. A reporter could not distinguish whether she was upset because she had forgotten it in the mirth or if she had to think of a place where it could be.

Anita turned around and pulled up her shirt but she couldn't hold her arm long so she had Penny take over. We all looked. It was right on one of the knobs of her backbone. It seemed to have fallen down within the skin as if the skin were not substance but air or cloud. A reporter felt as if he had been closed into a too tiny room.

It's blue, Gerald said.

Tears dropped off Penny's cheeks and hit the cardboard. I'm scared to death, she said.

Gerald got the Polaroid that was used to take the employee of the month and had Penny stand up next to the wall. She wiped off her tears and smiled. The picture slid out and she wanted to see it.

Let's go get them jars, said Gerald.

They went off to look and left a reporter and Penny alone and he didn't know what to do because she was crying and shaking again. If she tried to talk, her teeth chattered. So a reporter unsheathed another cherry sweet roll. Tonight, he wanted to eat on top of eating. It was like swinging a sword. Penny kept saying something and gradually he figured out it was the word *me* and finally he saw that it was, Look me.

Look me? a reporter said.

She had kicked off her shoes and taken off her pants and shirt to reveal her bones. Look me over for one of them moles, she said.

I can't do that, a reporter said.

I ain't taking off my panties, she said.

But she took off her panties. For a second, a reporter was proud. A girl had taken off her clothes, including her panties, right in front of him. It was a first. He thought for a girl to take off her clothes she had to like him, and he didn't like her back, so that made him feel blessed for a second. Another thought he had was of Daddy's magazine. He didn't hide it. It lay on the coffee table each month until Mama finally threw it away. But the bones in front of this reporter bore little resemblance. She had turned over on the cardboard. Start on my back, she said, shivering. My back is what I'm afraid of. I can't see my back. Ribs cut through her back, too. A reporter leaned down. She smelled like beer, cigarettes, and Pepto.

Don't touch me, she said, chattering.

Don't worry, a reporter replied.

I mean you can touch me. Don't *touch* touch me.

A reporter felt the emptiness of looking. It made him want to eat. He touched her and her flesh. She kept asking, Do you see anything? Do you see anything? They are so much I can't see. He told her no. He put his fingers in the slots of her ribs and they were almost too big to fit. He tried his hands all over her, but they were still empty.

Look in the back of my head, she said. They can get in your hair.

This next part a reporter remembered years later when his Daddy took him into the basement to weigh him on the feed scale. He had bought the feed scale expressly for this purpose. If a reporter was going to fatten to this hilarious size, by God he was going to be weighed. He was going to see to it. What happened was a reporter was draped over her. Years later, aboard the feed scale, he could still feel her breath blow out as if from a birthday balloon, and his whole self, including future girth, washing over her. I need to hold her down, he thought. I need to absorb her. At first, she tried to lie still as if he were conducting another part of the scan, some part she knew nothing about but needed, but then she tried to squirm and roll so a reporter had to hold on tight. He was lifted off, the way a crane lifts very heavy things, and she scrambled up naked and Anita was standing there with an armload of empty jars like a cluster of bubbles.

What are you all doing? she said.

Penny sobbed and sucked hard between sobs. I wanted him to look me for them moles, she said, but he got all over me.

Honey, it's your own fault, said Anita. You can't do like that.

She didn't want him to, said Gerald, turning away. Let's let her get dressed.

Penny got her clothes. They were impossibly small. A reporter tried to give her some sweet roll. He touched it right to her mouth but she turned her head away.

Stephen Marion is a native of east Tennessee, where he works as a newspaper journalist. His stories were published recently in the *Oxford American* and *Tin House*. He is also the author of a novel, *Hollow Ground*.

EUGENIA MARION

I was at the county jail one morning—the old jail, not the new justice center—and a couple of young women had just bonded out and were looking for a ride. One of them was a little shaky. I was already working on a long story about the life of a sportswriter who used to ride around the county a good bit in his car at night. The invitational attitude of the two women and the restlessness of the sportswriter seemed to me to fit a certain period of his life perfectly. And the plenty of the grocery store seemed the right place for it all to end when I discovered that both the sportswriter and the young women had the same secret.

Stephanie Powell Watts

FAMILY MUSEUM OF THE ANCIENT POSTCARDS

(from *New Letters*)

In April 1976 my Uncle Silas on my daddy's side got out of jail early after two years and five months of time served for arson. We welcomed him with dinners and back slaps, ignored the pink guilty splotches on his face, places on his skin that would never fully heal, regarded him with a child's wonder, his disappearing act a magic trick—now you don't, but now you see him.

July '76 was the bicentennial for white people, and though we agreed with our black Muslim cousin and black nationalist neighbor, "Whose 200 years of freedom?" we all marveled at the fireworks in town, bigger and better than usual, some of us with our arms crossed over our chests in protest, but all of us with faces tilted to the clear summer sky.

Most remarkably, late in that year, forty-one-year-old Ginny Harshaw, my mother's aunt's child, my cousin, though I called her Aunt Ginny, found a husband. We'd given up on her long, long ago. Just when she had ceased to be a variable in the world of change, Aunt Ginny shocked us with Gerald, five foot, maybe a little more, with a big round belly taut as a starving child's. Though Aunt Ginny was an imposing woman, tall and big boned, a woman's beautiful, "her cheekbones," the women said, her "long fingers like a pianist," they said, though no man ever noticed, apparently except for Gerald.

Our family talked. My mother, her sisters and brothers, wives of brothers, everyone had something to say about Aunt Ginny and Gerald. But none of our mocking importance or our jokes made Aunt Ginny twist in shame or doubt the certainty of her mind. Nothing stopped her from rushing like a teenager out her mama's door when Gerald's Grand Torino rattled up the drive. "He is not afraid," she said and neither was she as she launched herself into the world, sprung and released like a sharp stone from a slingshot. After all those years of living with her mother and her dead father, gone now for twenty-five of those years, she finally flew the coop. On the way out the door, her hard suitcase on the porch already (she would return for her personal things soon, she said), pillowcases of summer clothes packed in the trunk of Gerald's car, she bent to her mother's chair in the front room—her hair dyed black as a China woman's tickled Aunt Ginny's lips— "Bye Mama," she said. Once on the porch, she threw a kiss to her father. "Thank you, merciful God," she said aloud. At that same moment she thought she'd never again have to hear her father's dead steps in the attic or behind her, no more heavy breath, sour from old cigarettes, lingering in the dark places of the creaky house he put together with his own hands. *Enough* she thought, not sure if what she felt wasn't ecstasy. Poor Aunt Ginny. She didn't know (how could she?) how dangerous and foolish to count on anything for the rest of your life.

We didn't hear much from Aunt Ginny in those early months, though we saw her every week on Sunday at my grandmother's. She stayed close to Gerald, served him food like the other wives, patted his hand, looked at him with what we thought was longing when he stood up too early to take her back to their home. We tried to get him to talk and included him the best we knew how. His people weren't neighbors or friends of ours; they were poor blacks, what we called Boomer rats, who lived many in dark houses out on tangled dirt roads on the fringes of the county. Our own dirt roads and tiny houses where we lived were exempt from judgment. We thought we could make nice talk, let him know he was free to sit among us. We told him how Ginny cooked the best turkey, juicy, we said. Years ago, we said, Ginny's hair was a marvel, black and shiny as a satin sheet, long enough for her to sit on. One time, a white man tried to buy it right off her head in Charlotte. Ginny would run her hand through her now short curls embarrassed to have all that past called up. And though nobody told it, Aunt Ginny knew we were all thanking Gerald for making her (the one we'd all called the lost cause) as normal as any of the other women. Gerald nodded, squinted his eyes in concentration. "Is that right?" was the most he'd say.

A couple of times Aunt Ginny came to Sunday dinner alone, dumb and still as a cow, waiting for the best moment to make her excuses and leave. But soon, though no one is sure exactly when, Aunt Ginny stopped coming at all. "Too far," she said. "Busy, you know how it is," she said, deepening her voice, hinting at sexual delights she hoped the long-married women remembered and coveted. But we knew Gerald was to blame. He had been the only person to change Ginny, the only one to make her want to snap her inertia and escape, shedding the kidnapper's ropes and leaving them in a snaky heap behind her. Whatever roots he worked, prayers or curses he hurled on the air, we knew without fighting it that it was powerful magic. Our best hope was that Aunt Ginny was too happy not to play along with Gerald. We were, of course, disappointed.

Almost eight months after her departure, Aunt Ginny came back to us, with her lips grim and set in a freeze that even death couldn't remove. Aunt Ginny rode shotgun beside her mother in the passenger seat of the Buick, her clothes in pillowcases in the backseat, the hard case luggage, a high school graduation present, forgotten in the rush.

"My nerves can't take all this," Aunt Ginny's mother said as she parked in the drive, theatrically lumbering to her chair in the front room. "You ought not put me through it." Aunt Ginny rested in her room, tried not to look at the lumpy pillowcases and hastily stuffed polyester from their open tops. She kicked the bag off the edge of the bed and the rags exploded like confetti on the floor. "I'm back, bastard," she whispered, sure her father had heard.

We wouldn't say it to her. We are not cruel, but we knew all along Aunt Ginny would return. Late marriages can't take; we nodded in agreement. The old are tired, sapless; and try it, be our guest, but you can't make it without hope, the antidote to despair, that the old have irretrievably lost. Though we wanted different for her, we knew Aunt Ginny's story would take one of just a few predictable shapes. The way they told it, Gerald beat Aunt Ginny for being tall, for glancing at him without tenderness as he drifted to sleep, for trying to prove that he could be loved. Aunt Ginny would not say, but something brought her home in a hurry. We thought we understood.

Aunt Ginny tried; you have to give her that. We saw her trying, felt her stretching for something good. We knew that what she wanted was that glad day when the life with Gerald that she knew was just around the corner finally materialized, poof, in a cloud of sorcerer's smoke. "You'll learn fooling with low class niggers," Aunt Ginny's mother said, the smug joy in her heart obvious on her face, a cruel cutting brightness like a sunny winter sky. Now, Aunt Ginny would have no reason to ever again refute what her mother told her.

I suppose Aunt Ginny's return to Mills Road and her mother was the only reason she and I connected. She was then a forty-two-year old woman, not even a divorcée since she never really married like we assumed, and I was fourteen. To say we had a lot in common is wrong on the face of it, but same knows same, one desperation calls out without speaking to another, and we became friends. In the midst of the murmur of the family crowd, the occasional dolphin-high screams of the smallest children, the chatter: *Do we have more paper plates? Mama, can I have . . . ? Cal, turn down that television; is this the last of the cake? Linda, Joyce, don't let your boys play on the stairs,* Aunt Ginny retreated to the living room, forbidden for children, with her romance novel from Goodwill and a pencil.

"Are you looking for something?" she said.

"I'll know when I find it," I said creeping my way along the back of the stiff Victorian sofa, full of shiny tasseled pillows that had to be moved to allow anyone to sit. Above the fake fireplace, my grandmother had pictures of her favorite children, her son James, a rakish knowing on his face as he stood on the tarmac on some army base in Germany, and her youngest boy, the artist (still in Denver or has he moved again?), smiling wide, a beauty in his high school graduation cap and gown. I hesitated to look directly at Aunt Ginny, convinced that seeing her face would compel me to leave.

"What are you doing in here anyway?" I said.

Aunt Ginny sighed and held up *With This Ring,* her romance, an old one judging by the ragged cover of faded and almost disappeared lovers in a posed embrace, framed by the curve of overlapping wedding rings. "I'm reading my literature."

"Those books are trash," I laughed, unable to keep the smugness out of my voice.

"That's my business."

"They're all the same book."

"Oh, so you know everything? Is that how it is?"

"I never said I know everything."

"Really, I thought every twelve-year-old in the world knew it all."

"I'm fourteen, Aunt Ginny."

Aunt Ginny laughed, "Oh, excuse me, fourteen. Come back when you're thirty with a lick of sense." Aunt Ginny had clearly been asleep and her hair was matted on one side; her face was still slack with it. She didn't look like a person with knowledge of any true thing.

"Why don't you stay home if you want to avoid everybody so bad?"

Aunt Ginny sucked her teeth in disgust but didn't answer right away, like she was considering the idea and trying to think of a real response. "I couldn't tell you," she snorted.

Every week we talked, read, but mostly listened as Sunday moved along in the next room. My grandmother and her widowed sister sat at the kitchen table, their stomachs pleased and pouted in their cooking smocks, sighing with fatigue. Harold, the oldest, telling stories that ended with him righteous and victorious. "He's a dick," Aunt Ginny said and I nodded. I had suspected as much. From the basement, the rumble of male voices, my grandfather barking proper form for the free weights, his yelps punctuated by the routine of the click of metal on metal. My mother's voice swallowed in the clamor of women talk. Every Sunday, for months, I met Aunt Ginny in the living room as I passed by my own mama without a word. We often handled each other like we were hot around the edges, careful not to start another round of the war we both heard rumbling in the near distance. I felt my mother's sad eyes follow my back into the living room. Long years would pass before I knew to feel sorry for her.

My grandmother's house is on Mills Road, just off Highway 16, little more than a path used for years by loggers. When my mother was just a girl she loved to listen to the saws and the pull, then catch of the flat-headed blades in the meat of the trees. The jangle, then click of the metal chains twisting around the logs, dragging them from the woods. The trees were almost nude with most of the leaves and branches gone, the tops lopped off, headless, making them look more like skinned animals than wood. Once, when the working men used uncovered tractors in these hilly woods, a man hired to gather felled trees was killed, cracked to pieces by a massive pine that rushed to him, his back no obstacle to the tree's progress to the ground. The trees the men cut fall with tremendous noise, destroying without compunction or remorse the absent-minded or just unlucky, but still, they said, you could hear the splintering of the man's bones.

That story must have haunted my mother because every time she told it, her face glowed with the same amazement and surprise, the same awe. And though I no longer wanted to hear my mother's stories, I couldn't help but think about her standing where I stood, a girl too, schooled already in the language of last resort.

A hundred yards of grass separated the house from the rise of packed red clay above the highway. When we were children, my cousins and I threw rocks as big as eggs as hard as we could at the passing cars below, never once hearing the satisfying ping of the contact of the stone on glass or metal, a sound we reached as far as we could to catch, a sound that would break our hearts if it happened, though we believed it inevitable.

Aunt Ginny's house is only a quarter mile from my grandmother's, but lower on the hill, leaning against the downward slope of the road. You don't notice the house's lean at first, but once you see it, it's hard not to think of Aunt Ginny's house as an alive, stubborn thing pushing against the world for the hell of doing it.

In her backyard, Aunt Ginny's father had planted thick vines of muscadine grapes on wobbly looking wooden structures. You heard the vine and the contented buzzing of drunken bees before you ever rounded to the back of the house and actually saw it.

"Sounds like a giant hive," Aunt Ginny said, "but they won't hurt you as long as you take it easy." Aunt Ginny moved to the vine, picked a fat grape, smoothed the white film like gunpowder with her thumb from the grape's skin, and took a delicate bite with her front teeth. "So good," she said. "The little ones are pretty tart, but not bad. Come on. I'm not picking for you."

I watched Aunt Ginny as long as I could, but as she expected, I inched to the vine to pick for myself.

"I'm making wine this year. I always wanted to do that," she said.

"Yeah?" I said concentrating on the thick clusters, careful not to pinch the body of a yellow bee between my fingers. "How many grapes do we need?"

"I don't know. Enough. Let's get this pail about full and we'll quit."

"What else do you need to make wine?"

"Grapes make wine."

"If you're Jesus," I said.

"I'm getting a bucket, smart ass. Keep picking." By the time Aunt Ginny returned, my hands and mouth were full, and Aunt Ginny wasn't picking, just staring at me, the dusty bucket over her chest like a breastplate. "Do some things you want to do in your life. Hear?"

"Shut up, Aunt Ginny. God," I said, hating the lessons I was sure came to Aunt Ginny from hard experience.

"I'm serious. Don't wait around. Like sex. Do it as much as you can. I'm telling you the truth. One day, you'll look over your lifetime of being a good girl and doing all the things you were supposed to and you'll be as mad and crazy as I am."

"Okay, Aunt Ginny, I'll have sex with everybody I know, even dogs. Will that make you happy?"

"You've got a filthy mouth on you," Aunt Ginny said as she shook the grapes to settle them. I was embarrassed at my joke. But it wasn't that bad, maybe stupid, but any other time Aunt Ginny would get it.

"Did you see my daddy?" she said, pointing to the house. "In mama's room." Aunt Ginny's glimpse of her daddy had changed her mood. I don't know if it's possible to hate someone you've never met, but I hated her daddy. But I wouldn't look. If I saw him in the window, then every other face with his same turn of jaw, every hungry looking man cupping his rusty knuckles to keep the match flame alive, sparing it from the air, scratching his leg with the back of his dirty shoe, in Denver, Kansas City, Ohio, Winston-Salem, or even in my dinky small town would forever move me to hate.

Some of the dead you feel like warmth, their presence a consolation, or so I've heard. My only experience with the dead was with my father's mother, her presence the intensity of a clenched fist. She'd never forgiven me for coming into the world two weeks before she died. But I knew from the cold rage coming off of

Aunt Ginny that her daddy's presence was no comfort to anybody. "Yeah," I muttered, my mouth full of grapes, making my
lips pucker with juice. I knew enough about Aunt Ginny's father
to fear even the flutter of a panel of curtain he moved. I turned
my back so Aunt Ginny's father couldn't see my face either. "Tell
him to leave," I said.

Aunt Ginny dropped her handful of grapes in the pail one at
a time; the soft thuds seemed a comfort. She chuckled, "Are you
used to things being easy?"

A few weeks later, Aunt Ginny waited for me outside my grandmother's house, leaning on her Buick, reading. "Hey Bebe. Roger,"
she nodded to my parents. "You want to go to the store?" I was
already halfway in the car before my mother could answer. "Bebe,
you don't care, do you?" Aunt Ginny asked, her hand on the door
handle.

My mother hesitated, tried to catch my eye as both a warning
and a talisman against harm. I wouldn't meet her stare. "Come
right back," Mama said.

Aunt Ginny reached across the bench seat and tossed a sweater,
some shoes, and a couple books to the back. "Get in. We've got
to hurry," Aunt Ginny said too loudly, mostly for my mother's
benefit. Once on the dusty road, Aunt Ginny rolled her eyes to
me. "*My* mother said bring back an onion," she said, and we both
laughed at our mothers and their worthless concern, like the two
of us were girls together.

"Where are we going?"

"Do you care?" Aunt Ginny rolled down her window, letting
the air flip her curls in every direction.

"Not really." I picked up one of Aunt Ginny's books from the
floorboard. Everywhere Aunt Ginny went, every room of her
house, my grandmother's and now obviously her car, she left these
romances scattered like she molted them. I read aloud: *Her hair
flowed and swirled gloriously like honey against the smooth silk of the
lavender sheet. Am I beautiful? she whispered. Yes, yes, a thousand times*

yes, he said caressing the down of her perfect cheek. "Man, how do you read this?"

"Just wait, little girl. You're going to feel just like that some day. Mark my words. Then don't come to me with none of this, 'but Aunt Ginny, I love him. But Aunt Ginny, he's my everything.'"

"Oh, God, if I ever say, 'he's my everything,' I want you to kill me."

"Not if, when. When, little girl."

"Yeah, okay, we'll see," I said pleased to be talking about my future romantic life, even my refusal of it making that shadow world possible and even legitimate. "What do you need from the store, anyway?"

"Nothing. Just felt like taking a drive."

We turned onto a dirt road barely big enough for one good-sized car, to a brick ranch house, tiny by today's standards. Not like the new houses that have sprouted up everywhere with extra rooms and even extra floors of rooms that more often than not go unused, leaving behind the deflated sense of the wrong promises fulfilled. But this was a starting-out place that people were happy with years ago (this year the hardwood floors, next year the addition), full of possibility. The house didn't look lived in. Not that it wasn't neat or was unkempt, but it was a house without intention, even the grass was filled in with lush green clumps here or there, but bald as sand in the next patch. Aunt Ginny killed the engine and we waited.

"Whose house is this? Gerald's?"

Aunt Ginny nodded her head.

"Are we getting out?"

"I don't think so," Aunt Ginny said.

"He'll see us. You know that don't you?"

Ginny rolled her window all the way up. "Lock your door," she said. "He'll come out in a minute."

"What are we doing here?"

"You want to meet your Uncle Gerald don't you?"

"I've seen him plenty of times," I whined.

Gerald poked his head out the door. I thought he might be annoyed or even that his face would flash with anger, but he didn't look surprised. "Ya'll coming in?" he yelled. In those days, I scrutinized every aspect of a person's appearance, and I knew all there was to know about Gerald's clothed body, but he looked kinder outside of my grandmother's house. His feet were bare and flat like snowshoes, and he wore a T-shirt oversized to accommodate his belly that made him look square and wide as a freezer. "Come on, if you're coming," he said.

"Let's go," Aunt Ginny grabbed my hand. "Is it all right?" she said. Aunt Ginny's desperation embarrassed me, but I couldn't let her see that I wanted to please her.

"We're here now," I sighed.

"Who is this?" Gerald said as if he suspected a trick.

"She's my niece, Gerald. Act like you've got some sense."

"I didn't say nothing." Gerald turned to go back inside. "How you doing?" he threw over his shoulder. Aunt Ginny smiled at me like I had passed some test. "Ya'll want cake? My sister brought over some coconut cake."

Gerald's house was dark, with mahogany paneling and floors, curtains pulled together like a modest lady's towel on her bosom, each room pinched with every door possible closed to the visitor's eye. Gerald led us to his sparse living room with only a dirty plaid chair and a low-riding sofa to match, *Heimliched* against the room's longest wall, and a console television stacked with years of *Ebony* magazines.

"I set up my poker games in here," Gerald grinned. "We're not fancy."

"It's nice," I said, embarrassed that Gerald had to explain.

"You've got good timing, Ginny; I'm in the middle of the game." Aunt Ginny shifted on her feet like she was embarrassed.

Gerald quickly added, "The Redskins will choke up anyway. They always do. Especially if I have some money on it." Aunt Ginny giggled and accepted his apology, as pleased as if Gerald had said something charming.

"You can turn it, but I don't get but two channels down here," Gerald said to me.

"Where are you going?"

"We're going to talk a minute," Aunt Ginny said. "Will you be all right?"

"Talk?"

"Just right there," Aunt Ginny said as she motioned to the bedroom, an uncharacteristic softness in her voice. "Just a minute."

I rolled my eyes at Aunt Ginny. What did she want me to do?

The other channel on Gerald's television came in only weakly, a dim pulse; Gerald had been generous about getting two stations, but both were just football games anyway. I turned up the volume to cover the mumble coming from the next room. If I'd been thinking, I could have gotten one of Aunt Ginny's romances. All I could think about was being alone and uncomfortable and feeling like my mother who hated being alone. My mother imagined that the rest of the world was invited to a great party with laughing people, too swaddled and secure to experience the abjection of the lonely. Her invitation never arrived. Through the years, I watched her stare out the window, a withering in her eyes, a sad turn on her already-frowned lips. I was determined to duck and dodge loneliness, and when that didn't work, I begged it away, though it never listened for long, except when I was with Aunt Ginny.

The living room was about as inviting as a hypodermic needle, but the outside didn't look much better. Above the largest couch was a picture window like a large television screen, but the show was pines straight as soldiers in a dark copse across the road. If I explored those woods, like the muscled and strong nature girls I envied, would I have to find a graying bone sticking from the underbrush of pine needles or a swarm of insects crawling over each other like the bubbles in boiling water? I believed I would.

I will feel this way again; in less than two years, I will be sixteen with my best friend in her grandmother's house, when her boyfriend will emerge from the kitchen with an ancient rubber from his wallet filled to bursting with water, his face all teeth and light as he offers it to us, the reservoir tip of the condom pointing hard and up like a nipple. My best friend will betray me by thinking this hilarious.

In that very moment, Aunt Ginny will come to me with the completeness of plunging into a tunnel, and I will remember that day, two years before, when Aunt Ginny and Gerald are together, and I am only a room away. I will see them as clear as an honest memory: Aunt Ginny and Gerald intertwined. She grips his back, her fingers dimpling his fatty flesh, his face lovely now in its proximity to hers. I know it does not come to mind, the bulge of his body or even her own ungainly proportions, but she will concentrate on his fingers and knees, smooth baby skin of his ear, the scrub of his kinky hair on her legs. Lazarus died twice. The second time for good. Not every miracle lasts. And I will breathe a few choking sighs (sighs my friend will mistake for muffled laughter), glad at last that Aunt Ginny brought me with her to Gerald's to share with her as much as I could, the biggest and most complicated miracle of her life.

A large green car rolled into the driveway behind the Buick, looking like a parade float, with the back end of it extended into the road. I was angry with Aunt Ginny, but I didn't want her humiliated and ran to get to the front porch before whoever was in that car tried to come into the house.

"Hey," the woman yelled.

"Hey."

"Where's Gerald? Is he here?"

I looked to the door not sure what to say. "Yeah. I think so."

"I'm his sister. They call me Sister. I know he's here. Tell him to come out."

"He's busy."

"Busy? You a Harshaw? You look just like them with them chinky eyes. Is Ginny Harshaw in there?" Sister got out of her car and moved quickly to the house. "She's in there sure enough. Stupid, stupid ass. Not Ginny, baby. My brother. How long they been at it?"

"I didn't time them."

"Don't you get attitude. I'm just asking a question. You know as well as I do what's going on." Sister leaned her skinny frame against the closed door of Gerald's house. Her face was Gerald's, the same big eyes and round jolly cheeks. "If he's like any man I know, we shouldn't be waiting out here but a minute," Sister giggled, but I was years from understanding that joke. Besides, I was annoyed that she had indirectly insulted Aunt Ginny.

"Gerald's nobody's prize," I said.

Sister laughed, "who said anything about all that. I'm just saying the both of them need to start acting like grown people. Gerald ain't got sense. I know it. I'm by myself and you don't see me acting a fool all the time, sneaking around like a child." Sister shook her head, twisted her mouth into a scowl. "If you want a woman, get one. Damn. I'd rather he find the Lord. You won't catch me listening to those Jewish fables, but they do some people a whole lot of good."

Sister stuck her head in the house, but appeared to change her mind and didn't go inside. "Look at you standing out here looking right lonesome."

"Nowhere else to be," I said, sounding more pitiful than I meant.

"You hungry?"

"I'm all right."

"You'd say that, wouldn't you? My house is on the next road. I've got food cooked if you're hungry."

"I'm all right."

"Your Aunt Ginny is not studying you right now. Come on. I'll take you to the store then. There's the *Run In* a minute from here. You can get a bar of candy or soda."

"Can you take me to my grandmother's?"

Sister paused and looked at her watch, but shook her head, like the ticking hands on the face had made her decision for her.

"This ain't a Yellow Cab," Sister laughed. "By the time we get back, your Aunt Ginny will be ready for you."

Sister and I pulled up to a small box of a store. "Here's a dollar," she said. But I had money in a sweated wad in my pocket. "No, thanks," I said. Sister returned her dollar to her purse, shrugged her shoulders, a whatever-you-want expression on her face.

Run In was only big enough for a couple of rows of candy, chips, soup, and cola, the few boxes of Kotex and motor oil covered in a film of dust. An older man, maybe as old as twenty, sat on a wooden stool behind the counter talking to a boy I had seen at school, lurking in the smoking section beside the basketball court. The clerk nodded hello to me, barely letting his gaze land on my face. I was a child to him, invisible and unimportant.

"I've never seen you in here," the boy from school said. I didn't realize that he'd ever seen me anywhere since he'd never before raised his hand in greeting or looked directly at my face. I grabbed the nearest candy bar, Chunky, a thick kind with nuts and raisins I hated, and an orange soda, and brought them to the counter.

"We'll let you stay with us," the boy said, winking at the clerk. "You want to give us a try?" he whispered as he leaned toward me. "We'll be sweet to you." The clerk laughed, but kept his seat, his rough fingers tickling my palm with the change from the dollar. I wanted to stay and let something more significant happen to me, an event I would savor in the retelling. But even then, I knew better. Why tears filled my sinuses, the hurt, a pressure like a slap all over my face, I don't know. I threw the soda down as hard as I could close to the boy's feet. I hoped to hear the thick can crack, see the orange fizz explode out like a hydrant all over his shoes. Though the can hissed, it did not pop open, but rolled like a loyal dog to the boy's feet. "What the hell is wrong with you?" I heard at my back as I wiped my eyes and reached for the door to leave.

Aunt Ginny and Gerald were already outside when we got back. I expected to see visible relief on Aunt Ginny's face as I appeared or at least an acknowledgment, but neither she nor Gerald did more than glance up at us for the briefest moment before returning to their conversation.

Sister honked her horn as she pulled out of the driveway. "Stupid ass," she yelled to Gerald, hoping he would have the decency to at least show a little shame.

"Ginny, I'm tired of this shit," Gerald said picking his hair straight up. "Goddammit," he said, but he sounded like he might cry.

"Aunt Ginny, let's go," I said.

"I'm coming."

"Let's go now."

"I'll see you," Aunt Ginny said as she turned her back to Gerald and walked the few steps to the car.

"What are you waiting on?" I said. Gerald watched us, his ugly toes exposed and pleading. I kicked the dashboard of the Buick, leaving the footprint of my shoe on the burgundy vinyl. "Did you even know I was gone?"

"I don't know. Let me think," Aunt Ginny said, her head on the steering wheel.

"Just go."

Aunt Ginny started the car, though we still didn't move.

"Go on, then. I don't want you," Gerald yelled, his voice cracking like a growing boy's. Aunt Ginny pretended not to have heard.

I rolled down my window, leaned as far out of the car as I could. "You go straight to hell," I screamed.

"Don't, don't," Aunt Ginny pulled on my arm, coaxed me back down into the car. Gerald said nothing. In fact, the three of us sat, the way people do when they wait for the life-changing moment to come.

"I used to really love him," Aunt Ginny said.

Gerald finally turned around and went back inside his house. At any minute I was sure he would return with a flower, a baseball bat, with a love poem or grenade, but he didn't come back at all.

"Aunt Ginny, go," I said.

"He's coming back," Aunt Ginny said, though she backed the

car from the drive, turned her head to the dusty road. It would be years, but just as Aunt Ginny predicted, I would feel this kind of love for myself, desperate, stupid, the way Aunt Ginny did or the ways I hoped my parents did (though, in fact, I knew better).

My family arrived at my grandmother's early the next Sunday. Though the front door opened many times, Aunt Ginny did not come. I didn't get to listen to the sounds of the house with her, or see her pretzel her long legs under her body as she read her book about white people in rich, implausible adventures. Just before dark, I walked to her house, to the green paint glowing in the fading light. I could hear her waiting inside, her holding out behind the door. "Aunt Ginny, let me in," I yelled. I was fourteen and in my worst, most painful year. I wanted to tell someone about it, confess it all but there was no one, and worse than that there was nothing to tell. But still I made a vow that when my own daughter is fourteen, I will fill the gap for her. I will not let her flounder disconnected and alone. I believe I would have followed through on that promise. I know it to be true. But although I felt her in quick flashes of being in my belly over the years, she was just as quickly gone. It would be years before I would finally accept that she would never arrive.

In the car, the very next Sunday, my father made his usual speech full of the dread of his in-laws, people who forever thought him too common. "Seven o'clock. No later, I mean it, Bebe." But my mother had decided that her life amounted to these Sundays. She would stay as long as she pleased.

I was sure Aunt Ginny would not be at my grandmother's, but there she was, in the kitchen, cutting herself a slab of dense chocolate cake. "There's my girl," she said. "Come help me eat this."

So much happened in the coming weeks. The grapes we picked turned to wine by themselves, the bucket forgotten and abandoned outside to become crunchy with insects and drowned bees. A boy I considered falling in love with rammed his hand between my legs on the bus, fluttered his dirty fingers in my lap while his friends hooted like sports fans. For a quick, sweet moment, I thought that meant I was desired. And late one Saturday night, the phone rang long and lonesome, not the discordant ring of the wrong number, or the quick bright ring of my mother's sisters, but the drawn-out moan of bad news. Aunt Ginny was in the hospital unconscious from a bottle of pills. If her mother hadn't come back early for the forgotten thing on the kitchen table, Aunt Ginny would be dead.

"I'm going to the hospital." My mother wrapped the stretched yellow cord of the telephone around her hand. "Come on, go with me?"

I did want to go, but I was more afraid than I'd ever been. For weeks my mother and I had spoken in the language of long pauses and slammed doors. We tried as much as we knew how, but the eye of whatever was passing over us had moved on and we were in the storm of it. How can I tell you how hard it is to want not to love your mother? How much and in how many ways I would struggle not to let her know that anything she says means a damn. "Why is Aunt Ginny's sister buried in their yard?" I said. My voice trembled.

"You listen to me," my mother said, her face rabid with anger and pain, "your Aunt Ginny is sick. You're old enough to understand." My mother sighed, holding the top of her head like it might fly off.

"I don't like liars," I said.

My mother's face dropped.

"It's not even her sister, is it?" I taunted, knowing the truth but not yet realizing how dangerous and insignificant the truth is in a life.

"We don't have time for this. Let's go," she said, talking slowly like she was talking to an incompetent. My mother was trying hard not to hate me. I knew it and I blamed her, though I hated me, too. The only difference between us was she could forgive me. We had been close friends for years, better than friends, but in that moment and many like it, neither of us understood that we would be friends again.

"I'll go when I get ready," I said, careful to stay just out of range of her arm.

"You make me sick," she said, and snatched her pocketbook from the table, jingled her keys for comfort. "Suit yourself. But you always do, don't you?"

The next Sunday at my grandmother's, two days after the funeral, the mood was quiet. At least for a while. Aunt Ginny's story was played over and over, *her hair, you should have seen it. That Gerald, he's to blame. A shame, a shame. Did you see him at the funeral crying, looking as pitiful and ignored as an ugly child? He should cry,* we all agreed. But Aunt Ginny's mother didn't blame Gerald. All day long and for the rest of her life she'd find a way to insert in conversation that Aunt Ginny died of pneumonia. She told that lie so many times, her face as clear and untroubled as a turnip, she finally convinced herself. In no time at all, two hours, three, we ate, became many, generations in the small rooms of my grandmother's house, and we closed over the hole Ginny's passing made—a stone dropped into a lake.

It has been years, nearly twenty, since Aunt Ginny lived in that old house on Mills Road, a gravel road now with fine gray dust from pulverized rock in layers over the red clay of my childhood. Now my cousin Mavis and her kids live there, but they will go soon. Nobody stays in that house long. Nothing works right in the old place, and newer is better, we all know that. I was thirty-three, old as Jesus and had just buried my mother the last time I went inside.

My mother, Bebe Marilyn Harshaw Thomas, had always said that she wouldn't live to be old and she was right. It is a cliché to say she was right about a lot of things. It also is true. The old green house was stuck in the same stage of decay it had been twenty years ago when Aunt Ginny invited me in. Aunt Ginny's room was the room Mavis's daughter shared with her toddler brother, the little boy too young to have any opinion, so Aunt Ginny's old room was still a girl's room.

Though Mavis's child plastered the wall with Disney and television cartoon characters, all I could still see were Aunt Ginny's music boxes in a row on her dresser, dozens of fraying romances, her record player with the handled carrying box, the neat stack of her 45s we danced to one afternoon, until we got tired of her heavy jumping skipping the needle, her twin bed covered in a white cotton bedspread like a corpse, and in the closet, heaps of clothes Aunt Ginny could scoop up in a hurry if somebody ever waited for her in the driveway again.

And her father. Still there. But not after that day. I would stay until he came in the room, as long as it took, until I felt him vibrate on the air. He would not be staring over a child this time. That day he would face me, a woman who never desired to love him. A woman, sure she'd lost for the second and final time, the person in the world who loved her most. You don't get too many people who love you like that. For them, I would force him out of that house for good. I would scream at him, fight him if it came to that. For Aunt Ginny, still and forever forty-two. For my mother, whom I would never see again in this life but would feel when I woke every morning, her palm warm on my forehead. "You have to get up," she'd whisper, and I'd jerk awake, eager to follow her voice.

"Get out, get out, out, out." I'd make him hear it until my throat was raw and sore. And he would. May God strike me dead if I lie, but before I left that house for good, I heard his retreating steps, the mincing steps of a coward. I heard the creak of the front door, the draft, colder than it should have been. I feel it still. Seconds before the front door slammed, shaking the frame, final as an axe blade, closed and closed.

———————

Stephanie Powell Watts was born and raised
in Lenoir, North Carolina, where most of
her short fiction is set. Her stories and poems
have appeared in a number of journals including the *Oxford American, African American
Review, New Letters, Tampa Review, The
Pushcart Prize,* and *New Stories from the South.*
Stephanie teaches creative writing at Lehigh University in Bethlehem,
Pennsylvania.

*W*hen I was a kid, my mother was friends with a single, childless
woman in her forties who still lived with her mother. One Sunday
afternoon, my mother asked her friend if she would like to take a drive with
us. My mother's friend obviously wanted to go, but her mother clearly wanted
her to stay put. In a rare act of defiance, my mother's friend got into our car.
"Bring me back an onion," her mother yelled to her from the porch. I was
eight or nine but the tug of war between the women, the strange desperate
bonds between mother and daughter, were easy for anyone to see. On one of
my trips back home to North Carolina a year or so ago, I passed the house
where these women used to live and that moment came back to me so strongly
I thought for a second maybe I'd dreamed it instead of remembered it from
twenty-five years before.

Geoff Wyss

CHILD OF GOD

(from *Image*)

There is nothing more delicious to teachers than a student getting pregnant.

The moralistic hand-wringing of the older teachers, whose lives have become a thin gruel; the knowing grins of the twenty-somethings, still racked by their own bottomless appetites; the general adult glee of watching carefree youth dragged into the confraternity of woe; the secret satisfaction all teachers feel when their admonitions, ignored, are made flesh: a student pregnancy offers something for every taste. Teachers are scavengers. We'll eat anything if it's free, and we are no more discriminating in the gossip we consume. Like the kids who make their lunch from the candy machine and know their diet is death, we gorge on the abundant, sugary whisperings of our high school, too overworked and too polluted to search out better fare. Given the way the pregnancy of our soon-to-be valedictorian appealed to our deepest gut, it was only fitting that we were discussing it at the lunch table.

"Bye-bye, college," sang Jason Pete, our assistant basketball coach. He listened to what he'd just said and giggled, blackly and helplessly, the way you might in response to the death of the last giant panda. "Bye-bye."

"Where'd she find the time, is what I want to know." This was David Bonvillian, the chemistry teacher, warming up his toothy smile. David got away with saying the things no one else could say because he said them in a voice so loud everyone's internal censor ducked. "Yearbook. Cheerleading. Student council. Fucking. There's got to be a daily planner involved."

Jason Pete mimed the act of writing.

"Monday: wake up and vomit. Tuesday: wake up and vomit."

"Wednesday." David again. *"Observe softening and expansion of own pelvic bone. Physics quiz."*

Jason and David enjoyed their usual chorus of tittering women, mostly first- and second-year teachers whose clothes were a little too nice. Claire Guidry, a counselor in her seventies for whom the body had exhausted its joys and who therefore thought the body an uncouth topic, stared at her Styrofoam lunch and chewed cheerlessly.

"The boyfriend works at Winn-Dixie. Got gold highlights in his hair," Jason said, a comment meant to indicate that Ashley Brimmer, our best student, an early admission to Emory, had opened her legs to the great average of our suburb, a shiftless, self-segregated exit ramp of economic helplessness, inarticulate rage, and bumper-sticker nationalism. That she had, in other words, made the choice so many of our smart girls had made over the years. I recognized in Jason's comment, and in David's response—"Maybe she did it to fulfill her service hours"—the jealousy of men who wished Ashley had, in some hypothetical universe where only men's minds can travel, chosen them instead, or pined away chastely for lack of having them. I was readying a statement that would triangulate our cynicism and heartbreak into something truer than either, a beacon we could navigate toward through this dark day, when Ted Infante entered the lounge.

Ted was the senior faculty member at Our Lady of Perpetual Succor, the chair of religion. A near-miss priest, he had married and raised a family and come to identify this most conventional of choices as saintly virtue. The most important lesson Christianity had taught Ted was smugness, and as moderator of the student ministers he sowed this smugness through the religious life of the school. But the word *smug* suggests the confidence of special knowledge; Ted was smug the way the word sounds, like a creature hunched and snuffling in a cave, dumbly hugging a beloved totem tighter and tighter to its breast. Ted hated knowledge. You could track his ignorant path through the faculty lounge by the trail of crosses he drew with fine-point marker on every object he touched—his coffee cup, his briefcase, each new memo he pulled from his mailbox—to make it safe for use. Ted further defended himself against the actual with a stock of good-cheer phrases and an incessant mask-like smile, his eyes bunkered into slits. When you spoke to Ted, most of what you said, along with most of the evidence of the world, burnt up before it could pierce his outer atmosphere. But Ted didn't need global threats to feel embattled; he felt embattled, apparently, by the act of running copies, using the microwave, or taking a pee, because he threw up a barricade of constant mumbling against all these activities, his voice rebounding off the proscenium of the urinal as he dandled his sanctified penis. His students and most of the younger teachers saw him as a harmless goof, cute and pettable, but I knew he was capable of making treacherous swipes with what he believed was a holy sword.

Jason and David fell silent when Ted entered, not because they feared his judgment, but because there was no way to involve him in the conversation that would not produce deep ennui; it would have been like playing pinball without the flippers. This left Ted to fill the vacuum with his dingbat buzzes and whistles: "All right, whew!" (Mopping his brow theatrically.) "We live to fight another day! It's halftime, ladies and gentlemen, halftime!" (Now squinching his nose to elevate his glasses and peer at people's lunch trays.) "Okay, let's see what they're serving us here. Shepherd's pie. Heh, heh. Question is, what's in the herd?" (A joke he had told a thousand times.) "That's the question. Could be anything! Never know. Never know," and he drifted off toward the mailboxes like a car in traffic trailing music of surpassing stupidity.

"Wilkins," Jason said to me some moments later, "you're pretty quiet today."

I felt my lips purse. I nodded, keeping my peace. Until Jason had spoken to me, I hadn't realized how tired I was. It's usually after lunch, when my resolve has gone soft as a pillow and all I want to do is lie down on it for a nap, that I wonder how the hell I'm going to do this for another twenty years, like Ted.

On my way to class, I dropped off some forms to Gilda, the assistant principal's secretary.

"Where would you like me to put these?" I asked.

"I'd tell you the truth," she said, "but I don't want to make you come in your pants."

"Who says I already haven't."

"Sick puppy," she said, her leer turning feral. Gilda was the most profane person I knew, and I was very fond of her. She was a genius of naughtiness, patently smarter than most of the teachers, a woman who had given her intellectual energies not to science or history, but to her borderless marriage and its catalog of sexual languors, which she would recount upon request. Gilda could make a double entendre out of *anything*. For most people, sex toys were punch lines, never escaping the jokes they appeared in; for Gilda, they were everyday household tools which I knew she kept in a briefcase under her bed because she had told me the story of her grandchildren discovering them. She liked me because I acknowledged her sexuality; because, being unmarried, I was not anchored to dutiful propriety like my colleagues; and because (championing libertinism in the abstract and sometimes enjoying its publications) I could keep up with her dirty talk. As for actual bad behavior, she was much better equipped for its rigors: three inches taller and eighty pounds heavier than I, she had the physical presence of a linebacker fortified by weaponized breasts and an audacious gush of platinum curls.

"You heard Ashley Brimmer's pregnant?" I asked.

"Ye-es," the word developing slowly, her eyes glinting, as if her secret society had secured the membership of an important and unlikely soul. I might have suspected Gilda herself of impregnating

Ashley, if that were possible—and as Gilda bit her lip and bared her gums, I wasn't so sure it wasn't.

"You hated girls like that in high school, didn't you?"

By *girls like that* I meant student-body-president, cheerleading-captain, homecoming-queen, treasurer-of-student-ministers girls— all the things Ashley Brimmer was.

"I did. But I loved their boyfriends. And their boyfriends loved me."

We stood enjoying the rich aftertaste of this joke in the window-less room where our lives had washed us up.

"At least she'll be able to finish out the year." In the archdiocese, we hide our pregnant girls away at an alternative school when they begin to show, but since it was already April, that wouldn't apply in Ashley's case.

"Well, they're discussing it this morning. Ted's pushing to get her out now."

My face compounded all the things it wanted to say into a pair of startled eyebrows.

Gilda shrugged.

"I just figure that, like every other man on campus, Ted's angry he wasn't the one who got to fuck her."

The bell interrupted whatever pithy summation I was going to make, and three minutes later I was teaching AP English with Ashley Brimmer in the front row.

We were wrapping up a quarter on the Greeks. Among the modern titles I had assigned was Forster's "The Road from Colonus," which ends with a tree falling and killing a Greek family of five in the very spot where an Englishman had considered spending the night.

"Fate works in mysterious ways," said Candice Monroe in answer to my question about theme. She had pulled one leg up underneath the plaid skirt our girls wear and wedged it at a youthfully impossible angle onto the seat. Hair exploded from her left temple in an insouciant brown spray. How wonderful it would be to be her, with her perfected teeth and her stacks of silly CDs, her oversized ballpoint pen with its translucent cushioned grip and her sunny spot in the third row!

"God has a plan for all of us?" I asked, paraphrasing her. "There's a cosmic purpose?"

"Yep."

I paused to give the others a chance to weigh in. These pauses— their length and weight, the questions I follow them with, the larger point I want to make about this story and all the stories I teach—were known to me from long experience, like lines in a one-man play of extended running, and in the quiet of my heart I considered Ashley Brimmer.

She sat in my foreground blur, in the desk right in front of me, clicking out and reinserting the lead of a mechanical pencil with the only part of her that was less than beautiful, her fingers. Those blighted nails were the first thing I'd noticed four years earlier, when she pointed to a question on my pretest in English I. I knelt beside her desk. "Is this an introductory adverb clause?" she whispered. I reread the item; I had omitted a comma that changed the answer. "Oh, my. You're right. I'm sorry." I was about to stand and announce the change to the class when Ashley whispered, "It's okay," and looked at me for the first time. At thirteen, a pretty girl's prettiness is transcendent. Ashley's skin and hair still carried the glow of their minting, untouched by time's trade and tarnish. Her body, all shoulders and elbows then, held itself light and straight in the desk, a posture that believed in everything except for evil and gravity. But it was her eyes that elevated her beauty from a thing to an idea: they were so direct and defenseless, so deeply black-brown, that I could barely muster the courage to meet them. Over the coming weeks, as she proved herself to be not only a magnitude brighter than the other students but also just as earnest as that first encounter foretold, Ashley's eyes and their expectations of me— that I be good and patient and self-sacrificing and honest—began to cast a radiant heat upon my cheek even when I was looking at other students. How many times in the last four years had I awoken to my morning alarm with Ashley's eyes staring from my preconscious, their blackness floating forward from the blackness of my room?

"Which character in the story makes a statement about providence similar to what Candice has just said?"

"Ethel." One of the boys in back.

"Where is it? Let's find the quote."

"I got it: 'Such a marvelous deliverance does make one believe in providence.'"

So, Ashley's eyes. Ah, but those bitten fingers! She did so many things with them, from handstands at pep rallies to ticket collection at dances to playing piano at mass, that there would have been no way for her to keep them nice anyway, but I finally caught her with them in her mouth. It was a changeover between classes during her junior year, the halls astream with students: I was standing in the doorway to my classroom pretending to be attentive to hallway conduct when I noticed Ashley gazing with complete stillness into the interior of her locker. She had lost track of the world, her eyes blind to the book she had begun to select with her left hand as her right hand unconsciously worked its digits one at a time into her mouth for a few tiny, complacent nibbles. It was one of the most tranquil and engrossing scenes I have ever witnessed, like watching a delicate bird groom itself on a silent ledge. When she finally snapped back to awareness and fluttered off down the hall, I remember thinking that the difference between voyeurism and sight is whether you mean to use what you have seen or to keep it safe inside you.

"And what sort of person is Ethel? What does Forster think of her?"

"She's just a daughter trying to look out for her father."

"Is she?" I asked. "Why does 'looking out' have to mean bullying him out of what he wants to do?"

"Well, where he wanted to stay is where the tree falls. It was fate that she made him leave."

Ashley's handwriting was as elegant and restrained as her general bearing. She wrote in slanted print, with pencil, and I had

watched her lettering grow sleek and functional as it shed its girl-
ish serifs and cinched its inefficient gaps. The word *Clytemnestra*
upside down in Ashley's notebook was an architectural feat,
a graceful unity of column and frieze. Where a girl in twenty-
first-century America learns to practice grace, I have no idea, but
grace characterized Ashley's handwriting and her posture and the
motions of her thought, and I knew she was laying out of these
sloppy early stages of the discussion the way a gifted high jumper
waits patiently while lesser opponents grunt and mash their way
through the lower altitudes and then overleaps them so simply
and so without ego that they feel grateful to have witnessed their
own destruction.

"Fate," she said finally, jamming the pencil behind her ear, a
characteristic gesture, "is the same thing in this story as it is in the
Oresteia—a word people throw around to justify their actions. The
death of the Greek family has no meaning."

"So. Ethel's talk about providence is just a way of putting a bit
of fancy wrapping on her will. Like Antigone."

"Like Agamemnon. Like Clytemnestra. Like Orestes."

"Fate's a platitude for the shallow."

"And for the manipulative."

"Because what quote-quote purpose has the Englishman been
saved for, do we find?"

"For complaining about the noise in his plumbing," she said,
smoothing the page with the flat of her hand. "Hardly a greater
purpose."

"So Jocasta's right. Chance rules our lives, ignore everything
but the now."

"No," Ashley said, enjoying the quaint trap I'd set as she nimbly
side-stepped it. "That's the conclusion of O'Connor's Misfit. It's a
false either/or, Mr. Wilkins." Neither of us had blinked in thirty
seconds. "You told us that either/or is what makes tragedy."

My heart was a happy jumble. To have sown so diligently and
to have the fruits of my labor returned so bountifully—I was
overwhelmed by the beauty of the thing Ashley and I had made

together, and I looked away in what could only be called embarrassment, even as Ashley's eyes fell shyly to her notebook.

Candice wanted very badly to be part of the fun.

"I think God knows what he's doing," she said with perfectly
irrelevant sweetness.

After Ashley's class, fifth period, the rest of the day was a dull-
ness and a drudge. I had two more sections of senior English, but
they were non-honors, which means that, far from a quickening
of the mind that leaves the body receding to a vanishing point, I
could look forward to repeating myself with heavy eyelids, performing broad, senseless gestures to compel attention, and using
my face as a weapon of surveillance and deterrence. Every day of
teaching involves at least one episode of conscious sweating. It
happens at cafeteria duty, with the humid chewing of five hundred
mouths around you, or when your arm is lodged in the guts of an
overheated copier and you need double-sided quizzes for a class
that starts in five minutes. This is the key to the unique exhaustion
of teaching: the mind is called upon to do delicate work inside a
constantly jostled container, like a painter made to paint inside a
lurching public bus.

At the bell, I humped my twelve pounds of books through the
shouldery mosh of the hallway to the locker of sophomore Nick
Melville where, in a finely modulated light yell that only he could
hear, I got him to admit that he had cheated on a test. Then, learning from a secretary that Doug Johansen, our assistant principal,
had gone outside to watch football practice, I trekked across the
blazing sward, and, with the sun glinting directly into my brain,
I nudged the conversation with surgically cool disinterest until I
learned that we had, indeed, decided to send Ashley away to the
alternative school without delay, precisely because of her promi-
nence on campus. Then I had to write a letter of recommendation
for a surpassingly average student, a task requiring a mastery of
faint adjectives and motionless verbs, a discipline much more de-
manding than actual praise, and I had to do so in a hard plastic

chair produced in numbers too large for an attention to ergonom-
ics and with a monitor whose blurriness I had to squint to correct
in a building that had begun to slow-cook its contents now that
the janitors had turned off the air conditioner. By the time I was
licking the triplicate envelopes and signing across the seals, I could
smell a uric, vaguely bookish reek coming off me. Then, at six
o'clock, I sat down at my desk, shut my stinging eyes, and turned
my mind to destroying Ted Infante once and for all.

It was, by now, the hour when people with families were putting chickens into ovens and huddling on couches, so I had the
faculty lounge to myself. Ted's desk was as clean as his brain was
cluttered, with only a radio, a crucifix, and a bonsai tree breaking up its broad expanse, and I navigated toward this queer trin-
ity through the other twenty-some desks in the lounge. Scooting
Ted's chair up behind me, I rubbed my hands together resolutely
and slid open his top desk drawer. There was little of interest there,
just some archaic office supplies, but I still experienced that brain-
shimmer of trespass, that tinkle behind the eyes. He had a Pink
Pearl eraser, its polygon edges scuffed a dull gray. He had an EZ-
Grader with sliding sheath and brass corner rivets, and he had lick-
able ring-reinforcers. These were old-school supplies, relics from
the age of paper, and they caused in me a feeling closer to pity than
to detestation, so I shut them away from sight and began to rifle
his file drawers.

Ted had penciled a tiny cross at the top of every document I
pulled from its file (worksheets on the patriarchs, flow-maps of
the sacraments), a crawling graphite infestation of crosses. Even
the file folders themselves had been scribed with crosses, a tiny
double-hatch on each tab alongside the description of its contents.
Inspecting a test on Moses, however, I noted that it had a cross at
the top of its first page only, leaving pages two and three unpro-
tected from the wiles of Satan. And really, the bottom half of page
one didn't look entirely safe to me, so far away from the citadel of
the upper margin. A cross beside each question would have been
a more responsible way to proceed—or better yet, between each

word. It might be prudent, ultimately, to replace each letter of each word with a cross to completely seal off all entry points for doubt and sin, though one would still need to consider a system for protecting each cross with a cross . . . I shut the drawer and swiveled the chair to the left.

The first file I pulled from this second drawer had no label, but halfway down its red flank, in Ted's penciled script, were the inevitable cross and the words, *Betrayals of Mission.*

The folder, which I laid atop the desk, was thick enough to call into service the widest pre-fold at its vertex; you could have written a nice fat title on its spine. I opened the manila cover and read the first page, which had been produced on a manual typewriter:

August 30, 1971.
Incident: Assistant Principal Linda Lekkerkerner was heard to remark
*   that the current pope was a political, not a religious, choice.*
Context: Faculty Lounge, seven members of faculty present.

After *Context,* there followed a paragraph in which Ted cited the doctrine that had been violated and the way this violation undermined the religious mission of the school.

I didn't know the principal in question. She had come a decade before my time at Perpetual Succor. But a couple hundred more pages sat waiting beneath this first one, and I began to turn them: accounts of catechistic errors by theology faculty, overheard doubts on the subject of transubstantiation, unsound discussions of Christ's humanity, the manually typed pages giving way in the 1980s to pages produced on an electric typewriter and citing teachers I had worked with. I knew Ted well enough to guess he'd been funneling these accounts to the archdiocese. I had the contents of the file spread rather haphazardly across the face of Ted's desk when the door from the copy room swung open.

Gilda took one step into the lounge with her armload of copies, pinned me with a sly glance, and said coyly, "What the fuck are you doing?"

She was wearing a red thing that on anyone else's body would have been called a dress, a garment of perfect respectability that Gilda's roadcrew physique had somehow turned into a mockery of respectability, and you do not temporize with such a woman, so I said, "I'm rifling through this motherfucker's shit. Come see."

I let her skim the top page to get the basic drift, and then I started thumbing the pages rapidly, looking for an *Incident* bearing my name. I didn't have to look far. Only two months into my first year at Perpetual Succor, Ted had slavered up to his Smith-Corona and typed the following:

October 20, 1981.

Incident: Teacher Gary Wilkins, while teaching Dante's Inferno, criticized the Church's stance on homosexuality by pointing out Dante's gentle treatment of homosexuals. "Homophobia is an Old Testament mindset. Jesus never condemned homosexuality. But most people, including the clergy, still aren't ready for the New Testament."

Context: I personally heard Mr. Wilkins's remarks as I stood outside his classroom. They were confirmed to me upon later questioning of his students.

There followed a list of Bible verses and papal statements which my teaching had countermanded.

"He's nuts," Gilda said.

"He's not nuts. He's evil."

But I wasn't angry. This was one thing teaching had done for me in the years since Ted had first added me to his dossier: by buffeting me daily with a hundred annoyances and insults, with a hundred opportunities for anger, teaching had taught me to batten down my temper and navigate it calmly toward its intended port. At the beginning of my career, I was a person who screamed in traffic and gritted my teeth at student misconduct, a man with a legendary forehead vein; now, after twenty years, getting angry is something I do once, maybe twice a semester, and I do it slowly, with none of the old panic, loading my cannons and bringing my bow around so deliberately that my target is compelled to admit the justice of my volley.

So it was with a sense of amusement, really, that I thumbed forward from Ted's report on me to the point, several years later, when Bill McGee became our principal. It had only taken Ted ten days to find an error in Bill's behavior, some problem with a comment he had made after our first mass of the year, and I lifted the remainder of the dossier out of its folder, some hundred pages, and carried it to the copy machine.

"What are you doing, Wilkins?" Gilda asked in the slightly hushed tones of espionage as she followed me into the little room. I turned, reached under her shoulder, and pulled shut the door to the humid, humming oubliette.

"You know what McGee'll do to Ted for this kind of disloyalty? I'm getting the motherfucker fired."

Gilda leaned back against the table in the corner. "It's all so male and exciting," she said, perfuming her voice with the same slutty musk she used for sentences like, *Why don't I ever get abducted?*—a parody of passivity as eerie as a wolf in your grandmother's sleeping bonnet. When I turned from the machine, having loaded the document handler, her eyes wore a challenging dreamy stare. "The way y'all are fighting over that little girl."

That little girl was obviously Ashley Brimmer, and while I didn't think Gilda's comment spoke to the truth of my actions, I knew that defending oneself against Gilda's sexual charges was like arguing with the Inquisition. It was easier just to admit guilt when the result was foreknown, so I turned and propped one foot manfully on a chair as the machine began to bump out its copies, and I said, "Can you smell the testosterone?"

"Smells like toner."

Ordinarily, I would have bandied the joke back at her—*It's pronounced "boner,"* something like that—and the volatility of the moment would have dissipated into the enervated sniggers and sighs of the modern workplace. But I thought I detected a vague insult in Gilda's quip, as if my life appeared dry and papery to women of full sexuality, as if I were not entirely real to them; and so, because I yearned deeply to enter that reality, and because I could think of no other way to do so than to blunder crudely forward, I took Gilda's hand, turned it palm upward, and cupped it between my legs.

"Does it feel like toner?"

I was swelling in her hand before she could unclasp my belt, which she began to do without looking down, smiling complacently as she dropped the buckle aside, twisted the tortoiseshell button beneath, and burrowed her hand warmly inside my boxer shorts. She was tucking me up against her breasts and waiting for me to fill her encompassing grasp when the door clicked open and Ted Infante's head and shoulders spilled into the room.

"Oh, *hi,* Mr. Wilkins! Just dropping in to make some late copies. Teacher's work is never finished! Isn't that the truth, by golly. Being busy's a blessing, I guess!"

Gilda and I were too deeply entangled to do anything but stand frozen. Ted was so short to begin with, and the almost horizontal bow he was performing through the doorway made him so much shorter, that his head was perfectly on level with the offending activity; he was speaking, in effect, directly to my penis. Yet, astoundingly, he saw nothing. Perhaps his optic centers registered a calming uniform gray; perhaps the dominions and powers of angels had arrayed themselves in glowing tableau betwixt his eyes and the occasion of sin. His face took on a sort of glaze as he backed out of the room slowly and clicked the door shut, sparging words in his wake: "No hurry, no hurry. Take your time! I'll be in the computer room—computer's our real boss! Just holler, no hurry."

"Jesus Christ," I said a few moments later, still pressed up against Gilda in a way that no longer seemed wholly appropriate. "Maybe he is nuts."

"Well, he's not an aphrodisiac," Gilda observed, releasing the wilted item in her hand. "Some other time?"

I took Ted's originals back into the lounge and refiled them in his desk. The copies I put in my own desk, and that's where they are still, in an unlabeled folder, supporting the illusion that I will one day use them. There is so much in my desk that's defunct: old tests based on grammar books we haven't used in ten years; student essays of note that I've never reread and never shared with my classes; old student-body telephone directories, most of the numbers now obsolete; letters of recommendation I wrote for people who now own their own law practices or perform neurosurgery or who have had four kids in seven years and will never return to college. I must have once perceived in these materials a potential energy. But energy leaks, sighing away into the air, and time replaces the life of every object with a memory of its life.

Ashley Brimmer came to my classroom at lunch the next day to tell me she was being removed from school.

"I don't want you to be disappointed in me," she said, her voice cracking.

"I'm not. How could you ever think that?"

"I'm disappointed in myself."

"Well," I said, looking into eyes that pleaded for me to say something important, "that's a feeling you get used to as you get older."

"Are you disappointed in yourself?"

The way she asked this question, with slight emphases on *you* and *yourself,* revealed that Ashley saw me, remarkably, as someone who had risen above the conventional adult mire of compromise, bitterness, regret, and despair. The shame I felt at having playacted my way into her esteem was surpassed only by the obligation to say something that would not further injure her.

"No. And you shouldn't be either. Go to confession or whatever, and then let it go. Leave guilt to the weak and stupid. They need it more than you do."

She smiled.

"Will you keep the baby?" I asked.

"Adoption."

We stood up from our desks and embraced, and she disappeared to the alternative school. But as I made my way back to the faculty lounge through an administrative back-hall of framed accreditation certificates and self-awarded plaques, the mendacity of my total being would not stop squeezing at my heart, and I was too tired to throw off its grip. It tightened as I walked, wringing loose a mist in my chest that rose and condensed in my eyes. I blinked at the moisture, but there was such relief in the blink that I could not bring myself to open my eyes again. There was nothing in that familiar hallway I could bear to look at, and I drifted forward through the lidded dark, leaving the known further behind with every step. Somewhere ahead there were secretarial desks, a potted tree, jagged file cabinets, but the darkness was too welcoming. Soon enough I would blow off course and end in wrack and ruin, but I understood that this was no more than the end I had been charting for myself all along.

Geoff Wyss's first novel, *Tiny Clubs,* was published in 2007. Wyss's short fiction has appeared in *Painted Bride Quarterly, Image, Northwest Review, Mid-American Review,* and others. His story "Kids Make Their Own Houses" was reprinted in *New Stories from the South, 2006.* A native of Peoria, Illinois, Wyss has lived for the last fifteen years in New Orleans. He spends his free time renovating his shotgun house and disciplining his cats. He can be reached at geoffwyss@hotmail.com

JACK CULICCHIA

I started this story six or seven years ago, when I was teaching at a high school in St. Bernard Parish that was later destroyed by Hurricane Katrina. The setting is largely borrowed from that place and time, or at least from my memory of it. Nearly all of St. Bernard was devastated,

Charlotte Holmes

COAST

(from *Epoch*)

Edisto Beach, 1968

According to Agnes, I've missed a lot, and she's put reading Rilke at the top of her list. I've built up the fire, and the smell of wood smoke is beginning to overtake the salt smell of the old room, and the warmth makes a dent in the dampness. Settled on one of the saggy, slip-covered sofas that have been here since my childhood, I open the worn clothbound volume, my first thought not about the poems but how her hands looked emerging from the cuffs of her black sweater, the long fingers with short-clipped nails pale against the gray linen as she handed the book to me.

"You speak German?" I asked as we sat drinking tea in her apartment last Thursday, and she said, "Henry, of course. We all learned German. And if I hadn't left, I'd speak Russian, too. Where I come from, adaptation's the name of the game."

She read the poem in Rilke's language, which I remembered a little from high school, though I didn't let on. I was too busy noticing that in her mouth, German wasn't guttural, was nearly as sibilant as the English translation she read next. She speaks English with hardly an accent—a result, she says, of leaving Poland when she was still young. Fifteen—already half her life ago.

I flip through the book, and when I find the poem, read it silently, then speak the words:

Who has no house now, will never build one.
Who is alone now, will long remain so,
Will stay awake, read, write long letters
And will wander restlessly up and down
The tree-lined streets, when the leaves are drifting.

From the other room, Lisa calls out, "What?" When I don't an-swer, she sighs, and I hear her feet hit the floor. I can feel her stand-ing behind me, across the room at the bedroom door. "Henry, did you say something to me?"

"No, love," I tell her, turning the page, letting my fingers graze the paper as gently as I'd touch Agnes's skin.

Lisa says, "This house is freezing," and comes to stand with her back to the fire.

"Surprising it gets so cold down here," I say.

"You'd think they'd have put in a furnace," Lisa says, fanning her hands out behind her. "Jesus, didn't your aunt ever stay here in the winter?"

I shrug, look back at the book, hoping she'll see she's interrupt-ing me. "Aunt Lou and Caroline were tough old birds. Maybe they liked the cold."

"Like you," she says.

"Like me," I agree.

She shivers and rubs her arms. "This house is freezing," she says again.

When my mother's aunt Louise died and left her beach cottage to me, I felt the weight of stepping into a fantasy. Aunt Lou'd known Jasper Johns when he lived down here, and evidently imag-ined me sliding easily into a life like his—a painter living cheaply in a remote Southern beach town, with few distractions.

I could (and did) make a long list of what she didn't take into account, and item number one was that I was twenty-five and still in art school, with no means of supporting myself here, unless I wanted to work a shrimp boat. Miffed at being passed over as

Lou's heir, my mother said maybe someday I'd appreciate owning a piece of oceanfront property. I guess I already do. Renting out the place from April until October allows me to just about break even with taxes and the considerable, necessary, endless repairs.

When Lisa turns to toast her front side, I say, "You can bring your book in here if you want to."

She looks back over her shoulder. "But you're in here," she says, "and I'm still angry with you."

Something small this time, a misunderstanding about dinner. I've never known Lisa to cook a main course more complicated than spaghetti, but last week she mentioned that she wanted to make Thanksgiving dinner. Not *help* to make it, but make it herself. It registered with me briefly, but before we left Philadelphia yesterday, I was the one who went out and bought the hen, packed the cooler, made sure we brought along what dinner required.

This morning we slept late, as we always do after the long drive. After breakfast, she went in to take a shower. Because she'd said nothing about cooking the dinner since last week, I made the pumpkin pie, put it in the narrow, inaccurate old oven to cook, and pulled the chicken out of the refrigerator. Lisa was out of the shower by then. I could hear her opening and closing dresser drawers in the bedroom, hear hangers moving in the closet. I went ahead and swabbed the roasting hen with olive oil and sprinkled it with sage, and made the cornbread dressing. I poured myself another cup of coffee and stood out on the front porch for a while, breathing in the smell of the ocean. I made a few rough sketches in my journal. I went for a short walk. When I came back inside, the house smelled of pumpkin pie, and Lisa was lying on the bed, reading. I figured she'd forgotten her offer to make dinner, but around three o'clock, I was just sliding the pan of chicken and dressing into the oven when she stalked into the kitchen and asked me what I thought I was doing.

Not, "What are you doing?" which she could see, but "What do you think you're doing?" an entirely different question, the kind my mother used to ask. I reset the oven temperature before I answered. "Obviously, I'm making dinner."

After being with her for so long, I know the routine: a spray of words, a slammed door, an hour or two of tense silence. But this time, she altered the performance. Tears began sliding down her cheeks. Surprised, I opened my mouth, ready to apologize, but she said, "You think I'm incompetent," not a question but a statement of fact.

If I'd been thinking faster, I'd have reminded her that she doesn't enjoy cooking, and I do, and that's always the way it's been. Before I had a chance to speak, she stomped off into the bedroom, closing the door behind her, hard.

Sometimes I wonder if the human tendency is to freeze in place at whatever age we are when we meet. My father sometimes still talks to me as if I'm his boy, though I'm thirty and married eight years. And the only way I can see that Lisa's responses have changed in the twelve years I've known her is that she's more comfortable making them. If we met now, perhaps we'd treat each other differently—we'd be kinder, more reasonable. We might act like the adults that other people see functioning in the world, instead of the college freshmen we seem to become when we're together.

"Well, do what you want," I tell her now, yawning to show I don't care what she does. "You can sit over there," I nod at the couch opposite, "and pretend I'm not here." I look back at the poem, and though I haven't finished reading it, turn the page.

She starts off into the bedroom to get her book, muttering, "You're not here. You're not here. You're not here."

The tide's coming in dark gray and churning, the rain moving in sheets across the water. Not much stands between me and the ocean—windows and French doors shut tight against the sea wind, the broad screened porch that embraces the house on three sides, and then a short plank walk down to a beach that erodes a few feet more each year.

Lisa used to insist that it was all a matter of perception—that

I thought even the beach was grander in childhood. But the one time she said this in front of my mother, Mom backed me up. Exhaling cigarette smoke, gazing out at the water with melancholy affection, she said, "Lisa, honey, from what I recall, you were never here when Henry was a child." And for once, my wife didn't have an answer.

Now she plops down on the sofa across from me, and drops a couple of heavy tomes on the coffee table between us. For four years, Lisa taught middle school music classes while I worked on my master's at Tyler and then got a job as a medical illustrator. As soon as we could swing it financially, she went back to school, earned a master's in music education and now she's studying for her PhD comps. Pale and small, she's developed muscles from hauling around these library volumes. She draws her legs up under her and wraps herself in the afghan, pulls one of the books onto her lap, and rubs her forehead.

"Jesus," she says. "I'm so tired." She used to complain that teaching adolescents exhausted her, that after a day at school, she had no energy left to read. Now she reads all the time and she still complains about being tired. She opens the book where her marker is, but after a few minutes I look up and she's staring across the room into the fire.

"Try driving for ten hours in a rainstorm," I almost say, but realize she'd only argue that she offered to drive half the distance before we'd even left Philadelphia. And then I'd feel compelled to point out that had she driven us, the ten-hour drive would have stretched to twelve. And lifting her chin, she'd say, "I drive the speed limit," enhancing her reason with an implied rebuke.

That argument played out, I look down into the open pages of my book and think about Agnes, spending Thanksgiving with her husband in a city hundreds of miles from here. Even though she says her husband barely knows how to boil water, I put him in the kitchen, allow Agnes to be in her studio, with the gray light from the window falling across her strong-boned face, strands of dark hair trailing down her neck from the bun that's always unraveling.

I think about her hands moving swiftly among the jars and brushes and tubes, mixing colors, and the smell of turpentine in the room. It clings to her, so when I bury my face in her hair, it's what I breathe in, along with a faint smell I couldn't place until I used the bar of soap in her bathroom.

Because she lives in New York, two hours from Philly by train, I've been able to see her only a few times in the two months since we met. What I know of her life, I've mostly collaged from scraps that form, I know, an incomplete picture. Once I asked her, "Where did you buy that sweater?" just so I could imagine her buying it. She looked at me, confused, and said, "I didn't buy it. I made it. Why?" but instead of the real reason, I said, "I like the color." She looked down at it. "It's black," she said, and raised an eyebrow at me. "I like the color on you, is what I meant," I told her, and she thanked me.

Our time together is too compressed to allow for the boring interludes where details of life fall in. Maybe that's why she's the one I want to turn to and say, "Do you hear that?" as the ocean pounds against the sand. I'd like her to smell the dampness in this musty room, so different from the smells of the usual rooms where we're together. Maybe I want to hear her say, "This reminds me of . . ." and have her fill in some blank about her life that I couldn't otherwise imagine. Maybe what I want is just to watch her take in the details of a place I know so well, see them filter into her consciousness and come back changed, infused with her own quirky vision.

The night we met, our breath clouded in the brittle air and she laughed and said the clouds were poems we had yet to find the words to. The next morning she woke and, before opening her eyes, laid her palm against my cheek and said my name. Last Thursday, I gripped her hands in mine as she arched above me, and I looked into her eyes and thought, *Who are you? What do you want from me?* Almost before the thought had finished forming, she leaned down and put her mouth over mine, binding me to her with the intricate threads of desire, so that *who* she was and *what* she wanted became secondary—tertiary—to the way our bodies fit together. For the first time in my life, I understood the meaning of "becoming one" with another person. That evening, standing on the platform waiting for my train, I carried the taste of her on my tongue.

Such intangibles—even the autumn light spilling through the salt-sprayed glass is more real.

With her resting in the crook of my arm, I told her: "Imagine light scrubbed bare, then gold-leafed."

I said: "The walls of the house are wood."

I said: "When I take you there, the seagulls will wake you every morning."

I leave her with impressions of a house she may never see. And the rest of what I leave is gone before I reach the corner—the teacups washed, the ashtray emptied, Agnes in the shower scrubbing me from her body with a soap that smells of sage.

I look up, and Lisa's staring at me, her eyes so intense, I can't think of anything to do except smile. When she doesn't smile back, I lay down the book of poems, cross the narrow band of floor between us, and kiss her.

We lie together, squeezed onto the narrow sofa. Lisa has one bare leg thrown across my legs. I wonder how many times we've done this, ended an argument with sex. Finally, it's easier. No one has to accept blame or puzzle out what really made us argue. Our bodies forge a resolution for a time. But then time passes, and though the circumstances change, someone is hurt again, someone slams a door again, someone leaves the house again, and we're no closer to understanding why.

In the almost two months I've known Agnes, I can't imagine trying to distract her from what she wants to say. In our conversations, she wants reasons, wants to ferret out my motives, make me admit what's on my mind. "Maybe some things don't need to be talked to death," I've told her. Smiling sometimes, she responds, "Why are you so afraid of what you feel?"

We've had two arguments, and I'm not sure the first (about the best way to prime a particular grade of canvas) qualifies as anything more than a minor disagreement. And the second might not have been an argument either, but her voice tensed when she said, "Believe me, I know you. I pay very close attention."

Because I had said, "You don't even know me. We've seen each other, what? A half dozen times?"

"Seven," she said.

Lisa slides her hands beneath my shirt and strokes my back, and after a moment she leans away enough to look up at me. She says, "What were you thinking?"

"When?" I murmur.

She tilts her head to indicate the other couch. "Over there," she says. "Before you kissed me."

"Mm." I pull her back to me and kiss her forehead. "I don't remember," I say. "Let's take a nap."

"Christ," she says as she struggles away from me and sits up on the sofa. When I ask what's wrong, she says, "I have work to do," and reaches down to the floor to separate her jeans and underwear from the tangle of clothes. Scowling, she stands, looking down at me as she steps into her pants and tugs the zipper up on her jeans. She picks up her socks and shoes and sits on the other sofa to put them on.

Watching her, I wonder when I came to feel so distant. I've left her as surely as if I'd walked out of the room. What remains is emptiness that I both cause and occupy. I don't want her to be unhappy. If I can avoid hurting her, I will. But as she sits on the sofa lacing up her shoes, I know that what I feel for her is simply the affection I'd feel for any other friend. Strangely, this realization feels like my true betrayal. Falling out of love is not what I expected.

"What's this you're reading?" Lisa says, looking down at the book on the cushion beside her.

I tell her the title, though she's reading it from the cover.

"Where'd you pick this up?" she says, beginning to page through it.

For a moment I can't remember if Agnes's name is on the fly-leaf, if she's made notes in the margins, marked favorite lines. But there's no edge to Lisa's question; I tell her the name of a used bookstore not far from our apartment in Center City.

She says, "Since when do you read poetry?"

I repeat what Agnes said: "All painters should know Rilke."

She flips through the book, pausing to read a line here and there, before closing it gently and laying it on the coffee table. She studies it for a few seconds before looking up at me. "If you haven't already read Rilke, how do you know that?" she asks.

I make myself meet her eyes, but I can't make myself speak. *Who is alone now, will remain alone.* After a pause, she gets up, goes to the hall, and puts on her jacket.

As she walks back through the living room, I say, "Going out?"

She opens the French doors and a cold wind pushes past her.

"Obviously," she says.

"I thought you had work to do," I say, but she's already closed the doors behind her.

For a while, I lie on the sofa, looking at the map my aunt painted, framed, and hung over the mantle when she and Caroline built the cottage in 1940. The paper's water stained from storms when the chimney flashing didn't hold—a situation I've come to know well since the roof became my responsibility.

Aunt Lou was an Atlanta architect, and the map is labeled in an architect's blocky hand: Edingsville Beach and Frampton Inlet and Botany Bay, and the network of tiny, meandering creeks that reduce the island to little more than chunks of sand surrounded by marsh and water. This house is a mark on the coast, and the Atlantic gradually darkens as it deepens away from shore. Lou drew a cross on the map to show where, on the road leading off the island, an historical marker delineates the high water of the worst coastal flooding on record, in the hurricane of 1899.

When I was a boy, I'd lie on the couch and study the map and think about the ocean covering up all the land where the house is, and the street behind us, the cement-block grocery store and the second row houses and even the third, all the way past what's now called Jungle Road because it looks more like something you might find deep in the lush interior, not a place where waves ever lapped the low-hanging branches of the palms. At night I had to sleep with the light on. I had nightmares of the waves slamming into the windows, the house filling with salt water.

"I guess it could happen again," Caroline had told me, ignoring my mother's frown. Practical and plain-spoken, my aunt's lover taught biology at Agnes Scott and didn't believe in soft-pedaling nature. When we walked the beach together, she'd take a stick to the body of a sea turtle ravaged by gulls, to show me its anatomy. Even at five or six years old, I delighted in this, knowing my mother would've tried to distract me from the carrion by pointing out the light on the water or an interesting formation of clouds. At night, in the absence of television, Caroline told stories about the early indigo farmers who settled the island and the cotton plantations that sprang up in the eighteenth century. Descendants of these planters still live on the island, and I was amused that the bedwetting, booger-eating Middleton boy I played with was the remnant of an aristocracy. My favorites among Caroline's stories were the tragedies: the planter's daughter drowned in a storm, the bride murdered on her wedding day by a spurned suitor. Caroline said with an authority not even my mother questioned that a ghost wearing a blood-stained wedding gown haunted the ruins of Brick House—ruins Caroline and I had explored together on sullen, mosquito-slapping afternoons when Aunt Lou and my mother sat on the porch drinking lemonade and trying to unravel their family's complicated genealogy.

"Who cares who married whom?" Caroline tossed out conspiratorially as I followed her to her car. "What I'm interested in is *living* history."

When I dared to point out that the ghost wasn't, technically, living history, she looked at me as if I were nuts. "Of course she is,"

Caroline said. "She's still *there*, isn't she?" Later, when I tried out this reasoning, my mother said, "Caroline has always thought a little differently from most people," and gave me a look that ended the discussion.

The first time I brought Lisa here was on the heels of a February storm. I promised Aunt Lou that "my buddies" and I wouldn't trash the place, and she agreed we could use the house if I promised to repair the porch screens. This was a few years before she died, not long after she'd lost Caroline, and I think now it was the test: Did I love the house enough to make repairs even when I was supposed to be having fun?

Lisa and I had been dating about six months, in the sheltered corral of a college campus. It's easy to forget sometimes how fast things change. Ten years later, it's another world—boys and girls living in the same dormitories, "free love" everywhere you look. In 1958 we could barely arrange to be alone together. Her parents thought she was spending spring break in Myrtle Beach with her roommates.

It doesn't take much imagination to construct the events of the week we spent here. But we were sloppy enough. By the time we returned to Pennsylvania, she was pregnant, although it took another month before we knew that, and yet another month before we found a doctor who could help us.

Going through that experience was bound to either draw us closer or break us apart completely, and I have to admit that when summer came, I still didn't know which way we'd fallen. I thought Lisa was holding up all right, so I didn't cancel my plans to study in Italy. I'd only been gone a couple of weeks when I got a letter from Lisa's mother, saying that Lisa bad been hospitalized for "nervous exhaustion," and not to worry if I didn't hear from her for a while.

Her folks have always been fond of me, and I imagine even if her mother had known about the abortion—which Lisa insists she didn't—she'd have remained fond. I have always been, as Lisa's mother likes to say, "a wonderful young man," by which she means

I'm polite, quiet, and generally cheerful, from a good family. She forgives me for being an artist because I talk sports with Lisa's father. She forgives my long hair because when Lisa and I visit, I clean the gutters, fix the leaking faucets, shovel the walks if there's snow. When Lisa and I disagree about something, I can count on her to take my side.

In the autumn of '58, when Lisa and I were back in school again, I realized that a sticky new web bound us to a path with marriage at its logical end. Lisa reminded me frequently that she'd "been through a lot." And having "been through a lot" apparently entitled her to my life, although I didn't really know why she wanted it. It seemed—still seems—a rough-hewn thing to me.

When I stand up from the couch to get dressed, I see that she hasn't gone far, just down to the ruins of the jetty. I'm putting on my shoes when I see her sit on the sand about ten feet from the edge of the tide. She wraps her arms around her knees and looks out at the ocean, and after a while she leans her forehead against her knees. I'd almost bet she figures I'm watching her, that the wistful pose is for my benefit.

I go into the kitchen to check on dinner, which I've lost my appetite for. Everything here is more than twenty years out of date—the pots dented, the knives dull—and I know before too long, I'll have to renovate if I want to keep on renting out the place. I can't even imagine the cost of such a project, but I'm certain it's one more thing I don't want to think about. I take the pan of dressing from the oven, jiggle the leg on the roaster to be sure it's done. I slice a few tomatoes onto a chipped plate, clean the broccoli—things that, had Lisa really had any interest in making dinner, she could've done once she saw I'd taken care of the main dish. I take a mug of tea out to the screened porch, thinking I might call Lisa in for dinner, but she's given up sitting on the sand—it must be damp, after all—and is now walking towards the mouth of the river. The shelling beach, Caroline and Lou called it—where the land curves out like a great arm, and sweeps in all the ocean's debris. A twenty-minute walk there, and twenty back—if that's where she's going, by the time Lisa returns, the dressing will be room temperature, the tomatoes leaking juice. I think for a minute about going after her.

Instead, I figure that whatever shape the dinner is in, it'll be more pleasant to eat if she's walked off her mood. I take my tea back into the house, turn off the stove and the kitchen light. In the living room, I stoke the fire, sit on the couch and open the volume of poems.

The day she gave me the book, Agnes told me that Rilke was married to a sculptor, a woman I've never heard of. Soon after their child was born, he left them. To my surprise, Agnes didn't say what I was expecting—what Lisa would have said—that the guy was a creep and a coward. She said, "He knew he couldn't live with them and continue to do his work."

"His wife must've hated him," I said, and she shook her head.

"They saw one another from time to time. His wife knew what he needed, probably as much as he did. Certainly she knew her own needs, although as an artist, she never had his genius."

"I can't imagine they really loved each other," I said.

Agnes sipped her tea. After a while, she said, "It's difficult to judge someone else's life."

As we sat there in her kitchen, Agnes's slate-colored eyes kept darting to the clock over the stove. I had a train to catch. The class her husband taught was ending soon. She had plans to attend a friend's opening. She could have been gauging the time for any of these events, or for none of them. Maybe checking the clock was simply a nervous habit. I didn't know her well enough to be sure. We were—are—still new enough together that if I were to catch my train and never come back, I'd be no more than an odd episode that ended as abruptly and mysteriously as it began. And while walking out of Agnes's life that way already seems impossible, I'd never thought I'd have an affair until the night someone who knows us both said, "Henry, here's someone you've got to meet."

I thought I knew myself pretty well. I trusted what I was capable of. As I sat at Agnes's kitchen table holding the volume of Rilke, she turned to me and said, "I love you," and I said, "You hardly know me," and she said, "Believe me, I know you."

On the front porch, Lisa's stomping the sand off her shoes, and in a moment she's in through the French doors and standing before the fire again, removing her jacket, shaking her long blond hair out around her shoulders.

"Dinner smells fantastic," she says, smiling. My mother often tells me what a good sport my wife is, and at moments like this, I understand what she means. I can tell by Lisa's voice that she's forgiven me, that somewhere between the jetty and the shelling beach, her anger became so much spindrift. I can almost guess that as she walked into the wind, she told herself, *Don't ruin the holiday. It's just a goddamned chicken. You should be grateful he likes to cook.*

I close the book and lay it aside. "I hope you're hungry," I tell her, "because it's just about ready."

She walks over to the couch. Her face is pink from the wind, and her blue eyes seem anxious as she looks down at me and extends her hands. I take hold of them—cold and a little damp—and she hoists me to my feet.

Charlotte Holmes was born in Augusta, Georgia, but for the past twenty years has lived in State College, Pennsylvania, where she teaches fiction writing at Penn State University. Her stories and essays have appeared in many journals, most recently in *Epoch, New Letters,* and the *Sun.* Among her awards are the D. H. Lawrence Fellowship in fiction, the Writers Exchange Award from *Poets & Writers,* and two fellowships from the Pennsylvania Arts Council. A story from her first collection—*Gifts and Other Stories*—was included in *New Stories From the South: The Year's Best, 1988.*

*H*enry is at the center of the book of multigenerational, interwoven stories I'm working on now. "Coast" is the fourth or fifth of these stories that I wrote, though chronologically, it comes first. I started writing it as a way to understand a situation I'd created in another story—told from Agnes's perspective—about Henry and Agnes's parting. I knew there were complicated emotional ties that kept Henry with Lisa, even though they have grown apart and their life together pales in comparison to the life he suspects he and Agnes might have shared. This story helped me to unravel those ties and to better understand his choice, which might be seen as an act of cowardice, or an act of decency, or one of sacrifice. That a choice can be both right and wrong, cowardly and decent, easy and difficult . . . most of the stories in the collection take this idea up in some way.

My husband often vacationed at Edisto Beach, South Carolina, as a child, staying in a beachfront house that his mother's friends owned. We stayed there early in our relationship, when the house was unchanged from the way it had looked in his childhood, and again when our son was small, by which time someone else owned the house and it was quite down-at-the-heels. Nonetheless, the memory of the place and the story of its origins made the passage into another generation in a vivid way. This is the house in the story. Although Henry is a Pennsylvanian, he has Southern roots on his mother's side. I wanted him to have the house because I knew he'd take good care of it and because I wanted him to leave it to his son, who is years away from being born when "Coast" takes place but is the protagonist of several of the other stories.

Kevin Wilson

NO JOKE, THIS IS GOING TO BE PAINFUL

(from *Tin House*)

We called them ice fights. They made things weird for a little while.

I had moved to Coalfield earlier that summer, after I lost my job as a checkout girl at the Bates supermarket in Mount Juliet. It wasn't a huge deal. I was stealing small amounts of money every once in a while and then I got caught and they didn't have any choice but to let me go. If they could have kept me, they would have. It happens.

I was living in a room above my sister and her husband's garage, just my computer, three fans, and a futon we found at a garage sale. For a few weeks, I just sat in that room, nothing but the hum of the fans, no friends, no money, not a thing to do, wishing I was drunk. It was not, truth be told, an uncommon situation for me.

At dinner one night, my sister asked if I'd explored the town and I shook my head. "There's a museum that's not too bad," she said, "and a roller rink that plays good music," and I smiled and felt like I might cry because, although my sister seemed completely oblivious to the kind of person that I was, she wanted me to be happy. I felt like, if I killed someone in front of her, she wouldn't turn me in, even though the guilt would cause her to commit suicide. "Can you drink beer at the roller rink?" I asked, and my sister got excited. "I believe so," she said, and though I never went, it was nice to pretend that I would.

My sister and her husband had a group of close friends, and, in an effort to get me out of the house, they invited me to come along for a barbecue at Danny and Erica's. After nearly a month of not settling in, I was beginning to think that talking to some capable and attractive and financially secure people might not be such a bad thing. I had devised a theory that if I had some friends I might not be so quick to want everyone around me to be miserable.

Danny and Erica had a huge, sprawling yard with a picnic table and a Frisbee that no one even touched and condiments attracting flies while the smoke from the grill got in my hair. These people were nice enough, but they were a little older than me; they talked about TV shows I'd never heard of and drank beer over ice with some lime juice mixed in, which was something that seemed strange and pointless. One of the guys, Eddie, told me when we were alone that my sister had said I was the wild sister and that he had been a little wild in college. "But not anymore?" I asked. He smiled and his face got red and he shook his head. "Not so much," he said, "no."

And then my sister found a fly frozen in an ice cube and plucked it out of her glass. "Gross," she said, holding it between her thumb and middle finger. Everyone was hooting and checking their glass like it was a party game. "Eat it," I said, and everyone stopped laughing. "Gross," my sister said again and frowned at me. Eddie, trying to be wild, said, "Hell, I'll eat it," but my sister shook her head and threw the ice cube in the grass. Wage, whose wife worked with my sister at the high school, said, "I bet you couldn't hit that tree with a piece of ice," pointing towards a dogwood about ten yards away. So far, Wage was the most interesting person in the group. He was cute but he also seemed, at times, to be mildly retarded. For instance, he had talked about a particular comic book character as if he was real. Another time during the party, he had mentioned that he could probably run a marathon this weekend without training, but his wife, Julie, kept saying that he'd never run a day in his life. He just shrugged and looked at me as if to say, "She has no idea what she's talking about." I thought out of everyone there, Wage seemed like the most interesting.

Eddie stood up from the picnic table and picked up a piece of ice. "Hell," he said, "I'll do it." He wound up and tossed the ice, missing the tree by a good distance. My sister's husband grabbed another chunk of ice and calmly tossed it at the tree, the ice shattering as it hit the trunk. "Game over," he said and sat back down. But everyone was getting a little drunk at this point and so the game was most certainly not over. We started winding our arms in big circles, testing our muscles, and then tossing ice into the air, waiting for impact. Wage had hit the tree seven times in a row, each time stepping back a little further. "I could probably play professional baseball if I wanted," he said, and then he hit the tree for the eighth time. "My hands are cold," Erica said, but no one stopped playing. Wage hit nine, then ten, then eleven. Everyone else stopped throwing, content to watch Wage continue his streak, twelve, thirteen, fourteen. My sister's husband had his hand on my sister's ass, rubbing it like a good luck charm. It seemed like it might be a good night after all.

On his nineteenth throw, it was like watching someone put correct change in a Coke machine, and I was getting bored. I fished a piece of half-melted ice from my glass and shook the excess moisture off. Then, as Wage began his windup, I tossed my piece of ice and hit him on the back of his neck. Without stopping his throwing motion, Wage spun around and winged the ice directly at my head. Julie gasped and then yelled, "Wage? Jesus Christ." I ducked and the ice sailed over my head and then Danny, who was spectacularly drunk by this time, shouted, "Ice fight!" After a few moments of hesitation, people looking around to gauge interest, everyone ran to the cooler, dumped their cups into the ice, and then scattered. Ice was flying from all directions, skittering across the grass as it landed. I could hear the sound of my heart beating in my chest, and I hurled ice at moving targets, rarely hitting anything, but I put every ounce of strength into the throws, as if I was trying to put a hole in someone.

When we finally stopped, the cooler emptied of ice, we were breathing so hard it was like we'd all been fucking for hours. There was the same kind of awkwardness that comes after an orgy, people sheepishly remembering what they'd done and who they'd done it to. Our hands were cold and clammy, wrinkled and pale. But it had been fun for those few minutes. "We should do it again," Wage said, and everyone laughed nervously. "We should," I agreed.

On the ride back home, I sat in the backseat while my sister and her husband sat in front. I had red, puffy welts on my arms that would be bruises by the next day and my throwing arm was already so sore I couldn't lift it above my head. "Eddie really likes you," my sister said, "I can tell." She was trying to be discreet about it, but I could tell she was giving her husband a hand job. "I don't know," I said. "Maybe. What do you think, Sammy?" He caught my eye in the rear view mirror, annoyed, and shrugged his shoulders. "How the fuck should I know?" My sister finished him off and he moaned a little under his breath and my sister said, "Well, I can tell with these kinds of things."

Two weeks later, still not looking for a job, I got an email from Wage, which was addressed to all the people who had been at the last party. The subject line read: *Ice Fight, Part II, Revenge of the Cubes, This Time It's Personal, Take No Prisoners.* He was inviting everyone to his and Julie's house for sushi and "more of what you got at Danny and Erica's." Was he sending this from work? Did he even have a job? I wanted to fuck him so bad but he seemed so strange that it felt like it would be illegal. I replied to the email and RSVP'd. "Watch out," I said, "I'm going to get you bad." Three hours later, he wrote back. "I'm going to bruise you up," it said and he had made an emoticon that looked like !-) which I think was a face with a black eye. I did a Google search for "ice fight" and found a bunch of videos of hockey players pounding on each

other. I wished I had some drugs, but I couldn't decide if I needed
to calm down or get excited, so I lay on my futon, all three fans
blowing on me, and thought about ice touching skin, how one
thing got cold while the other melted.

The party was tense from the minute we arrived. When we first
walked in, Julie said, "Wage bought so much ice it's embarrassing.
I don't know about this." Sammy said that he might not play because his arm was so sore the last time that he had trouble at work
the next day. "Erica doesn't want to play either," Julie whispered.
I felt my hopes for the night slipping away.

I looked out the window and saw Wage and Eddie in the backyard, placing coolers filled with ice at strategic locations around
the yard. There were also little red flags jammed into the earth,
though I had no idea what they delineated. Wage and Eddie saw
me at the same time and both of them waved. I nodded and they
entered the house. "You ready?" Eddie asked, and I said it didn't
seem like people were as excited this time. "How much alcohol do
you have?" I asked Wage, understanding that whatever he said was
going to be too little.

"You're giving them too much time to have second thoughts,"
I said. "Just let me throw a piece of ice at Sammy and we'll get
started right now." Wage shook his head. "I promised Julie we
would wait." His face looked like he had only just now realized
that maybe Julie was trying to screw him over in regards to the ice
fight. "Shit," he said.

Dinner was quiet and awkward; the sushi was a little warm. My
sister and her husband told everyone about a complicated movie
they had seen the day before. "Someone is bad, but not the one
you think," my sister said. Her husband shook his head and said,
"Well, I had thought he might be bad, but then I forgot about it
after a while." Everyone else just nodded and smiled.

Once the plates were put away, everyone standing dumb and
nervous, I finally said, "The ice is melting, I bet. We should probably do something about that." My sister shushed me and looked

apologetically around the room. Wage nodded. "It's a lot of ice," he said. "The guy at the gas station said that I must be planning some kind of party, and I told him it was going to be a better party than he'd ever seen in his life." Instead, we were just a bunch of people in a room, calculating our desire for something stupid and senseless. Julie touched Wage on the shoulder and said, "Maybe people would rather sit down in the living room and have some coffee and play a board game."

"Not me," I said and my sister shushed me again. Wage looked at Julie like she'd just suggested that he put his favorite pet to sleep. "But I bought all that ice," he said. It looked like he might honest to God start crying and I wanted to punch Julie in the face. If we couldn't have an ice fight, I was thinking, I'd settle for a real fight. But there was my sister and she kept staring at me, her eyes saying, "Be a grownup; this is how normal people live." So I said, "Maybe we can vote on it." Wage and Eddie and I raised our hands in favor of an ice fight and the rest of the group voted for coffee and a board game. "Fuck," said Wage, and Julie asked him to come into the kitchen to help her with coffee.

As the rest of us sat in the living room, looking through the board games in one of the cabinets, we could hear them arguing. "This is a little awkward," Danny said, holding an empty glass, afraid to go near the kitchen for a refill. "Well, Wage is always a little awkward," Eddie said, and Erica and my sister began to giggle. Sammy fiddled with the TV remote but couldn't get it to work. "Sometimes I think that guy's got a screw loose," he said, and again the women resumed giggling. I got red with anger and without thinking I said, "I guess that explains why I want to fuck him so bad." Then the room got silent and I told my sister I was going to wait in the car until the party was over.

From the backseat of the car, I could just barely see them through the living room window, Danny pretending to ride a bicycle while the others watched with confused looks on their faces. Exasperated, Danny pedaled even harder. I thought about throwing a rock through the window but the desire passed and it was just me in the car, the windows rolled down, too hot for much of anything. And then something hit me in the face, just above my left eye, and I fell back against the seat and moaned, low and heavy, like I'd been kicked in the gut. I'd been kicked in the gut before and it was the exact same sound I'd made then. I looked down and there was a piece of ice in my lap, and then there was Wage's face just outside the car door. "I got you," he said, smiling.

A half inch lower and I'd be blind in that eye, but I grabbed his shirt and pulled him into the car. We made out for a few seconds, his feet hanging out the window, and then he said he had to go. "Julie thinks I'm getting some more coffee," he said, and I told him that Julie was a fucking moron. "She's not so bad," he said. He straightened his clothes, stepped out of the car, and walked back inside the house. I watched the living room window until I saw him standing in front of the rest of the group, his turn to play, pretending to be a robot or maybe someone with stiff joints. My sister shouted something and then she and Sammy exchanged high fives. I ran out of the car, into the backyard, and knelt over one of the buckets of ice. I jammed my hands as deep as they would go, the ice numbing my skin, and I stayed like that, hidden in the shadows, until I couldn't feel my hands at all.

Back in the car, the night over and everyone going home, my sister turned around in her seat and said, "You probably know this already, but you can't go out with us anymore. And you better not do anything to Wage." I didn't say anything and the rest of the car ride was silent until Sammy said, "If you and Wage had a baby it would explode the minute it was exposed to air." My sister shushed him, but after a few more seconds of silence she started to giggle.

Three days later, I got an email from Wage. The subject line read, *"Ice, Ice, Baby"* and the email was short and to the point. "Meet me at the kids' park across from the library. Tonight. 9:30 P.M. I'll be hard to see because I'll be wearing all black but I'll be there, and if you come, I'll be happy."

At dinner, my hands shaking from the anticipation, my sister asked if I'd found a job yet, and I told her that I had not. "You should try harder," Sammy said. "There aren't enough cash register jobs in this town," I said. My sister then spread out four different job applications from places like the Beauty Barn and the Sharp Shopper. "Sammy and I talked about this," she said. "By next week, you need to have a job." Sammy nodded and then looked at me, the first time all night, and said, "Don't tell them you got fired from your last job for stealing." I poured out the rest of my iced tea over his mashed potatoes and left the table with the applications in hand. "I didn't get fired for stealing," I said. "I got fired for not telling them that I was stealing."

I put on a black T-shirt and walked along the empty sidewalk, everyone's house on the block lit up with the glow from TV screens. As I walked past each house, I pressed an imaginary button with my thumb and pretended that everyone inside the house was now dead. I did that until I got bored, which was longer than I had anticipated, and then I was at the park. I didn't see Wage, which was to be expected. I imagined that Wage was the kind of person who put a lot of effort into hiding, so I walked over to a swing and sat down, my feet tracing designs in the dirt.

I heard something shift in the bushes behind me and then there was Wage's voice, whispering, "No joke, this is going to be painful." I turned around and he was holding two bags of ice, bright and sweating in the darkness. "Good," I said.

He dropped one of the bags of ice and then sprinted across the park into the shadows, and I tore open the bag and filled my pockets with ice. A shard winged past my face into the grass, and I tossed a handful of ice in what I believed was his direction. It was so satisfying, the way the ice moved through the air, and how each piece seemed like the physical embodiment of a wish that I was making, hoping that it would connect with Wage and knock him silly. I saw him roll in the grass and then run towards the merry-go-round, and I side-armed a piece of ice. It smacked against his arm and I heard him mutter, "Shit!" I ran back to the bag of ice and reloaded, confident in my aim. I hit him three more times, once in the mouth, the satisfying sound of it clacking against his teeth, and he bounced a piece of ice off of my ear, which made me dizzy and nauseous. When the ice had been exhausted, melted into the earth, no trace of our having ever been there, we made out in the bushes, the tips of our fingers like a dead person's, our skin tender and angry. I managed to get his pants down and though it was thrilling, it wasn't as good as the ice fight. Once it was over, we sheepishly crawled out of the bushes, brushed ourselves off, and sat on either end of a seesaw. We talked in low whispers to avoid detection.

"If a cop comes by," Wage said, "tell him that you just found out you were pregnant and we're trying to decide what to do about it." I decided that Wage was smarter than anyone gave him credit for and I felt smarter for having discovered this.

"I have to get a job," I said. "I want to keep seeing you," he said. We agreed that I would get a job and we would keep seeing each other. He got off the seesaw without warning and I slammed onto the ground. He ran over to me and asked if it hurt and I said that it did not hurt as much as I wanted it to. We made out again, my mouth swollen and tingling, and then we walked away in opposite directions. As I passed by the same houses I had passed before, I pushed an imaginary button that brought everyone inside back to life.

I got a job at the Dixie Freeze, making cones and handling change. I loved the sound of the register making decisions, and I wondered if it was embarrassing to admit that you enjoyed working retail. People don't want you; they want the thing that you're holding, and that makes things so much easier.

I met up with Wage three or four nights a week, different locations, bags of ice weighing him down. We'd throw out our arms and make anonymous bruises on our bodies and then we'd find some hidden place to put ourselves together.

"How can you get away at night?" I asked. "Doesn't Julie get suspicious?" He kept touching my hair, pulling his fingers through it, which normally I don't like but it was okay with him. "We sleep in different rooms," he said. "I go out my window and she doesn't even know I'm gone."

"You sleep in different rooms?" I said.

"I talk in my sleep," he said, not really paying attention to the conversation. "It freaks Julie out."

One night, hiding up in the branches of a tree, dogs circling suspiciously beneath us, Wage asked me to tell him something strange. "It doesn't matter what," he said. "Just something that you don't tell other people." My legs were going numb from being in one position for so long, but I ignored it and tried to think of what I should tell him.

"When I was a sophomore in high school," I finally said, "I got invited by some big-shot senior to go to prom. My sister was a senior and she didn't get asked so it was kind of weird for the whole week leading up to it. That night, I got really drunk and got into a fight with the guy, who was an idiot, and so I just came home and everybody was already asleep and the house was dead quiet. I went into the room that my sister and I shared and I could tell she was awake, but she wouldn't say anything. I put my hands under her shirt and I was trying to kiss her and she told me to go to bed. And I don't know why, but I wouldn't stop. I was trying to kiss her and she kept turning her head away, until finally I got into my bed and went to sleep. The next day, she didn't say a word about it, and I thought maybe I had dreamed it all. And I'm still not exactly sure if it really happened. When my sister is on her deathbed, I'm going to ask her about it and maybe then I'll finally find out."

"You tried to kiss your sister?" he asked, and I nodded.

"I tried to kiss your sister, too," he said, as if it was confusing to him that we had both done something similar.

"When?" I asked, genuinely intrigued, the idea of his mouth against my sister's.

"Some party at Eddie's house, I think," he said. "We were in the kitchen and it was late and I tried to kiss her and she giggled and pushed me away."

"Are you sure that it really happened?"

"Yeah, because she told Sammy about it and he told me that he would kick the shit out of me if I tried it again."

We threw acorns at the dogs below us until they scattered, and then we went our separate ways.

Of course, everyone in town found out about us and everyone in town hated us and everyone in town hated me a little more than they hated Wage. That's the way it works, I guess. At dinner with my sister and Sammy, there was nothing but the clanging of silverware against plates.

"What?" I finally said. "Did you not expect this?" My sister shook her head. "You steal everything," she said. "You just take things and it doesn't matter if you really want them. You just take them to see what it feels like in your hands." She pushed away from the table and walked off. I looked at Sammy, who was focused on his food.

"Wage tried to kiss her, you know," I told him, and he nodded. "I know," he said, "So you're not his first choice." He finished his meal and walked away from the table, and, with a wide motion of my arms, I swept all the dishes onto the floor, the glass and ceramic shattering and splintering at my feet. I waited for someone to come running into the room, to see the mess I had made, but no one came. I figured it was time that I found somewhere else to live.

Julie made Wage move out and so he got a tiny apartment in the town square. I grabbed my computer and one of the fans and walked awkwardly through town until I was at his door. Suddenly, we were together and there was no point in meeting in the middle of the night in public places.

I made cones and took people's money and Wage stayed at the apartment and typed on his computer. It turns out he wrote original content for some website about electronic gadgets. It turns out they paid him a lot of money to do this. "I could buy a lot of things that I don't need," he said. We bought bags of ice and left tiny dents in the walls of the apartment, pools of water on the floor. My arm was nearly paralyzed from throwing and Wage had chipped a tooth that he did not bother to fix. When we went outside, we carried ice in our pockets, which melted and left our pants embarrassingly damp, though we did not care. We took a clock radio apart and made it look like a bomb and left it in front of the county courthouse. The next day, we checked the newspapers and there was no mention of it. We began to get the impression that people, if asked, did not take us seriously

On my days off, Wage got irritated with me, sitting in front of my fan, wishing I had a joint to smoke. "You breathe so loud," he said. "It's distracting. Julie did not breathe at all when we were together." I told him that this was impossible and he said, "It sounds impossible when I say it out loud, but that doesn't mean it's not true." He took his computer into the closet and shut the door behind him.

In bed, after we had fucked and we finally fell asleep, Wage made tiny yelps, without interruption, for the entire night. It sounded like he was being bitten by small animals in his dreams, and I found that I could not sleep beside him without imagining that, in his dreams, it was me who was biting him.

"I thought you said you talked in your sleep," I asked him in the morning.

"I do," he said. I asked him what language he thought those sounds were, and he said, "A language that you do not understand." For a split second, I thought about kicking him in the gut and leaving him on the floor, but then I realized I had nowhere else to go. Instead, I bent his finger back at an awkward angle and, as he yelped in pain, I kissed him with so much force that our teeth clacked together. I felt him get hard at the same time that his legs turned to rubber. "Do you understand that?" I asked. He smiled and then nodded. "Yes," he answered, "I understand."

Julie and my sister came by the Dixie Freeze and I instinctively reached for something heavy, expecting a fight. "We just want to talk," they said, and I told them to give me five dollars each and when they did, I pocketed it and told my manager I was taking a fifteen-minute break.

"I miss him," Julie said. I nodded and looked at her like, "that's not going to get you your five dollars back." My sister touched my arm and motioned towards the sky or maybe some building in the distance. "This is just some place for you to pass the time," she said. "We live here and we'll still be living here when you move on." I shook my head. I wasn't allowed to be happy, just because I didn't have a place of my own to live?

"That's not it," Julie said, "but do you have to make other people miserable in order for you to be happy?" I stood up and walked back to my register. "You were miserable long before I ever showed up," I said. Julie started to cry and my sister put her arms around her. I made myself a cone of soft-serve and went into the employee bathroom. I smeared the ice cream all over my face and hoped that in a few minutes I would not want to kill someone nearly as much as I did at that moment. When it had passed, I washed my face, and when I walked out of the bathroom, my sister and Julie were gone. I went back to my register and touched the buttons to add up numbers too large to mean anything.

It wasn't more than a few days later that Wage decided he was going back to Julie. "I think if we stayed together," he said, "we might end up doing something that would get us in a lot of trouble." I grabbed his shoes out of the closet and tied the shoelaces together in complicated knots to slow him down. He packed up his computer and some clothes, ashamed to look at me, and I took out an ice tray from the freezer and emptied the cubes into the sink. I threw one of the cubes and it landed flush against the back of Wage's head. He shrugged from the pain of it, but kept on packing. I threw another piece and it missed and cracked the mirror in the bedroom. I threw another piece, and then another, and by the time the sink was emptied of ice, Wage's nose was bleeding, and I thought it wouldn't be so bad if I was dead.

"The rent for the apartment is paid up for the rest of the month," he said. "You can stay." I guessed this was what it felt like to love something, wanting to kill it for leaving you, and I kissed him so hard that my mouth was smeared with his blood.

"I'm already wishing I wasn't leaving," he said, and then he left. I ran to the freezer and took two more cubes of ice and held one in each hand, my fist squeezing them into diamonds. I squeezed until the thing that I held had disappeared and then I lay flat on the ground and stared up at the ceiling.

I thought about that night after the prom, how I'd forced myself on my sister, wanted so badly to be against her. I remembered how she had said, almost crying, "You're going to hate yourself so much for doing this." I pulled away from her, stunned, and I whispered, "You think I don't know that?" I felt the anger become dense inside of my chest and then I walked over to my own bed and crawled under the sheets. I kept my back to my sister's bed, but my eyes were wide open. I lay there and waited for her to come over to my bed, to place her hands on me, and to make me feel happy. The entire night, I lay there and waited, but she never came, and I wished that I had only tried harder, had made myself so necessary that I could not be refused.

Kevin Wilson was born, raised, and still lives in Tennessee. He is the author of the short story collection *Tunneling to the Center of the Earth*. His stories have appeared in *Ploughshares, Tin House, One Story,* and elsewhere. He currently lives in Sewanee, Tennessee, with his wife, the poet Leigh Anne Couch, and his son, where he teaches fiction at the University of the South. This is his third appearance in *New Stories from the South*.

LEIGH ANNE COUCH

*W*e called them ice fights. They made things weird for a little while. In the summer, I work on the staff for the Sewanee Writers' Conference, where our main objective is to make sure there is a steady supply of ice for the cocktail parties. We spend a lot of time hauling coolers filled with ice from event to event, wearing out ice machines on campus. A few years ago, a group of us were cleaning up after a reception, very stir crazy, perhaps a little drunk, and we started chucking ice at each other. Things quickly got out of hand. People were bruised. Someone's eye was swollen shut. Our hands were numb.

After that, we could not wait for nightfall, when we would carry buckets of ice to private locations in order to hurt each other. It's all we thought about. I exchanged about twenty emails during the year after that conference with my friend Caki where we shared our intricate designs for chain mail, how to reconfigure a 1987 Cormier bazooka so that it would shoot ice, debates on square versus round cubes. In one of these emails, I said, "No joke, this is going to be painful."

The story came not long after that.

Stephanie Soileau

THE CAMERA OBSCURA

(from *Nimrod*)

It's the most embarrassing things that get you: how he pours salt into his hand before sprinkling it pinch by pinch onto his asparagus; the way he looks up over his glasses with eyebrows arched and magnified eyes startled that the world is in fact right-side-up; the green button-down shirt with the cuffs rolled to the elbows and the unflattering jeans and the thick white socks and the white rubber gardening shoes, none of which have been changed in the three days since you started to notice him at all and maybe longer; and the way he catches you watching him pinch salt onto his asparagus and blinks giant eyes at you with purpose, with resolve, because you did something like this two days ago when you noticed him watching you deliver your lunch tray to the dish cart, and he's caught on, and this is flirting, and he's going to give it a whirl. Not to mention, of course, certain pertinent details of your own personal life, namely, that you are, as of a year ago and admittedly with some lack of enthusiasm—yes, in hindsight it seems like a grave mistake but, at the time, how *had* you felt at the time?—married.

He lingers at the lunchroom table with no food or drink in front of him, and you realize of course that you've communicated your interest a little too clearly and he's lingering just for you, and after he's finally given up and left, your fellow teachers at the table say with revulsion (and with some affection, too) that he seems so "out of phase." What do you do when this ticklish absurdity masquerades as persistent, budding joy? What do you do?

You wander casually into his photography studio as you and the other teachers have been invited to do, to come and enjoy the camera obscura that he's made of the room, lens boxes in every boarded-up window and bedsheet partitions catching the light and colors like butterflies in a net. The outside is inside: shadowy, silent, upside down.

It makes unfamiliar what is familiar, but for you, who are new to this high school, this town, called away from a life in a city a thousand miles away, where you had spent the last decade content with the limits of your map, for you, in this room, this new place is doubly strange. It is dizzying, this disorientation.

So you push aside a bedsheet and step through a shaft of projected light that contains in its colors the orange of a school bus, the gray-green of late summer grass, the fish-school fluttering of students dismissed. The photographer is leaning there, arms crossed like a museum guard.

You pester him with inane questions, growing bolder and clumsier by the minute. You ask how it works, the camera obscura. You ask him to show you his lens. You ask why the leaves seem to move so slowly, why the room feels so still, and you ask this unrelated thing that you've always wondered and been too embarrassed to ask—and he seems like the kind of man who would know, so here goes: *How come we're not upside down in mirrors?* You ask this and begin to understand the physics of mirrors at the very moment the words are leaving your mouth, and by the time he blinks that slow, deliberate blink and embarks upon an epic explanation, through which words and logic are applied at last to intuition, you understand completely the principles of reflection.

You find yourself crowding him into a corner and cut short your questions to kiss the strange mouth that you can't believe is the same mouth that smiles such a warm and charming smile (he does have a very nice smile, everyone agrees on that) but then snaps at a strawberry like a toad swallowing a moth, in three jerking, chomping bites. You remove the glasses from his eyes and say, in a voice like Ingrid Bergman's—is it Ingrid Bergman? no, it's some-one irrelevant from some movie you don't like, but you're going to do it like Ingrid Bergman—so you say, *Oh darling, you had me at angle of incidence.*

Actually, you do not do—would not do—would you?—any of those last few things although you loll for an hour in bed one morning thinking them up while your husband clatters and clinks things in the kitchen and finally—how you wish he would stop, just *stop*—brings you coffee with a touch of cream, no sugar, just like you like it, and two pieces of toast, one buttered, one jammed, just like you like them. He is feeling good today.

In only a year much has been revealed, including the presence in your husband's liver of a virus, the treatment for which is more ag-onizing than the disease itself, which will eventually kill him, but not now, not soon, maybe not for many years—years and years!—so why must the treatment come now, in this fragile, fumbling first year of marriage? The daily doses of poison leave him worn, desiccated, and patchy-haired. Yet he is unaccountably cheery! It is his nature, as it is the duck's to quack, the scorpion's to sting. Why now?

So much must be struggled through, a lifetime of struggling—how could you not have considered the outrageous length of the life before you?—with this man whom admittedly, admittedly, you love but—well, why not say it?—who came with an array of exasperating qualities that predated the discovery of the virus and have continued unabated even now, quite disproving the saintli-ness of the gravely ill. It's the mislaid paychecks, the professional cooking classes slept through or flunked, the birthday-gift Vespa purchased on your credit card and stolen before you even knew it was yours (he forgot the keys in the ignition), the time he left the window open and the cat fell three floors to the pavement and broke two legs.

It's other things too. It's even the things you love. That the animal he would be if he were any animal—if he could *choose* to be any animal—is a duck. You married a duck, you think now. How could you have married a duck? And yet, you can't bear to imagine forgetting these things. You can't bear to think that one day, your memory of his face will be foggy and painless, that one day (not soon! not soon!) you will not be there for the final moments, to bicker with nurses, sign forms, sleep in armchairs, and stroke the forehead of your ailing duck.

And now, this morning, after a period of grave dehydration and two days in the hospital hooked to pumps that filled him up again with fluids, he is cheery (of course) and almost wild with life. He wants to thank you, to do for you as you have done for him all these months, but how reluctantly, how peevishly you've done for him he hasn't noticed, or has refused to. You are a good wife. He brings you coffee and toast.

When later that same morning you bump into the photographer in the halls of the art annex where you've gone specifically to bump into him, you feel yourself turning quite red, and then—oh vampiric treachery (or, more concretely, your refusal to eat the lovingly toasted toast)—you feel yourself turning quite pale, and you know you are going to faint, and in fact, the floor and the ceiling change places and you come out of the faint sprawled in his arms with that face hanging upside down over you. It's truly a troubling face.

It's the voice that's most confusing. It lumbers out like a friendly bear from a cave and says, "Just lie still until you're sure you can stand." And though he's still in that awful green shirt, he smells like sawdust and his hand is warm and enormous and sweeps the hair back from your forehead and holds it back and the voice rumbles, "She's okay. No, no, I've got her, she's okay," to the crowd of your colleagues and students gathering in the hall. The principal says to you, "Are you ill? Do you want a doctor?" and you say, "No doctor," and the Latin teacher with the crazily curled hair, the closest thing you have to a friend in this new place, squats down, leans in close to your ear, and whispers, "Maybe you're pregnant."

You can see that he's heard this too, and there is an embarrassing, unspoken implication, though if pressed you couldn't name it, and he blinks his eyes, but you fling out your arms in search of the tile, knocking away his hand, and finally you distinguish up from down and you're standing and he's still on the floor. Now, you snatch up your things. You bolt.

When you see him again at lunch, he says, "Have you recovered from your *spell*?" and you say, "I have," and while you eat you find yourself leaning slightly in, slightly toward him, and you're afraid your colleagues will notice the leaning, but lean you must, so lean you do. He crosses his legs and his rubber shoe rests lightly against your shin. You pretend to be the table.

For the next day, you celebrate, secretly. You feel you have passed a test, and you will allow yourself outrageous and wicked flights of fancy. You are a somewhat pretty woman and you have always had suitors, some of them, including the one you finally (and unenthusiastically?) married, somewhat pretty themselves, but your heart has chosen—well, it's overstating the case but—your heart, after all these years of not knowing in the least what it wants, has finally chosen—something else? You could be Beauty to his Beast, Princess to his Frog. Concave to his Convex. You will pack up your things, move out on the husband, divorce, and marry immediately this brilliant, odd-looking man, and you will have brilliant, odd-looking children, and you will adore them all, and you will make them sometimes change their clothes, and you will defend your miserable brood from contempt, and everyone will wonder how such a delightful woman ended up with such a categorically graceless lump of a man, or better, how such a categorically graceless lump of a man could deserve such a delightful woman. It will be saintly, how you adore him.

This almost, but not quite—not nearly—actually only vaguely assuages the guilt of even thinking of abandoning a man who will one day—not today, not tomorrow, not even soon!—be laid low by his own liver. It is amazing how often this slips your mind. You are appalled at the bifurcation of self that has allowed such thoughts. At the forgetfulness that, among other things, causes you in the middle of a grammar lesson, in front of fifteen mystified fifteen-year-olds, to laugh hysterically at the double entendre in a dangling (dangling!) modifier.

You concoct elaborate reasons to enter a room where he is, and once in that room, you panic and make abrupt, inexplicable exits. At school events you try to sit near him, not next to but directly behind, perhaps. At an assembly in the old colonial church that serves as a lecture hall and theater, he is in front of you, just to the right, and about fifteen minutes into the principal's tirade against uncited or fallacious internet sources, against plagiarism, against cheating, you see him gazing at the ceiling, taking mental measurements of the room, of the windows, and he turns around and says softly, "I'm going to turn this place into a camera obscura." You notice that he has changed his shirt.

For a week you see him crossing from studio to woodshop to lecture hail and back again with little wooden boxes and mirrors tucked under his arms. He boards up the windows in the lecture hall one by one. You run into him in the teacher's lounge, and in a convulsion of glee he pulls from his wallet a mail-order invoice for two dozen lenses. He rattles it at you. "By the end of the week!" he says. Over lunch, he will speak of nothing but focal lengths and apertures. In that he is speaking at all, this is a vast improvement in his social behavior, but in another sense this development is, for your colleagues, excruciating. You listen, conspicuously and intensely. To everyone's chagrin, you invite elaboration.

On Tuesday morning, between the usual announcements for quiz bowl practice and yearbook orders, he proclaims over the intercom the unveiling of the camera obscura. After the last bell, you come in with a group of other teachers, and you all take seats and drop your heads back to see the puddles of light on the ceiling above each window. One by one the others get up, say into the darkness *This is amazing, good work there buddy,* and exit, and you finally realize that you and he are alone in the camera obscura.

He emerges from the shadows near you and says, "I've found that the best way to experience this is to lie down." And you both lie down in the aisles and watch the clouds move across the ceiling, the leaves flutter slowly in the trees, no accompaniment to this movement but the creaking of floorboards under your back, the rush of your breath, and the electric crackle (are you imagining this?) between your feet and his, no that's the click and hiss of an IV drip in the stillness of a hospital room, like the steady click and hiss of a camera on time-lapse, or actually it is his camera on time-lapse and it's recording the reflected movement of clouds. On the ceiling just above you are the main road and the gas station across from the school, its empty parking lot, utter stillness, and when a blurred human exits the gas station and moves away, toward the frayed edges of projected light, and then disappears into shadow, it's like discovering a code in the static of space. It is frightening and ominous and sad, it is a glimpse of the future of a memory.

You think: *We are watching forgetting. This is what forgetting looks like.*

You take a breath and say this, and there is no answer.

Half an hour passes and the two of you manage this much more conversation:

"Is it Tuesday?"

"Yes, it is Tuesday."

Finally, with nothing else to say, you pick yourself up from the floor, dust yourself off. You're right in front of the lens box, your head is blocking the sun—you can feel the hot coin of it on the back of your skull—and you idiotically make hand-shadows of an octopus swimming across the sky. There is no response. As you shuffle up the aisle, he says from the darkness, "Thanks for coming, come again," and you wonder if he means today, tomorrow, or nothing at all.

One buoyant blue morning you are inexplicably crackling like cellophane, trembling with *agapē,* you are Isis, *agapē theon,* in spite of it all. This morning, this joy is a balloon that you tap with the tips of your fingers, a slow volley to the janitor, and he taps it back to you, and to the principal, and he taps it back to you, and to the Latin teacher with the crazy hair (now absolutely certain that you are "expecting," and you are, but what? what are you expecting?)—tap! with a flourish of wriggling fingers—and each of them smiles a true smile, a this-morning-in-June smile (although it is, of course, not June but nearly November).

It's the weather. It's only the effect of the weather.

It compels you to ask the photographer if he would like, after school, to go for a hike. When you call your husband, you don't even bother to lie. He has seen the photographer, granted, from a distance when picking you up from school, and you have composed a careful portrait besides—the rubber shoes, the off-kilter remarks. This could not be more than simply a hike. Your husband says, "Sure, okay. I can't do that with you. I want you to have someone to do that with."

He has a cowboy-ish walk, very straight, and he strolls over boulders with no change in his posture, never bending, never grappling for a foothold, not at all like the scrambling squirrel you are. You and he climb up and up, up, and up. Finally, you reach the top, the end, the vista, and there at the vista, there is a bench, only feet from a fierce drop-off.

You both sit on the bench with a little space between you. You hear him swallowing. A tumble of frivolous questions presses, but you wait. Your teeth are chattering, you are shivering, although it is easily seventy degrees. You pretend to enjoy the beautiful view.

"So," he says. "You moved here from the city."

"Yes."

"What did you like to do. In the city. For fun."

"Um," you say. You answer.

"I've never been to that city," he says.

"Well." You say something—too much—about the wind and the cold and the possums in the alleys. About the trains and the lake and the skyline and the ball teams and the bums, corners, taverns, noise, markets, neighbors, feral cats.

"You're homesick."

You are, you say. You are, but this is nice. It's nice to be out for a hike.

He blinks and you blink. There is something yet that needs to be said.

"Did you have a," he says. "A boyfriend."

"No—"

"In the city."

"I. Um."

When the word "husband" bobs to the surface like a drowned corpse, you feel like the world is upended and you will be shaken off. It's gone over the cliff, whatever it was that sat between you, you kicked it over the cliff and you can hear it whistling all the way down until it hits the bottom in a little puff of dust. Clearly, this is a bigger problem than you thought. You begin the funereal march back down the trail.

There is silence for the first fifteen minutes of the journey, and you wonder through this silence if there is something required of you, an apology, an abandonment of ethics, but then, suddenly, he is merciful. He points up into a tree, blinks once, twice, triumphantly, he says, "Look. Do you see it? A titmouse!"

You are in a state of vapid waiting. Your skull is a lean-to and you're camped out under it, waiting for a change in weather. There is no change in weather. You start to blurt cryptic things to the colleagues, to the husband. Things like: *My skull is a lean-to and I'm camping out under it.* You feel you are speaking in rebus. You have trouble stepping outside the situation enough to determine exactly what is a problem, and exactly how much of a problem the problem is. You begin to suspect the problem is probably you.

At home, your husband resorts to antics. He requires your attention. (Of course he does. Of course, he requires your attention.) He begins with little gestures, like startling kisses on the neck while you stand petrified before an open cabinet in your kitchen, arrested by despair in mid-reach for a coffee cup. Or he grabs you in a hug, pins your arms to your body, and holds tight against your squirming, saying *Who's my testy little kitty? Who?* Things escalate: he buys a wig, attempts soufflés. Finally, he throws up his hands and says, "I just don't understand."

"What?" you say. You poke with indifference at a deflated muck of egg whites and crabmeat that he's set before you for dinner. The wig, more joke than vanity—the "Special Bargain Quasimodo" that he ordered online in a fit of doubled-over hysterics, too red, not more convincing as hair than a clump of dried pine needles— is carefully arranged, seriously donned. His eyes are bloodshot. He looks dry again. His fingers. His ears. One spark and the wig would burst into flames.

"The sad," he says. "I just don't understand the sad."

You decide to come clean. You will take your chances with your one friend, the Latin teacher, with her wild, mythic hair. A unicorn, she appears only to virgins, the pure of heart. Her eyes are wide and dewy, her gait is graceful, rolling—where her hips go, the rest of her follows. She told you once that she has exceptional— even mystical—powers of empathy, and you, earthbound flesh, believed her. You are beginning to know better, but all the same, she is a friend, your only friend, so you confide everything—the virus, the camera obscura—and when you do, she cringes from you, shields her face as if you have struck her. As if you have *struck* her, truly, and you think, my god, is it so awful, my god, is *this* my nature? She says, "Why are you telling me this? Why are you doing this to me?"

"To you?"

"This assault. On everything. On vows and love and—"

"But I didn't," you say, "I didn't *do* anything," and for the first time, it occurs to you this might be true. As for the unicorn, she will appear to you no more.

But screw the unicorns, you think, let's be more objective.

The fact *is,* before all this, before the obligating virus, you had been nearing thirty and thinking that you'd better just pick someone to love already and be done with it. Love, you told yourself, after two critical, devastating failures, is a choice and not a visitation, is not the shared transport of a 4 a.m. binge on Borges and a can of sardines, is not transcendence or revelation, has no empirical epistemology. It is like-mindedness on questions of dinner and dishes and laundry. It is, you have learned now, tolerance of peculiar sounds from the bathroom, the daily jamming of needles into thighs. You pick someone, that's all. You pick someone you like well enough and dig in. Ritual evokes reverence; every injection, every slice of buttered toast conjures affection. Was this cynicism or was it faith?

At home, your husband has excused himself from living. He has quit his job, or been fired—it is unclear which—and your health insurance is the only thing between him and—what exactly? This is also unclear. He plays video games. He has drawn the living room curtains and sits cross-legged on the floor, his hands working the controller, in darkness except for the glow of the television, and surrounded by plates of shriveled pizza, crumpled taco wrappers, empty or half-full bottles of sports drink, all toppled and scattered. When you ask him how he is feeling, he says, cheerily, "Fine, fine! And how are you doing?" You might as well be greeting each other over cantaloupes at the supermarket.

As one does in times of trial, when the truth is clear except to the self, you have a dream. In your dream, your husband is a plate of sushi. He is laid out in fleshy pinks and whites upon a bed of rice and wrapped up neatly in cellophane. You peel back the cellophane—a naked, private, alarming sound—and pat the shrimp. "I'm sorry," you say. "I'm sorry this is so hard."

At school, the photographer doesn't blink at you anymore, and in fact each of you pointedly ignores the other, but sometimes you still manage intentionally accidental contact. One day, you have somehow both landed on a park bench in the courtyard outside

the annex. He is, incongruously, the sponsor of the school yearbook, and three art girls dash over and flutter around him, they
want the key to the darkroom, and they cram themselves onto the
bench, shoving the two of you together. They tug and nip at him
like puppies at an old hound dog. "Oh, Mr. So-and-So, you know
you can trust us!" There is gray at his temples, and—you see that
you were wrong, he is actually quite handsome. How could you
have been so wrong? The art girls dash away again, leaving you
thigh to thigh on the bench.

You say—you try to say—what can you say? You say nothing.

He says nothing.

Neither of you says anything.

When the fifth-period bell goes off, you rise together, and in
the confusion of walking away, out of a habit that was never actual
but only imagined, the two of you grab hands, you enfold fingers,
you squeeze.

This startles both of you. It will never happen again.

————————

Stephanie Soileau grew up in Lake Charles,
Louisiana, but has spent the last decade or so in
Chicago and San Francisco. She is currently the
Nancy Packer Lecturer in Continuing Studies
at Stanford University, where she was also a
Truman Capote Fellow in the Wallace Stegner
Fellowship Program for 2007–2009. Her short
stories have appeared in *Tin House, Gulf Coast,
StoryQuarterly, Nimrod, New Stories from the South
2005* and *2008,* and *Best of the South: From the
Second Decade of New Stories from the South.* She is working on a collec-
tion of stories and a novel about fishermen, oil, and erosion in coastal
Louisiana.

CHRIS REMPLE

*O*ne of the visual artists in residency with me a few years ago built an installation like the one I describe here, and my first notes for the story were blind, nearly illegible scrawls of half thoughts and half images set down in the dreamy half darkness of the camera obscura. The first line I put to paper was, I think, a version of "This is what forgetting looks like." There was something very peaceful and lovely but also sad and lonesome about being in that dark, quiet space, spying on the world through a pinhole. I tried to build a story around those feelings and images.

MAGIC WORDS

(from *Narrative*)

Because Paula Blake is planning something secret, she feels she must account for her every move and action, overcompensating in her daily chores and agreeing to whatever her husband and children demand. *Of course I'll pick up the dry cleaning, drive the kids, swing by the drugstore.* This is where the murderer always screws up in a movie, way too accommodating, too much information. The guilty one always has trouble maintaining direct eye contact.

"Of course I will take you and your friend to the movies," she tells Erin late one afternoon. "But do you think her mom can drive you home? I'm taking your brother to a sleepover too." She is doing it again, talking too much.

"Where are *you* going?" Erin asks, mouth sullen and sarcastic as it has been since her thirteenth birthday two years ago.

"Out with a friend," Paula says, forcing herself to make eye contact, the rest of the story she has practiced for days ready to roll. She's someone I work with, someone going through a really hard time, someone brand new to the area, knows no one, really needs a friend.

But her daughter never looks up from the glossy magazine spread before her, engrossed in yet another drama about a teen star lost to drugs and wild nights. Her husband doesn't even ask her new friend's name or where she moved from, yet the answer is poised and waiting on her tongue. Tonya Matthews from Phoenix, Arizona. He is glued to the latest issue of *Our Domestic Wildlife*—his own newsletter to the neighborhood about various sightings of wild and possibly dangerous creatures, coyotes, raccoons, bats. Their message box is regularly filled with detailed sightings of raccoons acting funny in daylight or reports of missing cats. Then there's the occasional giggling kid faking a deep voice to report a kangaroo or rhino. She married a reserved and responsible banker who now fancies himself a kind of watchdog Crocodile Dundee. They are both seeking interests outside their lackluster marriage. His are all about threat and encroachment, being on the defense, and hers are about human contact, a craving for warmth like one of the bats her husband fears might find its way into their attic.

Her silky legs burn as if shamed where she has slathered lavender body lotion whipped as light as something you might eat. And the new silk panties, bought earlier in the day, feel heavy around her hips. But it is not enough to thwart the thought of what lies ahead, the consummation of all those notes and looks exchanged with the sales rep on the second floor during weeks at work, that one time in the stairwell—hard thrust of a kiss interrupted by the heavy door and footsteps two floors up—when the fantasy became enough of a reality to lead to this date. They have been careful, and the paper trail is slight—unsigned suggestive notes with penciled times and places—all neatly rolled like tiny scrolls and saved in the toe of the heavy wool ski socks in the far corner of her underwear drawer, where heavier, far more substantial pairs of underwear than what she is wearing cover the surface. It all feels as safe as it can be because he has a family too. He has just as much to lose as she does.

And now she looks around to see the table filled with cartons of Chinese food from last night and cereal boxes from the morning, and the television blares from the other room. Her son is anxious to get to his sleepover; her daughter has painted her toenails, and the fumes of the purple enamel fill the air. Her husband is studying a map showing the progression of killer bees up the coast. He speaks of them like hated relatives who are determined to drop in, whether you want them to or not. Their arrival is as inevitable as all the other predicted disasters that will wreak havoc on human life.

"Where did you say you've got to go?" her husband asks, and she immediately jumps to her creation. Tonya Matthews, Phoenix, Arizona, new to the area, just divorced. Her palms are sweating, and she is glad she is wearing a turtleneck to hide the nervous splotches on her chest. She won't be wearing it later. She will slip it off in the darkness of the car after she takes Gregory to the sleep-over and Erin and her friend to the cinema. Under the turtleneck she is wearing a thin silk camisole, also purchased that afternoon at a pricey boutique she had never been in before, a place the size of a closet where individual lingerie items hang separately on the wall like art. A young girl, sleek, pierced, and polished, gave a cool nod of approval when she leaned in to look at the camisole. Paula finally chose the black one after debating between it and the peacock blue. Maybe she will get the blue next time, already hoping that this new part of her life will remain. Instead of the turtleneck, she will wear a loose cashmere cardigan that slides from one shoulder when she inclines her head inquisitively. It will come off easily, leaving only the camisole between them in those first awkward seconds. She tilts her head as she has practiced, and with that thought all others disappear, and now she doesn't know what has even been asked of her. Her heart beats a little too fast. She once failed a polygraph test for this reason. She had never—would never—shoot heroin, but her pulse had raced with the memory of someone she knew who had. Did she do drugs? Her answer was no, but her mind had taken her elsewhere, panicked when she remembered the boy who gave her a ride home from a high school party with his head thrown back and teeth gritted, arm tied off with a large rubber band while a friend loomed overhead to inject him, one bloody needle already on the littered floor.

You can't afford to let your mind wander in a polygraph test—

or in life, as now, when once again she finds herself looking at her husband with no idea of what he has just said. Her ability to hold eye contact is waning, the light out the window waning, but the desire that has built all these weeks is determined to linger, flickering like a candle under labored breath. Somewhere, her husband says, between their house and the interstate, are several packs of coyotes, their little dens tucked away in brush and fallen trees. The coyote is a creature that often remains monogamous. The big bumbling mouthful of a word lingers there, a pause that lasts too long before he continues with his report. He heard the coyotes last night, so this is a good time to get the newsletter out, a good time to remind people to bring their pets indoors. Dusk is when they come out, same as the bats, most likely rabid.

The kids are doing what they call creepy crawling. Their leader picked the term up from the book *Helter Skelter*. They slip in and out behind trees and bushes, surveying houses, peeping in windows, finding windows and doors ajar or unlocked. Their leader is a badly wounded boy in need of wounding others, and so he frightens them, holds them enthralled with his stories of violence or murder. They might not believe all he says, but they believe enough to know be is capable of bad things. As frightening as it is to be with him, it is more frightening not to be—to be on the outside and thus a potential victim.

To the kids he looks tough with his tongue ring and tattoos, his mouth tight and drawn by a bitterness rarely seen on such a young face, some vicious word always coiled on his tongue and ready to strike those who least expect it—though he has to be careful when bagging groceries at Food Lion; he has been reprimanded twice for making sarcastic remarks to elderly shoppers, things like *You sure you need these cookies, fat granny?* He has been told he will be fired the next time he is disrespectful, which is fine with him. He doesn't give a shit what any of them says. Dirt cakes the soles of his feet, like calloused hooves, as he stands on the asphalt in front of the bowling alley, smoking, guzzling, or ingesting whatever gifts his flock of disciples brings to him. He likes to make and hold eye contact until people grow nervous.

When Agnes Hayes sees the boy bagging groceries in the market, her heart surges with pity, his complexion blotched and infected, hair long and oily. "Don't I know you?" she asks, but he doesn't even look up, his arms all inked with reptiles and knives and what looks like a religious symbol. Now she has spent the day trying to place him. She taught so many of them, but their names and faces run together. In the three years since retirement, she has missed them more than she ever dreamed. Some days she even drives her car and parks near the high school to watch them, to catch a glimpse of all that energy and to once again feel it in her own pulse. She still drives Edwin's copper-colored Electra and has since he died almost two years ago. She would never have retired had she seen his death coming, and with it an end to all their plans about where they would go and what they would do. One day she was complaining about plastic golf balls strewn all over the living room, and the next she was calling 911, knowing even as she dialed and begged for someone to *please help* that it was too late.

The school is built on the same land where she went to school. She once practiced there, her clarinet held in young hands while she stepped high with the marching band. Edwin's cigar is there in the ashtray, stinking as always, only now she loves the stink, can't get enough of it, wishes that she had never complained and made him go out to the garage or down to the basement to smoke. She wishes he were sitting there beside her, ringed in smoke. Their son, Preston, is clear across the country, barely in touch.

Sometimes creepy crawling involves only the car, cruising slowly through a driveway, headlights turned off, gravel crunching. There are lots of dogs. Lots of sensor lights. Lots of security systems, or at least signs *saying* there are systems. The boy trusts nothing and no one. He believes in jiggling knobs and trying windows.

When asked one time, by a guidance counselor feigning compassion and concern, what he believed in, he said, "Not a goddamn thing," but of course he did. Anyone drawing breath believes in something, even if it is only that life sucks and there's no reason to live. Tonight he has announced that it is Lauren's turn to prove herself. She is a pretty girl behind the wall of heavy black makeup and black studded clothing. She wants out of the car, but she owes him fifty dollars. He makes it sound like if she doesn't pay it back soon he'll take it out in sex. She is only here to get back at the boy she loved enough to do everything he asked. She wants him to worry about her, to want her, to think about that night at the campground the way she does.

The leader reminds her often that he was there for her when no one else was. He listened to her story about the squeaky-clean asshole boyfriend, feeding her sips of cheap wine and stroking her dyed black hair the whole time she cried and talked and later reeled and heaved on all fours in a roadside ditch.

"He's an asswipe," the boy had said. "He used you." And then later when she woke just before dawn with her head pounding and her body filled with the sick knowledge that she had to go home and face her parents, he reminded her again how much she needed him, couldn't survive without him. "I didn't leave you," he said. "Could've easily fucked you and didn't."

And now she is here, and the boy who broke her heart is out with someone else or maybe just eating dinner with his parents and talking about where he might choose to go to school. He is a boy who always smells clean, even right off the track where he runs long-distance, his thigh muscles like hard ropes, his lungs healthy and strong. He might be at the movies, and she wishes she were there too—the darkness, the popcorn. She wishes she were anywhere else. She had wanted her parents to restrict her after that night, to say she couldn't go anywhere for weeks and weeks, but they did something so much worse; they said how disappointed they were, that they had given up, how she would have to work really hard to regain their trust, and by *trust* it seems they meant love.

The leader is talking about how he hates their old math teacher. "And I know where she lives too." He circles the block, drives slowly past a neat gray colonial with a bright red door, the big Electra parked in the drive. "What's the magic word?" he mimics in a high Southern voice and reaches over to grab Lauren's thigh, then inches up, gripping harder as if daring her to move. He motions for her to unzip her jeans, wanting her to just sit there that way, silver chain from her navel grazing the thin strip of nylon that covers her. Lower, he says, even though there is a boy in the backseat hearing every word. She feels cold but doesn't say a word. Her shoes and jacket and purse are locked in the trunk of his car. "For safekeeping," he said. She is about to readjust the V of denim when he swings the car off the side of the road behind a tall hedge of ligustrum, where they are partially hidden but can still see the house. "Like this," he says and tugs, a seam ripping, and then he slides across the seat toward her, his mouth hard on hers as he forces her hand to his own zipper. The boy in the backseat lights a cigarette, and she focuses on that, the sound, the smell; she can hear the paper burn.

Erin and her friend, Tina, sit in the backseat, and Gregory is in front with his Power Ranger sleeping bag rolled up at his feet. Paula will drop him off at the party and then go to the cinema, and then she will still have time to sit and collect herself before driving seven miles down the interstate to the Days Inn, where he will be waiting. The children have said that this car—their dad's— smells like old farts and jelly beans. They say he saves up all day at the bank and then rips all the way home. Gregory acts this out, and with each "Ewww" and laugh from the girls, he gets a little more confident and louder. He says their grandmother smells like diarrhea dipped in peppermint and their grandfather is chocolate vomick. They are having a wonderful time, mainly because it's daring, the way he is testing Paula, the way they all are waiting for her to intervene and reprimand, but she is so distracted she forgets to be a good mother. When he turns and scrutinizes her with a mischievous look, she snaps back.

"Not acceptable, young man, and you know it," she says, but really she is worried that they are right and that *she* will smell like old farts and jelly beans when she arrives at the motel. Her cell phone buzzes against her hip, and she knows that he is calling to see if they are on schedule, calling to make sure that she doesn't stand him up again.

"Aren't you going to answer that?" Erin says. "Who is it, Dad looking for underwear? Some lame friend in need of a heart-to-heart?" The laughing continues as Paula turns onto the street where a crowd of eight-year-olds and sleeping bags is gathered in the front yard of a small brick ranch.

"One of my lame friends, I'm sure," she answers but with the words pictures him there in the room, maybe already undressed, a glass of wine poured. They have already said so much in their little notes that it feels not only like they have already made love but like they have done so for so long that they are already needing to think up new things to do. Her pulse races, and she slams on the brakes when Gregory screams, "Stop!"

"Pay attention, Mom," Gregory says. "See, they're everywhere," and she thinks he means her lame friends, or kids at the party, but he picks up one of those little gourmet jelly beans, tosses it at his sister, and then jumps from the car. "Thanks, Mom," he says, and Paula waves to the already frazzled-looking mother who has taken this on. Thank you, Ronald Reagan. That's when the jelly bean frenzy started, and then after her husband said something cute and trite about sharing the desires of the president since he was now a vice president at the bank, all his workers gave him jelly beans because what else can you give someone you don't know at all who has power and authority over you? He got all kinds of jelly beans. And now if people hear about the neighborhood wildlife, it means many more years of useless presents—coyote and raccoon and bat figurines and mugs and mugs and more mugs. She will

write and send all those thank-you notes. She will take all the crap
to Goodwill.

Sometimes Agnes watches television in the dark. She likes a
lot of these new shows that are all about humiliating people until
they confess that they are fat and need to lose weight or that they
are inept workers who need to be fired or bad members of a team
who need to be rejected and banished from the island. Her pug,
Oliver, died not long after Edwin did, and she misses the way he
used to paw and tug and make a little nest at the foot of her bed.
She misses the sounds of his little snorts in the night. How could
there have been a moment in life when she wished for this—the
quiet, the lack of activity and noise? The clock ticks, the refrigerator hums. She could call Preston. She could give him an apology,
whether or not she owes it. What she could say is that she is so
sorry they misunderstood each other. Or she could call him and
pretend nothing ever happened. She keeps thinking of the boy at
the grocery, trying to place what year she taught him. Who were
his parents? What is his name? Some children she gave things to
over the years—her son's outgrown clothes and shoes—but then
she stopped, dumping it all at the church instead, because the children never acted the same afterward, and that bothered her. They
never said thank you, and they never looked her in the eye, as if
she had never made a difference in their lives, and that was what
hurt so much when she thought of Preston, how easily he had let
a few things make him forget all that she had done for him in his
life. She stated the truth, is all. When Preston planned to marry
Amy, she told him how people might talk about them, might call
their children names.

Right after Edwin's funeral, he called her Miss Christian Ethics,
Miss Righteous Soul. He told her he wished he could stay and
dig into all that ham and Jell-O but that Amy was at the Holiday
Inn waiting for him. "They let dogs stay there too," he said and
lingered over the prize rod and reel of his father's she had handed
to him, only to put it back and leave. She hasn't seen him since.

Now her chest is heavy with the memory, and her head and arm and side ache.

The parking lot stretches for miles, it seems, kids everywhere in packs, snuggly couples, the occasional middle-aged, settled-looking couple Paula envies more than all the others. The Cinema Fourteen Plex looms up ahead like Oz, like a big bright fake city offering anything and everything, a smorgasbord of action and emotion as varied as the jelly bean connoisseur basket her husband's secretary sent at Christmas, a woman Paula has so often wished would become something more. Wouldn't that be easier?

"He's here," Tina says and points to where a tall skinny kid in a letter jacket is pacing along the curb. "Oh, my God. Oh, my God."

"Puhleeze," Erin says, sounding way too old. "Chill out. He's *just a boy.*" And then they collapse in another round of laughter and are out of the car and gone. Paula's hip is buzzing again. Buzzing and buzzing. What if it's Gregory and the sleepover is canceled? Or he fell on the skate ramp and broke something or needs stitches and her husband can't be found because he's out in the woods with a flashlight looking for wildlife? Or maybe her husband really does need her. He just got a call that his mother died. Does she know where he put the Havahart trap? And when is the last time she saw *their* cat?

Lauren is feeling frightened. The other boy, the one from the backseat who is always quiet and refuses to talk about the bruises on his face and arms, has announced he's leaving. He can't do this anymore. The leader slams on the brakes and calls him a pussy. The leader says that if he leaves that's it, no more rides, no more pot, no more anything except he'll catch him some dark night and beat the shit out of him. "I'll beat you worse than whatever goes on in that trash house of yours," he says, but the boy keeps walking, and Lauren feels herself wanting to yell out for him to wait for her. She has always found him scary and disgusting, but now she admires his ability to put one foot in front of the other. He says he's bored with it all—lame amateur shit—but she sees a fear in him as recognizable as her own. "Let him go," she whispers. She is watching the flicker of television light in the teacher's upstairs window. "Please. Can't we just ride around or something?"

"Afraid you won't get any more tonight?" he asks and leans in so close she can smell his breath, oddly sweet with Dentyne. The lost possibility of his features makes her sad, eyes you might otherwise think a beautiful shade of blue, dimple in the left cheek. He pulls a coiled rope from under the seat. "You gonna stay put, or do I need to tie you up?" She forces herself to laugh, assure him that she will stay put, but she makes the mistake of glancing at the key in the ignition, and he reaches and takes it.

She cautions herself to keep breathing, to act like she's with him. "Next one," she says. "I need to collect myself."

"Well, you just collect," he says. "I'll be back to deal with you in a minute." She doesn't ask what he plans to do. His outlines of all the ways such an event might go are lengthy and varied, some of them tame and pointless and others not pretty at all. He has already said he wants to scare the hell out of the old woman, let *her* know what it feels like to have someone make you say *please* and *thank you* every goddamn day. The girl watches him move into the darkness, numb fingers struggling to finally zip her pants back up, to pretend that his rough fingertips never touched her there. She will get out and run. She will leave the door open and crawl through the hedge until she reaches the main road. She will call her parents, beg for their forgiveness. There is no way now to get her shoes or phone, but she moves and keeps moving. She thinks of her bed and how good it will feel to crawl between clean sheets, to stare at the faces of all the dolls collected before everything in her life seemed to go so bad. Now all the things she has been so upset about mean nothing. So what if she let the handsome, clean-smelling track star do everything he wanted to do? She liked it too, didn't she? Not making the soccer team last year, being told on college day that she had no prayer of getting into any of the schools she had listed, most of them ones he was considering if he could run track. But losing or getting rejected—that happens to a lot of people, doesn't it? She can still find something she's good at, go *somewhere*. Right now she just wants to get home, to shower herself clean with the hottest water she can stand, to soap and scrub and wrap up in a flannel robe. She once watched her uncle skin a catfish, tearing the tight skin from the meat like an elastic suit, and she keeps thinking of the sound it made, a sound that made her want to pull her jacket close, to hide and protect her own skin. She feels that way now, only there's nothing to pull around her, the night air much cooler than she'd thought—and she keeps thinking she hears him behind her, so she moves faster. She is almost to the main road, the busy intersection, the rows of cars heading toward the cinema. Her foot is bleeding, a sliver of glass, and she is pinned at a corner, lines upon lines of cars waiting for the light to change.

Paula's cell phone buzzes again, and she takes a deep breath and answers. "Where are you?" he asks. She can hear the impatience, perhaps a twinge of anger, and his voice does not match the way she remembers him sounding in the stairwell. When she pictures his face or reads his tiny penciled scrawl, it's a different voice, like it's been dubbed.

"Almost there," she says and tries to sound flirtatious, leaving him a promise of making up for lost time. Then she glances out her window and sees a girl she thinks she recognizes. Shirt torn and barefooted. They certainly won't let her in the theater that way. The girl is so familiar, and then she remembers—her daughter's school, story time in the library. But that was years ago when the girl's hair was light brown and pulled up in a high ponytail. She knows exactly who she is. This is a girl parents caution their *good* girls against. She is rumored to be bulimic. She locks herself in the school bathroom and cuts her arms. She once tried to overdose on vodka and aspirin and had to have her stomach pumped. She gives blowjobs in the stairwell of the high school in exchange for drugs.

She has blackened ghoulish eyes and jet black hair, silver safety pins through her eyebrows and lip. Paula has heard parents whispering about her at various school functions. They say, "Last year she was perfectly normal, and now this. She was a B student with some artistic talent and a pretty face, and now this." She is the "Don't" poster child of this town, the local object lesson in how quickly a child can go bad.

Agnes is trying to remember what exactly it was she said to anger Preston so. She had tried to make it complimentary, something about skin like café au lait. She had often seen black people described that way in stories, coffee and chocolates, conjuring delicious smells instead of those like the bus station or fish market across the river, which is what a lot of people might associate with black people. Her maid once used a pomade so powerful smelling Agnes had to ask that she please stop wearing it, but certainly Agnes never held that against the woman; she couldn't help being born into a culture that thought that was the thing to do.

"Sometimes it's not even *what* stupid thing you say," Preston shouted, the vein in his forehead throbbing like it might burst. "It's *how* you say it. So, so goddamned *godlike.*" He spit the word and shook all over, hands clenched into fists. But now she wants him to come back and be with her. She didn't know coffee would be insulting. She is going through her phone numbers, she has it somewhere. That same day she reminded him that even the president of the United States said things like that. The president had once referred to his grandchildren as "the little brown ones," and why is that okay and chocolate and coffee are not?

It's your mom, she practices now. *Please talk to me, Preston.* She is dialing when she hears something down on her front porch. The wind? Her cat? There was a flyer in her mailbox just this evening saying how she should not leave the cat outside.

Lauren shivers as she stands there on the corner. She expects to hear his car roar up any second and wonders what she will do when that happens. She will have to tell her parents that she lost her purse, that it got stolen, and her shoes and jacket. She shudders with the thought of the boy pawing through her personal things, a picture of the track star cut from the school newspaper, a poem she was writing about the ocean, a pale pink rabbit's foot she has carried since sixth grade when she won the school math bee with it in her pocket. The light is about to change, and she concentrates on that instead of imagining her parents' reaction. Just once she wishes one of them would pull her close and say, "Please, tell me what's wrong," and then she would. She would start talking and not stop, like a dam breaking; she would tell them so many things if there were really such a thing as unconditional love. But instead they will say, "What is wrong with you? Why are you doing this to us? Do you know what people are saying about you?"

"Do you need a ride?" A woman in an old black Audi leans out the window and motions her to hurry. "I know you from school."

She does know the woman, the mother of a girl in her class, a girl who makes good grades and doesn't get into trouble. Not a popular girl, just a normal girl. A nice girl who smiles shyly and will let you copy her notes if you get behind. Erin from Algebra I freshman year. This is Erin's mother.

She hears a car slowing in the lane beside her and runs to get in with the woman just as the light changes. "Thank you."

"My daughter goes to your school," the woman says. She is wearing a low-cut camisole with a pretty silver necklace. Her black sweater is soft and loose around her shoulders. The car smells like crayons and the woman's cologne. "I'm sorry my car is so messy. My husband's car, that is." Her cell phone buzzes in the cup holder, but she ignores it. "Where are you going, sweetheart?" she asks. "It's too chilly to be out without shoes and long sleeves." Something in her voice brings tears to the girl's eyes, and then her crying is uncontrollable. The woman just keeps driving, circling first the cinema and then many of the neighborhoods around the area. The girl sinks low in her seat when they pass the teacher's house, that old Pontiac still parked behind the hedge. She can't allow herself to imagine what he is doing, what he will do when he finds her gone. They drive out to the interstate and make a big loop, the woman patting her shoulder from time to time, telling her it's okay, that nothing can be that bad. Every third or fourth time the woman asks for her address, but for now the girl just wants to be here in this car riding. The woman's cell phone keeps buzzing and buzzing. Once she answers it to the loud voice of her daughter from the movie lobby saying she will need a ride home after all. "Are you mad, Mom?" the girl screams. "Is that okay?" And the woman assures her that it is okay. It is fine. She will be there. Then she answers to say she saw their cat early this morning. And then, apologizing when it rings again, she answers and says little at all, except that so much has happened, she just might not get there at all. "In fact," she whispers, "I know I can't get there." And Lauren knows there is a good chance that she is part of what has happened, but the heat is blowing on her cold feet and the woman has the radio turned down low with classical music, and her eyelids are so heavy she can barely keep them open. When she was little and couldn't sleep, her parents would sometimes put her in a warm car and drive her around. Her dad called it a "get lost" drive, and he let her make all the choices, turn here, turn there, turn there again, and then she would relax while he untangled the route and led them back home, by which time she would be nearly or already asleep. There was never any doubt that he could find the way home and that she would wake to find herself already tucked in her bed or in his arms being taken there.

Preston's answering machine comes on, and Agnes is about to speak, but then she hears the noise again and puts down the phone. She wishes she would find Preston there—Preston and Amy, waiting to embrace her and start all over again. Preston in his letter jacket like he was all those nights she waited up for him and said, "Where have you been, young man?" And Edwin would be in the basement smoking, and Oliver would be rooting around at the foot of her bed.

Her chest is tight with the worry of it all. She swallows and opens the door. Nothing.

"Here, kitty," she calls in a faint voice. She steps out on the stoop into the chilly air. The sky is clear overhead, a sliver of a moon. There is a car parked way down at the end of her drive, just the front bumper showing beyond the hedge. It wasn't there when she came home. Perhaps someone had a flat or ran out of gas. She calls the cat again and hears leaves crunching around the side of the house. She waits, expecting to see it slink around the corner, but then nothing. There is more noise beyond the darkness, where she can't see. And it is coming closer, short quick sounds, footsteps in the leaves. She is backing into the house when she thinks she sees something much larger than the cat slip around the corner near her kitchen door. She pulls her sweater close and pushes the door to, turns the dead bolt. The flyer talked about coyotes and how they have been spotted all over town.

The girl finally tells Paula where she lives, a neighborhood out of town and in the opposite direction from the motel. Paula's cell phone beeps with yet another message, but now she ignores it. She doesn't want to hear what he has to say now that he has had time to shape an answer to her standing him up yet again. She parks in front of a small brick ranch. The front porch is lit with a yellow bulb, all the drapes pulled closed.

"I'm happy to walk you up," Paula says, but the girl shakes her head. She says thank you without making eye contact and then gets out, making her way across the yard in slow, careful steps. Paula waits to see if a parent comes out, but the girl slips in and recloses the door without a trace.

Paula sits there in the dark as if expecting something to happen. And then she slips off the cardigan and pulls her turtleneck over her head. The message is waiting. He might be saying this is the last time he will do this, he has wasted too much time on her already. "Why are you fucking with me?" he might ask. Or, "Who do you think you are?" The chances of him saying he understands completely and they will try again some other, better time are slim. She imagines him there in the room, bare chested and waiting, already thinking about his other options, his better options. And she imagines her own house and her return, sink full of dirty dishes, purple nail polish and Power Ranger figures everywhere. A litter box that needs scooping and clothes that need washing and an empty pantry that would have been filled had she not been out buying lingerie all day.

She saw a coyote just last week, but she didn't report it. She was standing at the kitchen window and glanced out to see a tall, skinny shepherd mix—except just as her mind was shaping the thought about someone letting a dog run loose in the neighborhood, it came to her that this was not a dog. It was wild and fearful looking, thin and hungry, and she felt a kinship as they stood frozen, staring at each other. Everyone wants something.

The leader can see her in there, old bat, holding her chest and shaking. She looks like a puppet, her old bitch of a body jerking in time with his jiggling the knob. "I wore your fucking boy's shirt," he will say. "Thank you so much. That little polo fucker really helped turn my life around." She lifts the phone and pulls the cord around the corner where he can't see her, so he jiggles harder, leans the weight of his body against the door. "Loafers! Neckties! *F* in fucking math." He creeps around and climbs high enough on a trellis to see that she is slumped down in a chair with the receiver clutched against her chest. "Say the magic word," he says and covers his fist with his shirt before punching out the window. "Say it."

When Paula pulls up to the theater, Erin and Tina are waiting. A tall, thin boy in a letter jacket trails alongside Tina, his hand in her hip pocket in a familiar way, and then they kiss before the girls get in the car. Paula is about to mention the girl she picked up but then thinks better of it. She wants to say things like, "Don't you ever . . ." but the sound of her daughter's laughter makes her think better of it.

"I can't believe you, like, ate face in front of my mom," Erin says, and Tina blushes and grins. She is a girl with cleavage and braces, betwixt and between.

"Jesus, Mom, let some air in this stinkhole car," Erin laughs, and then the two girls talk over the movie and everyone they saw there as if Paula were not even present. Paula can't stop thinking about the girl and how she came to be on that busy corner with no shoes, how she looks so different from that clean-faced little girl in a library chair, and yet she is one and the same. And what will she write and slip to her co-worker on Monday, or will she avoid him altogether and pretend nothing ever happened, that she never ventured from her own darkened den in search of excitement? She imagines the coyotes living as her husband has described, little nests under piles of brush, helpless cubs curled there waiting for the return of their mother.

"I'm sorry if I messed up your time with your lame friend," Erin says sarcastically and then leans in close. "Really, Momsy, I am." She air-kisses Paula and smiles a sincere thanks before turning back to her friend with a shriek of something she can't believe she forgot to tell, something about cheating, someone getting caught with a teacher's grade book. She has licorice twists braided and tied around her throat like a necklace, and her breath is sweet with Milk Duds.

The old woman is dead or acting dead, the recorded voice from the receiver on her chest telling her to please hang up and try her call again. It's one of those houses where everything is in place, little useless bullshit glass things nobody wants. She looks as miserable dead as she did alive. It makes him want to trash the place, but why bother now? He didn't kill her. He didn't do a thing but pop out a pane of glass. He searches around and then carefully, using his shirt so as not to leave a print, takes a golf ball from the basket beside the fireplace and places it down in the broken glass. Television is too big to lift, no purse in sight, not even a liquor cabinet. She gives him the creeps, and so do all the people looking out from portraits and photographs. He'll tell the girl that he just scared the old bitch, threatened to tie her up and put a bullet in her head until she cried and begged for his mercy and forgiveness. He'll say he left her alive and grateful.

The moon is high in the bright clear sky when Paula ventures outside to look for their cat. She pulls her sweater close and steps away from the light of the house, the woods around her spreading into darkness. Her husband is sleeping, and Erin is on the phone. There were no messages other than the one on her cell phone, still trapped there and waiting. She hears a distant siren, the wind in the trees, the bass beat from a passing car. *Please,* she thinks. *Please.* She is about to go inside for a flashlight when she hears the familiar bell and then sees the cat slinking up from the dark woods, her manner cool and unaffected.

Jill McCorkle, a native of Lumberton, North Carolina, graduated from UNC-Chapel Hill and received her MA in creative writing from Hollins University. She is the author of five novels—*The Cheer Leader, July 7th, Tending to Virginia, Ferris Beach,* and *Carolina Moon*—and three short story collections. Her new collection, *Going Away Shoes,* is forthcoming fall 2009. Her work has appeared in the *Atlantic, Ploughshares, American Scholar, Best American Short Stories, New Stories from the South,* and the *Norton Anthology of Short Fiction,* among other publications. The recipient of the New England Book Award, the John Dos Passos Prize, and the North Carolina Award for Literature, she has taught creative writing at UNC–Chapel Hill, Tufts, Harvard, Brandeis, and Bennington College. She is currently on faculty at North Carolina State University.

*T*he whole idea for "Magic Words" came out of my thinking about the way please *and* thank you *are often taken for granted and spouted without any sense of what is really going on. I was struck by the weird extremes in usage from the polite superficial "please" to someone pleading for his or her life or the polite superficial "thank you" to an honest sense of gratefulness. So, that's where I started—a sense of the surface action being completely out of balance with what is being thought, felt, known below it all. The various characters are in such a place, their actions masking their real desires and needs. I consciously placed them all in what felt like a minefield, with threatening turns all around them. When Paula looks out and makes eye contact with the coyote and acknowledges that everyone wants something, she is speaking to the whole cast, each character having come to a place of needing a kind of acceptance.*

That's a common enough story, but I was surprised where I wound up when their lives began to intersect. I had fully intended that Paula would make it all the way to the motel and consummate the relationship she has been flirting with and that the boy would intentionally hurt Agnes and that the cat would likely never come home. For whatever reason, as soon as Paula made the decision not to go, the volume turned way down on all the others, and I found myself more focused on the fragility of their lives and the moment.

The image from reality that fed this story was my own moment of being surprised by a coyote in my own backyard. There was about one second where I thought it was a dog and then just as quickly knew it was not *a dog. We made eye contact, both of us frozen in place, and I remember taking note of where my children and pets were and thinking the word* please. Please go away. Please don't come closer. And needless to say, I was thankful when he turned and darted back into the woods. I could only imagine that he was feeling the same.*

Tayari Jones

SOME THING BLUE

(from *poemmemoirstory*)

In Scottsboro, Alabama, there is a warehouse store that sells everything that people leave behind on airplanes. This is where your mother has found your wedding dress.

You are apprehensive. What ever happened to "something old, something new"? What you have so far is something mortgaged—this would be your childhood home. (Storybook weddings are far more costly than anyone imagined.) There is also something pawned—your engagement ring, one and one third carats, clear as drinking water. (Your fiancé Marcus, being both book-smart and streetwise, haggled with the pawn broker for almost an hour.) And now, there is this lovely gown—something ditched. Because let's face it. No one just loses a dress like this. (The designer is famous and photogenic; her picture is printed in gossip magazines.)

But how can you complain? Marcus is a good guy. He is a podiatrist. More importantly, your mother is happy and she is *alive*. Only two years ago, she lay bald and dying, weeping because she would never be a grandmother, never wear the mother-of-the-bride dress she bought six years ago on sale at Filene's.

At the time, she really *was* dying, not yet in hospice care, but fading, so you didn't tell her that lately you'd been dating women and that you loved one in particular, an artist who designed elaborate

160

jewelry from bottle glass. Who would have benefited from such a confession?

Instead, you sat beside your dying mother and promised to name any son of yours Benjamin, for her father, and you'd call any daughter Iris, in her memory. And while you were promising, you promised God you'd be a better daughter were you given just another chance.

And just like that, she recovered. So appealing was your offer that God actually took you up on it. Call it a miracle. Call it a contract.

So now you stand in the makeshift dressing room of the warehouse-store laced into this gown which was abandoned by a woman whose obligations were far less urgent than your own. The bodice is old-fashioned, rigid with whale bone but lush with beadwork. The organza sleeves are light and thin as Bible paper.

Your mother waits on the other side of the curtain, eager and restless as a child, her face shining with joy and with health. You love her. You love her. She is your mother. How dare you, even for one moment, regret trading your own life for hers?

Tayari Jones is the author of the novels *Leaving Atlanta* and *The Untelling,* winners of the Hurston/Wright and Lillian C. Smith awards. Her stories and essays have appeared in *McSweeney's,* the *Believer, Callaloo,* and the *New York Times.* She teaches on the MFA faculty of Rutgers-Newark University and is a red velvet cake enthusiast.

RICHARD POWERS

This story came about as a challenge from the PEN/Faulkner Foundation: write a story that can be read in three minutes or less on the theme of "Lost and Found." I have always been obsessed with the Unclaimed Baggage Center in Scottsboro, Alabama. My mother is pretty obsessed with bargains, and I have no doubt that she would love to wear a mother-of-the-bride dress one day. I put all these things in the blender of my mind, and this story is what poured out. I didn't intend for it to be as sad as it is; I had imagined a funny story, but art often has its own agenda.

Stephanie Dickinson

LOVE CITY

(from *Short Story*)

I like the way the moon weakens in the sky when the sun's eye pops open but we have no time to admire it. Desiree and I creep along the far reaches of the Fountain Inn Motel hoping that no one sees us on our way home to Cabin #7. The pool glows from all the flickering candles and the liquor is going down quick. "Say drink drank drunk, man," LeAndre's middle brother shouts before LeAndre cannonballs into the pool. It's a workday dawn, but around the pool, it's still an early summer night. Kids, that's all they are. Four, six teenagers not much younger than me, age fifteen.

The baby and I stop to admire the Indian paintbrush. "See, Desiree, how the white moves." I point to the moths suckling the purple buds, one pair of wings lighting above the other until it looks as if the paintbrushes are about to fly away. She nuzzles against me and smacks, a happy baby, long eyelashed and taffy-lipped.

"Hey, skinny," one of them calls out and I know who they mean and I mean to ignore them and walk right on by.

Taking a deep breath, I pat the baby's bottom before we set out across the courtyard where the pool bedazzles surrounded as it is by pieces of families who live in these cabins of nicked doors and low ceilings. Yesterday a stray bullet called a small boy's name as he climbed out of the swimming pool. Luckily for him, it missed.

"Take a look at what the dog's dragging in." There's a hoot and a holler.

Desiree's in and out breathing as she rides against my ribs comforts me and I wish for the hundredth time that our cabin unit was far from here.

LeAndre has climbed back onto the diving board and is drinking shots from a Dixie cup and swigging it straight from the bottle. He yells at his girlfriend, a coffee-skinned Cinderella, "Gimme the Johnny Walker Black." She sprawls in a chaise lounge like she washed up there in her size five glass slippers.

"We got Old Grand-Dad and tequila." A glass slipper, this one bigger and in the shape of a liquor bottle, appears in her fingers. LeAndre's little brother grabs it up and delivers it to the diving board. The sun pries open its other eye but night keeps on going.

LeAndre refuses to sit and lifts the new bottle. "This stuff knocks people on their butts. Shoot, I can drink a bottle straight and still be standing on my feet." The flickering red candles stretch their cat scratch shadows. Buckwheat Zydeco pumps his accordion on some old person's tape player. They all shout and accuse one another of having sexual relations with their mothers.

"Man, you've got boogers for brains, you know that," Baptiste says, sneaking out from behind the soda machine. "You should hook up with the skinny girl with the dog muzzle for a face."

I stand frozen, looking. Baptiste is beautiful. Tall, smoke on ice, and his face valentine-pretty like somebody else got cheated for his to shine so. LeAndre for one. Baptiste peers out of sullen gray-lynx eyes with a droop to their lids. "You drink that bottle and you'll fall in the pool." There goes his loud surly mouth. Tormentor. Both LeAndre and Baptiste were raised in the Chef Menteur Houses. Both came through the flood. Baptiste keeps on. "Three feet of water is all it'll take to drown you. Or maybe that mouth of yours can hold you above water."

Drowning. We all dream of water closing over our heads, a trapdoor slamming. Water banging and bleating, black greasy water, salamanders.

"LeAndre, don't take guff from that copper thief." His girl-friend lifts her arms over her head and cracks her knuckles. Her fingernails slice the first rays of sun.

Baptiste keeps strands of copper wire in his pockets and an L pipe. He doesn't care if he feeds on ripped open chests. It's the growth industry in Orleans Parish—stripping out new pipes and copper wire from folks just finished remodeling their houses, folks ruined twice.

"Ain't she a rock star," Baptiste catcalls. "The hand lady."

Heads turn. It's the white woman, who has hardly any hair and always wears a blue jumper, stumbling from the laundry shack. She paces at all hours of the day or night, holding her hand to her ear and talking. "Scotch thistle. Foam flower. Yellow archangel." She appeared one day with the hospital band still encircling her wrist. "Lavender meadow mist."

LeAndre's girl shouts, "Copper thief. Baptiste, you're a rat star. Gnawing copper."

He doesn't answer her, instead he spots me trying to sink past. He growls, his teeth spark like just struck matches. "Hey, chickie, hey carpenter's dream. Walk your skinny legs over here. I want to talk to you." Baptiste wears a white cutaway T-shirt and white sneakers. Like the white stead in the old time photos of soldiers on horseback, a whole army mounted on brown horses except for one man on a white stallion. Baptiste acts like he's the white stallion man.

His teeth take an edge of the breeze and then grind it with his saliva. "I got something up in my room that'll make you hot as a ripe peach. Do you hear me, skinny Bible girl?"

No thanks, my silence says. I take another step and then another, hoping he won't keep taunting me. I'm not a Bible girl at all. Just not pretty.

He steps in front of me, cocky smirk on his lips. An upside down looking smile, the kind girls like. "Church looking thing, I'll fix you. Homely little oyster on the half shell, I'll slurp you up." He leans down, puckering his lips and coming closer and I know I should move but I don't. I remember the storm born over the water, and how it traveled like an angry sky whale feeding on the warm air, licking and smacking and growing bigger, the gnawed water rising into giant waves. Baptiste moving closer, each step feels like those waves. I blink. His lips are dark beignets, every cent thrown away. His mouth almost touches mine and then he jumps back as if a wasp stung his lip. "She puckered up. The dog chick thought I was going to kiss her. I wouldn't touch this one with a ten foot pole."

Redness fills my cheeks and forehead. I hum until it goes quiet in my mind.

"Leave her alone," LeAndre says. "Put your fists up, Baptiste. Let's duke it out."

"I'll hurt you. I whopped you back in the third grade."

"Yeah, Baptiste, you were in fifth grade and I was in third," LeAndre blurts out like he's been harboring that sorrow.

LeAndre's mom Chandra listens through the window. She bosses her kids around night and day yet it was Chandra who helped me with Desiree's hair, twisting tiny braids and snapping barrettes, Chandra who taught me how a baby should be rubbed about the U-shape, massaging the belly from the left hip across the navel to the right hip to relieve gas.

Maybe I'm homely, but Desiree is pretty with her strange gray-green eyes and dark skin.

LeAndre tilts the bottle, bouncing himself on the diving board, his pants sagging. He's short and slight with not much of a chin that you notice and feel sorry for. Chandra lets him keep a spider in a glass tank and buys him the crickets to feed it. Living crickets. The kids like to watch the tarantula spin his web.

"You're nothing but yellow chicken meat," LeAndre calls. "Chicken meat. Yellow."

Baptiste climbs up on the diving board and begins to bounce. He jumps and lands hard, stomping the diving board and LeAndre loses his balance. Oh, no, he mouths and splashes into the pool where he flounders, beating his arms and sputtering before dog paddling to the ladder and heaving himself up.

Chandra curses from the door crack of blue Cabin #5. I picture the stud in her nostril like a roofing nail. Then with a dazzling slam she explodes from her unit in a billowing housedress coming to the rescue of her son. Desiree and I rush for the safety of the green cabin. Hurry hurry. I bump my shin on the microwave oven discarded outside one of the cabins. When I cry out, Desiree joins in. "Hush, my love. It's nothing." The woman in the blue jumper is tripping along too and muttering the names of flowers into her hand. "Elephant toe tree. Ponytail palm. Giant bird-of-paradise."

At last I twist the key, enter, pull the chain lock. I let out a dry cleaning bag of pent up breath. Desiree and I are home. The walls that I painted a pale green are glad to see us. After minding the Fountain Inn's front desk for Mister Leonard while he minded his girlfriend I'm tired. I pull aside the mosquito net and plop on the bed with the baby.

"I'm going to pretend I'm a moth and fly right between your toes." She loves it when I stroke the bottoms of her feet and blow bubbles on them. I use my thumbs to kiss and tickle each toe. Toes have mouths too. I warm Desiree's spiced apples in the microwave. "Didn't momma make a nice room for us?" Around the door and window I used crayons to color cypress trees and blue flower trees and leaves with caterpillars asleep in hammocks and I stapled ruffles to the lamp shade and spread little green rugs on the floor. "One spoonful at a time. Open your mouth wide." Desiree eats too fast because she loves food and can't get her burps out.

There's a knock on the window and I try to ignore Baptiste who presses his lips to the glass. "I want your soft . . ." He's knocking and calling and yammering, wanting to touch me, wanting a suck face butterscotch sundae. "Let me in. I need your sweetness. Bible chick, I can teach you verses." Fingers tapping the window, he snickers because I'm just playing hard to get. He flat out starts to pound. I put Desiree down and crack the door leaving the chain lock on. Baptiste's knee jams itself against the frame. One eye, a meringue lash, one white sneaker.

"Go away, Baptiste. Please, the baby's trying to sleep."

"I can give you something that'll make you sleep real good. A meat inoculation."

It's just us without an audience and I'm wanting to tell him to stop bothering me and in the middle of my words I hear a firecracker. I don't let Desiree play next to the door or get too close to that window. Because what Katrina stirred up besides tree roots is not settling down any too easy. Another firecracker and Baptiste's lips unstick themselves from the door jamb and his eye widens like it's about to somersault. Oh, no. Another backfiring muffler pushes Baptiste until his chin hooks the chain on my lock. I try to push him from the door, I'm sorry please go away, I press myself against the door. The lock gives. "Baptiste," I whimper. He's crumpling over my welcome mat, his white cutaway T-shirt bleeding, getting up on one elbow, then a knee.

"Can't breathe."

I run for towels. I'm a crab keeping close to the floor. A trickle of red runs down his chin and from the hole in his back. Baptiste coughs. Poisoned water that they pumped back to the great lake. Please, don't shoot. I don't know what to do. Desiree cries. I smile into his golden brown skin and eyes and his Roman nose. I smile at the ninety degree August day on its way almost a year from the flood. I smile at the ceiling. Please don't hurt us.

"Elephant toe tree." The hand woman in the blue jumper stands in the door with her fingers against her ear. Someone hovers behind her, made of mist and smoke, the shoulders of fire I refuse to see, the hand holding a gun. "Peace lily. Gardenia," she says.

Baptiste's legs pedal and his knees rise and then shiver.

"Cape jasmine," she says. "Transylvania sage."

He settles in a pool of grease like a fried catfish in a jacket of rust colored breading.

A shiny bright ambulance careens down the expressway its siren singing as it goes. People from every unit gather outside my door.

The EMS men arrive and sweep Baptiste away. Maybe they can save him. Maybe, maybe. Fingers crossed. The two red-haired twin girls from Tallahassee. Mrs. Phillips, the nicest person and my only friend here. The sun climbs higher into the sky before the police pull up. I am holding an injured towel.

"Miss, you must have seen something," the policeman says, cleaning a thumbnail on his belt buckle.

I shake my head. "The hand lady was in the way."

Someone points her out and the police ask what she saw. "Lavender meadow mist," she says. "Screw pine."

His turn, the policeman's, to shake his head.

She is here all by herself, alone except for her hand. Maybe she uses it to talk to God. "Ponytail palm. Giant bird-of-paradise." God.

I am still holding the towel.

The green mosquito net slopes above us like a willow grove. Three days have passed since Baptiste was alive. I take Desiree into my arms and rock her to sleep. My tongue feels cut. Beyond the hum of the air conditioner, I hear the man who cleans the pool meaning everyone has gone home. He lugs around a wooden crate with a funnel in the slats and a sign that reads WATER ME. His cat, a one-eyed calico, accompanies him wherever he goes. He's taking no chances of Banjo getting stranded. A white man with a dyed Mohawk and tattoos covering his neck, arms, and chest, he's the same man who stocks the soda machine. After skimming the water, he lights a cigarette, and I smell wisps of smoke, a firefly he breathes in and out. He marches to the soda machine, and with a thump down rolls the orange Fanta. Breakfast. Newport and a soda.

I roll over. In the next cabin, LeAndre and his mother, Chandra, fight and his little brothers are crying and you can hear each and every word through the wall. Four of them are crowded into that one room where you'd be crying too. "You let him push you around," Chandra bullies.

"Baptiste wasn't pushing. We had words is all."

"I'm talking about that cop. I wanted a man for a son. You're acting like a wiggly thing."

A door slams and they're shouting by the outdoor Coke machine. My eyelids need toothpicks and I can't keep them from covering my whole head when they close. I'm tickling my sweet Desiree's foot. A school of black trout swim by my head, then an uprooted tree trunk. I'm trying to dive between the slippery eels. I open my eyes and the baby lies with her feet in the air and it looks like she's trying to climb with her ten toes. There's a calm inside Desiree and I think of the first time I set eyes on her in a Styrofoam ice chest floating in the floodwater of Katrina, her little brown body not wearing a Pamper and covered in red ants. When you've lived through the black water and red ants you can live through anything. She's mine. I saved her life and she became mine.

I turn on the pillow to look at her lashes, comparing them to my own, which are shorter, trying to blink back the sun the drapes let in. A leaf smell seeps from her. Then I squint and the hairs rise on the back of my neck. Someone is sitting in the room's one chair, his legs crossed. I cover the baby's eyes and make myself look at his gory sneakers that make slippery sounds when he gets up and marches to the door and back to the chair. I try not to see into his eyes—stars that have gone black. His handsome face like embalmed cold rain. I want to ask what he knows about the drowned ones but instead I tell him to get out. I'm sorry that he's dead but he can't stay. He won't go until I reveal who that figure of mist was. LeAndre or Chandra or both. *Bible girl, my back was turned but you were looking that way. Who shot me? Who? Did you have a gun too?* The air conditioner is a hoax in the window. It sweats and cries long tears and exhales lukewarm breath but right now I'm freezing. I tell him the truth, which is the same as I told the police. The crazy hand lady was in the way.

There's a knock, two shorts followed by a pause and another knock. Chandra is giving the signal but I don't need it. I know the sound of everyone who lives here. Mrs. Phillips is my only friend but she never comes over here. I blink and search for the red sneakers, for the visitor wearing them but nothing. Baptiste disappears. Then I crack the door. Chandra and Pernell, the youngest of LeAndre's brothers, stand right where the outline of Baptiste could have been drawn but never was. The toddler hangs onto his mom's hip-hugging bell-bottom jeans and her tote bag, which could carry a picnic. Do I want her inside my cabin? No.

"Can Pernell use your bathroom?"

I don't move to slide open the chain lock. "Hey, pretty boy," I say to the toddler.

Chandra yanks off her sunglasses. Her eyes take me in, her pupils dilated like so many folks around here. "We've got plumbing problems. The toilet's overflowing next door and Mister Leonard just now sent for a plumber."

"I have to go pee pee," Pernell says.

I open the door and step aside. Pernell gallops to the wall where a pelican fishes the woodwork. I drew it from a magazine and tried as best I could to make the feathers look like you could pet them.

"Bird," he laughs, pointing.

"Pernell, you get into the bathroom this minute. You hear me? Before I slap your behind." Chandra wears funny bell-bottoms that she's cut into fringes from the knees down and high heels. She moves in a cloud of designer perfume and stale bread that makes Desiree sneeze. I take a deep breath and hold it.

Pernell runs to Desiree to kiss her and pounces on the bed. Desiree smiles when she sees him, the same way she always smiles. Like violets.

"Get off there with your dirty tail. I'm going to wash his bottom in your tub. Go right in that bathroom and I'm not playing Pernell. Get your business done." Chandra's mouth shimmers and twists in wintergreen lip gloss like a meat juice warm from the oven. The rose tattoo on her neck sharpens its thorns.

"Come here, little man." I reach in and turn on the bathroom light for Pernell. Blue shower curtain, blue towels, blue rugs.

The plump two-year-old in green flip-flops and soiled pink

shorts dives and hides under the bed. Chandra snaps her fingers and orders Pernell out from his hiding place, yanks him into the bathroom, shuts the door and locks it. After three flushes and bathtub water running for a good long time, they come out. Chandra's tote is open. "Ivory, hey. We're a little short of cash." She is wondering if I could spare a twenty since she knows I do little errands for Mister Leonard and watch the desk.

"Chandra, I can't do that. You know I save everything for the baby."

"You work for that old motel man." Her mouth sets itself hard. "I see a ten dollar bill right there coming out of your purse." I remember her stories of how she was married to an old guy who she divorced because he couldn't take care of her bodily needs. The story changed to a husband who jumped into the floodwaters off a tin roof during Katrina to swim to her and went under. A real nice churchman she tells me. He dove in and she swears a water moccasin big as an alligator unhinged its jaws and slurped her nice churchman in. No life insurance. No money.

"Chandra, that's for formula."

A furrowed forehead stares me down. "You didn't tell no tales to those cops, did you?"

The black water rises up, splashes into my mouth.

She blurts, "I saw those cops over here twice three times."

"Twice, Chandra." Shrugging, I give her the ten dollar bill and two jars of strained peas and carrots for the kids.

"You better have told the cops the truth."

"I did."

"Do you have another ten stowed in that bag of yours?"

She's taller and bigger than me and I don't like her coming so close with that big space between her front teeth. I back up to the door so I can stay facing her. Pernell hits the pelican drawn on the wall. "Fly, fly," he demands. She's so busy coveting what everyone else has it makes her guts itch. You tell me how to scratch that. Pernell slaps another pelican and another. "Fly."

The pelicans on the walls shift and the ceiling moves with the black tips of their wings flashing. I smell their salmon-colored bills. Their breathing ruffles the hair on Pernell's arms. I imagine them, scooping Desiree and me up and flying us into the treetops. Then they settle back into their feathers. Only crayon drawings on a wall.

"You look in that bag and get me another ten dollar bill. You better not be thinking it was LeAndre who brought that boy down. I taught all my kids to stand up for themselves but not like that. You don't shoot anyone in the back like a weakling. You face your trouble eyeball to eyeball. Twice you say the cops came. You can bet if it was a white boy lying on the ground they'd have come ten times. Some people are saying it was that crazy hand lady. Other folks are saying it was you." Chandra looks me straight in the eye, sighting like a rhinoceros, that one big horn. "That's right I've heard people say it was you."

I feel like she's gored my stomach. "Me?"

"Yeah, Bible girl, you're the one he couldn't stop making fun of. How many times did he call you butt-ugly in front of a crowd? Plenty. People say you'd had enough and snapped."

I hear it again in my head. They hoot and holler and Baptiste wolf whistles. "Ivory. That little hottie's hot for me. Look at the chickie. I can't tell her butt from her face. That big hole in the middle of it must be her mouth. Bible girl, practically wearing her baby and want to know why she has to safety pin the kid to her. Want to know?" More catcalls, sure they want to know. "Because any baby would run away from that big nosed ugly a momma." I cover Desiree's ears and I hum until it goes quiet in my mind and I'm away from Baptiste's mouth. My face feels hot like a candle holding its little tears of wax.

"Pernell, get over here. We're leaving." Chandra palms open the door. She startles and lets out a gasp. The hand lady is right there staring at her. "Get away from me." The hand lady is red-cheeked from where she presses her fingers. "I like listening to the walls," she says, dropping her hand to her side. "I like hearing the flowers." The red marks on her face are smeared.

"Get out of my way, you crazy loon," Chandra snaps. Then before I can get between them, she shoves the hand lady.

I can't tell whether she knows she was pushed. "Peruvian birthwort. Peace lily," she mutters.

Something's different in the room, something added not subtracted. I go through the bathroom slowly, lift the base of the toilet, looking in all the TV places to hide a gun. Then I fill the bathroom sink with water and pick up Desiree. "Time to splash splash." She gurgles. Toes, hands, precious underarms. I tell her that someday we'll have a nice bathroom with carpet soft as a meadow and a real kitchen, one of those with a breakfast bar and solid beech wood stools imported from Italy and brass fisherman's lamps. It's when I'm digging under the sink for Mr. Bubble that I nudge the Kleenex box and find the gun stuffed inside. I find what they left in my bathroom. Anger rushes around inside my head once again. I believe I'm holding what killed Baptiste. A 38-caliber pistol made of plastic and zinc. A junk gun. The chill runs up and down my spine and I don't touch it except through tissue. How do I get rid of it especially if Chandra is on the lookout? My left eyelid begins to twitch. Should I bother or dare to call the police and risk being set up as a snitch? I pack my red patent hatbox suitcase. I wish I could peel off the wall drawings and fold them like I do Desiree's soft blanket we call limey.

I feel eyes everywhere, all over me. Charred stick eyes, the marked children of the flood eyes, the old folks with hair in their ears eyes, blown light bulb eyes.

"Should we go see Mrs. Phillips? We'll stop and say hello to her and Beauty." I bundle up Desiree's diaper bag with formula and baby food and Pampers. I don't care that much about me but I need to save myself for Desiree. I fold the pistol into one of her Pampers. I can smell the history of the gun. Like a history of the lake, all the shotgun camps and crab lines that spilled into the Ninth Ward and the city pumped its corpses, and its Mr. Clean and Touch of Glass and toner cartridges right back. I can almost sense the first hand that touched this pistol. I see a tall man walking around Royal and Dante Streets dressed in a silver suit. That man is the pistol's daddy.

I still feel all those eyes watching. The gut-it-out eyes, the talking-to-my-hand eyes, the bus driver eyes, dyed red eyes, button not zipper eyes, long white cigarette eyes.

Night. Music shudders from speakers and makes the Indian paintbrushes quiver. If they weren't rooted, they would disappear into the clouds and gauzy moon. I can see the purple stalks in the night. The white wings. They settle outside in a beautiful shivering, they are there and no one notices. In the cabins, the young guys and girls are fighting and bragging and laughing and making love and making plans and selling things to make you feel better than people are supposed to, or things so as not to feel at all.

I knock on the door of the watermelon-pink cabin and Mrs. Phillips answers. Her hen is clucking as soon as she cracks the door. Beauty is her name, a yellow-eyed, dingy white-feathered egg-laying hen with red comb that escaped from a hatchery during Katrina. Mrs. Phillips rescued her and has kept her ever since. Beauty lays beautiful eggs for Mrs. Phillips and Desiree loves that chicken better than anything on earth.

"Well, come in Ivory and Desiree," she says with a welcoming smile although her bottom denture is already out. "You come right in." Mrs. Phillips is a little wrinkled leaf of a woman who wears a bathrobe from another century. Her hands look like tree roots from all the janitor jobs she did to put her son through school. She still picks up the garbage from around the pool for a little extra jingle, and before bed, she sticks a piece of masking tape between her eyes so she won't squint while she sleeps. "Come in, Ivory and Desiree. Are you hungry? You must be hungry from that boy dying on your doorstep."

"We're not so hungry."

Desiree and I don't like to bother her with visits too often because she always insists we eat something like an omelet or egg salad.

"I can just see you're starved." Mrs. Phillips puts her scrawny arms around me. "Put a smile on your face, Ivory. You can't help that poor boy anymore."

Suddenly I want to lie down on the floor. I want to be stroked and told I'm pretty. I want to be taken care of. But Mrs. Phillips reminds me of how old she is, how the flesh loses its muscle and only scraps of sinew keep it going. "Almost eighty and I still have two strong arms. Almost eighty and I hope the food isn't too dried out. I don't want to serve you crippled food." Once she made us potatoes and buttermilk biscuits in her toaster oven and carrots chopped into pennies. Everything always tastes delicious.

Almost eighty. Grandma Flossie was only fifty-nine.

"Ivory, you better sit down and forget about all that business out there. They all have too much time on their hands, and nothing to do with that time, or their hands. That's why there's all that trouble out there."

In her half-pint refrigerator Mrs. Phillips keeps a hundred margarine and yogurt tubs filled with tiny pieces of things—one cauliflower, an apricot, onion peels, walnuts. Desiree likes to watch her shift her food items from one tub to the next. Out of all the tiny containers come nice things to eat. Before too long we're sitting at a cramped table.

"I'm afraid, Mrs. Phillips."

"What are you afraid of? That you saw something and now they're watching you?"

I shrug. "Something like that."

"It was never this bad in my day. Although I did have a fine second son named Rock after that actor because my Rock was just as handsome. He went in the Army and came back in one piece but one Saturday night he went to a nightclub and who did he bump into? Well, he bumped into Blondell Lighty and caused her to spill some of her drink. Accidents do happen but Blondell who thought pretty highly of herself threw the rest of her drink in Rock's face."

Mrs. Phillips' voice trails off. I pat her hand and both of us tremble.

"Why did Blondell have to throw that drink? When she did that, Rock slapped her, and he shouldn't have slapped her. I believe he did that out of reflex because he was Army trained. Blondell's brother was standing at the bar and he went home and got his gun and came back and shot Rock dead. That boy went to prison but I got no satisfaction from it. Nothing and no one could bring my Rock back."

Mrs. Phillips talks with her mouth full as if the words are more important than the shreds of coleslaw and the meatloaf cut into tiny squares with a strange bright sauce. Desiree lies on her limey on the floor watching Beauty who roots in the top drawer of Mrs. Phillips' dresser. Then I glance up and see the red man inside the mirror and behind him is the figure of mist. It's like I'm being beckoned to a place of green stones and cobwebs. Baptiste extends his arm, *Hey skinny, I need some friends. Come into the mirror and we'll talk.* The wall shakes, sounding like glass hitting something, shattering.

"What in the world is that?" Mrs. Phillips asks. "Must be a bottle of beer because not much else comes in glass these days. Those gals next door enjoy their beers. I'm going to bring some cookies out. Ivory you could stand to gain some weight. A few cookies aren't going to hurt a young pretty girl like you."

Almost eighty, poor Mrs. Phillips can't see far enough to know I'm not pretty. But it's nice to hear, like butter on a burn.

I want so badly to tell her about the gun, how it was left in my bathroom. I'd like to ask her what I should do and where I should go. And the tears come and I'm afraid of them. Why is Baptiste following me? He knows I didn't touch him, I didn't see, and maybe I wanted not to see.

Mrs. Phillips goes to her dresser, lifts Beauty, and reaches under her.

Ten one hundred dollar bills. One thousand dollars. I've never seen so much money at once. "I'm going to call a taxi and have them carry you and the baby to the bus depot. I'll miss you and Desiree. I don't have anyone who listens to me. It feels good to talk."

She shows me what she saved from her house and those things smell—shawls hand knitted and Sunday dresses. "When I die you can have all of this. You can come back from wherever you are."

I try on clothes and I laugh at myself swallowed by floppy collars and purples and hot pinks with zippers that don't zip. Her eyes shine touching her old frocks. The chicken clucks from its roost of a drawer pulled open.

There's a knock at the door. I look out the window first afraid that it's Chandra or the same police officer who talked to me before. "Gardenia. Gardenia. Gardenia." It's the hand lady stuck on a single word. Yes, it's only the hand lady. Then she burrows her lips into her fingers and mutters pieces of words that hurt, dirty water words fed back to the fishes.

As we leave, the baby and I pass the orange cabin on the dark side where the guys sell drugs and the pretty girls hang around and laugh. They sparkle with necklaces and rings, red ice and white diamond ice for their earlobes. There's the yellow cabin where the red-haired twins live who like singing along with country western radio. They're from Tallahassee and climbed on a Greyhound bus and found their way here just in time for Katrina. Two days ago, another stray bullet called a name, but it missed all the gigglers and braggarts by the swimming pool. Like always Desiree's in and out breathing as she rides against my ribs comforts me and all I need to do is get us to the taxi that Mrs. Phillips called. It's a workday midnight around the pool but it's always an early summer night. The red boy and the mist figure follow us but only so far. They can never leave Femaville. Pretty soon all these motel cabins and kids will sink down into the black liquid thereafter. There's the taxi waiting. Desiree giggles and so do I.

Stephanie Dickinson has lived in Iowa, Texas, Louisiana, and now New York City, a state unto itself. Her fiction appears in *Salamander, Short Story, Natural Bridge, African American Review, Fourteen Hills,* and *Gulf Coast,* among others. Along with Rob Cook she edits *Skidrow Penthouse* and is an assistant editor at *Mudfish.* Her story "A Lynching in Stereoscope" was chosen for *The Best American Nonrequired Reading 2005,* edited by Dave Eggers. "Dalloway & Lucky Seven" was reprinted
in *New Stories from the South: The Year's Best, 2008.* Rain Mountain Press recently released her collection of stories, *Road of Five Churches.* Her first novel, *Half Girl,* which won the 2002 Hackney Award (Birmingham-Southern College) for best unpublished novel of the year, is now published by Spuyten Duyvil.

I'd been working on my New Orleans novel when Katrina struck. The floodwaters found their way into the next draft, and soon I had an overflow of scenes and characters. Some of them, fearing they'd never see the light of day, fled the novel and made off to a short story. Other characters joined them. Like the superintendent of my East Village building who befriended a hen that somehow escaped slaughter—when you passed her apartment, you heard its clucking. "What is that?" "Oh, Christina has an egg-laying chicken in there." Two summers ago I took a Greyhound to see my mother many states away. I'd traveled on buses as a child but didn't remember the overwhelming poverty of the passengers or Greyhound's abysmal treatment of its riders. Lines to be waited in all night, doors slammed in weary faces. In one of those lines a pale woman with a buzz-cut head stood wildly talking to her hand, a hospital bracelet encircling her wrist. She conversed with her fingers all the way from Pittsburgh into the heartland, through delays and transfers, and no one asked if she needed help. Yet she made it. The egg-laying hen and the hand woman joined the Katrina survivors in "Love City."

Michael Knight

GRAND OLD PARTY

(from *The Oxford American*)

Finding the address is as easy as opening the phone book. Howell Tate. 1414 Druid Lane. Ivy on the bricks. The neighborhood a dream of landscaping and old houses. Older oaks. Spanish moss. The .12 gauge in your hands couldn't feel more out of place. No sign of your wife's car, but maybe she parked in the garage. Use the barrel to ring the doorbell. This is what a man does when he's been made a fool.

Inside, a dog barks at the sound. A moment later, a shadow moves behind the leaded glass and a moment after that, the door swings open to reveal Howell Tate. Must be him. He's wearing khaki pants and a bathrobe, open over his bare chest. He's holding a black standard poodle by the collar. The poodle bucks and strains, nails ticking on the hardwood. Howell Tate takes in the shotgun, puts his free hand in the air.

He drags the poodle back from the door and bobs his head as if to agree with some point you have made. "Don't shoot, all right? I'll put the other hand up when you're inside. If I let go now, Clarence T. here is long gone and I'm already in hot water with the neighbors."

When you ask if he knows who you are, Howell Tate says, "I thought you were the Chinese food but I'm beginning to have my doubts."

When you identify yourself, he says, "*Right,*" drawing the word out, stalling, sorting through the situation as he speaks. He's handsome enough, fifty-something but fit, plenty of hair, face creased in a way that ruins women but looks okay on a man. This is an election year, and two nights a week your wife and Howell Tate volunteer for the local chapter of the GOP, pestering people over the phone about fundraisers and rallies. You imagined someone younger, a kid (who else besides housewives and college students would be so willing to give time away?), and you feel, suddenly, almost as wounded by the fact that Hannah is betraying you with someone your own age as you are by her betrayal.

Tate starts nodding again. "I think I get the picture," Tate says. "I'd say we're looking at a misunderstanding of some kind." His voice is respectful but unafraid and you can't help admiring his composure.

Tell him you have caller ID. Tell him Hannah carries the phone into the bathroom when it's him. Tell him she has dropped his name a few too many times, as in "Howell Tate thinks Florida's in play this year" or "Howell Tate believes it's a mistake to cozy up to the moderates." Don't tell him how the sight of her makes you feel. Whatever you do, don't tell him that. Tell him to turn around. Tell him you want to look upstairs. Tate will do as he is told.

Clarence T. bounds ahead, then waits, panting, on the landing. You trail a few steps back. You doubt Tate will try anything but it's probably best to keep your distance just in case.

He glances over his shoulder. "You a hunter?"

Don't answer.

"That's a nice piece," Tate says.

You have been married thirty-one years, decent years, not perfect but good enough. You have three grown children, two boys and a girl. Douglas, after Hannah's father, and Weyland, after yours, and the youngest, Marianne, all of them married and living their own lives. No grandchildren yet but surely those will come. Hannah has her volunteer work, plenty of friends. You own a string of hardware stores. You've added two locations to the original, established by your father more than sixty years ago, and you're proud of that, no matter that the big chains have chipped your profits down to nothing. You give money to charity. You don't cheat on your taxes. You vote the party line. Barely an hour ago, you were sitting in the dark at the kitchen table, running all this through your head, when that hollowness in your stomach, the feeling that's been nagging you since suspicion first took root, gave way to something more dense, something altogether darker than the kitchen, and you retrieved the shotgun from the attic. Tate's right. It's a beautiful weapon. Black walnut. Engraved plates. You treated yourself to it on your fiftieth birthday, six years ago last month.

Tate says, "I want you to know I'm a staunch advocate of the Second Amendment," and right then a door opens at the end of the hall and there's Hannah in her bra and half-slip, hugging herself, her hair a mess, her whole body gone soft with age, but still beautiful, still capable of inspiring desire, all of her silhouetted by the lamplight at her back. The fact that she doesn't speak makes her appearance even more startling, as if she's not herself at all but a vision of herself, an image from some uneasy dream.

"Huh," Tate says to her. "I figured you would hide."

Clarence T. trots around the bedroom from Tate to Hannah to you, sniffing knees and whining like he understands that something important is under way though he's not sure what it is or what's expected of him now. Eventually, he settles at his master's feet and swipes at an itch behind his ear, clinking the ID tag on his collar.

"I don't blame you for being pissed," Tate says. "She's your wife. I get that. I think the shotgun's a little much but I'd be pretty hot, too, if I was in your shoes."

He and Hannah are perched on the end of a king-sized bed, a discreet yard of empty space between them. Like it or not, you're obliged to ask how long they've been carrying on. Both Tate and Hannah start to reply, then stop out of deference to the other. Tate waves for Hannah to go ahead. Hannah raises her eyes. Her gaze is frank and sad.

"This is only the third time. I don't suppose that makes a difference."

Don't admit that you're relieved.

"I'm sorry," she says. "I don't guess that makes a difference either."

Tate says, "Of course it does. Of course it makes a difference."

Hannah says, "Howell, please."

"All right," Tate says, "but look, we're all grown up here. These things happen. Doesn't mean anybody should get shot."

As if to punctuate his remark, the doorbell rings and Clarence T. scrambles to his feet, barking, and bolts out of the room.

"That'll be the Chinese food," Tate says.

He claps his hands on his knees, makes as if to stand. Remind him that you're armed. Tell him not another word.

Softly, Hannah says, "You're not gonna shoot anybody. You're not that kind of man," and even though what you hear in her voice is more like affection than contempt, tell her you didn't think she was the kind of woman to be unfaithful but here she is and here you are and you never know what a person will do so could she please, please, please, please, if she ever really loved you, now would be the time to shut her mouth.

The world is quiet for a second before the doorbell rings again. Clarence T.'s bark echoes up the stairwell in reply. He sounds revived. Warning off strangers, that's something a dog can get his head around.

Tate raises his eyebrows in a question, turns his hands palm-up.

In some more pragmatic chamber of your mind you understand that allowing him to answer the door is a bad decision (surely the deliveryman will go away, surely there are mix-ups and prank calls all the time), but mostly you're thinking here's an opportunity to get the night moving forward again, no matter where it leads. You instruct Tate and Hannah to stand, march them single file into the hall and down the stairs. You install Hannah on the sofa in the living room, then take a position where you can keep an eye on your wife and monitor the door.

"All set?" Tate says.

You nod and Tate opens the door and just like that, Clarence T. is gone, skittering out between the deliveryman's legs. The deliveryman is, in fact, Chinese. An old guy with a birthmark on his cheek. He watches Clarence T. vanish into the dark, then holds up a paper sack and reads from a receipt stapled to the side.

"One orange beef, one General Chin chicken, two spring roll, one snow pea, one wonton soup."

"You got fortune cookies in there?" Tate says.

The deliveryman says, "Always fortune cookie," and you have the idea that you know what's coming, that you've been expecting it. You're not at all surprised when Tate ducks past the deliveryman and leaps the porch steps in a stride. You bring the shotgun up but your wife is right, you can't pull the trigger and Tate is moving fast besides, head down, zigzagging tree to tree. The deliveryman looks at you, waiting, his expression bored, disappointed. He pays no attention to the gun. How long must a man live before the world is drained of fear and wonder? His birthmark, you notice, is shaped like Tennessee. He raises the sack again and shakes it in your face.

Because your hands are full—Chinese food in one, shotgun in the other—you close the door behind you with your foot.

Hannah says, "It's not right you had to pay for that. There's money in my purse if—"

Don't let her finish. You'll never recover if you do. Tell her that you're hungry. You're not, of course, but you're quite absolutely on fire with rage and humiliation and the last thing you want is to be pitied. Order her into the kitchen. Tell her to make a pot of coffee and when she does, try not to think that she's indulging you. Tell yourself that she really is afraid of what you might do. You prop the shotgun in a corner, set the food on a marble-topped island, hoist yourself onto a stool. While you unpack the cartons, Hannah pulls drawers until she locates a fork and you accept it without meeting her eyes. Take no comfort in the fact that she doesn't know where Tate keeps his silverware.

Hannah says, "He'll get the police."

Hannah says, "Believe it or not, I love you."

Hannah says, "Talk to me . . . please . . . we're into something now. I don't know what to do."

You understand that she wants you to forgive her, or condemn her, to acknowledge the gravity of the situation, anything, and you feel like a child sitting there, stirring snow peas with the fork, but you can't imagine what to say, nothing real at least, nothing true, nothing that hasn't been said a thousand times.

"All right," she says. "I know you're hurt. You should be. I need to put some clothes on now." She looks tired. She's pinching the bridge of her nose. "There's no excuse for what I've done," she says, letting her hand fall to her side.

What can you do but let her go? As she passes, Hannah touches your shoulder, fingertips warm through the fabric of your shirt, and like magic, you really are hungry all of a sudden. You've never felt so empty in your life. Here's chicken, beef, peas right before your eyes. Spring rolls. Go ahead. Eat. Don't think about the end of your marriage or the probability of jail. Let your mind go slack. You're all consumption. Rice. Wonton soup. No taste. No satisfaction. You're eyeing a fortune cookie when Clarence T. clatters into the kitchen, tail wagging, looking pleased to see you, and you hear Tate's voice down the hall saying, "That's his car out front," and you wonder how much time has passed since Hannah left the room.

Another voice, a woman: "You stay put. I mean, you stay right here on this spot until we secure the premises."

Tate says, "Ten-four."

Footsteps thudding up the stairs.

Still not thinking, exactly, still operating on the surface of yourself, you wipe your mouth and retrieve the shotgun and open the back door. Something stops you at the threshold. Perhaps it's the pool, rimmed with slate, lit up like it's filled with neon, a little waterfall going in the shallow end. In the moment of your indecision, Clarence T. shoulders past you into the yard and prances around the perimeter of the privacy fence and you realize that you can't bear to leave your wife alone with this man Tate. Duck into the walk-in pantry on your left. Press your eye against the door seam. You can make out a half-inch sliver of the kitchen. A few minutes pass before a policeman edges around the corner, does a quick survey of the room, holsters his pistol. He's big, soft-looking, face round and pink, forearms doughy beneath his sleeves. You lose sight of him when he moves off toward the island.

"All clear," he says.

Another cop appears a moment later, a black woman, smaller than her partner by at least ten inches and some hundred-odd pounds, younger by ten years.

"You sure?"

"Back door's wide open." His voice is muffled and blurred like he has something in his mouth and you know he's snacking on the remnants of the Chinese food. "Must have fled on foot."

"Hell," the woman says.

"At least there's coffee."

The woman looks at him a moment with her lips pursed, part irritated, part amused.

"Tell me something, Hildebran," she says. "What do you think about all this?"

"All what?"

"These old white people carrying on."

The man doesn't answer right away and you picture him gazing out the door into the night, chewing thoughtfully, mulling the insect sounds, shrill as whistles, and all that ambient light: floodlights, pool lights, porch lights, moonlight, the warm light of other people's windows.

"Everybody's crazy," he says. "Especially in love."

An hour after the police have gone, you're still hiding in the pantry. It's dark in there but for a rectangle of light around the door. The shelves are mostly empty. The air smells like dogfood and trashbags. Now that some time has passed you can appreciate the absurdity of your situation. It would have been better all around if you'd given yourself up. You've never committed a crime. You're what people call a pillar of the community. Surely the police would have been willing to deal. You've been trying to come up with a way to extricate yourself without making your presence known (that would only put you right back where you started and this whole night has been a bad idea), but all you can think of is to wait until they go to bed. Your back aches from standing so you lower yourself quietly to the floor and cradle the shotgun in your lap.

Listen.

"I can't believe he ate all this," Tate says. "It's not enough to bring a shotgun in my house, to threaten my life?"

"He wouldn't have hurt anybody," Hannah says.

"He had a gun. I don't think I'm going out on a limb when I assume he meant to use it."

"You don't know him."

"I know he ate my orange beef."

"He paid for it," Hannah says.

"Look," Tate says after a moment. "Maybe you'd feel better if you spent the night in a hotel. My treat. I think maybe that's a good idea."

When Hannah doesn't answer, he says, "This isn't what I bargained for."

You understand what's come to pass. How strange to bear witness as this man dismisses your wife, at once tragic and enraging and a source of vindication. All that food, it's like gravel in your stomach. In the silence that follows, you can hear Clarence T. scratching to be let in from the yard.

"I can't believe I let this happen," Hannah says, but even as she speaks you have a sense of sagging down through the layers of how you're supposed to feel, blood rushing in your ears as if from the swiftness of your descent, to some truer, deeper reservoir of feeling in which you are liable for the sadness you can hear in Hannah's voice. Think of all those quiet hours that seemed to you like peace. How is it possible you overlooked her discontent?

"Pass me that fortune cookie," Tate says.

You expect him to read it aloud but he only makes a noise in his throat and Hannah has to ask him what it says.

"It's blank." He sounds surprised. "Somebody fouled up on the assembly line somewhere in the People's Republic. The Party will not be amused."

Clarence T. whines and scratches.

"Let the dog in," Hannah says.

A moment later, the door creaks open and you hear Clarence T. skitter in over the tile, hear him make a happy lap around the island. When he swipes at the pantry, your bones go brittle in your skin.

"Here's what we'll do," Tate says. "I'll take you to the Radisson and you can stay there on me until your husband is in custody. Then we'll meet for dinner one night, do proper good-byes."

"I have my car. I'll just go home."

"The police didn't think that was the best idea."

"I'm not afraid," she says.

Clarence T. paws the pantry door again and you push to your feet. Your knees and ankles pop, as loud to your ears as snapping fingers, but neither Tate nor Hannah comments on the sound.

"Don't make this harder than it has to be, Hannah. I didn't set out to hurt you. Your husband showed up with a gun."

"You're a coward," Hannah says. "You left me here."

"I went for help," Tate says.

Hannah laughs and you can hear that she is close to tears. "Say what you want about my husband, you can't call him a coward. I think it's romantic what he did."

"That's one way of looking at it," Tate says.

Again, the scrape of claws.

"Feed your dog," Hannah says. "I'm going home."

Her sandals slap as she storms out of the room. It's easy enough to imagine Tate on the other side of the door. He's got one hand on his brow as if checking for a fever and his cheeks are puffed with air. He's wondering how he got himself into such a mess as this.

"Clarence T., my old friend," he says, "I'm just not sure it's worth it."

The thing to do is to be waiting with your hands up when Tate opens the door. Your wife is headed home, despite everything, and you're a good man in your heart. But the weight of the shotgun is somehow reassuring, something to hold on to, the trigger slim and cold as jewelry to the touch, and you can't convince yourself to put it down. Crazy, that policeman said. Romantic, Hannah said. You have the idea that this night has been bearing down on you forever, dogging you like time itself, and as the knob begins to turn, you can feel your whole life funneled hard into the here and now: nothing before this moment, nothing after.

Michael Knight is the author of a novel, *Divining Rod;* two collections of short stories, *Goodnight, Nobody* and *Dogfight and Other Stories;* and, most recently, a collection of novellas, *The Holiday Season.* His fiction has been published in magazines and journals including the *New Yorker,* the *Paris Review,* the *Oxford American,* and the *Southern Review* and has been anthologized in *Best American Mystery Stories, Best of the South,* and *New Stories from the South.* He lives in  Knoxville with his wife and two daughters and directs the creative writing program at the University of Tennessee.

I wrote the first draft of this story almost five years ago now. What I wanted was to try to bring something new to a very old dramatic premise—a cuckolded husband catches his wife in the act—and one of the ways I thought to do that was to have the protagonist feel compelled by the nature of the premise, by the very fact that it was familiar, with familiar roles for the players, to behave in a way that went against his nature. In my conception, then, the premise itself would operate on this super-cool thematic level. Of course, that stuff never works out the way we plan. The original draft was written in third person and most of the scenes were more or less the same. I liked plenty about the story, but it was clear that something was off from the beginning. The main problem was that I kept writing sentences like "And he felt compelled to behave in such and such a way." Maybe not quite that bad, but you get the drift. So the story lurked quietly in the nether regions of my computer until one day when I didn't have anything else to work on. I pulled it out and switched the point of view to second person, not because I had any big ideas about what would happen, but because switching point of view is just something I try now and then—I don't think I'm the only writer in the world who does this—in an effort to reinspire myself, to find new ways into fiction that's not working the way it's supposed to. But all of a sudden the second person, the imperative in the voice, began to shore up some of my original ideas about the innards of the story, and I was able to cut all those really bad lines explaining the protagonist's behavior and just write the story itself. I sent the new draft to Paul Reyes at the Oxford American. Both he and Marc Smirnoff made some excellent editorial suggestions, and the story is much improved for their assistance. I am grateful to them both for helping it into print.

Rahul Mehta

QUARANTINE

(from *The Kenyon Review*)

"Y ou will see him only the way he is, not the way he was."

Jeremy and I have rented a car and are driving to my parents' house. He has never been to West Virginia. All week he has been looking forward to seeing the house where I grew up, my yearbooks, the wood paneling in the living room where I chipped my tooth, the place by the river where I drank with friends. He is annoyed that I am talking about Bapuji again.

"Don't you think I know by now how you feel about your grandfather?" he asks.

"Yes, but I am warning you. When you see him, you will feel sorry for him. You will forget all the stories I've told you."

"I won't forget."

"You won't believe me."

It is late by the time we reach the house. My parents hug me at the door. They tell Jeremy how much they enjoyed meeting him in New York last year. They are awkward. They half hug him, half shake his hand. They are still not used to their son dating men.

"Make yourself at home," my mom says to Jeremy.

"Bapuji is in the living room," my dad says to me.

We remove our shoes and go inside. Bapuji is sitting in a swivel chair. The lamp next to the chair is off. In the dim light it is difficult to see him, but when he stands up and comes closer, I see how loose his face is, the deep, dark eye sockets and sharp cheekbones, the thin lips oval and open, as if it is too much effort to close them or smile.

I bend down to touch his feet. The seams on his slippers are fraying, and his bare ankles are crinkled like brown paper bags. He lays his palm on my head and says, "Jay Shree Krishna." Then I stand and he hugs me, my body limp.

"This is my friend Jeremy," I say. Jeremy nods and Bapuji nods back.

Last week when I called my mom to discuss plans for our trip, she said it was better not to tell Bapuji that Jeremy is my boyfriend. "There is no way he could understand," she said.

My mother warms up some food and, even though they are leftovers, Jeremy and I are happy to have home-cooked Indian food, to be eating something other than spaghetti and microwave burritos. After dinner, my mom tells us we can make our beds in the basement. She and I spoke about this on the phone, too. She said we shouldn't sleep in the guest room because there is only a double bed there, and it will be obvious we are sleeping together. Better we set up camp in the basement where there is a double bed and a single bed and a couch. She said "camp" like we are children and it is summer vacation. She hands us pillows and several sheets of all different sizes and says she is going to sleep.

I make the double bed for Jeremy and the single bed for myself. Jeremy suggests we both sleep in the double bed and that we can mess up the single bed to make it look like one of us slept there. "I don't think it's a good idea," I say. "What if we sleep late, and someone comes down and sees us?"

As we are falling asleep, Jeremy asks, "Why did you touch your grandfather's feet?"

"It's a sign of respect."

"I know, but you don't respect him."

"I respect my father."

"You didn't touch *his* feet."

"Don't be funny," I say. "He is Americanized, he doesn't expect such formalities. But if I didn't do pranaam, it would hurt my grandfather's feelings, and that would hurt my father's feelings." A few seconds later I add, "It's tradition. It doesn't really mean anything."

"Yeah, tradition," Jeremy says, sighing, sleepy-voiced. A few minutes later, I hear him snoring from across the room.

Whenever I see my grandfather, I have to touch his feet twice, once when I first arrive and again as I am leaving. Each time I hold my breath and pretend I am bending over for some other reason, like to pick up something or to stretch my hamstrings. He always gives me money when I leave, just after I touch his feet. I never know what to do with it. I don't want to accept it, but I can't refuse. Once I burned the money over my kitchen sink. Another time I bought drinks for my friends. Once I actually needed it to pay rent. But it didn't feel right. It was dirty, like a bribe.

Now, as I try to sleep, I toss and readjust, trying to get comfortable. I am not used to sleeping alone. I don't know what to do with my body without Jeremy's arms around me.

The basement where we are sleeping is where my grandfather lived when he first came to America. I was ten then, and Asha was eight. Bapuji came a few months after his wife, Motiba, died. At first he tried to live on his own in India, but he found it too difficult. He couldn't take care of himself, didn't even know how to make tea. He shouted so much that whenever he hired new servants they would quit within a couple days. In the end, my father took it upon himself to bring Bapuji to America. As the eldest of five brothers and sisters, he thought it was his responsibility to take care of Bapuji, which, I quickly learned, really meant it was my mother's responsibility.

My mom says Bapuji wanted to live in the basement because the spare bedroom upstairs was too small and he needed more room. After I left for college, he moved upstairs into my old bedroom, which was bigger.

When Asha and I were young, we'd hardly ever go all the way

into the basement. We'd only go partway down the stairs and hang on the railing like monkeys and spy. The basement smelled of Indian spices and Bengay. Bapuji made my mom hand wash all his clothes, because he said the washing machine was too hard on Indian cloth and stitching. He didn't like the smell of American detergents. He made her scrub his clothes in a plastic bucket with sandalwood soap and hang them to dry on clotheslines he strung across the room. He tacked posters of Krishna and Srinaji to the walls, and he played religious bhajans on a cheap black cassette recorder that distorted the sound, making it tinny and hollow, as though it were coming from far away. Asha and I called the basement Little India and my grandfather the Little Indian.

Those early years in a new country were difficult for him. He barely spoke English, and there were no other Indian families in our community. He couldn't drive, and our housing development wasn't within walking distance of anything. He wasn't used to the cold. Even in the house he would have to bundle up with layers of sweaters and blankets and sit in front of a space heater. Now and then my parents would try to take him to the mall or the park, but there was nothing he wanted to buy, and he claimed the Americans looked at him funny in his dhoti and Nehru hat.

But if it was hard for him, he made it equally hard for everyone else, especially my mom. She took a couple months' leave from her job in order to help Bapuji settle in. He made demands, and as far as he was concerned she couldn't do anything right. He wanted her to make special meals according to a menu he would dictate to her each morning. He insisted my parents add a bathtub to the basement bathroom, even though they couldn't afford it and there was already a standing shower. He would call my father's brothers and sisters and tell them his daughter-in-law was abusing him, that she was lazy and disrespectful and a bad housekeeper. He would say his son shouldn't have married her. When my mother was cooking in the kitchen, he would sit at the table and say, "This isn't how Motiba made it."

Years later, my grandfather even claimed my mother was trying to kill him. Bapuji was a hypochondriac, always complaining about his health, aches in his joints, a bad back, difficulty breathing. He had started complaining about chest pains. My mom was sure it was heartburn. She said she had seen him sneaking cookies and potato chips from the kitchen cupboard late at night. She said he should stop eating junk food and then see how he feels in a couple weeks. But Bapuji called everyone, my aunts and uncles, even relatives in India, saying his daughter-in-law was refusing to let him see a doctor because she wanted him dead.

When my mother told Asha and me Bapuji claimed she was trying to kill him through neglect, I said, "If only it were so easy."

"You shouldn't joke like that," my mom said. But then I looked at Asha and Asha looked at me, and we both started laughing, and my mother laughed, too.

My mother and father often argued about Bapuji, never in front of us, but we could hear them shouting in their bedroom. Sometimes they'd go for a drive, or sit in the car in the driveway. Once after a tense dinner during which my mother served Bapuji rice and dhal and Bapuji looked at the plate, dumped all the food in the garbage, and went to the basement, my mother took my father onto the back porch. Asha and I peeked through the window blinds. It was winter, and my parents hadn't put on coats. We couldn't hear what they were saying, but they were pointing and pacing and when they spoke their words materialized as clouds.

On the Saturday evening after Jeremy and I arrive, Asha visits us with her husband, Eric. They live a couple hours away and are both in med school. Jeremy and I spend the morning in the kitchen helping my mom roll and fry pooris.

After dinner we play Pictionary as couples: Dad and Mom on one team, Asha and Eric on another, and Jeremy and me on the third. Bapuji sits in a corner while we play.

Asha and Eric are winning, mostly because Asha is such a good drawer. When we were kids, she drew the most beautiful pictures, mostly horses. She loved horses. They were so good my mother framed a couple and hung them in the living room. My drawings were terrible. I threw them away without showing them to anyone.

It is Asha and Eric's turn, and the word is "snatch." Asha guesses it quickly, but when I look at Eric's drawing I am horrified. He has drawn something vulgar. I hold up the picture and show it to my parents and say, "This: from a future doctor." My mother giggles and blushes as though she is twelve. I tell Eric and Asha that they should be disqualified from the round because the category is "action" and he drew a noun. Eric says he can draw whatever he wants, as long as the person guesses the right word.

"Uh-uh," I say. "Look it up. It's in the rules. Plus, your drawing was rude, so you should lose two turns." Everyone is laughing and arguing. My grandfather comes over to see what's going on.

"Do you want to play?" Jeremy asks him. I look at Jeremy like he shouldn't have done that, and he shrugs.

Bapuji shakes his head no.

"Then you should go sit down," my mother says. "Otherwise, it's too crowded around the table."

Bapuji goes back to his chair. Two rounds later, we are all racing to see which team guesses "diminish" first. It's in the "difficult" category. My mom is frustrated because it is difficult, and it is her turn to draw for her team and my father is guessing all wrong. "Look!" she says, pointing emphatically at her paper. "Just look what I've drawn. Look what's here. Can't you see?" Bapuji comes over again, and he is leaning over my mother's shoulder looking at her drawings. He starts to guess "little" and "smaller" and my mother says, "Please go sit down." She continues drawing and he continues guessing "tiny" and "shrink," hovering over her, leaning closer and closer until his chest is touching her back. My mother slams her pencil down on the table. "Bapuji," she shouts. "Please, just quit it!"

We all stop. Bapuji looks around at us. Then he walks over to the swivel chair and sits down. After a couple minutes, he collects his shawl and goes upstairs without saying good night.

No one wants to play Pictionary anymore. Asha suggests we watch one of the movies my father rented. It is a big-budget comedy, one that I would never rent, about a man and a woman who don't like each other at first, but end up falling in love. The movie is formulaic, the dialogue horrible, but the actress has such a stellar smile and the actor is so goofy and good-looking, we are all charmed. We laugh loudly at the bad jokes. We guess the ending, but the predictability is comforting, and we are all smiling as we tidy the living room and prepare for bed.

The next morning Asha and Eric leave. My father challenges Jeremy to a tennis match. He is eager to show off the fancy country club with the indoor courts, which he joined last year. He's always wanted to join, ever since he came to this town.

My mom and I go to a café by the river for bagels and coffee.

"I'm sorry I made a scene in front of Jeremy," she says.

"It's no big deal," I say. "It seems like things are getting better, though. For you, anyway. I've noticed Bapuji mostly spends time in his room now. Not like when Asha and I were kids and he followed you around the house, barking orders."

My mother takes a sip from her coffee. "I don't like who I am when he's around. I don't like how I behave. I know I am mean sometimes."

"You're not mean."

"Do you know what it is like to have someone living in your own house who hates you?"

"He doesn't hate you," I say.

"It would be easier if your dad would take my side. When we're alone he says yes he understands, yes Bapuji is difficult, yes he disrespects me, but he doesn't say it to Bapuji. He doesn't stand up to him."

"How can he?" I say. "Bapuji is his father."

"I am his wife."

I finish my bagel and coffee, and my mother pays at the cash register. When we get into the car in the parking lot, she says, "Forget it. I'm sorry for bringing it up. I want to have fun with you and Jeremy before you leave." She puts her hand on my knee for a minute, then starts the car.

I was sixteen the year my mother's father died. She hadn't seen him in years. She got a call from Bombay that he was ill, and left the very next day. By the time she arrived, he was dead.

When she returned, she was different, quiet. She didn't go back to her job right away. She stopped cooking. She spent most of the time in her room with the drapes closed.

My father tried to keep house. I helped too. We took turns cooking dinner: burned rice, over-cooked vegetables with too much chili pepper and salt. After ten days Bapuji said to my father, "How long is this going to last?"

"I don't know," my father said. He was rummaging in the fridge.

"It is her duty to take care of us. You must tell her."

"Her father died."

"My Motiba died. You didn't see me behaving like this. She is selfish. She has always been selfish. Why must we suffer because of her?"

My father picked up the phone and ordered pizza.

I went upstairs to my parents' bedroom. The door was slightly ajar, and I wondered if my mother had heard them talking. I knocked twice and she didn't answer. I opened the door fully. It took several seconds for my eyes to adjust to the darkness. My mother was lying in bed on one side, the covers pulled over her head.

"Are you OK, Mom?" I asked, still standing in the doorway. She didn't answer. "I'm worried. Please, Mom. Do you want to go out? I can take you for a drive. Maybe some fresh air. We can get buckwheat pancakes at IHOP."

My mother was silent. I walked toward the bed, and as I approached I could hear her crying beneath the covers. I stopped, not sure what to do. I wanted to put my hand on her shoulder, sit on the edge of the bed stroking her the way she would stroke me when I was a kid and I was sick or upset. But I didn't. Instead, I turned around and left, pausing for a moment in the doorway. "I love you, Mom. Please get better."

A couple days later, my mother returned to work. She started cooking again, but she still didn't talk much, and she didn't smile. I saw her standing at the stove one evening, stirring the dhal. My grandfather was sitting at the kitchen table, watching her.

I want to take Jeremy on a road trip. There is a town seventy miles up the Ohio River, famous for three things: ancient Indian burial mounds, after which the town is named; a state penitentiary; and a large Hare Krishna commune.

When I was young, my family visited the commune often. It is beautiful, set atop a hill with views of the river valley. There is a temple and a Palace of Gold. My family went a couple times a year to worship. In those days, there were no Hindu temples nearby, and my father figured the Hare Krishnas were the next best thing. But my mom was wary. She thought they were weird.

"This isn't our religion," my mother said.

"Krishna is our god," my father said.

"These people aren't our people," my mother said.

When we had visitors from India, my father always took them to the Palace of Gold, which the Hare Krishnas called the Taj Mahal of the West.

One summer, he tried to send Asha and me to summer camp at the commune. He showed us a brochure. He said he wanted us to learn something of our culture, to understand where we came from. But looking at the children in the brochure, their white faces blank as they sat in the temple while a white man in a saffron robe read from a book, I couldn't understand what my dad meant. Asha, on the other hand, was lured by the pictures of kids riding horses. In the end, my mom refused to let us go. Even Asha, who had seemed so excited, was relieved. She was nervous the Hare Krishnas would shave her head.

Now, as Jeremy and I plan our trip, my father warns us the

commune isn't what it used to be. He says there was a murder a couple years ago, and the head of the commune was arrested for tax fraud and embezzlement. Still, I insist on showing Jeremy.

It is my father's idea to invite Bapuji.

"He'll get in the way," I say. "We'll have to stop every five seconds so he can pee."

"C'mon," my dad says. "He hasn't been to temple in years. Besides, he can use an outing."

I tell my dad I'll think about it. Later, Jeremy says to me, "If we stay late it will give your mother a break from your grandfather. Think of it as a favor to her."

The three of us drive up the valley on the two-lane road. We drive through one-light towns with old church steeples and country general stores, and picturesque hills broken only by the spitting smokestacks of the chemical plants that have proliferated along the river.

When we reach the town, it is even more depressed than I remember. The penitentiary was shut down a couple years earlier when the state ruled that the prisoners' cells were too small, that keeping inmates in such cramped quarters was cruel and unusual punishment. Many people lost their jobs. The town is still suffering.

To get to the commune, we have to take a narrow road that snakes up a large hill. It is separated from the rest of the town. Both the Hare Krishnas and the town's residents prefer it that way.

The Hare Krishnas own the whole hill, including the road. It is in such bad condition, I have to drive extra slowly. The sign for the temple is so faded I almost miss it. Once there were cows on the green hills and white men with shaved heads wearing necklaces made of tulsi beads, and women in saris with hiking boots and heavy coats in the winter. Now the hills are empty. Many of the houses are boarded up. The cows are gone.

Our tour guide at the Palace of Gold speaks with a Russian accent and explains how, in Moscow, under the Communists, he had to practice his religion in hiding, at secret prayer meetings. He is lucky to be in America, he says.

The palace isn't heated, and Bapuji shivers beneath his layers— two flannel shirts that don't match, two crewneck sweaters, a heavy jacket that once belonged to my dad. He pulls the coat collar closer to his neck.

Outside, much of the gold leaf has flaked off the structure, and inside there are cracks in the ceiling. The marble and wood need polishing. One stained-glass window is broken. The tour guide tells us we should come back in summer when the rose garden is in bloom. "It's really beautiful," he says.

After the tour we eat a late lunch with the devotees. There are only a dozen of them, and we all sit silently in rows on the floor eating off stainless steel thalis. The food is modeled after Indian food, but it is nothing like my mother's. It is bland and tasteless— beige and brown and gray.

When we go to the temple, the alcoves with the statues of gods are all covered with velvet curtains. A devotee tells us they won't open them until the arati at five o'clock. He says we should stay. Jeremy and I decide to take a walk around the commune, and Bapuji says he'll wait in the temple. He is talking to the devotees when we leave him.

Jeremy and I find a pond flanked by fifty-foot-high statues of Radha and Krishna dancing. Their hands are joined in the sky, forming an archway. Small cottages, modern-looking with large windows, surround the pond. I tell Jeremy that one year my father wanted to rent one so we could visit on weekends, but my mom refused. I tell him there used to be peacocks. We walk around searching for them. We find deer and swans and rabbits, but no peacocks. Not even a feather.

When we return to the temple, the arati has already begun. The curtains have been lifted, revealing a gold statue of Krishna in the center and Hunuman and Ganesh on either side. They are layered with garlands and surrounded by candles. My grandfather is standing in the front of the room before the statue of Krishna. To our surprise, he is leading the arati, chanting "Hare Krishna, Hare Ram." He is holding a large silver platter with coconuts and flowers and a flame and burning incense, and he moves the offering in clockwise circles. He seems too weak to carry such a heavy platter; I wonder how he is managing. Everyone is watching him, following him, echoing his chanting. Jeremy and I sit in the back silently.

Afterwards, several devotees talk to my grandfather. They want to know about India. Are the temples beautiful? Has he been to Varanasi or to Mathura, birthplace of Krishna? He is smiling and gesturing, and he has more energy than I have ever seen. It is only with great difficulty that we are able to pull him away.

When we return to the car, it is almost dark. Bapuji is quiet again, moving slowly. I ask if he wants to sit in the front seat. He shakes his head no.

After twenty minutes in the car my grandfather says, "I want to go back."

"We are going back," I say.

"No," he says. "To the Hare Krishnas."

"Did you forget something?"

"I want to stay there," he says.

"You can't," I say.

He taps Jeremy on the shoulder so that Jeremy turns around, and then he whispers, "I am not happy."

Jeremy looks at me.

"Don't talk nonsense," I say.

The road winds around a corner, and I can see the moon reflected on the river up ahead. After a couple minutes, Bapuji says again, "I want to go back."

I grip the steering wheel tightly, and my shoulders tense. "Be quiet, Bapuji."

"Your friend understands me," he says, tapping Jeremy on the shoulder again.

"He's not my friend," I say. "We are a couple, like you and Motiba were."

Bapuji is silent for a few minutes. Then he says, "Your mother is a bad person."

"Do you want to talk about bad people?" I say. My hands are shaking. "You are a bad person. You are the worst person I know. You have caused nothing but pain in my family."

"Be careful," Jeremy says. "Watch the road."

"Your life is nothing anymore. Look at you. Pathetic. Let my mother be happy."

I look in the rearview mirror and see my grandfather's face in shadows. It catches the light from a streetlamp, and through his glasses I can see his eyes and cheeks are wet and he is trembling.

Jeremy screams and grabs the wheel. I hear a horn and look forward and see flashes of light.

When we finally come to a stop, our car is in the grass beside the road, facing in the wrong direction. A car honks loud and long as it passes us, and the sound disappears in the distance.

I flip on the overhead light and look over at the passenger seat. Jeremy is OK. He is staring at me, trying to catch his breath. I look in the backseat. I can see my grandfather's seat belt is fastened, but his head is down, his chin on his chest. "Bapuji?" He doesn't respond. "Bapuji?"

I get out of the car and open the back door. I put my hand on his shoulder, shaking him gently. Even with all the layers of clothes, his shoulder is thin and narrow. My grandfather looks up. His glasses have fallen on the floor and the lenses are cracked.

"Are you OK?" I ask. He nods.

I walk around the car a couple times to see if there is any damage. We try the engine, and it starts. Jeremy drives the rest of the way home.

When we reach the house, Bapuji goes straight to his room.

"Is something wrong?" my dad asks.

"He's probably tired," I say.

My mother asks us if we are hungry and we say we already ate. I tell them I am tired and we have to leave early the next morning so we should go to sleep. Even though it is early and it is our last day, my parents don't argue. My mother says she is tired, too.

A few years ago, while I was away at college, Bapuji contracted tuberculosis. At first, we couldn't figure out how he got it. We had never heard of anyone getting TB in America. Then my father remembered that Bapuji's younger brother had died from it when they were both children. The doctors said Bapuji must have been exposed to the bacteria then, and that it had been dormant in his system all these years, waiting for his body to weaken, waiting to attack.

For the first few days of his illness, Bapuji was quarantined in the house. He wasn't allowed to leave his room except to take a bath and use the toilet. The doctors said he could be dangerous to others. They advised my parents to limit their contact with him, and not to let anyone else enter the house. Later, when his health got worse, he was admitted to the hospital and isolated in a room with special ventilation. Whenever people visited, they had to rub antibacterial liquid on their hands and forearms and wear masks and gloves before entering the room, and they could stay only for a short time.

My mother visited the most. She brought him homemade food during lunchtime and sat with him every evening. My father came less frequently. My mother said it was too difficult for him.

One weekend, I flew home to visit my grandfather. Just before going to the hospital, I gulped coffee and ate nachos. When I put the mask on, I couldn't believe how vile my breath was. I couldn't escape it. I thought, *This is what's inside of me.*

Bapuji seemed disoriented and didn't recognize me at first. He was tired. The mask must have made me look strange.

In the car, on the way to the hospital, my mother had told me that when Bapuji's brother was dying of tuberculosis, and he was miserable and in pain, Bapuji would let him rest his head on his chest, and sing to him until he fell asleep. This is how Bapuji got exposed to TB. I couldn't quite picture the scene. Such tenderness didn't fit with the grandfather I knew.

Bapuji said he needed to use the toilet. My mother helped him to the bathroom. When he got up, I noticed a brown stain on his bed sheet. His gown was open in the back, and I could see a bit of dried excrement on his backside and his skin peeling like birch-tree bark. I remembered my parents telling me the TB medication made his skin dry.

When Bapuji was finished, he called for my mother, and she went into the bathroom and helped him clean up. I buzzed for the nurse to change the bed.

Watching my mother, I realized this could be her future; he could fall seriously ill, and she could spend many years taking care of him. My mother also knew this. I could tell by the matter-of-fact way she went about her tasks—cleaning him, rinsing his drinking cup, flipping his pillows—the blank look on her face while she did them, as though she were the one fading away.

Jeremy and I wake early the morning we are leaving my parents' house. We eat cereal while my mom makes sandwiches for our car ride. She has cooked some extra Indian food for us to take with us, and she puts the curries and subjis and rotis in a small cooler and sets them in the foyer next to our luggage. "Everything is cooked. All you have to do is heat it up when you're hungry."

We are all standing in the foyer.

"I'm glad you guys came," she says.

"Me too," my dad says. "Bapuji!" he shouts up the stairs. "The boys are leaving."

It is silent upstairs. My father shouts again, "Bapuji!" Still nothing.

"He is tired," I say. "Let him stay in his room. I'll go up."

His bedroom door is shut. I knock, but he doesn't answer. I open it. The room is dark. Bapuji is in bed. His broken eyeglasses are on the bedside table, on top of the Bhagavad Gita. He has the covers pulled over his head.

"Bapuji," I say, quietly, "I am leaving." He doesn't answer. He is either asleep or ignoring me.

I remember so many years ago, my mother in bed after her father died, the covers pulled over her head, me approaching, hearing her cry, not sure how to comfort her.

I remember also my grandfather's story about comforting his brother as he was dying.

Now, I don't approach my grandfather. I don't know whether he is crying under the covers. I stand in the doorway another minute, watching him, and then I leave.

When I go downstairs, my father asks if I did pranaam, and I say yes.

Jeremy drives most of the way home. We don't talk much. I fiddle with the radio, which usually annoys him, but today he doesn't say anything.

Back in New York, our apartment smells terrible, like we forgot to take the garbage out, or something died between the walls. Even though it is cold out, we open a couple windows.

I walk into the living room to open another window, and I see the answering machine is blinking the number eight. I figure some of the messages are from my friends or from Jeremy's friends, but I'm sure some are from my family. Probably my mom or dad. They'll want to know we arrived safely. Maybe one is from Asha. Maybe there is one from my grandfather. I don't play the messages.

I go into the kitchen, take my mom's food from the cooler and put it in the freezer. Jeremy is in the bedroom unpacking, and I can hear him opening and closing dresser drawers.

"Are you hungry?" I ask.

"Starving," he says.

Jeremy wants some of my mom's Indian food, so I take out a couple Tupperware containers and pop them in the microwave.

As for me, I can't stomach it. I reach for a box of spaghetti and set a pot of water on the stove to boil.

Rahul Mehta is a graduate of the University of North Carolina at Chapel Hill and of the MFA program at Syracuse University. His fiction has appeared in *Noon*, the *Kenyon Review, Fourteen Hills*, and elsewhere. Born and raised in Parkersburg, West Virginia, he currently lives in Alfred, New York, where he is completing a short story collection and working on a novel.

JOHN LAPRADE

*Q*uarantine" is fairly autobiographical.

Perhaps I shouldn't admit that. It was very difficult for me to write; after finishing it, I held onto it for a long time before sending it out. When I learned it had been accepted at the Kenyon Review, *I mailed the story to my brother. I am very close to my family, and I was anxious about how they would react. My brother didn't respond for a month, maybe two. When he finally called me, he asked, "Why did you write this?" His tone wasn't accusatory; I think he genuinely wanted to understand. I was talking to him on my cell phone, wandering around a Brooklyn neighborhood I was completely unfamiliar with. I felt disoriented, lost. "I can't control what I write about," I said. Even as I spoke, I wasn't sure I believed it; but my brother seemed to accept this explanation. He, like the sister in my story, is a doctor, and as a doctor, he knows how things can arrive unexpectedly, grow uncontrollably, eat away at a body. "What about Mom and Dad?" I asked. "Should I send them the story?" He said, "It will hurt them."*

Thank you to Bob O'Connor for his insightful comments on an early draft.

Elizabeth Spencer

SIGHTINGS

(from *The Hudson Review*)

Mason Everett, a man who lived mostly happily in his own mind, hadn't any idea why his daughter Tabitha had come to visit him. It's true they never saw much of each other. Maybe it was a shame. He was neutral on the subject. He had long loved her at a distance, but now she was close she brought back shadows. Still he was willing to find out what she wanted. Her mother, in far-off Maryland, was maybe the one to ask. On the other hand her mother might be the very reason she headed his way. She arrived about twilight in a cab from the airport.

"But I would have met you," he protested.

"Too much trouble," she answered and came right in with her duffel. She looked like all the rest of the ones her age, but also bore a resemblance both to him and Celie. He remembered that when young he too had done unexpected things. She went upstairs to the spare room. She shut the door. Mason waited downstairs and thought about dinner.

Other ideas trundled through his head. Was she into a love affair, was she on drugs, did she drink, did she need money? If she needed money, why did she take a taxi from the airport? Everything went in a circle until he heard her step on the stair coming down. She drifted around the living room. Did not turn on the TV. "How is your mother?" he inquired. Tabby said her mother was okay. He had not counted on monosyllables. He tried several other directions but finally gave up. "Is a steak all right?" She said yes. She also said, when asked, that she liked it medium.

During dinner he asked if she was in school. She replied that she had had to leave. "Had to leave?" he repeated, inviting her to explain. But she did not say anything more.

Mason wondered why he didn't push her further, but then of course he knew why. It was a habit formed long ago, not to go too deep, not to quarrel. If they quarreled, they would get back to the accident, that blue blinding flash, that had brought guilt in, and blame, wordless until her mother got into it and a real quarrel started, the kind that spiraled downward till it reached a depth charge.

He was walking his dog Jasper the next evening when old Mrs. Simpson, who occupied her front porch as a regular thing, called out, "I hear your daughter's with you."

"Yes, ma'am," Mason answered, adding, "She can walk the dog."

She had walked Jasper twice now, once with Mason, once alone. He seemed content in his private way. Airedale mix, had looked forlorn in the shelter when Mason chose him out of others. But choosing didn't change him; he still looked forlorn. Tabby didn't pet him but seemed to like him.

"What's her name?" asked Mrs. Simpson.

"Tabitha. We call her Tabby."

"Tabby and Jasper," said Mrs. Simpson.

Mason agreed that was it.

In the years since Cecilia left, Mason had framed up his life in an adequate way. He missed her but not what she had turned into. But he liked a woman to be somewhere in his life; and when passing through one of the town malls, he observed a likely one who owned a knitting and handwork shop. She was doing some sort of fancy stitching when he walked in. He introduced himself and found she knew him already. She had had some acquaintance with Celie. He said that Celie had moved away. Yes, they were separated. Too bad, she said, but things happened. Her name was Marsha. He asked if he could call her. She thought a minute and then laid aside a bright length of wool to write down her number. So it was easy as that. She had had two husbands, both long gone. He agreed that things did happen. Though he didn't see her often, he liked to know she was there.

Tabby began to catch the bus in the afternoon and to be absent until dark. He didn't ask where she went. But one afternoon he called Marsha, who didn't work on Thursdays. Mostly, he wanted to talk about Tabby.

"Can't you call her mother? Seems to me her mother should have called you."

"She did call. The evening Tabby arrived. I said, 'Yes, she's here. Yes, she's fine.' I hung up."

"You ought to have asked some questions."

"That's the very thing I don't want. I don't want Celie's side. I want Tabby to tell me what she wants to when she wants to tell it. None of this ought-to business."

Marsha laughed. "Well then you'll just keep rocking along for months and years." She sat in her big chair, doing handwork.

"It's fine with me," said Mason and added, "She likes Jasper."

"Does Jasper like her?"

"He doesn't say."

"How old is Tabby?"

He counted back. "About sixteen, I think." He grinned, sheepish. "Actually, I'd have to look it up. I forget."

"I think you just better come right out and ask her what the problem is."

He didn't really want to. He remembered the terrible day she had blinded him, the flash of blue light in his face when he was trying to fix the electrical motor for her CD player. He was threading the wires together, holding them close to squint at when she had connected the plug to the outlet. His eye streamed water and blood, and she yowled *I'm sorry* till her mother made her stop. It seemed to him every time he looked at her, she was yowling it yet, for his sight never entirely came back. Did it matter? He could read and work as he did before. The surgery had been delicate, one eye all but blind, the other intricately damaged. The accident gave him the chance to work at home instead of at the office. He wore glasses with thick hexagonal lenses and had to have special equipment to work with figures. Insurance supplied the major expense. So what did it matter in the long run? Sight-damaged people went successfully through life. It was well known. But he read it as a constant theme in his daughter's eyes whenever they met his, never to be erased. *I'm sorry, I'm sorry.* And instead of *It's okay, forget it,* he said now, *Why are you here?* No answers so far, but as Marsha told him, he had to try.

Tabitha had volunteered to cook dinner and turned out something done with hamburger meat that was edible. When he had praised her and eaten enough, she brought out some ice cream, and he ate that too.

"Listen, honey," he started. "We've got to talk."

She looked up. He thought he heard *I'm sorry.*

"I haven't asked you yet. I was too glad to see you. But why did you come? Just to visit? No other reason?"

She played with her spoon. She let Jasper lick it clean. She leaned to pet him. "It's mother," she said.

"Well, what about her?"

"She wants to marry somebody. I think he's terrible."

"Terrible or not, I can't stop her. What's his name?"

"Mr. Bowden." She winced on the word. "I told her, if he didn't leave, I would. She got mad. I think he's an alien."

"From where?"

"Outer space alien."

"Oh." After a silence he said, "But if she's happy with him . . ."

"Nobody could be," said Tabby.

He sighed. He was a little bit jealous; unavoidable, he supposed. "Have you heard from her?"

"I told her I was coming here. She was mad and shaking."

"She gets like that," he recalled, speaking half to himself.

The next day Tabitha got a letter. Mason, who went for the post, saw it before she did. The lettering of the address was stiffly upright, like printing. He gave it to her to open, and she read it aloud.

I know your mamma misses you, she says so all the time. I wish you would come back. We can all go out to restaurants and the movies. You wouldn't have to go unless you want to.

> *Your friend,*
> *Guy Bowden*

"You see what he's like?" asked Tabby.

"Maybe he means it," said Mason.

"He's stupid," said Tabby.

They alternated cooking. Tabitha improved. Mason asked Marsha to dinner. Tabitha wore a bright blouse, brought up out of that bottomless duffel. She ironed her jeans and put on lipstick. She made a veal concoction, which was edible. Mason opened some wine.

"I'll teach you to sew," Marsha offered.

"Maybe I ought to learn," said Tabitha and got dreamy.

"She's like you," Marsha told Mason. "She's pretty though."

"Are you going to marry her?" Tabitha inquired later on.

"Nothing like that," Mason replied.

"What you mean, 'like that'? You sleep together, don't you?"

"Mainly we're just friends."

It was a week since she came. Jasper now slept in her room, lying near the door sill. Sometimes he snored.

There was bound to be a foray.

When the phone call came, Mason was alone in the house and had no idea what to say. "I can't direct you here unless you tell me where you are." It was Celie, traveling with Guy Bowden. She thought they should all get together and talk. "We've got to understand things," she said. She had forgotten how to get to the house. The new highway had confused her sense of direction. They had stopped at a mini-mart to telephone. Mason knew where it was.

"Tabby's not here now," he floundered. "Get something to eat and call us back."

"We've eaten already," Celie wailed. She had taken on her desperate sound.

"Everett! Guy Bowden here." The voice was commanding. "We would like to see you."

Mason hung up. He wasn't going to be bossed around. Where was Tabby? Letting Celie know he'd no idea where she was—that would cause a flare-up. He shrugged into a jacket and took Jasper for a walk, hoping to think things over.

When he turned the corner to return home, he saw the strange car parked in front of the house, also Tabby, approaching from the bus stop. And now he freely saw what he had been thinking all along without knowing it: *It's her and me. It's WE. And they are THEM.* Big question: *Did Tabby think so too?* In just one week it might have happened.

He hastened to her, heart beating with unexpected love that now came on full force, out in the open. How urgent it was. To love and to know.

"Honey," he said, "it's your mother."

"Oh, God," said Tabby and thrilled him.

He caught her hand. Jasper wagged to see her. They huddled, a party of three.

"I bet he's with her," said Tabby, adding, "Let's go somewhere else."

It seemed such a good idea that Mason almost thought it might work. But he was not entirely lawless yet, and they went in.

They were both in the living room. Celie looked as if she still belonged here and had just told Guy Bowden to sit down. That was the first thing. The next was how nice they both looked. Mason recognized that he and Tabby did not look nice. They looked scruffy.

Guy Bowden was a beefy fellow, large arms, thick legs, heavy feet. But wearing a nicely pressed grey suit, a satin tie. Celie was trim, she was a word he used to think about her: petite. It rhymed with neat. That was long ago when he was proud of her.

Guy Bowden was looking all around without approval; but when Mason and Tabitha entered, he at least stood up. Celie had rushed to Tabby, who now was getting her hug. Jasper growled.

"Leaving me!" Celie wailed. "It's been just awful, you leaving me!"

"Your mother's desperate," Guy Bowden said and sat back down.

"How about some coffee?" Mason offered. "How about a drink?"

So was he being weak? It was what she accused him of, often in the past.

Tabitha got glasses and poured them out some Diet Coke. "The lawn looks nice," said Celie, as though she had jurisdiction.

"I still have Aaron," Mason said.

"Don't feel up to it?" Guy inquired.

"Don't really like it," Mason admitted.

"Tabitha, we've come to take you home with us," Celie said firmly, and though it once may have worked, Mason saw it wasn't going to work now. She's grown up, he wanted to say, but didn't.

Tabby sat on a footstool with her arm over Jasper's neck. "Suppose I don't want to?" she said.

"Well, now," Guy pronounced, "there's been a legal agreement, as I understand it, and I think you have to, young lady." He spoke in a teasing way.

"I'm not going," said Tabitha.

They were silent.

Mason Everett regarded his ex-wife, judging that she hadn't changed all that much. He wondered to what degree he had changed. He wouldn't doubt he was showing his age. More wrinkles, a haircut overdue. Celie worked at exercises, she tried different diets, she measured her waist. She talked a blue streak about uninteresting things. She was talking now. There was a group she belonged to. They discussed single parents, problems with preschool children, problems with school-age children, problems with adolescents. They called in experts and listened to lectures. There was this interesting woman from Canada. . . .

"What do you do here?" Guy Bowden asked Tabitha, leaning forward. He sounded intently kind.

She took her time about answering, then said, "I'm studying at the library. I'm going to go to college."

"Oh that's great!" said Celie. "I'm glad of that! But you can do that back home! I'll arrange it for you."

"I'm going to do it here," said Tabby.

It came to Mason that this was all a lie. He didn't know where she spent her time when she left the house, but it was the freedom sense he saw in her. He thought that was what she took with her wherever she went. It was what he wanted her to have.

Celie turned to Mason. "So you're doing that for her?" She seemed shocked.

"First I've heard of it," said Mason, "but if she wants it—sure."

"Taking things away from me," Celie said and sprouted tears. So they would be back into it, Mason thought, and saw the whole flawed fabric of human relations form, the present now becoming like the past, the future scrolling out ahead looking just as always, torn, stained, blemished. No change. He winced.

"How are your eyes?" asked Celie.

"Same as always." Silence.

For Guy Bowden, the moment had arrived. He leaned toward Tabby as if he were right in her face.

"Tabitha, you've got to understand that your mother and I just want the best for you, and what we think is that the best, the very best, is coming back to us. I know I upset you with some things I said. I'm just a rough fellow sometimes. But my heart's in the right place. If you only knew how I mean that. More than you could ever know. I mean it! I mean it! And where is my heart? It's right with you, honey. With you and your mother, she's just so fine."

Tabitha and Jasper both looked at him. Mason tried to look elsewhere.

"Don't you see, Mason?" Celie appealed.

"I think it's up to her," said Mason.

"Unfortunately, it is not up to her," Guy said. "I mean as I understand it, you two agreed—"

Tabitha jumped up and ran in the kitchen.

Guy Bowden rose with resolution and followed her, his heavy feet like a marching drum. They could hear his voice, muffled but persuading, "Now sweetheart, you just need to listen. And think . . . you need to think . . ."

Mason and Celie were left alone.

"Is he what you want?" he inquired.

"He's just so good to me," she explained.

Now was the moment to say, *So you think I wasn't good to you.* But he didn't. He'd had enough of that. What is separation, together or apart, but one long silence?

Two birds chirped outside the window. It did sound like a conversation, he thought, and wondered what they were saying. From the kitchen they heard something shrill, a sound as if it came from a stranger.

Tabitha ran. She shot through the hallway and was out the front door, running like a deer. Jasper was right after her, he made it through the door. Maybe he thought she was playing.

Mason jumped right in front of Guy Bowden, who was chasing her. "What do you think you're doing?"

"She's the one." Bowden was rubbing at his face. Had she hit him?

"I was trying to be nice to her. Damn it all, I'm always trying to be nice to her. She won't let me."

Mason walked out the door. He looked up and down the street, but neither dog nor girl was in sight. She could have made it around the corner, or into the next yard. But which one? He called her once, "Tabby!" then decided not to call again. It was exactly as if she'd caught the bus. He stood on the sidewalk, looking all around. Next Celie and Bowden would come to the door and start talking.

He walked deliberately away. From the door Celie called after him. "Mason! Where are you going?"

"I have to find her," he said, not looking back.

He did look for her quite some time. No Tabby, no Jasper either. He telephoned Marsha. Marsha said that Tabby was there, but she hadn't seen Jasper.

Mason got the car and drove to find them. Tabby was in the kitchen eating cake. The three of them sat and thought things over. No Jasper.

"Aren't you allowed to have her with you at all?" Marsha asked in an experienced way, two divorces and a grown son somewhere.

"It was something I could have arranged. But they let me know a fixed arrangement meant I could only see her at allotted times."

"And you wouldn't?"

"At the time I wouldn't. I was tired of fighting. Celie—you see Celie can keep on fighting forever. Nothing stops her."

"Maybe they'll go away," said Tabitha.

"Maybe they'll stay and just keep the house," said Mason. Mason's reading equipment was in his house, also his workload from the hospital. Mason's present project was research in genetic statistics as related to disease. Figures from the computer flowed under his crafted Dome magnifier, a glass balloon large as a grapefruit. Specially enlarged from his machines, they arrived sometimes in complex pairs, wavered and spread apart; at other times they approached, hesitated, then matched up and marched together. He checked results and tabulated conclusions.

When Tabitha called, Marsha had left her shop with the assistant. She had driven to her house where she found Tabitha, sitting on the steps. Marsha was a good-natured woman, tolerant of human mistakes.

She gave a drink to Mason and a Pepsi to Tabitha. Then she talked in a quiet sort of way, about a time when she had lived out West, married to her former husband. She got out some knitting. In and out, the long needles kept to a steady rhythm.

Yes, it was her second husband she remembered most. Brad. The first she had been too young to evaluate now or ever. The second she had loved deeply, but he had always wanted to travel. His business was mainly in investments for himself and other people. He could carry his office everywhere—a computer, a cell phone—set up every needed connection in fancy motels. This was West Coast life. They journeyed, up into the Northwest—Seattle, Portland, sometimes into Canada. Then he'd take a notion to go south.

Mason sat and watched his daughter with his fragile eyes. If he only had a vision device to see into her being, discern her aim and direction, for even at so young an age she must feel something of the sort.

"You didn't want to keep me," she suddenly accused.

"That was then," he replied. "This is now."

Marsha knitted on. She kept journeying on as well. In the south, Brad liked to go to San Diego and especially always took a day or so for Coronado. There was an old resort hotel out there near the beach. He would switch for once from motels just to stay there. The food was good. He never stayed anywhere there wasn't some special restaurant to explore.

"Didn't you ever go home?" Mason asked.

"Oh yes, the house. It was in LA. It was nice enough, everything in order. He left it with one of his assistants, a boy who practically lived there. Very nice young man, but then he—" Another story.

It was growing late. The rhythm of the long needles was steady. Tabitha yawned.

Mason was not supposed to drive after dark. Impressions blurred. He sometimes thought he saw someone cross the road in front of him when no one was there. Wary of arriving, he drove slowly home.

"I bet she was going to tell how they went to Mexico next," Tabitha said.

"Probably."

Tabitha said she was out of money. He said he would give her some.

He dared then to ask, "Bowden. Did you hit him?"

"No, I bit him. He bent my arm back till it hurt. He did that before. That's how I got close enough. So I bit him."

"Why do you go uptown? What do you study?"

"I don't study. I made that up. I just hang out. I met a boy I liked, but he's gone away."

Mason remembered the day they removed bandages from his eyes. He remembered blinking. Though dimly, dimly yet, he could see. He had felt a burst of joy, like a bubble.

He turned into his own street and crept nearer. The visiting car was gone. The house was dark. A shape was waiting at the door.

Tabby gave a cry of delight: "It's Jasper! He's come home!"

"And so have you," said Mason and was happier than he could say to hear no denial.

Elizabeth Spencer was born in Carrollton, Mississippi. She received an MA from Vanderbilt University in 1943. Her first novel was published in 1948; eight other novels followed. Spencer has published stories in the *New Yorker,* the *Atlantic,* and other magazines. She went to Italy in 1953 on a Guggenheim and met her future husband, John Rusher. In 1986 they moved to Chapel Hill, where Spencer taught writing at UNC until 1992. Her most recent book is *The Southern*
Woman: New and Selected Fiction. Her other titles include *The Voice at the Back Door, The Salt Line, The Night Travelers,* and *The Light in the Piazza,* which was made into a movie in 1963 and premiered as a musical

production on Broadway in Spring 2005. It received very good reviews and won six Tony Awards in June 2005. Spencer's writing has received numerous awards, including the Award of Merit from the American Academy of Arts and Letters. She is a member of the Academy and a charter member of the Fellowship of Southern Writers. In 2007 she received the PEN/Malamud Award for Short Fiction. Her latest award is the Lifetime Achievement Award from the Mississippi Institute of Arts and Letters. Please see her Web site (www.elizabethspencer.com) for more information.

The story "Sightings" came to my mind after seeing a friend with vision problems using a huge glass magnifier, oblong, about half the size of a volleyball, to read some poems we were discussing. I am acquainted with various appliances for magnifying texts because my cousin has a degenerative eye affliction. So I invented a character with eye problems and soon saw that he had a dog named Jasper, after meeting a friend in Seattle who had a dog named Jasper. I also discovered that my character was divorced and had a daughter he seldom saw. The daughter reappears. Why? We go on from there.

George Singleton

BETWEEN WRECKS

(from *River Styx*)

The kid's mother stole my pallet of river rocks stacked out by the driveway, she said, to complete the thousand arrowheads on order from Cheap Chief Charlie's roadside attraction down near Myrtle Beach, among other places. The woman introduced herself as Sally Renfrew, and claimed that the chalcedony vein below Andrew Jackson Prep—her son Stan's school—finally "ored out." Sally Renfrew said that she had run a fake arrowhead business for fifteen years; that she now understood Malthus's notion of supply and demand; that it wasn't easy being a single mother anywhere on the planet but seemed particularly difficult off Scenic Highway II some twenty miles from at least an Auto Zone, Staples, public library, grocery store chain, GNC, or hardware store that specialized in durable chisels; that she couldn't return what flat rocks she'd already slowly stolen (and I never noticed, seeing as I'd allowed the family river rock business to fail while I hopelessly worked on my low-residency master's degree in southern culture studies) over the past month; and that she was worried miserably that her boy wasn't going to follow through with college once he graduated from high school in the next year. She rattled on. I thought that maybe she feared I would tie her up, throw her into a secret back room, and torture her for the unspeakable crimes she performed upon a man, namely me, whose pregnant wife took off on him in order to raise their child far from South Carolina. Then I felt so guilty about standing there on my own land on the banks of the Unknown Branch of the Saluda River, blocking Sally Renfrew's exit strategy, that somewhere during her manic monologue I agreed not only to help her load rocks, but also to be a "big brother" of sorts. She chattered on and on about how Stan recently met his biological father, the father died in a motorcycle accident, and the kid had it in his mind that he could skip college and become a stand-up comedian. I looked down at the river. I wondered if my father or grandfather ever had poachers of this sort, and tried to think of how they might handle the situation.

I said, "Shut up. Get all the rocks you want. I tell you what—make your arrowheads, and give me ten percent of your gross profit. I know all about the arrowhead market," which was a lie. I looked at Sally Renfrew—if she had a seventeen-year-old son she must've had the kid at age sixteen, I thought, for she appeared to be my age—and stuck my hand out.

"We live about two miles away. I promise that I haven't stolen from you before this past month. I didn't steal back when your dad pulled river rocks out and sold them to landscapers, or even those couple years when your father kind of slacked off after your mother's death, or when you gave up altogether in order to go back to studying full-time. Or when Abby took off for Minnesota."

I kept eye contact. "You certainly seem to know enough about what goes on around here." I wondered if she *knew* that I was trying to complete a low-residency master's degree program in southern culture studies from Ole Miss–Taylor, and that I waited daily for some kind of omen to send me in the right direction in regards to a new and daring thesis.

Sally Renfrew shrugged. She placed a nice flat piece of slate that might've been part of my house's roof some sixty years earlier. She said, "I'll tell Stan to come over here tomorrow. He's not much into sports. But he eats. Maybe y'all could go hang out and eat breakfast. Tell him how important it was for you to study all those things you studied before you came back here with Abby and gave up. How many bachelor's degrees do you have anyway? And as for the southern culture studies thing—good God, man, there's a term paper a minute going on around you."

I said, "Hey, wait," but then forgot what I was going to ask her. It had to do with scams, the South, and people, maybe.

When she left I think she might've called out the open truck window, "Five percent."

Stan Renfrew said that he now pronounced his name "Stain," and that it was his biological father's idea. He said it would get him more attention on the comedy circuit. We sat inside Laurinda's, the closest diner from my house, in a square brick building that over the years had housed an auto body repairman, a florist, an office supplier, biker leather goods, a bait shop, a lawn mower repairman, and a number of other people running their money-laundering, drug-selling, slave-trading fronts. There was no valid or business-rational reason for a florist to set up shop in an area where houses stood about three per square mile, on a two-lane road that only connected ridges, hilltops, and valleys. I hadn't yet figured out what Laurinda did illegally, and my visits to her good diner went from twice a month to about daily after Abby took off to birth and raise our child in the upper Midwest without my help.

Because I didn't want this Stan kid snooping around my property, I drove over to Sally Renfrew's place and found him waiting for me at the end of their quarter-mile driveway. He leaned against the mailbox tall and skinny, but not with the ubiquitous ennui-ridden look on his face that most seventeen year-old kids perfected from watching bad situation comedies. Stan got in my truck, said, "I hope you're Stet Looper," and stuck out his hand to shake.

I said, "Your mother must be the top saleswoman in all the world. I realize that you probably don't want to hang out with an old guy."

He nodded. He apologized. Stan said, "I just spent ten days with my father. He died on me. But he was seventy-seven years old. So I'm kind of used to old people."

I U-turned and headed toward the diner, trying to do math in my head. "Your father was *seventy-seven*? Good God, man, how old is your mom?"

"It's a long story that involves a famous visiting professor named Stanley Dabbs and a starry-eyed college senior who wanted to be an art critic. I'm what came out of all that."

I grinded my gears and didn't look at the road. I knew Stanley Dabbs's name. I thought about how I might have had a book or two the man had written, from back when I was either a philosophy or history or anthropology major. Dabbs was the last of the great social critics and commentators. "Stanley Dabbs is your father?"

"Was," Stan said. "Are we going to Laurinda's place? I used to go there when it was a driving range. There used to be a tree farm with migrant workers back behind the place, and everyone yelled out 'Quatro!' after hitting tee shots."

I didn't remember it being a driving range, but that sounded about right. I said, "Do you play golf?" I tried to think of all the correct and relevant golf terminology I'd amassed over the years. I said, "What's your handicap?"

I drove past my own long driveway. A vee of geese flew overhead. Stan said, "That was all just a joke. Quatro! I made that up. Hey—if the Special Olympics had a golf tournament, would it be all right to ask competitors what their handicap was?"

I stepped off the accelerator and looked at Stan. He didn't smile. This is a different kind of boy, I thought. "So your mother wants you to go to college, huh? She told me that you wanted to forgo college and be a comedian." I pulled over into Laurinda's, which seemed to have more cars in the lot than usual. "I have a feeling your momma isn't going to like my advice."

Before Laurinda—she worked as cook and waitress, somehow—got to our booth I looked outside and saw a man who, I thought at first, suffered from an inner ear problem. I'm that way mostly, I swear. I ignore people's vices. I told Stan, "That guy either has an inner ear problem, or a gimpy leg." The man weaved around the newspaper rack outside, then looked east up Highway 11. He took four mini-steps to turn around and look uphill in the other direction.

Stan said, "I've been thinking about going to the vocational school to study construction. Then I'm going to build a wooden house entirely out of yardsticks for the exterior. I figure it'll make it easier to prove the square footage when it's time to sell." He didn't laugh.

The man came inside, doffed his stained cap that advertised Celeste Figs, then sat down at the counter. "Chicken truck turned over three mile thataway, and a three-car wreck the other," he said loudly to no one in particular. Laurinda flipped a round mold of hash browns over on the stove.

She said, "Coffee?"

"Well, two cars and a van of illegal aliens, you know."

I said to Stan, "Order whatever you want. Except the sausage or bacon. I don't want you clogging your arteries. Or the chicken, seeing as I guess we can drive down the road and get chicken for free."

Laurinda came around the counter and said, "Stuck, too?" I didn't nod or shake my head. I must've stared blanker than corn-fed trout. "Are y'all stuck between the two wrecks, too?" she said.

Stan Renfrew said "No ma'am," like a regular gentleman. He said, "We're out looking for our trained cadaver dogs that got out of their pens. Is there a cemetery nearby, by any chance?" Laurinda said, "Oh my God." She set her coffeepot down on our table. "You mean those dogs go round pointing out dead beneath the rubble?" When she held her mouth open I noticed that she chewed two separate pieces of gum.

"I've heard both of those jokes, Stain," I said. "The one about cadaver dogs. The one about yardsticks. Just order. There's no snare drum inside here for rim shots."

Laurinda stared at me. She closed her mouth and, with a look of impatience, shook her head. "Okay. You boys ready to order?"

The man with the inner ear problem folded his cell phone in half, swiveled our way and said, I thought, "Ford ate." Maybe he talked about himself in third person, I thought. Maybe he left a buddy named Ford at home, seeing as Ford had already eaten breakfast.

Laurinda turned over our coffee mugs without asking what we wanted to drink. She poured both cups to their rims without asking if we wanted milk. To the man at the counter she said, "Hours?"

"Yeah."

I said, "What's he saying?"

"Drunk say ford ate hours before the roads get cleared."

Four to eight, I thought. "He's drunk all ready?" I kind of whispered. And I felt like a hypocrite, seeing as I'd been known to partake of bourbon shortly after sunrise. Laurinda nodded and looked out the window. Stan Renfrew asked if she served muffins, and I waited for some kind of off-color joke that he never delivered, even after she said, "Haven't yet. Mostly serve hungry people, honey."

"I've been to your house before," Stan said. Laurinda brought him two pieces of toasted white bread cut into circles, scrambled eggs, and a hotdog. "Before and after you moved back there."

"Did you know my father?" I asked. Abby and I moved back to my childhood home only two years earlier, after I'd finished my fifth bachelor's degree, and after Abby—who had a lisp—realized that she wasted her time trying to get an on-air reporter job at a TV station. My father had promised to let me "study myself out," as long as I promised to return home to operate Carolina Rocks, our family business for three generations.

Laurinda brought me a plate with six over-well fried eggs stacked atop each other. I had ordered pancakes. Stan said to me, "I never met your father, no."

I said to Laurinda, "This isn't mine."

She checked her order pad, then looked at the booth parallel to ours. A family of four bowed their heads in prayer. Laurinda swapped eggs for pancakes, quietly, right beneath the praying woman's nose. Six fried eggs! I thought. Who eats a half-dozen fried eggs at one time?

Laurinda placed her finger on her lips and asked us to keep the secret. Stan said, "That is so cool." He leaned over and whispered, "Second Comers," which were members of a religious cult that chose northern South Carolina to bombard with believers, thus taking control of the area after running for various councils, et cetera. As far as I'd heard, only one family ever emigrated, and here they were stuck between scenic highway wrecks. Stan got up, grabbed both of their syrups, and placed them next to my plate. He reached over again and took the man's fork, then smiled at me. I wondered what a proper, responsible Big Brother or mentor would do in this situation. I probably should've said, "That's not appropriate behavior," or quoted something about having and having not. Instead, I nodded and smiled, and took a glass of water from their table. Stan said, "I know all about these people."

I said, "Go ahead and finish the joke."

Stan said, "No joke. But to answer your question: Nope. Never met your father. But I helped your wife move out, sort of."

I looked across at him. The drunk guy at the counter got up and saluted two men who walked in. He said, "Ford ate hour. Y'all hear? Y'all scared check point, too? *Got*-damn. Can't get to the red dot store now."

Stan said, "I really *smoked* a sex education course I had to take. I made a sixty-nine. I think it was the oral exam that put me over the top."

More people walked into the diner. Laurinda came by and said, "Either y'all ever cooked, washed dishes, or waited tables before? I need me some help. I should order up some wrecks more often. Or a rock slide."

I said to Stan, "Whoa, whoa, whoa—you met Abby? You came onto my property and met my wife at some time?"

Stan said to Laurinda, "You ever hear the one about the popular blind waitress who spent most of her time shaking up bottles of ketchup? I got to work on that one. Something about how they're not really bottles of ketchup, but men with their pants down."

Laurinda went off saying, "I'll comp your meal if you pitch in." She turned around to the Second Comers and said, "Y'all's food's getting cold. My booths aren't rented by the day."

I didn't have time to think about theories of synchronicity; or why we're all put on this planet; or the plays of Samuel Beckett, Harold Pinter, or Jean-Paul Sartre wherein characters are stuck endlessly against their wills; or Martin Luther King's "Letter from a Birmingham Jail"; or how the best way to kill yellow jackets is to let them all get in their underground nest at dusk, then pour gasoline into the hive hole and light it; or how sharp fronds prevented fish from swimming out of baskets used by prehistoric Native Americans, thus trapping them; or the history of alienation in regards to psychology; or how helpless, distraught, confused, frightened, and relentless squirrels can be, once caged.

Well, no, I did have time to think about that last part, because the man at the counter announced to everybody, "I got enough squirrels in my cage. I don't need none of *that*."

I said to Stan, "I'd be willing to bet that that guy's just as irrational sober as he is drunk."

The Second Comers remained bowed. I reached over and grabbed the father's bacon. Stan leaned over and said, "I didn't know she was leaving you. If I'd've known you back then, I wouldn't've helped your wife move out. She didn't seem to know how to use bungee cords, and luggage wouldn't stay up on the roof rack, you know. I was walking down the road picking up aluminum cans 'cause it's free money, and the more I save the easier it is for me to buy gold, and then I'll turn in the gold bullion later in order to fly to Illinois and get a cell phone with a valid area code so my mother thinks I'm truly at the University of Chicago, and then I'll still have enough money to pay for my apartment up in New York while I'm doing the comedy circuit and telling my mother and dead biological father that I'm attending and passing all of my American studies, philosophy, art history, linguistics, classic rhetoric, and interpretive dance classes. Anyway, there I was with my burlap bag of crushed Budweiser cans—you know it only takes about twenty-five cans to make up a pound, and aluminum's going for fifty cents a pound—and your wife was hunched over the hood of her car half-crying. I said 'Hey, you got any beer cans in the backseat?' and she said she didn't. I tied up her trunk and couple suitcases, she handed me two dollars, and I walked back home realizing that I probably wasn't going to find another two hundred cans on that particular afternoon. It'll get worse if more of these Second Comers show up, seeing as they don't tend to drink a lot of beer and throw their cans out moving car windows like the rest of us."

Stan finished off his hotdog. I said, of course, "You selfish little bastard. I knew you'd turn on me sooner or later. Sometimes you really scald my testes. Ingrate!" for I felt sure that it's what a regular father might say. Then I got up to help Laurinda with the dishes.

The drunk said, "Ford ate hour" as I passed him. I listened to Stan slide out of the booth in order to follow me.

I leaned over the man, smelled plain beer, and said, "Bush ate whole years." I thought, What hour did you awake in order to get this intoxicated?

My protégé Stan called out, "Wait up."

Here's what I thought, perhaps. Here's what I thought up elbow deep in dish water, without a Hobart machine in the kitchen of Laurinda's diner: If I were a father, I would want my son to know manual labor. I thought, If my son were a stand-up comedian, I would want him to know that there's not much funny in working for minimum wages, which in turn, somehow, made it all that more comedic. Why would anyone choose to wash dishes for a living unless he either had lost hope altogether, or never knew that there were self-satisfying vocations out there, like digging holes in the ground and filling them back up. Stan worked beside me with large white towels draped over both shoulders and one in his hand. I said, "This is not how I planned to spend my day. But we must pitch in and help the community. We're not doing a bad thing, understand. If there's a heaven, maybe we'll be remembered for helping out Laurinda. Even if there's not, we can feel sure that by helping her out, she won't later go nuts from being inundated, then go off on a shooting spree. Shooting sprees aren't good things."

I wished that some of this was on tape, so I could show both my rational side and my stern side to Abby up in Minnesota. Then maybe she'd return, give birth to our child, and believe me when I said that this place was the best of all possible areas to raise a child, four to eight hour road congestion or not.

Stan smiled. He handed a plate back to me and pointed at some egg yolk. "You don't officially have to do all this," he said. "You can ask my mom out on a date if you want. Ya'll've been watching too much TV. In the real world I don't think prospective boyfriends really have to hang out with the mother's kids and act all cool and normal."

I handed Stan the rewashed plate. I looked through the kitchen porthole and noticed that the Second Comers finally began their meals. Laurinda cooked, and talked loudly over her shoulder to the customers. A state trooper walked in the door and took off his Smoky Bear hat. I said to Stan, "What? What're you talking, man?"

"It's a great idea if you ask me—my mom has the arrowhead business, and you have the rock business. You're single and she's single. Even if y'all end up not liking each other—and you will, because you're both smart and stuck in a place where brains isn't exactly the first organ mentioned when people ask to list them out—it's a smart idea business-wise. Economically speaking, you know. Like a family that owns the Pepsi distributorship, and another that owns the bottling company."

"Maybe you can get a job running one of those Meet Singles agencies if you don't go to college or end up making it as a stand-up comedian, Stan." I pronounced his name "Stain," like he wanted.

"That's 'Pimp Daddy Stan' to you, my man." *Pimp Daddy Stain* didn't sound very hygienic.

I unstoppered the sink. I said, "I'm still married. I'm not looking for a girlfriend, I'm sorry to say."

Stan smiled at me. He loaded a caddy of clean silverware. "I'm thinking about joining a Hermits Anonymous group, but I have a feeling that no one will ever show up to the meetings." He looked at me. "Would it sound better as 'Hermits Anonymous,' or 'Misanthropes Anonymous'?"

I said, "I used to be a member of Cannibals Anonymous. Great buffet."

This might be selfish on my part, but I enjoyed spending time with Stan Renfrew not for the right reasons: To be honest I didn't give a crap about his self-esteem, or the so-called weighty decision before him involving whether to forgo college to make people pay money in order to laugh. As far as I could tell—and I wasn't but some sixteen years older than Stan—no children made less than a B in high school or college anymore, and then they graduated and found high-paying jobs without ever having to know the discomfort of blisters. I had read an article somewhere about a group of college graduates who *didn't* get high-paying jobs, and successfully sued their alma mater. Pissants.

We caught Laurinda up with clean dishes, pots, and silverware, then took to reloading spring-action napkin holders, checked on the salt and pepper shakers, gathered up wet dishrags and tossed them in a take-home hamper. Stan and I walked around with coffeepots, topping off people's mugs. I didn't have time to think about my low-residency master's degree projects that I would probably never finish, about the prospective theses that I didn't want to undertake. And I didn't have time to think about my confused, determined, wayward, pregnant, and estranged wife.

"Y'all sit down and have some pie," Laurinda said. "I wonder if I'll have everyone here for dinner, too, what with the road blocked."

"Ford ate hour," the drunk man said, though his eyes looked much clearer.

I hadn't paid much attention to the Second Comers, who had finished their praying somewhere along the line, and eaten their meals—I assumed—without complaint. I said, "I'm still full," to Laurinda.

Stan said nothing, but turned to look at the patriarch of this particular religious cult family. The father stood up and held both hands up high. To me Stan said, "Here it comes. Here's the reason why they have to pray so long." I waited for him to finish up a joke of some sort. He didn't.

"Why y'all are all trapped here I guess it's as good a time as ever to make you an offer."

"They're grave robbers," Stan whispered to me. We leaned against two stools adjacent to the drunk man. "I've followed them around before. They're grave robbers."

The man must've only stood five-five at the most, which I couldn't tell when he kept his head bowed. His blue jeans showed patches of red clay at the knees. I leaned forward to see both of his children staring down at their empty plates, appearing embarrassed. The wife looked up at her husband in that beautiful, hopeful, dreamy way that only women can pull off. Abby once looked at me that way when I added transmission fluid to her car, I remembered.

"As y'all may or may not know, the price of gold has skyrocketed what with our being in a war, and amid high fuel costs, and on the brink of upcoming inflation. Not to mention the end of the world as we know it, praise Jesus."

I started to laugh. Stan said to me, "Hallelujah."

"Anyways, gold's now upwards of six hunnert dollar a ounce, and I'm talking the good kind of gold the dentist puts in your teeth. Anyways," he reached into his pocket, "I got here with me a nice collection of gold teeth I'd be willing to sell right at half the price of what they got it going for up in New York and down in Hong Kong."

I looked at Stan, and craned forward to look at what the man held in the palms of his hands. Stan turned to me and said, "I told you so. That's why they pray for so long—in case grave robbing's frowned upon by God. And of course it won't be, seeing as God told them to chisel gold out of dead people's heads."

"Sister Rebecca?" the man said. She stood up—her pants held mud stains, too—opened her purse, and pulled out a set of scales best known to small-time drug dealers.

I said, "Damn. What's the world coming to?"

The drunkard blurted out, "Why'd anyone want to buy gold if it's the end of the world like y'all're saying? I thought you couldn't take it with you, end of the world and whatnot." He stood up, and for a second I thought he was going to attack the family of grave robbers. He said loudly, "Does *any*body have a *got*-damn bottle of *booze* stashed in your car outside?" and banged his right fist against his thigh.

The grave robber, of course, said, "We have some communal wine out in the van we'd be willing to sell."

Stan smiled. He said, "Man, I'm going to get a whole mother lode of jokes out of this place. Get it?"

I kind of wanted some booze, too, at this point. I wasn't proud to say that, since Abby had taken her "necessary sabbatical," I had gone from stealing a shot or two of bourbon a week—maybe a can of beer if I was interviewing prospective southern culture studies subjects worthy of a thesis—to a good near-fifth a day. I had gone from telling myself I wouldn't drink until dusk, and then that went backwards to Happy Hour, and then that went backwards to as soon as the sun was one degree past its zenith. I had made a point not to've slugged down a sixteen-ounce plastic cup of bourbon and Pepsi before going to pick up Stan. I rummaged around the cupboards until I found a pint of boysenberry-flavored vodka—Abby's—and glug-glugged a couple shots into my coffee. I learned that, if I ever lived in the Land of Only Boysenberry-flavored Vodka, I would be a sober man.

"You ever had a drink, Stain?" I asked Stan. The grave-robbing Christian and the drunk had left for the parking lot. "Maybe you and I could get in on some of that wine action. I think it's my duty as a Big Brother to make sure you know how to handle your ine-briants, or whatever. Your beers, wines, and liquors." Let me say now that I felt like an idiot saying all this. I understood that Stan was smart enough to figure out my ulterior motive.

Stan said, "I spent ten days with my biological father. Then he died."

I took that answer as meaning that he'd been drunk, and he'd done some drinking afterwards in order to ease his guilt, pain, wonder, misery, flashbacks, Oedipus complex, no sense of worth, anxiety toward college, and/or panic attacks about jokes that don't get laughs. I said, "Let's you and me go meet Mr. Gold and see what kind of deals he has, seeing as we're stuck here."

We aren't stuck, I thought as I was shaking the Second Comer's hand. *Stain and I can drive right back home between the two wrecks.* The drunk man said, "Ford ate hours. I can't wait that long. This is my idea of Hell."

The Second Comer man said, "I could tell by the look on your face that you didn't believe my gold to be gold. I promise on a stack of Bibles that I ain't done no alchemy tricks."

Stan said, quietly, "Double negative." I wanted him to be my younger brother. I wanted him to be my son. He looked at me and said, "I know what you could go investigate." Understand that he shouldn't have known about my life whatsoever without doing some detective work. "There's a man who buys fake arrowheads from my mother. He walks from North Carolina to Oklahoma throwing them down on the ground. Part of what he's doing's political, and part of it's plain crazy. He says that he's filling the Earth back up for what we've extracted. He says that he's also making sure we never forget the Trail of Tears. He calls himself Johnny Arrowhead."

I said to the Christian, "I believe you got gold. I'm more inter-ested in the wine."

He handed me an unlabeled bottle and said, "Muscadine. It's good. It's what Jesus drank. Five dollars."

Stan took the bottle, took the cork out with his teeth, and tipped the bottle up like a professional. I said, "Hey." I said, "Hey, hand that to me." I gave the Second Comer a ten dollar bill, and he handed me over another bottle from the trunk of his car. I looked inside and saw two shovels, eight muddy boots, a crowbar, a pair of pliers, and a map with highlighted yellow circles. The drunk went back inside with one bottle.

Stan's mother, of all people, drove into the parking lot of Laurinda's diner. Stan said, "My mom. Damn."

He handed me his bottle. She got out of her car wearing heavy leather gloves. She looked at her son, then at me. She smiled. "I just heard on the news about some big wrecks. Thank God y'all are here. Oh my word the whole drive over here I thought it would be y'all." She wore some tight blue jeans, that's all I have to say. I don't know if it was on purpose or anything, but she had these scuff marks on her thighs that pointed straight up like arrowhead points, toward her zipper.

The Second Comer man knew enough to close his trunk. His wife and children came out of Laurinda's diner and got in the car. He took off, and I assumed that he either squatted on nearby land, or he would sit in a traffic jam, waiting. Stan stuck out his hand to shake his mother's. He said, "Ford ate hour, Mom. Ford ate hour."

She said, "Are you drunk?" She looked at me. She said, "Are you not the man of whom I thought?"

Stan said, "Now that's some good English."

I looked toward Laurinda's front windows. Inside there were people feasting on good bad food. I said to Sally Renfrew, "I'm just trying to do the best I can. I'm just trying. I didn't sign up for this particular mission, you know."

Sally said, "Go on inside, Stanley."

I said, "Stay, buddy."

She kind of sidled around, as best I could figure. I think I'd seen my wife, Abby, sidle, maybe near the beginning of our marriage. Sally Renfrew ebbed and flowed left and right, shifting her weight. She said, "Go inside and see if they have any toothpicks. I need some toothpicks."

Stan said, "Yes, ma'am."

I said, "Don't you do it, Stain. It's a trick."

What the hell? I laughed, and looked off in the distance in the same direction as to where the Second Comer drove off with his family. Stan said, "Ford ate hour, ford ate hour, ford ate hour," and walked back into the diner. For a second I wondered if he suffered from echolalia, or Asperger's syndrome. To his mother I said, "Well. Here we are. How long have we been neighbors?"

She said, "I've lived off Highway 11 for sixteen years. I moved here right about the time you went off to college the first time. I'm older than you are, Stet. Not by much, but I'm older than you are."

I offered her my bottle of wine. "It ain't bad, really. It's good. It's not bad. It's different. It's bottled by a Christian of sorts. It's not bad. It's good."

Sally took the bottle and turned it up in the same manner as her son. She wiped her mouth with the back of her hand. Overhead, some ducks flew by. Way above, a jet flew north, or toward the Midwest. Or West. It didn't fly south. Sally said, "Well. Here we are."

I didn't say, "Yes." I didn't say, "I get along well with your son, and maybe we can all move in together." I didn't say, "Hoo-whee ain't it weird all these cars piled up and we're stuck at a diner?"

I said, "You don't look older than I am."

Sally nodded. She looked at me in the same way that women always looked at me—as if I'd said something about the correct way to boil Brussels sprouts wrong—and said, "Right." From inside Laurinda's Diner I heard someone say, "It doesn't matter," and wondered if that person talked about his eggs not being sunny side up. Did he say it didn't matter about hash browns, or grits, or toast? Sally said, "Yeah, people tell me I look too young to be

Stan's mother. But I am. I think they're being nice. Like you're being nice. Well, you have to be nice for letting him drink wine."

I was officially married. I didn't need complications or temptation. I noticed how I, too, began shifting my weight involuntarily. I held my right elbow with my left hand, and swung my right forearm back and forth. Sally Renfrew said that she wanted me to write about her. She wanted me to write my low-residency master's thesis in southern culture studies on the way she invented a prosperous fake arrowhead empire, and how she had finished an unpublished scholarly treatise on the philosophy of craft.

Stan came out of the diner smiling, and holding something up to the sky. The Second Comer grave-robbing Christian had dropped one of his gold teeth on the linoleum. Stan said, "Would this be bad luck or good luck?"

I said, "I think it's good."

Stan's mother said, "Bad."

Stan got behind the wheel of his mother's car, and I opened the door to my truck. I told Sally I would go get my tape recorder and notepad, then come over to see how she manufactured fake arrowheads. It seemed like a good idea at the time—I couldn't imagine anyone else writing such a thesis. Stan put his mother's car in reverse by accident, and backed into my truck. He said it was a joke. Sally told me to bring my own protective eyewear.

George Singleton's the author of four collections of short stories, two novels, and one book of advice. He lives in Dacusville, South Carolina.

GLENDA GUION

I wrote a short novel about Stan "Stain" Renfrew, a boy who wanted to become a stand-up comedian instead of attending college. His mother had had an affair with a famous social commentator of sorts, and Stan was the result. The

THE WORLD, THE FLESH, AND THE DEVIL

(from *Image*)

My knights and my servants and my true children, which be come out of deadly life into spiritual life, I will now no longer hide me from you, but ye shall see now a part of my secrets and of my hid things.
—Sir Thomas Malory, *Le Morte D'Arthur*

The aviator had been hearing the howling of the dog pack for some time. He didn't live on this long ridge high in the Alleghenies or anywhere near it, so he couldn't know that the raucous bugling meant that death was on its way. His head was full of what had just happened to him: the dark bird impacting the canopy of his Phantom at low altitude, blood and feathers and howling wind and blindness. Groping for the ejection handle, he had managed to punch out as the uppermost branches of the trees lashed the fuselage, as the forest pulled him down. The aviator didn't know what had happened to his backseater. He felt weak with guilt. He didn't belong on the ground.

He sat at the edge of a clearing, on one in a squat line of tilting stone blocks, an archipelago of order in the chaos of the forest. Around him lay maybe an acre of open ground punctuated by sprawling clumps of rambler rose. He had been drawn to the clearing by the spikes of golden sunlight that drove downward through the green forest roof. They reminded him of the light-shafts that often penetrated the cloud cover when he was skimming along in the thin margin between the cloud bottoms and the mountain ridges.

Fat squirrels dashed among the tree-limbs, chittering, staring down at him with frantic, bulging eyes. Overhead, boughs squeaked and grunted and thumped against one another in what sounded to his ears like sober conversation. Insect life burrowed beneath his flight suit, into his skin. He had a growing sense of the forest as a single great organism, one that he imagined was slowly becoming aware of him. *I am here,* he thought, *in the vegetable kingdom.*

He had lost everything in his tumble through the forest roof. When his eyesight cleared, he was already sliding into the treetops, the silk of his parachute tangling in the branches. Caught high in a monster oak like a discarded marionette, concussion blurring his vision, he had pulled the razor-sharp KA-BAR knife out of his belt and, in a sudden access of terror, slashed the shroud lines of his chute, his torso harness, the lanyard that attached him to the seat pan with its survival gear. He had cut himself free and left it all irretrievably behind. Flares, smoke, compass, mirror, radio beacon, flashlight. Gone.

He'd slipped and slid and bumped his way down the many-limbed trunk of the oak, slowing his fall with an outflung arm here, a foot against a bough there, dragging stripped-away branches after him, green twigs snapping and cutting into his neck and cheeks, bark scraping the skin from his palms. When he landed at last with a breath-stealing thump on the thick carpet of decaying leaves on the forest floor, he found himself in the midst of a tribe of shaggy wild mountain ponies, who took a single eye-rolling look at him and dashed off into the undergrowth, tails flying. Knowing of no better direction in which to start the search for the wreckage of his jet and for his backseater, he had stood on shaky legs and followed them. He kept walking into spider webs strung invisibly between bushes, seeing their elaborate architecture only in the instant before he was into them, the sticky threads adhering to his eyelids, stretching over his nostrils, across his mouth.

There had once been buildings in the clearing where he now rested, and their half-hidden foundations still divided the open ground into squares and rectangles. The aviator took comfort from the straight lines of them, here where nothing was straight. He could recognize the hand of his kind in such a thing. It didn't occur to him to wonder where they had gone, the people who had laid these foundations, what might have swept them away.

In his fall from the oak, the aviator had twisted his ankle. It ached savagely, and he could feel the hot swelling of the flesh and the soreness in the tendons. The leather on the toes of both his boots had been peeled away by contact with the Phantom's dashboard as he ejected, and the steel toecaps shone dully through. He heard the dogs, but dogs in his experience were pets. They ran and played in the grass. You fed them; you picked up their poop. He himself didn't own a dog, but he knew plenty of people who did. He dismissed the sound.

The gray dogs raced like floodwater through the undergrowth, fifty of them or more, driven by the coming of spring and by their hunger. Everything alive on the ridge they pushed before them: white-tailed deer, possums, raccoons too terrified to remember that they could escape into the trees. Even a cantankerous old black bear, shaggy and leaned out by the winter, looking for early berries, heard the murderous howl that rose from their many throats and took to his heels, shambling along beside the humbler animals. Nothing stood against the tide of the gray dogs.

The pack's frontrunner was young and fast on his delicate feet, if not particularly strong. None of the dogs was strong, not alone, all of them stringy, feral mutts bound together at the mad edge of starvation. Deep in the frontrunner's brain lay the puppy-memory of a place of regular meals and fences and collars, fragmentary, fragile as a cobweb, of a world away from the ridge where he had answered to a name. His name. What had it been? The wild cry that issued unbidden from him tore the memory to shreds. Now he was as gray as dust, as gray as the rest of them, and crazed with fury and hunger. His dog's heart soared because everything on the ridge fled them.

He slowed minutely to snatch a stick insect from the branch of a bush, swallowed it down without tasting, and the rest of the pack surged around him, pushing him hard from beside and behind, their panting breath hot on his hindquarters. The next swiftest of them, a lanky prick-eared dog, ran at his shoulder, as close to him as a littermate at their mother's teats, as close to him as a brother.

Run run run, he cried, they all cried with one voice. The hunger gnawed at them, the agony of appetite hurled them forward, scrawny backs bowed, bony shoulders hunched, empty bellies drawn up tight as drum-skins against their spines, eyes slitted against the wan light that filtered down to the forest floor.

In sixteenth-century Europe, the legend once bloomed that birds of paradise had no feet and that they never lighted anywhere. Instead, the fabulously plumed birds were said to drift forever on the winds, consuming nothing but the dews of heaven, and they descended to touch the earth only when they died. The myth arose because the lustrous skins of the birds arrived from New Guinea preserved in poison, with the feet removed for shipping, and the men who unpacked them, and the people who bought them, none of them ever saw a living bird of paradise.

The aviator could tell you firsthand, though, that to light nowhere, always to fly, to press forever against the taunting edge of the envelope of flesh and mechanism; to watch and strain and yearn as your engines sucked hopelessly at the thinning oxygen, as your enemies spiraled about you, desiring nothing but to see you vanish in flame and smoke and tatters; as the controls bucked and fought and ceased to respond; to see the leading edges of your wings gleam red as blood against the impossible disk of the sun, to grope upward into the darkened freezing curve of the stratosphere, and then always to fall back. . . . To light nowhere and always to fly: the aviator could tell you that this is paradise.

A family of bobwhite quail broke out of the dense thicket of rambler rose near which the aviator sat. They flashed away into the sky, their panicked wings thumping at the warm, still air. A thrill ran through the aviator's barrel chest, a shiver of delight to see them fly. He was twenty-nine years old, and that was what he wanted more than anything, to be able to take to the air in a fraction of a second, like a bird. No ready room, no rush across the hot tarmac, no cinching himself solidly into a fabulous gizmo of metal and plastic and Plexiglas. He was a creature of the sky. Only among the cloud-tops did he not feel trapped in his own flightless body, excluded from what he thought of as *the true life*. The time on the ground between hops was endless, dull, insufferable.

The aviator's eyesight was excellent. He made out swift movement, small innocuous animals crossing the creek that bounded the clearing, chipmunks and rabbits and even a frightened fox, scurrying out of the tree line and crossing the rocky clearing where he sat. The smaller animals channeled their way through the lush spring grass and the patches of flowers, forcing their bodies into gaps between the close-grown stalks of rambler rose. The fleeing creatures were silent except for their desperate gasping and the scrabbling of their little hard feet against the earth. A doe and her spotted fawn flashed by, droplets of creek water flicking from their delicate legs. A mouse skittered over one of the aviator's boots. The howling of the hunters rose behind them.

A bear lumbered through the clearing, smelling of half-eaten fruit. The aviator started—he thought someone, perhaps in the survival training classes in which he now wished he'd paid better attention, had told him to roll up into a ball if he was ever confronted by a bear, to pretend that he was dead—but the old bear kept on without even a sideways glance at him and passed out of the high meadow.

Vague shapes clustered at the edge of the forest. Gray and low against the ground, like a terrible mist, they advanced across the fast-running stream and out of the undergrowth, many of them moving in a single body.

The frontrunner had not been alone in—how long? No way to tell. There was that faint sense that he had of the life he'd lived before the gray dogs: the life of plentiful food, the life of lying quiet in a cool place and resting, the life shared with men. And then there was the life of the pack, which was all of his life since. It was a life of riot, of constant noise and hunger, of wolfing down any bit of flesh that came his way, no matter how hard, how bitter, how rotten, of running through the dark, constant running, and of falling down to sleep only when the others fell down around him, curling himself over and against the closest dogs, his nose to his neighbor's tail for warmth, the neighbor's nose likewise digging into him.

He snatched at ragged sleep, in which he would sometimes dream of the life of food and the soft voices that came with it—*good dog, good dog*—but in which more often he would dream that he was running, running, seeking after something to eat, the world fleeing before him, only to wake and find that he was already pounding along with the pack on the trail of some terrified quarry. The dust raised by their relentless passage settled over their coats until they became a single uniform gray.

He had been slow at first, always in the rear of the pack, struggling to keep up, always at the fringes of the group when they flung themselves down to sleep, always cold, always farthest from the kills. Never full, eating only when the feast was so great that the pack leaders couldn't eat more, when they were so gorged that they couldn't be bothered to chase the starvelings away but instead lay a few yards distant, eyes half-closed, bellies bulging, while their inferiors fought each other for the leavings.

Sometimes he would find dry bones in the foliage, usually small—voles, squirrels, perhaps the partial skeleton of a coyote— and he would suck on them, afraid to bite down because he knew that the sound of the cracking bone would draw the attention of others who would snatch the secret morsel away. Sometimes he would strip berries from nearby bushes, but they made him vomit as often as they nourished him.

Soon enough, though, he found his stride lengthening, his legs growing stronger, his pace quicker, and he took his place in the midst of the surging pack, the foot-draggers left far behind him. The gray dogs never looked backward. Always on the move, eyes searching for the kill, anything to keep the specter of starvation away for yet another night and yet another run. His prospect was a lake of bobbing backs and heads and shoulders, the sweep of the tail ahead of him.

When prey was scarce, the pack at some unfathomable signal would wheel, and a shudder of greed and terror passed through their ranks. This was the moment they all feared and dreaded, when the pack whirled on itself the leaders sweeping in behind the stragglers and overtaking them, knocking them off their feet. The pack would consume its laggards. The frontrunner wasn't innocent of the cannibalism, when the killing went far enough. As dogs drifted in to join the pack—strays gone feral, lost hunting dogs, abandoned mutts—others surrendered their bodies to the multitude. The lame and the halt fed the leaders.

In time, he found the ranks before him thinning. He shoved his way forward in the pack, striving for all he was worth, until there were no dogs in front of him. He flew through the forest, and the frontrunner's howl broke from his throat, and the dogs behind him took it up, adding their voices to the awful wail. They trailed him, matching their pace to his. Down the fern-shrouded hillsides they flew, along the ravines, across the ridges and through the deep forest, pressing behind him so that he was fearful to stop, lest they should bowl him over and, seeing him weak for a moment, devour him. Only when he felt the horde flagging could he slow his pace. Only when they collapsed from exhaustion, their scrawny sides heaving, could he stop.

•••

The aviator fled. He wasn't aware of any impulse to run: one moment he was at rest, watching the dogs advance, and the next he was thrashing his way through the rambler roses, which tore at his Nomex flight suit, at his skin. The watery light in the undergrowth was confusing after the brilliance of the clearing. His strained ankle protested, the swollen flesh pressing against the tight lacing of the boot, but the closing cry of the dogs kept him moving.

His mind went for a moment to the knife, the KA-BAR with its seven-inch blade, secure in its sheath on his belt. He was a man; he was fit and strong, in the prime of his life. He had been trained to fight, to survive, to prevail. He had killed other *men*, for heaven's sake, though never at close range. The idea that he might be eaten by a bunch of dogs seemed faintly ridiculous to him. But the reddened eyes, the lolling tongues, the bodies bunched together, clenched like fists and then flexed on the bound, the long legs tirelessly eating up the distance, most of all the fangs, the numberless teeth in the gaping mouths—if he faced them, he would die. The aviator knew himself as prey.

He followed the trail of the other animals. His sharp eyes picked out the brown, humped back of the bear, maybe thirty yards ahead of him through the light bracken, lolloping along at its best pace. Why didn't it fight? It struck the aviator as wildly unfair that something as strong and fierce as the bear should be fleeing. The bear should rightly be between him and the dogs.

The face comes to the aviator, with its high cheekbones and dark eyes: his backseater, Geronimo. And with the face, a blaze of shame. Had the aviator ordered Geronimo to punch out, or had he left him behind? The altimeter unwinding like a nightmare clock as the forest reached upward.

Outside the scratched Plexiglas bubble of the canopy, before the impact, the sky was bright, and the aviator picked out details on the ground below. A skein of silver lines, rivers, broken here and there with white, where rapids boiled. The carpet of endless forest, which furred the rough outlines of the mountains and made them seem soft as pillows. The thousands of hectares of it spread out on all sides, to the horizon. Behind a dam, one of the rivers blossomed into a lake. He eased the stick forward, and the fighter stooped like a hawk. The aviator wanted to make a low-level run through the mountains.

They were deadly men in a deadly machine, one so fast that, pushed to its maximum, it could outpace the turning of the earth. They could run westward with the sun, and night wouldn't ever fall on them. An endless day. The stink of jet fuel and rubber and stale air filled the aviator's nostrils, the stench of his own sweat. The seat-pan hard beneath his buttocks. Over the intercom, he could hear Geronimo's breathing, high pitched and stertorous. Strange to have breathing in his ears like that, like a lover sharing a pillow, but in a hundred missions he had grown used to it.

The Phantom descended, the forest rising up to meet it. Suddenly, Geronimo laughed, at some private joke, at something glimpsed on the ground below them, at nothing, and the sound, distorted over the intercom, came to the aviator as a meaningless blast of sound, flat and crackling, like gunfire. He could picture Geronimo's face beneath the oxygen mask and helmet, the eyes amused. Impossible to know what another man was thinking. No one closer than a pilot and his navigator, and yet they might have been worlds apart, connected only by the slender static-filled line of the intercom. Neither of them could see the other, each in his own universe of panels, instruments, lights, cramped and familiar and homelike.

The dark bird shattered the canopy.

The Phantom F4B weighed thirty thousand pounds empty. It carried twelve thousand pounds of fuel in an internal tank. At the time of the bird strike, the aviator's jet was fitted with two drop tanks, which brought its initial fuel load to eighteen thousand pounds. The aviator didn't know precisely how much of the fuel they had burned before the collision. Geronimo would know. The back-seater managed mundane tasks like navigation, communication, fuel consumption. Say they had consumed five thousand pounds. At impact, the Phantom had weighed well over twenty tons, counting the twin pods of Zuni rockets slung under the wings.

A turkey buzzard—that was what it had to have been, the wingspread wider than the span of the aviator's arms, the glimpse of that ugly, naked head, like something peeled and red—weighed about five or six pounds. It had impacted the canopy at just under four hundred knots. Shards of glass from the shattered heads-up display had gashed the aviator's forehead and the bridge of his nose but spared his eyes. If the vulture hadn't caromed off in some unknown direction, it would have decapitated him.

As he ran, the aviator kept hoping to strike a debris trail, trees sheared at a descending angle, with the twisted hulk of the plane's wreckage at the end. Had the plane burned when it struck? All that fuel, it should have blazed like a torch. No smell of smoke reached him, no flicker of flames to tell him where to go. If Geronimo had ejected in time, then he would search for the wreckage of the Phantom as well. The aviator could imagine the backseater leaning nonchalant against the massive tail section of the smashed plane, amused but unsmiling. What was he, maybe twenty-one? A kid. Everything amused him. The two of them could hold off the dogs. Two men together had nothing to fear from a pack of dogs.

The frontrunner made out the shape of the man in front of him, hunched and running but nonetheless upright—*two legs*—and the scent was strong in his sensitive nose, the scent of another carnivore, fat on meat and marrow and bone. He had never pursued a man before. Nothing was forbidden the gray dogs; but this? For a moment, the frontrunner was two dogs, and each dog possessed a separate history. One history was ten thousand years of servitude and loyalty and symbiosis, of corrective blows and caresses and the sweet leavings of the master's table.

The other was the history of a million years, and a million years before that. The history of the timber wolves and, behind them, of the dire wolves that ruled the fantastical prehistoric jungles, too fierce to run in packs, too deadly even to their own breed for any kind of companionship. The lanky dog at the frontrunner's shoulder lunged forward, and the frontrunner pushed hard, to stay out in front.

The aviator struggled up out of the ravine, knees quaking, lungs burning. He knew that he was only moments ahead of the dog pack. They were screaming at his heels. He felt that he might almost be able to bear what was going to happen to him—it would at least stop the agony in his ankle, the drowning sensation of the carbon dioxide waste building up in his blood, the unbearable tension of the endless sprint—if it weren't for the awful howling. The howling drove him on. The bear had outdistanced him, and the other animals as well. The aviator was alone with the gray dogs.

He dodged an upright stone, hip-high, skirted another, and a third, topped by a crumbling seraph. Grave markers. He was passing through a cemetery. One great central monument, twice the aviator's height, bore the figure of a bandaged man, twisted, misshapen, propped up on clumsy crutches. Little granite dogs twined around the man's bandy legs. If he'd had the breath, the aviator would have laughed at the coincidence.

The graveyard sprawled out on all sides, vast and full of moving shadows. To the left and right, the suggestion of tilting buildings, bracken grown up around them, trees pushing through shattered roofs, thrusting their limbs through glassless windows. Ahead of the aviator, cloaked in trumpet vine, a crumbling brick wall. And in the wall, nearly hidden in the gloom that spread beneath the encroaching trees, a door. The aviator lunged for the door, thrust downward on the great wrought-iron handle, hauled it toward him. It refused to open, and he tasted death, more surely than he ever had in combat, more surely than he had when the vulture had burst through the Phantom's canopy.

Push. He put his solid shoulder to the upper panel of the door and shoved for all he was worth. The door gave before his weight with a terrible scream of age and disuse, and he spilled inside. He found himself in a high-ceilinged building, dark, dust-coated, disused. A church? He took no time to look around him, but kicked the heavy door shut, leaned his weight against it. His breath came in sobs as the howling dogs flung themselves against the wood.

The frontrunner struggled to stop short of the closing door but couldn't manage it. The others were too close and moving too fast. He went headfirst into the hard wood of the door's lower half, stunning himself. The lanky dog at his side screeched and bounded, bounced off the door as well, and fell back into the scrambling horde. They were piling up, two and three deep, those behind shoving those in front, dogs' bodies washing into the doorway like waves against a cliff, legs splayed, tails tucked under. They yowled and squealed and bit one another, rolling over and over, dog after dog piling blindly on, the prostrate frontrunner bottom-most.

The aviator recognized the building as a barracks, abandoned for some considerable length of time: long and narrow, with a tall, pitched roof and small windows. It was a room in which, he felt sure, many lonely men had passed the loneliest hours of their lives. What had they been? Soldiers? Prisoners? Monks? The building would have sufficed to house any of them. The roof had given way in places, and pale light filtered through to piles of rubble on the floor, but he noted with relief that the walls appeared to be sound. Sanctuary. Behind him, the door held, despite the pounding and thumping and wailing of the gray dogs.

The dogs began scrambling at the sides of the building, growling and griping, seeking another way in, a way to get at him. He hustled around the periphery of the room as fast as his bum ankle and his short breath would allow, making sure that it was as solid as it had seemed at first blush. He was a practical man. The place had been securely constructed. Here and there lay piles of ruined furniture: smashed bedsteads, half-burned mattresses, wrecked chairs, an empty trunk, the leather that bound it cracked and green with mold. Outside the walls, the dogs bawled their frustration.

Elated, the aviator howled at them in return. He tilted his head full back, closed his eyes, inflated his lungs, and roared. He had never in his life done anything like it. The sound of his voice bounced back to him from the sagging rafters, loud and reassuring, and he kept on, his teeth bared, spittle flying in high arcs. His head ached with the echoes. His nails bit into the palms of his hands, and cords stood out on the sides of his neck, blood vessels began to rupture, but he couldn't bring himself to stop. It felt as though there were a dozen of him, a score, all lifting their voices up in protest against the death outside.

A reply came. Not from the dogs. It came booming from deep within the wilderness, wordless and chthonic. The aviator continued screaming for a moment longer, but the great call from the forest was overwhelming, and he felt how small his own voice was, raised up against it. Even the dogs fell silent. It wasn't a challenge, like one bull elk defying another over a female or territory. This was a declaration of dominion: calm, deliberate, absolute. The bellow came again, vast beyond comprehension: the voice of the forest.

The aviator found himself praying—he who never prayed— praying and begging that he would not have to face whatever it was that he had called up.

In the refectory of the military school the aviator had attended as a boy, there was a stained-glass window that he particularly admired. It had been installed to honor the graduating class of 1943. Most of the colorful images set into the window meant little to him, a mishmash of Jesus Christ as a human and as a lamb, King Arthur holding up a clumsy sword, his noble knights arrayed around him, the Grail floating above their bowed heads, shedding rays of light. The central figure, though: as he ate, the boy who would become the aviator often lost himself in contemplation of it, and had to be jostled back to awareness of his surroundings by his classmates.

He found it a little humiliating, to be so entranced by the picture. It wasn't even, he didn't believe, a very good piece of art. A man surrounded by doves descending and ascending, bordered by bursting stars, by smoke and long trails of flame. A man in the garb of an old-time combat flyer: leather helmet, goggles, Mae West, parachute harness, leather boots. His coveralls were gleaming white, and he seemed to float above the ground, his feet pressed tight together, his toes pointed downward, his palms outward in a beseeching attitude. His face was bland, his features frustratingly regular and unmanly, his lips full and lush. His hips were strangely wide, and he appeared to have a little pouch of a belly that thrust his flying suit outward.

The man in the stained-glass window was not heroic. He was a bit silly in his passivity, his apparent gentleness, his androgyny. The boy would have preferred that the doves had been hawks, or eagles, with their cruel talons and their hooked beaks, their all-seeing eyes. The smoke and flames seemed to indicate that the man had been defeated in battle, his plane had gone down, he had died. One of the reprobates at the school—the academy was full of them—had thrown some hard thing at the window at some point in the past, and the flyer's right eye was dark, as though it had been shot out.

The boy would rather have been interested in any of the other martial figures in the window, or none of them, but it was this embarrassing image to which he came back again and again, despite the mockery of his table companions, many of whom would fight and die courageously in wars yet to come. Whatever his flaws, this man in the window, he was a being of the air. He was, as the boy knew himself to be, an aviator.

The forest whispered with a million vegetable mouths. The aviator found that he didn't want to sleep. He had discovered in this dormitory setting a kind of calm, a repose of the spirit that was better than sleep. He would be sought out soon by men much like himself; he would be judged on how he had handled the bird-strike and resulting crash, would be either hero or goat—but for the moment, he desired only to exult in the familiarity and solitude of the barracks.

The forest murmured, and the dogs kept their vigil. The aviator wanted to take off his boots, but he didn't dare. He would have had to cut the boot off of his injured foot, so severe was the swelling, and he knew that he would never get it on again. For the first hour or so after hearing the voice from the forest, the aviator had hurled pieces of wood and chunks of masonry from the windows in an effort to get the dogs to leave him be. He had managed to brain one lanky dog, and its body lay unmolested in the leaf-filtered moonlight among the gravestones. The gray dogs were either too weary or too agitated to eat it.

The aviator had ceased to want them to depart. The gray dogs were not company, but they were . . . What? They were not the forest. There was something terrible waiting out there among the trees—or perhaps it was the trees themselves that were waiting, watching. The aviator could almost bring himself to believe that the patrolling dogs were guarding him from whatever it was that walked in the darkness, that dwelled in the shadowed hollows out beyond their protective circle. He regretted having killed the one, and he was grateful to the others for their noise and their animation.

Most of the graves that he could see from the windows were graced with a wretched man of rags and tatters more or less similar to the one on the monument, sometimes crude, sometimes elaborate. The figure was always accompanied by numerous dogs, and it was hard to tell if the dogs were being affectionate with him, or if they were plaguing him. The aviator had worked out, in the hours that he had stood at the window peering out, who the man was: Saint Lazarus, the leprous beggar who died outside the rich man's gates, where the dogs licked his sores.

This building and the surrounding graveyard had not been part of a prison, not a monastery or a military installation. It had been a leprosarium. The aviator had heard of such places, stuck far away from population, in the swamps, tucked away in barely habitable regions of the deserts of the southwest. In the mountains, on the high, lonely ridges, where contact with the uninfected was nearly impossible. No crime had been committed by those who had lived in this dormitory, but confinement here had been life-long, without hope of mercy or parole. The forest had been the walls.

He yawned. He knew that, if he had suffered a concussion, he mustn't sleep. Sleep for him could mean death. For the lepers, to enter the forest was death. To try to return to civilization was to perish. The uninfected ones who lived in the valleys and the flat-lands away from the ridge, what would they have thought of the lepers? Their features ravaged, fingers missing, feet irretrievably lamed, skin luminous with infection. Monsters. Perhaps banishment was the kindest solution, for all involved.

The frontrunner roused himself, the foul dark taste of his own blood on his tongue. Only a moment before, as it seemed to him, all had been noise and fury, the shrieking of his packmates as they piled into the closed door and landed atop him. Then darkness like sleep, and a voice that called to him, a voice that spoke his old name. Now silence hung over the place. He stood and shook out all his limbs, checking for serious injury. There was none.

He saw that the lanky dog that had run along at his shoulder lay unmoving out in the middle of the field of standing stones. The rest of the pack milled about aimlessly in the open space between the building and the nighttime forest. There was a man in the building, he knew, the man he had been chasing. The dogs looked to him, and he knew as well that, were he to begin running, they would follow him. He would once again be the frontrunner, and they would once again be the gray dogs, and everything alive would flee before them.

Instead, the frontrunner lay down on the threshold of the door. He would wait on the man to emerge. Resting his aching head on his paws, he turned over in his simple brain that name, the name by which they had known him in the days before the coming of the pack. He had once been called *Attaboy*.

"Dead to the world, be thou alive to God."

The voice woke the aviator, who had fallen asleep, propped in a sitting position in a corner of the dormitory, half-wrapped in a flimsy, scorched mattress. The room had grown cold. Before the aviator stood a man covered in silver scales. He was naked, and he gleamed like a fish in a river. He glistened so brightly that it was difficult to make out any particular details of his appearance. His face was a shining caul, pierced only by his dark eyes. The aviator assumed that it was the silver man who had spoken, but there was nothing to prove it. The aviator couldn't make out whether the man even had a mouth.

In the old days, the aviator knew, the priests had given lepers a full funeral. Put them alive into a coffin, covered it with a pall, hauled them out to the cemetery. When they left the leper alone, to climb out of the casket on his own, forever after unclean, they had said those words over him, like a magical incantation. Dead to the world. Dead to the world.

The silver man turned from the aviator, whom he had been examining, and strode toward the door. His back, his buttocks, his legs—the coin-bright scales covered all. The aviator almost expected him to jingle when he walked. It occurred to him that this must be one of the lepers from the leprosarium's operational days. Surely the institution must have been closed for years? This might be the last leper, then, so far gone in the disease that he wouldn't wish to come down off the ridge even when it was allowed.

The silver man's hands and feet, fingerless and toeless so far as the aviator could tell, seemed to confirm this notion. He walked over the warped board floor of the barracks with a rolling gait, like a sailor in heavy seas. When he reached the door, the aviator struggled to find his voice, to shout out a warning.

And knew, in that same instant, that he had not warned Geronimo. He had punched out and left his backseater alone in the Phantom as the forest drew it down and consumed it. As the aviator floated into the foliage under billows of fluttering silk.

"No," he said. The silver man opened the door. The aviator's throat was raw, and it stung with his attempt at speech. "There's something out there." He meant the dogs, of course, but he also meant whatever was beyond the dogs, out in the forest. The forest itself. His hand found the haft of the KA-BAR.

"Go home. Go home."

Impossible, again, to know if it was the silver man who spoke. The words echoed in the tall-ceilinged room, and the aviator remembered with discomfort the howling that he had set up in the night, and the intolerable reply that had come. This voice was entirely human, humane. Gentle. The aviator could tell that the words were directed at the dog pack, but he thought that they were perhaps meant for him as well. The silver man stepped into the graveyard.

Home. The antiseptic BOQ at Oceana? The cramped cockpit of the Phantom? The dormitory of the military school? The Spartan bedroom in his boyhood home? He couldn't tell what precisely the word might mean, but he felt a strong impulse to rise, to search, to find it out.

When the aviator emerged from the barracks at dawn, favoring his injured ankle, only Attaboy awaited him. Tracks in numberless circuits around the building testified to the watch the gray dogs had kept over him during the night, and similar tracks led away, in many directions, winding past the ruined outbuildings of the leprosarium and into the trees. The pack was broken. There was no sign of the silver man, and no prints that looked to have been made by unshod human feet. At the aviator's appearance, Attaboy rose from the door's sill and stretched, head cocked at an attentive angle, as though he were waiting on a word of command.

The aviator slapped his palm twice against his thigh, as he had seen other men do to summon their dogs, and Attaboy trotted over to him, looking up with mild brown eyes. The aviator reached down and stroked the dog's dusty, bony head. "Left you all alone up here, did they?" the aviator asked. The dog pushed hard against the hand.

"All right then," the aviator said. He crossed the graveyard to the body of the lanky dog. The piece of jagged masonry that had broken the dog's skull lay nearby. Overhead, a pair of perfectly matched turkey vultures circled counterclockwise, their wings stiff and still as they rode the thermals, waiting with infinite patience and serenity on their chance to descend and feed. The aviator admired their flight for a moment—so effortless, so unforced—before he knelt and picked up the lanky dog, felt the stiffness in its limbs. He was intent before anything else on finding a place to lay the body where it could lie undisturbed. With the dog cradled in his arms and Attaboy at his heels, the aviator entered, limping, into the green sepulcher of the forest.

Pinckney Benedict grew up on his family's dairy farm in southern West Virginia. He has published two collections of short fiction and a novel. His stories have appeared in a number of magazines and anthologies, including *Esquire, Zoetrope: All Story, StoryQuarterly,* the *Ontario Review, Image,* the O. Henry Prize series, the *New Stories from the South* series, the Pushcart Prize series, *The Oxford Book of American Short Stories,* and *The Ecco Anthology of Contemporary American Short Fiction.* He is the  editor, along with his wife, the novelist Laura Benedict, of the 2007 anthology *Surreal South.* The second volume of the series, *Surreal South 2009,* is due out in October 2009. He serves as a professor in the English Department at Southern Illinois University in Carbondale, Illinois.

*L*ike most of my stories, this one's a hodgepodge of bits and pieces that became stuck in my psyche and needed to work themselves out. The stained-glass window, for instance, is real: I became obsessed with it as a boy in an extremely strict single-sex prep school very far from my home in West Virginia, and not a day passes that I don't think of it. I'm also quite an aviation buff, particularly military aviation, and when I was preparing this story, I'd been having long conversations with an older friend who was a Phantom pilot in Vietnam, which is where a lot of those details came from. The "Silver Man" is a nod to Kipling. When I knew I wanted to have a leper—or perhaps the ghost of a leper—in my story, I thought of the best fictional leper I know, and that's the Silver Man from Kipling's "Mark of the Beast." That's a lot of stuff. The story is maybe a bit overpopulated, but I'd rather make that error than have it be too quiet.

Holly Wilson

NIGHT GLOW

(from *Narrative*)

It's Labor Day, and it's our Friends of Friends Barbecue. I sit on the front porch waiting for people to show, which no one will because all we got is veggie dogs and a sooty yard, and all the neighborhood knows that much, they're not dumb. But Evelyn says, *Wait out there for folks, you never know.* But I know. People don't go outside here, no one's going to just walk by and see the wimpy sign Dad made. Evelyn and Dad think it's like old-fashioned times when people might sidewalk-stroll for fun. This is stupid, and instead I want to go inside to see what happens with Jeanie, our new Resident Friend.

Jeanie came yesterday afternoon via dirt bike. She vroomed up all crazy haired, no helmet, no stuff, parked off behind the carport like anyone might steal her dirt bike if they saw it. She wouldn't eat any supper, just went straight up to her room, where she started right away to curse and scratch up the walls, crying in quick little rips. I sat outside her room last night, slid cheese under the door, which she snatched up with tattooed fingers (snakes chasing spiders in the direction of her chewed-up nails).

So here I'm on the porch with thoughts of Jeanie when the screen door slams and out Jeanie comes, tall and grinning, her dark hair combed now and parted in wicked zigzags. She's got toast crumbs on her chin and a big spill of orange juice on her shirt.

Hey, little sister, I'll race you wherever, she says.

Now, I don't have a real sister, all I have is Dad and Evelyn, so of course I'm like, *Okay, let's go!* And like that she takes off for the carport, cutting through the raised onion beds, kicking up mud under her ratty K-Swisses. Luckily I've got on my LA Gear Heatwaves, so I go right after her.

She's fast and disappears behind the community van, where it's dark and where wild cats and raccoons live in the brambles. *Come here! Come here!* she shouts. I run up as if to tag her, but she's stopped with her arms crossed like she's got something important to say. She's got cat scratches all up her arms like some were clawing her here in the brambles, little scabbed dashes making up scratch lines. She grins, says, *I bet you haven't seen this,* and then she pulls her red Reebok shorts up on the inside side, and no panties! She fingers around, and I see a string hanging down from her soft lady pelt, and she says, *Go ahead, tug it.* I do it because I'm no pussy, but oh, nasty!

You can suck on that, she says, and I toss the bloody wad into the onion bed, and she turns and runs into the house doing a funny horse laugh while I'm on her heels, and we end up skidding into the community living room, where stupid fat Evelyn is there piling paper plates according to size.

Nine others used to live here in this building, nine plus Evelyn's Bruce, who died in the fire. They all left for Midwest Missions. Now it's just Evelyn and Dad and me, and now Jeanie. We walk up and down the new cement stairs like nothing happened, but we still smell the smoke. Dad stays up in his room or naps in the basement by his puppets while Evelyn spreads out all day in the community living room, watching her stories and staring at seed catalogs and crying for Bruce but saying she's crying for the people in her stories.

I mean that the house is normally quiet with no ruckus, and now here we are, me with Jeanie, and Evelyn looks down at the mud on our shoes, and you can just tell she's thinking, like, What of my onions!

Before she can say anything, Jeanie goes, *Oh, shit! Oh, shit! I'm late for Debra!* Debra, we find out, is Jeanie's parole officer, her P.O., is what she says.

I need those keys, Evelyn, Jeanie goes, meaning the keys to the community van Evelyn wears on a rope around her neck. *I need them right now.* Here she puts her hand out, like, Give them here! Evelyn sees her finger tattoos and goes for the keys straightaway, and right then I admire Jeanie's gusto.

It happens to be Outreach Day, and it's so clear Jeanie's just trying to get out so she won't have to go. *The rule is,* I tell Jeanie, *no un-Quaker person living in the building can just ask to borrow the community van and get to.*

Now that Jeanie's here I have things to explain and can get a break from the normal stuff I do. Usually what I do is sit around and write letters to Demarcus, my ghetto-kid pen pal appointed to me by Evelyn when we moved into House of Friends. It counts as my writing option for home school. Or sometimes I go hang with my best friend, Sweetie, who only wants to do gymnastics when I don't know how. All she talks about is her mom's girlfriend Helen's mouth cancer while doing tumbles on her fancy mat.

But compared to Jeanie, Sweetie now seems like just some retarded kid. I follow her out to the van to see how she walks when she's going someplace (like a gun dog trotting toward a shot-down bird, gleeful and ready for murder). She's still got mud splatters on the backs of her legs, like mud constellations, like you could pilot anything via her big calves. She stops all of a sudden and turns around to bend toward me and whispers in my ear so fast I can hardly understand. *We're going to fly my octopus kite sometime soon,* she says. *Then you can watch me ride dirt bikes with my old guards, Busty and Jerome,* she says. *We'll have good times, strawberry pop for you, Dr Pepper for me,* she says. I feel her tongue flicking on my ear as she says all this, but it doesn't bother me.

She straightens up and says in a normal voice that if she can manage it one day we'll do a hot air balloon, we'll throw whatever fun things we can think of over the sides, spiders, daggers, whatever. So the point is, when I look at Jeanie I cease to think regular things, instead I think: guns, fire, fun.

Jeanie goes off in the van, and I am left alone with Evelyn and Dad all day, as no one shows for the barbecue. Later Dad comes downstairs and says all gloomy, *Well, let's do this,* meaning Outreach. *Do you remember what to do?* he asks. Dad was blind until six months ago, when he bumped his head in the fire. He still wears those sunglasses, still knocks over the plastic porch gourds Evelyn thinks are pretty and autumnal.

I say, *Yes. Do you?*

Then we go do Outreach. We go door-to-door among the blacks in their apartment squares surrounding our building, and if a kid answers the door I say, *Is your mama here?* Then she comes, and Dad starts in with what's important about Organic Community Gardening, and Evelyn passes around pamphlets, and usually they let us in for niceness, but you can tell that it's like a life raft inside, or a small dinghy for them maybe, the way they move in groups around the living room crowded together and spilling out, with the big-boobed mama at the mast, and how one in the back is always about to get kicked out into the ocean but in this case the yard or apartment square. You can tell they don't give a shit about Organic Community Gardening. My job is: hand them their House of Friends Community Garden Treat, which was made by dopey Evelyn—chocolate pudding in a Dixie cup with Oreos for dirt and gummy worms for worms. I say, *It's like the ground, with worms, like a garden,* and *ooh,* they go, *ooh,* and they stick their fingers in all at once.

On the walk back Dad says, *I think we got some joiners.* Evelyn says, *Yes, those twin girls for sure.* Evelyn still holds Dad's arm when they walk down the sidewalk, and the effect is like he's a retarded old man. I walk way ahead and jingle quarters in my pocket. We should be having ice cream now, is what I think. We should stop off for pizza. We should go to the zoo. Instead, we do what we always do after Outreach, which is go see old Mom in the boneyard.

Dad stands gloomy over Mom's grave with his eyes closed, gives her the weekly update. *More rain,* he says, *Labor Day barbecue,* he goes. I bounce on my heels, imagine whose bones look like what, imagine what monster hell Jeanie and I could do here. Evelyn does the nice thing and tugs weeds away from other people's grave-stones, total dead strangers, then she goes and sits near Bruce's dirt, waves me over for a quizlet on Jesus as Peacemaker.

When we get home Dad goes straight to the basement, where his puppets and puppet stage are, which is now his job. He does them about the miracle of vision and how pretty the world is and all the colors, and his two main puppets are Petey, a grumpy boy who does not appreciate things, and Delores, a pretty girl with brown ringlets and dimples who reminds Petey to see beauty. He does these shows in schools and vacation Bible schools to lots of clapping, and he packs it all up, his puppet stage and puppets, in a special suitcase, hauls it all home in the community van.

After he bumped his head six months ago in the fire and could suddenly miraculously see again and he saw me (for the first time since I was a baby!) in the wild blaze on the stairs, he said I was different, that in his head he thought he really saw me all this time how I was, but that was with pretty brown ringlets and skin clear like a fish, with pretty red lips and eyes not too close together. And this is not what I look like at all. He said all this drinking some of Evelyn's bad coffee, and everything about his face was bitter, so I said, *Well I guess you were wrong,* and I shrugged my shoulders like no matter, and he said, *I still can't believe it's not true,* and I said, *Well, believe it.* My hair is red! And then he said that he imagined everyone as more like warm floating animals, and when his vision came after the bump we were really more like walking cacti with thick arms and legs and nasty juices inside. *This is why now we are Quakers,* he said, and then he went back to his room, where he keeps it dark.

•••

Today is the first day of October, the first day I can think about Halloween, and we have Jeanie's birthday, as her real one was in prison before she came here. In prison they don't give you anything for your birthday but maybe new shoelaces, and maybe only new to you. Debra the P.O. comes, and Evelyn's made a yellow cake, and we all eat, Dad too, in the basement by the puppet stage, where it's still sooty from the fire. You can tell Jeanie's embarrassed. She sits on her hands on the folding chair. She tries to make a speech, says, *Well, thank you all so much, thank you, Debra, this is just splendid, thanks for taking me in here, I've never been made to feel so comfortable.* Evelyn cries a little, and Dad talks about how people do change, look at him, look at Evelyn, who lost her Bruce. Debra says she's seen it happen for women who prioritize. Then Jeanie really breaks down, and Dad gets out the puppets and sings "Happy Birthday" in the voice of Petey first, then Delores, and we all join in. Afterward Dad goes back to his room, and Evelyn goes out hoeing, waiting for the little black kids to maybe show up. Upstairs I paint my fingernails with yellow highlighter while Debra talks to Jeanie woman to woman.

When Debra leaves, Jeanie comes into my room and says, *Let's go have a real party.*

We go to the gas station, and she gives me six smokes to suck up, and we play six games of Street Fighter, and she gets to be Ibuki while I'm just old nasty T. Hawk. I kill her two times and she kills me four, and then she goes in the bathroom but leaves her cool jean purse with me, and inside I see she's got a steak knife and two old muffins and ChapStick, plus a pool of change at the bottom, so I know when she says she's out of quarters she's lying, but I give it to her, as she's my elder. She goes, *Okay, what now, what about screwing with that crazy bitch's garden?*

I say, *Okay!*

She says, *But I want you to dig up all the radishes and take a bite of each one, and I want you to stick a carrot in your crotch and do Michael Jackson.*

I'm thinking, You *watch* me do Michael Jackson.

And like that we're shin deep in dirt, planning out Zombie Whore costumes for Halloween, and then Jeanie's shoving carrots down my top, calling me carrot tits, and I'm like, *Don't! Oh, don't,* but laughing, when Dad comes out, which is rare because sunlight colors make him nauseated, and besides, there's always historic peace church things to do and puppets to build, and anyways, he'd rather sit in his room covering his eyes, he says he sees when he doesn't see, but he comes out and says, *Girls, oh, girls. Don't you know it's free day at the zoo?* And I'm like, *Oh, please, please, let's go, Jeanie, take me, Jeanie, it's free, please, please,* and so on.

First we hit the American Prairie, and there's wolves and elk and buffalo. *I'm a wolf and your dad's an elk, and Evelyn is one fat buffalo,* Jeanie goes.

What am I? I say.

You're a dippy little prairie dog, she says. Then she flicks my hair!

No, I'm not, I say, but secretly I'm thrilling with contentedness.

We go to the Rain Forest, we go to the African Veldt, we sno-cone our butts through the splendid Asian Steppes. Jeanie gets more and more excited, going, *Look how clean it all is! All the zebras with the zebras, and the donkeys off by themselves.*

Yeah, what of it? I say. It's like she's being mystical and weird.

The monkeys are with the monkeys, she goes. *All the birds get the same place, and a net at the top to make them stick with it.*

If they don't separate them, I say, *they might all eat and chase each other.*

You're so smart, she says. *But look, they even keep the sexy guys together,* she says, meaning the five boys in white hats and sagging money belts selling ice cream by the Elephant House. They're looking at us, and we're looking at them.

Go look at those elephants, Jeanie says. *Let me have a break from you.*

And so I do what she says. I trot inside the tall dark hallways where elephants pass through, pooping their way to lunchtime with trainers. I read the plaques on the wall, memorize things for the quizlet Evelyn's going to give when I get back. These elephants, I tell myself to memorize, weigh up to eleven thousand pounds, they have a one-fingered trunk and a convex back.

They're all locked up now, but I can see through a window where one throws mud on its back and one pisses on the cement floor. I run out for Jeanie because she'd get a kick out of this, but she's gone.

But then sure enough there are noises from the men's bathroom, and so I walk in, and there's Jeanie with two of the ice cream guys, one pinning her up against the dirty wall with his tongue out, twirling it toward her open mouth, and one on his knees, sucking her knees. She doesn't see me, so I stand and watch, wait forever for her to finish, then finally she turns and sees me and is like, *Well, where the hell have you been?*

I point in a sassy way to the ground, like, right here!

She says then, *Time to go!* I ask her if I can go to the gift shop to look for my name on a key chain, and she says, *Why? You have no keys. So no.*

So we skip the gift shop, but then, in the parking lot on the way out, there's a hot air balloon tethered to three flamed 4x4 trucks, taking up all the left of the lot. The balloon is yellow, and the basket's painted black with a giant lightning bolt on each side. People are lining up to get tickets from a bearded man on crutches.

Let's do it, let's do it! I go a zillion times, but Jeanie's like, *Nope, out of money, you'll get over it.*

This makes me almost cry, though I've already got myself up in that balloon in my head. I see us up there floating, and I'm seeing below us the zoo, a million splendid animals fixed on us wondering if we're gods, a pool of black kids in the parking lot pointing up, jealous, and off far away Jeanie's dirt bike track, a rumbling cloud of dust, and in the other direction my friend Sweetie's house. Jeanie's got her jean purse up there with us, and inside, I know, those muffins, fun enough to throw, and that knife, big enough to cut rope.

She's messing in her purse now, and I think, she's caved! But no, she just pulls out a smoke. Well. I don't know how much a tethered balloon ride costs, but I think she could at least check.

It's Halloween afternoon, and Jeanie's already plowed through the candy corn Evelyn set out for the black kids. Now she's in the shower, which for her is at least thirty minutes, so after my math quizlet I sneak up to Jeanie's room to prepare myself as a Zombie Whore. I get out the shoebox where she keeps her makeup, and I get out some eyeliner and smear it good under my eyes for death, and then I draw some bugs like tattoos on my fingers, and then I draw with some of her slutty lipstick blood lines down my mouth corners. Then I go for her closet and double up one of her purple tube tops and stuff it with socks, and then I rat out my hair like she does before dirt bike riding. Then I check in the mirror, and I look good! And scary! So scary I hide in her closet, planning to leap out when she comes in. So I wait there.

After forever she finally comes in with an orange towel around her, but only partially, as I can see her butt sticking out (I can see her through the door slats), and she's lighting up a smoke, which she's not supposed to ever do inside because of the fire, so I wait just a second before leaping out and going, *Gotcha!*

Jeanie shrieks *Fuck* so loud, jumps back, her face goes white. I put my arms out like a zombie and turn in circles with my tongue hanging down. Instead of laughing, though, she's pissed, she's staring at her tube top, which now, I see, has lipstick all along the top where I pulled it over my face. I try to run, but she grabs at me and slaps the back of my head, and she's not letting me go. She calls me a nasty mosquito bitch, and I'm like, *Sorry! Don't hit me! Sorry!* And her towel comes off then while she thumps me harder and harder on my cheek and arms, and between hits I see she's got way more tattoos than I ever knew—mermaids and devils and a growling dog, even sea creatures on her big puffy boobs, which I bend into to protect my face from her thumps. I find my eye up against the eye of a green sneering octopus, which makes me think of the octopus kite Jeanie's never flown with me, the hot air balloon too.

And then Evelyn's there in the doorway going, *Sake's alive! Sake's alive!*

Now to me in my position this sounds like, Snakes alive! Snakes alive! And I don't know what to think, like maybe some garden snakes got in the house or maybe Jeanie's finger tattoos have come to life, I don't know, but I'm scared so I bite Jeanie right up under the octopus, which makes her shriek again, and I dive myself behind Evelyn's big body and am ashamed to say I whimper.

Jeanie just stands there naked, the fiercest look ever on her face, looking about to explode. Then Dad stumbles in and sees our scene and sees Jeanie and all her tattoos and her boobs, and suddenly he looks very, very sad, like, Just another sad thing I've got to see with my eyes these days, or, How will I update your dead mom about this.

He shakes his head, whistles low, says, *The calf and the lion and the yearling together, but still no peaceable kingdom.* Which is to make us feel guilty; which is what Jeanie would call a bullshit Quaker dictum, and just as I'm thinking that, Jeanie says, *Steven, that is such Quaker bullshit, and I don't have to listen!*

And I say, I don't know why, *Oh, yes, you do, that's Isaiah, you crazy bitch!* Now my eyes are aflame with tears.

Dad puts his hands up, says, *Okay, okay, girls. Let's all isolate and calm down.*

I go in my room and cry into the pillow. When I get up, I see that the result is: now I'm an even better zombie. I really look like I've just dug myself up. Later when I go downstairs it's clear Jeanie and I won't beg for candy or throw eggs like planned, she's still so pissed. She's slurped down the last of my Hawaiian Punch drink boxes out of spite and now waits at the screen door with her dirt bike gloves on for her dirt bike friends. Her ears are tuned to their downshifts, so she just leans on the wall, eyes closed, like life is so hard. I make a big show of not caring by walking out the door, leaving without telling where. Really I'm going to Sweetie's, who now doesn't seem retarded at all.

Sweetie's house is splendid nice, as Sweetie's mom and her girl-friend are architects. I stand on the porch and ring their doorbell, fancy and shaped like a silver ladybug. I hope it's okay that I'm here, as I was told not to come for a few days, as Sweetie's mom's girlfriend's mouth cancer is looking bad, but surely they're still doing Halloween.

Sweetie comes to the door looking very pretty with her ponytail ends curled and wearing the gymnastics leotard she let me try on once, except her face is splotchy with red and I know she's been crying. I wonder if it's possible she got beat up today too, but I want to stay cheerful, so I say, *Trick or treat, you leotard retard!* Then I friendly punch her in the shoulder.

Helen's in there dying, Sweetie wails. *It doesn't look good at all!* And then both her hands go to her eyes, and she cries into her palms.

I don't know what to say, I've always been able to skirt real dying. Sweetie's mom, Leslie, walks to the door to see who's there. She at first looks put off that it's me, but then she sticks her head out the door and looks down the street, where there is a group of Swamp Monsters already heading this way with sacks outstretched, and so then Sweetie's mom says, *Molly, it would be so helpful to us if you could stay on the porch and tell people we're having a family emergency and to please not ring the doorbell,* and then she limps back inside. (She met Helen in the car crash, she calls it her love limp!) Then she comes back with a big wooden bowl filled with apple-spice minibars that I'm to hand out, stares a bit at my messed-up face, my swollen cheek.

Sure, I'll do whatever! I say, and Sweetie steps out on the porch as if to stay with me, but then her mom grabs her by the arm and says, *No, Sweetie, you've got to be in there,* and before the door closes I see a grim-looking woman inside dressed as a nurse, and I'm con-fused as to whether she's a real nurse or just one for Halloween.

So I sit on the porch and toss the minibars at the trick-or-treaters before they can even walk up the steps. Sometimes I miss and hit them in the shins, but I don't care, I pretend I'm protect-ing Sweetie's family from real monsters. Behind me I hear people walk around in the house, sometimes slow, sometimes fast, and

I want to peek my head in the door to see what's going on. But I don't, I'm not nervy enough, though I know it's just what Jeanie would do.

All the Halloween kids going by on this street have nice shoes, either with wheels or red lights in the back, but I still like my Heatwaves with their orange bottoms. I bet my one other friend, poor Ghetto Demarcus, I bet he'd love a pair of light-up shoes. How awesome it would be if I could buy him some and mail them to Chicago and maybe not say who sent them, except for maybe like "a Friend" or something like that, but how he'd secretly know it was me, and he'd probably write me more than four times a year then and tell me how much he loved his new shoes, and it'd be this silent thing between us.

Recently he's begun to appear to me in dreams, always in cool hip-hop clothes. He stands at night in the brambles by the carport rapping a very sad rap song, like a rap song in a minor key, something slow and sorrowful to make you cry. His shoes are covered in coon shit, and he's got a golden hair pick stuck through his squared-off afro. When he opens his mouth to rap, light pours out, and when he does hand gestures to go with the rap, light shoots out of his fingertips and hangs in the air like a glowing fog. Just thinking about it wets my eyes.

I wonder what him and his friends are doing right now for Halloween, if their single mothers let them walk the projects dressed up as ghouls or not. I see Demarcus dressed as a Frankenstein, leading all his little sisters through a maze of gloomy skyscrapered streets. All I really know about him is that his mom works freezing frozen french fries and brings home bags of them for Demarcus and his sisters every Saturday, and he loves that.

It's dark now, the trick-or-treating has slowed, and suddenly all the lights go out in Sweetie's house, and then the porch light too. I stick my face against their dining room window, see only a slice of light from underneath the bathroom door in the hall. And then the bathroom door opens and the light's still on, and I half expect it to be mouth cancer Helen with her crazy red wig, who only last week helped me with my science option from her at-home hospital bed, but it's that nurse, and at first I think she's changed clothes, as she's got a purse on her shoulder, but then I see, no, she's still a nurse, so she's probably a real one. The nurse spots me, mouths *Go home,* then she shoos with her hands.

I walk home, two miles of split sidewalk and scabby stray dogs. I'm halfway there, already where the Mexicans sit out on their porches all night long, and I'm hoping they might yell something sexy at me so I can curse back, but then, vroom vroom, Jeanie rides up behind me on her dirt bike. She looks at my swollen cheek, says nothing, then says, *You may hop on, little zombie sister.*

I get on the back and put my arms around her and my cheek against her hair, and her hair smells like motor oil, and her body is an unmoving board, and she revs the dirt bike engine with her hand, coils those finger snakes around the handle, which spreads the snakes out fatter where her knuckles are, and it's like they're digesting a big rat, like they do, and just then that's one of my favorite things to see, it makes me woozy with calm.

Next day Jeanie says offhanded things to me all day long, like, *If I were any animal I'd be a big-ass boy lemur with a big dick.* This while we're peeling Evelyn's potatoes. And then, while we're doing the Friendly Monthly Mailers, she says, *I think your father may be a fag.*

The stunner is later, on the couch, during *Matlock,* after Sweetie calls to say Helen is dead. Jeanie says when I put down the phone, *The only person who ever really loves you is your mother.*

So what about me, then, I say, sitting up straight, which, with me, means I'm serious.

Your mom's dead, she says. *Don't be stupid.*

I am quiet for a long time. But then I'm like, *Jeanie, Jeanie, you are like my dead mom!* Which I have no idea if it's true, but: Jeanie's hands are just like mine, but bigger. When I nap in the big upstairs window during the quiet meetings in the basement, the boring no-ghost séances, she comes up smelling skunky, wraps herself around me like a mama cat does kitties, and sometimes she even purrs in my ear and I go right to bed, no big dreams.

But to this she sighs. She knows just what I'm asking. She says, *No, I'm not, I'm not anything like her. And don't ever say I have anything to do with you. Don't you know everyone needs a public that's theirs alone?* Here she looks off squinty-eyed in the distance, then back at me.

A public is like your own kingdom, she says. *My old guards are my public,* she says, *Rusty and Jerome. The dirt bike track is my public. You're a prairie dog, I'm a wolf. This is just where I'm living,* she says.

Oh, I go. *Oh. Then,* I say, *is Sweetie my public?*

She goes, *If you want. If you want a little fartface who eats her doughnuts with a fork to be your very special public.*

Next tragedy occurs. We've gone to Helen's funeral, splendid and bleak. We've gone again door-to-door about community gardening, spoken to the mamas and kiddies about dirt, which Evelyn's giving me science points for to make it worth it. Jeanie goes off most days to the dirt bike track, comes home covered in dust.

The day before Thanksgiving Dad comes out of his room, no sunglasses. He says, *Let's all go for ice cream!* He's feeling so good, he says, unlocking the community van, like a cloud has lifted from his vision. He opens the door for Evelyn, says, *What a sweater!* Her sweater's just an ordinary cat sweater. Evelyn sits up front, and Jeanie takes the back, puts her legs up so only she can sit there, so I take the middle seat and sit the way she does, which, normally, Dad's like, *Feet on the floor, please!* But he's so happy because he's come up with a new puppet show concept based on the main Quaker man, and all the way to the Ice Cream Treatery he sings "How Great Thou Art" in a throaty voice.

It's dark out now, and I know what the community van looks like to outside things we pass. The van's inside light won't turn off, so to the sidewalk strays we're like a suspended glowing space floating through the streets, like we're something intelligent on patrol.

When we get there it's almost closing, so we take our cones outside. It's windy, and we all do our licking braced against the blow. Dad asks Jeanie, *How are things going with your P.O., Debbie?* and she says, *Debra,* and he says, *Well, okay, how's it going with her?* And Jeanie says, *It's okay. Things are okay.* She scratches at her arm scratches, which she always does when Dad speaks.

Then we go the long way home, through nice houses on the outside of town, even by a field with cows. I am thinking about what will tomorrow hold. Will Jeanie take me to the dirt bike track finally, or will I play-judge Sweetie's gymnastic routine again? Will Evelyn have a heart attack in the garden, might Dad be restruck blind? I try to picture a day when all these things happen, one after the other, and it nearly crosses my eyes.

And then, over in a burned-down field, I see it.

In the field, all alit in splendid night glow, the lightning bolt balloon. The three flamed 4x4 trucks. There are cars and people, and I say, *Oh, please, Dad,* PLEASE! And he looks at me in the mirror and tries to twinkle his eyes and says, *Sounds fun. You up for it, Evelyn?* he says to be jokey, and she just old lady giggles.

We pull in, but the other cars are mostly leaving. I'm worried the balloon might close, so I jump out of the van and run to where the bearded man sits on a bucket, no crutches anywhere. He's got a roll of tickets in one hand and an empty beer cozy in the other.

The balloon is up with people in it, and it takes forever for it to come down. Jeanie catches up with me, and Evelyn's walking Dad slowly over like we have all night when obviously we don't, and Jeanie's like, *Do we have to?* And I'm like, *Yes! You said you would, so shut up!*

The bearded man says, *How many?* And I'm like, *Four, please!* Then we all stand in the light of the trucks waiting. Finally the balloon is down and the basket door opens, and when one person steps out, one of us steps in, except for Evelyn, who gets in after two people get out, because of her weight, she explains to me so no one else has to. The balloon basket is bigger than it looks and even has a kind of outdoors carpeting. Inside there's a man with an outfit like a sea captain. *I am your pilot,* he says. I wish he weren't here. I wish it was just me and Jeanie and no ropes.

The pilot fusses with flame knobs, and you can just tell Evelyn's thrilling, like, Oh, what the devil, or something like that she'd say. Jeanie is saying it's too cold, and I say, *Well, then, you shouldn't have worn those shorts, this is not Florida,* and Dad says, *Girls, let's just enjoy the beauty, okay?*

The bearded man closes the basket door and messes with some ropes, then pats the basket like it's the butt of a horse. In my head I'm like, Remember this, remember this!

Then the pilot turns the flame knob up a little, and I can even feel its heat on my forehead, and it feels so nice, and I'm already remembering what won't ever happen: us up in the night, a great lit thing rising up in the monster moonless sky.

Evelyn turns to me and says, *Tomorrow we'll read about balloons,* meaning for science option, but just as she turns back around she sees the pilot making the flame go higher and higher, and her eyes go so big, her not ever approving of open flames because of her Bruce. She says, *No, ha ha, I don't think so, not for me,* and she opens the door and steps out just as the balloon is lifting, and even before all the weight of Evelyn is out, we shoot up fifteen feet like a rocket, and the pilot is screaming *Abandon, Abandon!*

And then he jumps.

And then Dad does, and then I hear the snap snap snap of the tethers, and Jeanie's lifting me up and over and going, *Fuck, fuck, fuck!* And next I'm crumpled on the ground in the triangle light of the 4x4s. Dad and Evelyn shout, *What's happened! Oh no!* and Jeanie is floating away up in the real air, which is only dark dusky gloom.

Good-bye, I go.

•••

They find parts of the balloon the next day all burned and tattered at the zoo, on top of the Spectacled Bear enclosure. How this would thrill her! The winds were blowing eastward, the people tell Dad. But no sign of Jeanie. The bearded man took off in one of the 4x4s right after but lost sight when the balloon went over some monster trees. *Like she'd been swallowed by the night, like the night ate her up,* the bearded man said very slowly. Now everyone's searching in fields and shrubs for a broken tattooed body, even Evelyn, who feels the most to blame. The dirt bike men ride slowly along ravines and gullies, heads down in search, their mustaches frowning for their mouths.

I don't go on the searches, I go to Sweetie's for Thanksgiving dinner because Dad says I must. We all go around to say what we're thankful for, and Sweetie says gymnastics, and her mom says feeling love from beyond the grave, and I say, *I don't know, elephants, I guess. Tube tops.*

Weeks pass. Christmas comes, no snow, but the brambles by the carport go twiggy and wet. No Jeanie, dead or alive. I go to the zoo on every free day, sometimes with Sweetie, sometimes alone. I look for dirty, blood-spotted K-Swisses under bathroom stalls. I count the number of chickens in American Farm from week to week, and sometimes there's less than before. I take notes. I draw diagrams. I put it all in letters to Demarcus, and I'm waiting to hear back what he says.

If I keep coming I know I'll spot her, splendid among the wolves, maybe, or with the zebras or the elk or the giraffes. She'll be a new, wilder Jeanie, like Jeanie of the big-dick lemurs, Jeanie of the poisonous snakes. Jeanie not of the dirt bike guys, not of the House of Friends, not of people anymore. Her finger snakes will pulse with rats, she'll be lit up, she'll glow in the night. *Come here! Come here!* she'll say, and I will, I'll do whatever she says, just watch me, watch how I move, watch what I do.

Holly Wilson received an MFA from Wichita State University and is now a doctoral candidate at Florida State University. Her fiction has appeared recently in *Narrative* magazine, *Redivider, Northwest Review,* and *Opium.* She was raised in Kansas, makes her home in Tallahassee, and is at work on her first novel.

I *began this story just after I'd read Mark Richard for the first time and was really taken with his child narrators, these wonderful neglected creatures full of simultaneously weird and familiar longing. Also, I'd been thinking a lot about* The Wizard of Oz, *that penultimate scene where the Wizard goes off in the balloon, leaving Dorothy behind. Even now when I watch it as an adult, when the Wizard floats away and it seems like there's nothing Dorothy can do, it's such a kick in the gut! That scene was my first experience as a spectator to engineered pathos that I can remember, and I wanted to sort of celebrate it in one of my own stories, if only by having one of my characters float away in a hot air balloon, too.*

Clinton J. Stewart

BIRD DOG

(from *Louisiana Literature*)

Glenpool's wife said enough after six. Told him if it happened again he'd be out a house and a pregnant wife. Not
to mention half his paycheck, which she noted wasn't half what it
should be anyway.

"You seem to have things confused," Lee Ellen told him. "The
dog points, you shoot the *bird.*"

Glenpool was standing on the back porch knocking the mud
off his boots while Lee Ellen spoke through the screen door. He
nodded and turned, sat on the top step, bent over and rolled his
jeans to the knees. She started to say something else about hunting
so he quit listening. He reached down and untied his bootlaces on
both sides, pulled them out through the eyelets, and balled the
leather into his pockets.

"The right dog pays for itself," he said.

Lee Ellen waddled forward and pushed open the screen. She
took hold of the door frame and leaned out.

"I've never seen a dog pay for anything," she said. "*Especially*
itself."

He turned to explain but saw Lee Ellen had lost her grip and
stumbled out on the wooden slats. With the added weight over
her legs, she pitched headlong towards him, and had he not rushed
the steps when he did, she would have tumbled, belly first, onto

the porch. He gathered her in his arms and held until she stood and righted herself and he stayed holding until she relaxed. Her shoulders dropped and she tucked her forehead to his chest. He leaned down and whispered.

In the living room he led her to the sofa, sat and eased her under his chin. His cheek on her head. Several minutes Glenpool listened to her breathing, felt her rise and fall against him. He'd almost fallen asleep when she spoke.

"I'm worried."

Glenpool cleared his throat.

"And?"

"You're not fixing it," she said.

"Nothing's broke, Lee."

She stood from the couch.

"How's this," she said. "I'm nine months pregnant and you're filling our backyard with dead dogs."

"It's not like that."

"Yeah? What is it like?"

Glenpool sat back on the couch and started with his feet up to the table. When he did he saw the unlaced boots still on, the mud caked around the soles and smeared to the table's leg. He'd streaked it down the hallway and in through the living room, his footprints etched in the carpet. He started to speak but it was too late.

Lee Ellen turned her back and began to sob.

Glenpool stood and pulled her to his chest and put his chin behind her ear.

"Okay," he whispered. "No more."

Six weeks later he called a Guthrie phone number from an ad in Sunday's *Oklahoman* and spoke to an elderly lady about a litter of Brittanys. Her husband, she said, could tell him for sure, but as far as she knew if Glenpool drove out that day the litter pick was his. He figured three hours until Lee Ellen and the baby woke, so he wrote her a note, placed it on the bedside table, and kissed her forehead before he walked out. She didn't move.

Four hours later she was still there. Glenpool came through the doorway, the new puppy asleep in his arms. His infant son in hers. Lee Ellen was turned facing the wall and he stepped across the room, eased into the bed behind her, and kissed her cheek. The child was curled beneath the covers, its tiny hand extended. Glenpool laid the Brittany into the folds at his feet, reached over Lee Ellen and lifted the blanket.

"Quiet," she whispered. Then, before Glenpool could tell her, she turned onto the puppy and it bawled and jumped up, and Lee Ellen screamed and hauled back on the blanket. The whole bed shook, and it jarred Kendon awake. Lee Ellen scooped up the boy and began to sway and bounce him, her lips whispering to his forehead. Soon he was quiet again.

She narrowed her eyes at Glenpool and laid Kendon into the folds.

He had to promise her to keep it. As a pet if nothing else. But if things worked out they'd have a stud dog. One day the boy would need a pup of his own.

"If he wants to hunt," said Lee Ellen.

Glenpool reached and touched the child's hairless head.

"Why wouldn't he?"

Winter passed and an Oklahoma spring behind it. The child forming words by the summer, nearly standing on his own. In the evenings Glenpool trained the Brittany in the back yard, Lee Ellen and Kendon watching from the porch. He taught the dog *whoa*. Showed how, when he changed directions, it should change with him, always in front. Months later, with it half-pointed to a bobwhite wing tied at the end of a fishing pole, Glenpool knelt beside, whispering, lifting the Brittany's head, stretching its tail vertical.

"See?" said Glenpool, turning to his wife and infant son. "See how he's pointing, Kendon?"

Lee Ellen suggested they name it Solomon, after the wise king.

"He's so smart," she said, and Glenpool agreed. It was smart.

His son, however, sat quietly between his mother's feet, twisting his fingers into the fabric of her skirts. Reaching to the sparkle of her jewelry. Glenpool tried to take the boy and have him pet the dog, but the moment Solomon approached, Kendon retreated, squirmed from his father, and burrowed into Lee Ellen's arms.

This continued for several months, into the boy's second year. A third following, and still every time Glenpool approached, Kendon withdrew. He could sit for hours with her, oblivious to Glenpool. To the dog. *To anything,* Glenpool noticed, as long as Lee Ellen was close.

He was nearly five when Glenpool finally spoke.

"Wrong with him?" Lee Ellen asked. She was beside him in bed, reading. "What does that mean?"

"It means something," he said. "Means he panics if you leave the room. Means he won't pet Solomon or step foot in the yard. Lord help us he gets dirt on him. What boy's afraid of dirt?"

"What would you have him do, Glenpool?" she asked, tossing her book on the night stand. "Chase birds? Gnaw on a bone?"

Glenpool shook his head.

"He's scared, Lee Ellen. Of everything. Not just the dog. He barely lets me near him. And every time he cries, you come carry him off."

Lee Ellen turned her back, reached over and switched off the light. She left Glenpool sitting in the dark.

A moment of silence and then he stood, walked into the hallway and downstairs. He opened the back door, went out to the porch, and let the screen slam behind. Solomon jumped from underneath and met him halfway to the steps and Glenpool caught his forepaws. He took him by the jowls and played for a moment, palming the dog's muzzle. He let him down, walked over and sat on the top step. His dog sat beside.

Birthday seven. Father, mother, and child. Solomon in the corner. They sang "Happy Birthday" and the dog howled and rose onto his hind legs and turned in a circle. Glenpool laughed.

"He's something, isn't he?" he said, then watched Kendon make his silent wish and blow candles.

The first present was a paint set from Lee Ellen's sister. Below that, a miniature replica of a village to be assembled and painted. There were tiny figurines for the townspeople, small streets and cars, and a theater with a bright marquee. Kendon inspected each object, looked closely through the colors of the paint set, each brush in turn. After several minutes Lee Ellen stood and handed him a box wrapped in bright blue. She leaned over and kissed him on the forehead.

"I love you," she said.

Kendon loosened the bow, folded away the paper, then carefully arranged it and placed it aside. From the box he pulled several thin books tied together with string.

Before Glenpool could see, Lee Ellen burst out.

"It's sheet music," she said. "K's going to learn piano!"

"Good," Glenpool said. "Good for him."

He stood from the table and walked into the living room.

He returned with a large cardboard box in his arms and dropped it in front of Kendon. It was duct-taped over the top and on the sides and Glenpool reached into his pocket and retrieved a silver Swiss Army knife and handed it across.

"There's your first knife," he said. "Has everything. Open it."

Kendon turned the knife in his hands and began maneuvering the different tools, the various blades. After several moments he looked up at Glenpool, then over to his mother.

"Here," Glenpool told him, pointing to the edge of the box.

Kendon stood, extended the main blade, and cut.

Glenpool folded open the flaps, retrieved several items and began arranging them on the table.

A pair of leather hunting boots—*Gortex,* he said, showing the inside—then a pair of leather shooting gloves. A goose down jacket and insulated camouflage pants. Canvas overalls and a game bag. A camouflage rain suit. There were smaller things too: a compass; snakebite kit; an emergency blanket and binder twine. There were extra bootlaces, salt pills, and earplugs. A bottle of Hoppe's No. 9 gun oil and a chamois cloth. A container of SureGuard insect repellant, and a small flashlight that also held matches.

"That's watertight," Glenpool said. "Your matches stay dry."

Lee Ellen mumbled something under her breath while Glenpool pulled out the final item. It was a large camouflage backpack with a length of rope coiled and attached to the bottom.

"This is your survival kit," he said, extending his arms above the display. "Everything you need."

Kendon studied Glenpool's present.

"Thank you," the boy said. "What does it do?"

September ended, and the heat began to lift. There were hints of autumn in the sunrises. Lee Ellen and Kendon stayed indoors—books and music, and then piano lessons at the house. Then the local college. Soon a private instructor from Tulsa three days every week.

The boy had a gift, the man claimed.

Glenpool spent his days pumping stripper wells around the county, Solomon always along waiting in the truck while he scaled the gratings above tank batteries. He shot fluid levels and ran flow lines, tightened gasket heads and grease certs. Later each day, with his work done, he would put away his tools and the two would set out chasing scattered coveys until twilight. Still months before season, they'd maneuver through the black oaks and mesquite draws, man and dog, Solomon pointing and Glenpool flushing. He'd raise to his shoulder a phantom shotgun, swing the barrel across with the birds, squeezing an invisible trigger. He'd watch the singles spread and alight. He'd mark their descent, their paths to re-covey, and then set off again.

Most days he told Kendon to join but Lee Ellen would object, insisting they had practice. Hunting, she said, could wait.

Glenpool told her she was sheltering him. That she'd make him—

"Make him what?"

"Nothing," he said. "You know what I mean." He nodded toward Kendon. "Cooped up in here all the time."

"He's not cooped up," Lee Ellen said. "He has a gift."

"He might have others, Lee."

"Like what?"

"Like anything," Glenpool said. "*Every*thing. How's he gonna know?"

Lee Ellen stood and walked into the kitchen. Glenpool followed, still talking behind her.

The Southern Field Trials, he said, were next month at the Roos Ranch outside Otto. A breeder had called about Solomon and said he would be there with his Brittany—a *champion,* he'd claimed—and the man wondered was Glenpool interested.

"Kendon can see the dogs," he told her. "I'm taking him."

Lee Ellen wanted to know if there would be guns.

There is no fixing a gun-shy dog, Glenpool said.

He talked to Kendon while they watched two German shorthairs and the Brittany winding through the underbrush, trailing singles. Several men followed close on foot, two more on horseback. Glenpool and Kendon were in a larger group of spectators behind.

"You take the best nose," Glenpool continued, "and he's scared? Forget it. Nothing you can do."

Even Glenpool's father—not a hunter by nature—knew this. *A disease,* he'd said. *Starts when they're puppies. They flinch, cower from the sound of a shotgun over them. Some take to running. Others hide, dig into the earth, curl under your feet if you let them. It only gets worse with age.*

He looked over to Kendon. The boy was staring blank to the horizon.

"Hey," Glenpool said. "You hear me?"

Kendon nodded. "Gun-shy," he said.

Just then the animal they'd been watching spun and froze, its head low to the ground, the tail vertical and stretched taut. The two judges stopped their horses. With the shotgun held across his chest, the breeder crept to the Brittany, bent and spoke softly to it, then he stood and looked back. One judge nodded, and the breeder stepped ahead into the ragweed. Glenpool brought Kendon to his side and dropped to a knee.

"Watch," he said, pointing. "See he's holding that gun? He'll walk there and flush the bird and kill it. That dog'll hunt dead."

"Hunt dead?" Kendon asked.

"A dead bird."

"Why hunt a dead bird?"

"To find it," Glenpool said. "A dead bird's hard to find."

Glenpool started to explain, but the shotgun fired and he rose up to see the bird tumble into the brush and the breeder start towards it. Glenpool searched for the Brittany, but she was nowhere. The judges, he noticed, were leaned in their saddles, looking beneath their horses. He looked with them and there she was. The small mass of white curled in the weeds.

He stood, took Kendon by the shoulder.

"Come on," he said, starting back through the crowd.

When they were almost to the main road he spoke.

"You see that dog?"

Kendon said he did.

"When he shot?"

The boy nodded. "Gun-shy?"

"That's right."

They turned at the section line and continued walking toward the main entrance. Several large sponsor tents were pitched there, hunting gear spread across the tables. As they approached, a series of shots came from behind the tents. There was applause and laughter. Then two more shots.

Glenpool looked at Kendon.

"You want to see?"

The boy shrugged.

When they arrived a crowd was gathered behind the Browning display. Glenpool took Kendon to the front, saw a shooting

range was set with several stationary targets along one si\
were two skeet houses on the other pointed to the open\
young boy, not much older than Kendon, stood in a chalk\
holding a shotgun across his chest. He yelled *pull* and fo\   ⸜lay
pigeons flew from the houses and the kid swung the barrel across
and fired three quick shots, then two more, but the targets floated
untouched over the weed tops. They both sank and disappeared.

There was laughter, then applause when the kid turned, smiling.
He shrugged, handed the gun to the man at the table who in turn
held it up to the crowd and asked for volunteers.

A half hour later Kendon was handing back the same shotgun.
Smoke still twisted from the barrel's end and there was again
laughter and applause from the crowd—only now they cheered
from disbelief. They slapped one another on the shoulders, on
the back, laughing and shaking their heads and challenging each
other.

They asked Glenpool how old was his son, and how long he'd
shot, but Glenpool didn't hear. He watched Kendon walk back to
him, replaying in his head what he'd witnessed.

He'd led Kendon to the shooting pad and showed how to shoulder the gun and lower his cheek to the stock. Said to look straight
down and swing the barrel ahead of his target. He showed how to
keep it moving that way—to not stop, or jerk, but squeeze the trigger and continue the swing. He showed how to breathe. To relax,
he said. Then he stepped away, studying Kendon's expression.

He'd doubted whether his son would even fire.

But the first clay flew and Kendon shouldered the stock and
hit dead center. Glenpool laughed, and he clapped along with the
other men. He clapped again on the next target. Then the next.
He kept looking at Kendon's face for something, some sign, but if
anything was there at all it was only boredom.

He'd hit ten straight when the crowd called to give someone
else a chance.

Later, in the truck, Glenpool was still marveling.

"I told your mother," he said. He reached over and mussed the boy's hair.

Kendon sat still on the passenger side, his eyes fixed to the highway.

When he finally did speak they'd been driving in silence for several miles.

"Those dogs in the backyard," he said, the sound of his voice barely audible above the engine. "They were gun-shy?"

Over the years, Glenpool had sold bird dogs he knew would not make—dogs that wouldn't hold point, wouldn't honor. A few couldn't smell road kill had he shoved their jowls in. That didn't bother him so much.

"Most people wouldn't know a good dog anyway," he explained, glancing over at his son.

Gun-shy, though? That was different.

He sold one to a trainer over in Perser—a man named Cundiff who'd claimed he could fix any dog—but only because Lee Ellen was a month pregnant, and they needed money. Still he wouldn't have done it had the old man not kept after him. As far as Glenpool was concerned, you couldn't justify such a thing.

"It's like passing a disease," he said. "But the old man said he could cure it. He insisted."

A month later Glenpool had run across Cundiff. He asked if the dog came out of it, but the old man stared back at him, blank and silent. Glenpool was about to remind him who he was when Cundiff shook his head and said it couldn't be helped.

"Told me he sold it to his cousin," Glenpool said.

He had a two-year-old Pointer by this time, and he thought she was solid. The few times he'd ran her she pointed and held, followed his commands.

"She even retrieved," Glenpool said, glancing at Kendon. "Drop a bird right on my foot. Little tender mouth."

But he left opening day for the Panhandle, the dog riding alongside in the cab, and the moment the truck stopped and Glenpool swung open the door she'd jumped out, took off across the pasture, and disappeared. An hour later she came back, ran through a covey, and took off again.

That evening he spotted her in the sunset, running wide open straight from the truck.

He'd called to her several times. Whistled until his lips went numb. Once dark set, he gave up, loaded his gear, and drove home. He went back two days later and followed the circle of buzzards to her carcass.

"I brought home and buried what was left of her," he said.

He bought two pointers after that—litter mates—from an old man in Bristow. A month later they had red mange. Then he went through three German Shorthairs in four months. The first had heart worms. The other two couldn't smell a skunk.

And that's when Lee Ellen had started in on him.

The last one before Solomon was a liver-and-white Brittany.

"She had potential," Glenpool said. But the first time she pointed, he flushed the covey and dropped three on the rise and when he turned back to find her she was at a dead sprint. He'd found her burrowed beneath a sapling in a dried-out creek bed. She was lying on her side, panting, her legs half twisted beneath her belly and her tongue out and caked with dirt.

He'd knelt beside her and talked to her. He'd stroked the animal's back and her head. And then he stood and lowered the barrel.

"I buried her beside the others and that's when your mom put the stop to it."

Kendon looked up.

"What about Solomon?"

"I had to promise to keep him," Glenpool said. "Told your mom we'd turn him into a pet."

Glenpool reached over and nudged Kendon on the shoulder.

"I had a feeling though," he said. "He was pick of the litter."

Quail season opened November 1. A cold front off the Rockies dropped the temperature below freezing, downing the Oklahoma

Panhandle in a late autumn snow—wet and heavy and slushed with the muddied soil. There were wind gusts to 30 mph. Glenpool woke Kendon at 3:30 and they headed into it.

By the time he exited Highway 54 the truck doors were frozen. He turned onto a cattle road leading into the back end of the ranch, pulled to the gate, and looked over at Kendon still asleep in the passenger side. He had to shove himself into the door several times before it finally gave and he stepped out into the frigid air, the sun not yet over the horizon. The wind hit his face and Glenpool felt his cheeks tighten, his jaws clench. He walked to the gate, unwrapped the chain, and flipped the hitch over the corner post. He tried to swing it open, but it bounced back against the hinges.

When he climbed in the cab Kendon was awake. Glenpool reached over and put his cold palm on the back of the boy's neck.

"Chilly out there," Glenpool said, laughing, but Kendon didn't move. He stared out the side window.

Glenpool shifted into four-wheel drive and started toward the gate.

"What are you doing?" Kendon asked.

"The hinges are iced," he said. Then he eased the truck forward against the iron. The ice cracked, and the gate swung wide.

He drove into the field until the road ended at the section line. He turned the truck around, put it in park, and let the engine settle a minute before he turned it off.

Kendon, silent, looked out the passenger window.

"Come on," Glenpool told him. "I bet Solomon's about to freeze."

He stepped from the cab and went to the rear of the truck, opened the top of the dog box, and pulled out his coat and wool hat and a nylon check cord. He unhitched the side door and Solomon pushed his head out and Glenpool fixed the cord to the dog's collar. Solomon shook a few times and stretched his jaws and then raised up to Glenpool's chest, howling.

Glenpool tied him to the tailgate and went back in the box for his shotgun and game bag. He fastened the straps over his shoulders, buckled across the front, and from a side pocket pulled five shells and fed them one after another into the weapon's magazine. Then he jacked one into the chamber.

He untied Solomon, walked around to the passenger side, and opened the door.

"Get your stuff," he said. "C'mon."

Kendon slid from the seat onto the ground, turned, and reached in the floorboard for the backpack. He shouldered it to one side, struggling with the weight. Glenpool stepped over and helped with the other strap. When he did, he felt the boy already shivering. He closed the truck door, locked the cab and the two set off.

When they reached the fence at the section line, Glenpool rested the shotgun against a post, knelt beside Solomon, and untied the cord. The dog hurried under the barbed wire and set into the pasture.

He was about to show Kendon how Solomon held his tail when the dog whipped around and froze.

"Did you see that?" Glenpool yelled, at the fence with both hands. "Already on point."

He gripped the top two wires and forced the bottom ones with his foot, showing Kendon to duck through. The boy came forward, bent, and then he stumbled and fell through, catching a sleeve on one of the barbs. Clumps of goose down tore free into the wind. Kendon looked at the sleeve for a moment and then pulled a handful of the material and sifted it through his fingers.

"Quit that," Glenpool said. "You'll ruin it."

He stepped up on the second wire, grabbed hold of the post, and swung over one leg and then the other and stood down. He reached back over the fence and grabbed the shotgun.

"Come on," he said, nudging his son ahead. "Your first covey rise."

When they caught up with Solomon, Glenpool went to a knee and pulled Kendon beside him.

"Tell him 'good boy,'" he said. "He did good."

Kendon leaned forward, his arm and hand shivering from the cold, and when he touched Solomon's back, the dog lunged forward into the brush and the ground exploded with quail. Glenpool rose, clicked off the safety, and fired three times to the right, killing as many birds, then swung to the left and emptied the chamber and two more fell.

When the smoke cleared Solomon was already headed toward them with two dead birds in his mouth. He dropped them at Glenpool's feet and took off again to retrieve the rest. Glenpool looked back and saw Kendon had stepped several feet away. His hands were deep in his pockets. His whole body shook.

"Did you see him? Look."

Kendon nodded. He stood silent in the cold.

The remainder of the morning was the same. Glenpool and Solomon out ahead, the boy farther behind. Glenpool kept trying to bring Kendon out front, show him the dog hunting. How he worked the wind for scent, trailed the birds, held point until they arrived, and retrieved.

"You won't see a better one," Glenpool said.

He'd asked Kendon several times if he wanted to shoot. He placed the gun in the boy's hands, but Kendon declined. He said the recital was coming up, plus his mother.

"Your mother isn't here," said Glenpool. He reminded Kendon of his gift, and again handed over the gun.

Kendon shrugged and took the weapon. He walked with Glenpool to Solomon on point. When the covey flushed, Kendon shouldered the stock, fired twice, and two birds fell.

Glenpool laughed out loud.

By late afternoon, nearly dusk, they'd pushed nine coveys and Solomon was winding another. Glenpool pointed to the dog, turned, but Kendon had stopped far back of him. He was kneeling, fixed to something on the grain stalks. "Bugs," Glenpool said to himself. "Back there looking at bugs."

He cupped his hands around his mouth and yelled to Kendon to come on, it was getting late.

When they arrived at the section line Glenpool called Solomon over and retied the check cord to his collar. Kendon walked up and Glenpool handed it to him.

"Here," he said, "hold your dog," and he stepped to the fence.

He heard Solomon bark one time and he turned back just as the end of the check cord disappeared into the weeds.

His dog was not on point. He wasn't anywhere Glenpool could see. He started calling. Whistling. They walked all the way to the section line with dark settling. The temperature dropped, and the wind picked up. It was so loud Glenpool stopped hearing his own voice, his whistles. He looked down at Kendon, quiet and shivering worse than before. He thought he should take him to the truck, but it would be dark when he returned, and impossible to find the dog if it was in trouble. He snatched Kendon off the ground, hauled him onto his back and headed into the pasture.

After several minutes—Glenpool yelling, whistling—Kendon spoke.

"Stop," the boy said. "Listen."

Glenpool heard a faint cry. Then a yelp. Solomon howling. The wind picked up the sound and shifted it around them. He made his best guess and took off.

One hundred yards downfield, near to the next section, Glenpool nearly fell into it. He stumbled, caught himself with the gun stock and barely kept from pitching Kendon over his back and down the enormous hole now at his feet.

An old grain silo, grown to a sinkhole several yards across. No telling how far down. Glenpool's stomach turned when he heard Solomon cry from the bottom. He lowered Kendon to the ground, reached into the boy's backpack, pulled out the flashlight, and pointed it into the hole. The beam disappeared halfway.

"Stay here," he said. He knelt and gripped the boy's shoulders. "Do not move from this spot."

Kendon nodded. Glenpool laid the shotgun beside the hole and ran through the field, up the pasture at the top end. He jumped the fence, went to the truck and from the dog box grabbed all the rope he could carry.

When he got back to Kendon it was fully dark and he was breathing so hard he couldn't tie the rope. His hands were freezing. They were swelling and shaking. He could feel the perspiration down his legs and into his boots. He went to a knee, shined the light over the edge, and there was his dog, the hind legs broken and twisted beneath him. Solomon lifted his head and tried to bark.

Glenpool formed a lasso with the end of the rope. He tied the end of the first length to the next and began feeding it into the hole.

Kendon was standing beside, staring down into darkness.

"What are you doing?" the boy asked.

"I'm gonna pull him out."

Until he said it, Glenpool hadn't thought about a lasso—how he'd fit it over the head. He kept feeding the rope farther into the hole, trying to figure, when it reached, what he might do.

At the bottom, he tried to swing the loop over. But when he did, Solomon raised onto his forelegs and stuck his head through the opening.

"I'll be damned," Glenpool said.

He pulled the slack tight. Then he wound the rope on one hand and half-hitched it over his wrist. He dug his feet solid and started pulling.

It was much farther than he thought. Solomon wasn't halfway up the shaft before the rope was choking so bad Glenpool had to stop and let it back to the bottom. The dog yelped, howled when his broken legs hit. The sound echoed to the surface.

Glenpool shivered, caught his breath, and looked over at Kendon. The boy was quiet, staring into the hole. Glenpool thought for a moment, then stood and took the rope hand over hand and pulled as hard as he could. Again, halfway to the surface the dog began to choke, but Glenpool kept on. He turned a loop over the other hand for more leverage—bending, reaching for more while he heaved—but as much rope began to slip each time he pulled. Then more.

The dog moving in inches. Up. Then back down. Up again and back.

Glenpool braced for a moment and peered over the edge, saw

the dog suspended there, turning at the end of its tether in the middle of the shaft. He figured he choked it to death, and nearly dropped it right then, but when he started to feed the rope Solomon jerked, his front paws clawing at the cinch. Glenpool let the rope all the way down and the animal dropped to the bottom.

There was another scream up through the dark.

"What are you doing?" Kendon asked.

Glenpool bent again and gripped the rope tight as he could.

Halfway up, Solomon stopped jerking. First the hind legs went lax, then the paws, still clawing the open air, began to slow. The front legs stretched out for a moment, and then nothing. All dangling limbs.

Glenpool kept hauling. Hand over hand. Reach and pull. His fingers throbbed now, his forearms and shoulders. Despite the cold, he was heavy with sweat.

When he finally saw the head, Solomon's eyes were glassed over and pressured from the sockets. The dried tongue hung from the side of his mouth.

Glenpool kept reaching. He was pulling faster now. He was breathing so hard he thought he'd pass out. A foot at a time. And then two. His fingers went numb, but he kept moving his hands, the dog's body creeping up the shaft.

Several more feet and Solomon's head was to the surface. With one hand Glenpool secured the rope, caught the collar with the other, and falling backward, hauled him out and onto his lap. Solomon lay limp, motionless across his legs.

"Okay," Glenpool said, shaking the dog's jowls. He loosened the rope around its neck.

Solomon's eyes were closed. He wasn't breathing. Glenpool began rubbing over the head, up and down the animal's back and sides. He turned it over and with a fist lightly hit on the chest. He looked around for something, he didn't know what, then he turned back and hit harder. Much harder, until he was pounding the sternum. Until he heard something crack.

Then Solomon moved. He coughed, breathed, or something.

Glenpool leaned down and listened. He pried open the jaws.

"I hear it," he said, then he stood and stepped back to watch the dog's chest. He laid flat to the ground to see if it moved. He crawled over again, put his ear to the animal's nose. Back to the sternum.

He'd sat up, and he was about to bring his fists down again when the flash of light blinded him.

Glenpool went back to his haunches. His ears were ringing. There was the smell of gun powder, that hot blueing. He blinked several times, shook his head, and looked up through the smoke and Kendon was standing over the dog with the shotgun still braced against his shoulder.

In silence Glenpool watched the boy cradle the weapon in one arm, kneel beside Solomon, and grab the rope. He looked briefly, and then he began dragging.

Next to the sinkhole his son stepped over the dog and with one foot nudged the carcass to the edge. The rope whistled across the surface. The frayed end of it twisted and snapped, chasing the animal's body down into earth.

Born and raised in rural Oklahoma, Clinton J. Stewart grew up hunting and fishing with his father. After completing an MA in English at the University of North Carolina at Charlotte, he returned to his native state. He now resides in Oklahoma City and works for Chickasaw Nation Industries (he is Chickasaw Indian and a Citizen of the Chickasaw Nation). When he's not working, he hunts and fishes with his father. He is at work on a collection of stories as well as a novel  about coyote hunting in Kansas, and is eagerly awaiting a new Brittany pup this spring. "Bird Dog" is his first published story.

*T*he idea for "Bird Dog" came from a story my father told me about rescuing (successfully) a bird dog from an underground grain silo on a freezing night in the middle of pheasant season in northern Nebraska. He did virtually everything Glenpool does in the final scene, minus the son, the desperate attempt at animal CPR, and the dead dog.

My father is a master storyteller of the oldest order, and a master hunter of the only order, so when he told this story, and described the scene—the old windmill creaking in the wind, the corn stalks crashing, the faint whine of that dog from thirty feet below the surface—I knew it had to go into something. So I spent a while, sat down with the scene (I was in a graduate school fiction class under the tutelage of Dr. Aaron Gwyn), and drummed up a story around it. Which means, for me, I searched for a conflict. I found it in the tension between a father (not wholly unlike my own) and a son (very different from me). The rest is details. I found a conflict, which is to say I found what the story was about, and I had a scene I was working toward that would, in its resolution, deliver what I wanted the story to say about what it was about, so to speak.

For language, tone, voice, or style, there's never been much choosing for me, and there certainly wasn't here. There's no artifice when my father tells a story. The language disappears, lyricism (minimal) serves its master—the details of the land itself, the scene, and demonstrable action. I'm standing with him over a point, walking with him down into a plum thicket in western Oklahoma, shooting with him on a covey rise. I cling to that essential power of story, and traditional storytelling. It's what I know, it's how I've learned everything about hunting—and everything about life, my heritage, myself—and I try to practice it every time I tell a story. I hope that's what "Bird Dog" became.

HORSE PEOPLE

(from *Ecotone*)

Barrett Fenton believed his father really did love all his sons the same, Barrett and his six brothers. By October 1927, the oldest, John, was eighteen, and the youngest, Dudley, was two and a half. Barrett was next to last, almost eight. One Sunday, when church and dinner were over, Barrett was on the porch when his father started for the stable. His father said, "Want to go riding with me?"

Barrett knew he was just lucky, being out on the porch at the right time. They were going to fetch a cook, his father said.

But they already had a cook. "What about Nehemiah?" Barrett asked.

"Time for Nehemiah to go on home," Barrett's father said. "Retire."

Barrett could hardly imagine the kitchen without Nehemiah stoking the coal stove and the woodstove, snacking on biscuit dough, and sharpening knives. Nehemiah was old, but he still seemed fine. "Why is it time?" Barrett said. "Is he going to die?"

"My guess is, Nehemiah'll be around a good many years, but your mother wants to hire somebody younger." They would continue to pay Nehemiah every month, his father said, same as if he still worked for them. But they were going to hire Philip, a son from a different family, to be their new cook. Philip's father was sick, Barrett learned, and his own father had asked the doctor to go see him.

Barrett knew that his father, Richard Fenton, was an important man, a judge for the Orange County Juvenile and Domestic Court. People sometimes came to the house to seek his help outside of court. They might want a divorce or be worried about a wayward son. Barrett's father would sit with them on the porch, talking, and they'd leave with a lighter step. They'd tell Barrett, "Your father's a good man, a fair man."

His mother was not as fair. She had favorites among the boys, usually Alex and Miles, the second and fifth ones. These days it was Dudley, the youngest, because he was sick with scarlet fever. At the moment, Barrett knew, his mother was writing letters. She spent a great deal of time on correspondence with relatives, friends, and business associates. Aunt Iris, his father's sister, who also lived with them, was reading to the other boys. Barrett was supposed to be with them. He was on the porch only because he'd left a book there.

"I've spoken to your mother already," his father said, "and Iris."

Barrett set his book on the porch swing, and off they went.

It would be the first time Barrett had ridden since getting over scarlet fever himself. His father would ride Hurricane, a charcoal mare. Barrett had taken a long time to name his pony. It seemed to him that the best names were already taken by his mother's horses—Card Party, Florian, Arrow, and She Will. At last, he'd settled on Skedaddle, a word his father liked to say.

"Blood from the sire, beauty from the dam," Barrett's mother often said. Racing and horses were what she loved. Barrett knew his father didn't feel the same way, though Hurricane was a great favorite of his. He'd tell Barrett's mother to watch out for horse people. Barrett didn't understand: Weren't his mother and father horse people, too? They were foxhunters. They were on the board of directors of the county horse show. His mother, Nelle Scott Fenton, didn't trust people anyway, only horses and dogs. *Pride of Virginia,* her stationery said, with dark red letters and a design of a horse jumping a fence, and though Barrett knew *Pride of Virginia* meant the horses, he always thought of his mother's straight-backed posture. She was a Yankee and proud of it, daughter of a Philadelphia lawyer.

Barrett's father saddled up Hurricane and had Stanton, the stable boy, saddle Skedaddle, and Barrett and his father took off for the back pasture.

It was a blue-skied day, warm for October, "beauteous," Barrett's father said, leaning his head back and letting Hurricane carry him along the grass road within the pasture, a riding trail.

Usually, on weekends, Barrett's oldest brothers—John, Alex, and Gordon—were home from college or boarding school. They'd go hunting. It was a fine thing on a fall day, to know his brothers would be coming back to the house at suppertime with rabbits or quail they'd shot. Because Barrett had been sick, and Dudley still was, the older ones had to stay at school. Barrett had heard his mother on the telephone, her voice stern, which meant she was almost crying.

Very briefly—and not within Barrett's memory—Barrett had a different younger brother, a child born between him and Dudley, "a beautiful baby who died in his crib," his father told him once. "Don't ask your mother about him," his father warned. Barrett wished he could remember that baby.

Barrett rode beside his father. Above them, buzzards wheeled so slowly, Barrett realized how patient they were, as if they weren't hungry for whatever dead critter they were eyeing on the ground. Patience was something his Aunt Iris talked about, and the preacher, too, yet Barrett didn't think they meant the buzzards' kind of patience. Barrett's stomach clenched at the sight of them. He worried about his mother, worried she would fall from her horse when she was away from home, and that only buzzards would find her. Daily she rode, usually by herself.

"Beauteous," Barrett's father said again, and if Barrett hadn't known differently, he'd have thought his father was a happy man. There was somebody named Ben Burleigh who was causing bad feelings between Barrett's parents. Barrett didn't know exactly what was happening. The unhappy feeling, though, was a fact, like the buzzards, something sinister that was close and distant at the same time. Ben Burleigh was a horse person, too. Sometimes, when Barrett did his lessons with his Aunt Iris, he would realize that his mother was not at home, and he knew, somehow, that she'd gone to see that man. "Your mother's friend, Ben Burleigh," Aunt Iris dared to say once, darting a look at Barrett. Much as Barrett loved his Aunt Iris, he thought she shouldn't have said that to him. The comment felt like a poke in the eye.

The sun was getting hot. Barrett and his father stopped at a creek for the horses to drink. After a while, making their way up a hillside, they reached a barn Barrett had seen only a few times before. It was old, with boards spaced widely so that light came through the walls. The barn's open bay allowed horses to shelter in its central aisle.

Along with the thoroughbreds that Barrett's mother and father raised, a special horse lived in the surrounding field, a red horse with a coal black mane. Ben Burleigh had given the animal to Barrett's mother. The horse appeared now, as if he knew Barrett had been thinking about him. He whipped along the crest of the hill, and when he was close to where Barrett and his father sat on their horses, he kicked up his heels and raced away. Hurricane jerked at her bridle. Barrett's father said a quiet word to her.

The red horse never let other horses get near him, Barrett noticed, never formed friendships the way the others did, grazing together or just standing side by side. He was the most beautiful animal Barrett had ever seen. Barrett's father never mentioned him. Barrett could almost believe, around his father, that the dancing, fiery figure was something Barrett's mother had only imagined.

His father led the way into the barn. Even in the dimness, Barrett saw hoof prints in the packed red clay that was the floor. How fine it must be to take cover there in the dark or during a storm. His father unlatched a door at the rear of the barn, and they rode through it into a brushy field. No horses lived back there.

Barrett recalled the purpose of their trip. Soon, Nehemiah would leave, and a new person would be there instead. He didn't think Nehemiah would miss them. Around Barrett's mother, Nehemiah spoke softly, but his jaw was tight. For Barrett's father, he had a quick smile but kept his eyes cast down. Nehemiah's ancestors, who'd been slaves, were buried along the fences in the field, Barrett's father said. That was the old way, he said, pointing to the rail fences. The ground was soft underneath, easy to dig.

They reached a wall made of rocks, with a gate in the middle, and passed through it. "This is where we leave our land," Barrett's father said. They entered deep woods. All around them, bugs made a glistening sound. The black walnut trees were already bare; they lost their leaves first. Other trees were still green, or just turning. There was a tall tulip poplar, Barrett's favorite kind. He loved persimmons, too, with their sweet fruit on the ground like a picnic.

Barrett was worn out. Scarlet fever had kept him in bed for days and made the grown-ups ban his brothers from his room, but Dudley caught it anyway and was even sicker than Barrett had been. The doctor came every day to see Dudley. The doctor still asked Barrett how he felt, holding his stethoscope against Barrett's chest and telling him to eat eggs and go to bed early.

A cabin came into view, a welcome sight.

And what was that happy sound, like a party? The cabin door swung open, and people spilled out of it, a big colored family with several children, greeting Barrett's father.

An old woman said, "Mr. Fenton, that boy . . ." And she doubled over, laughing.

"Philip got a pet chicken, named Emmy," a younger woman explained.

A girl about Barrett's age said, "We put the chicken down the chimney, to clean it." She made flapping motions with her arms.

"Well, let's take a look," Barrett's father said, swinging out of the saddle and holding out a hand to help Barrett climb down from Skedaddle. For a second, Barrett's legs buckled, but his father didn't seem to notice. He said, "Meet my next to youngest—Barrett."

The family said Barrett favored his father, and Barrett was pleased. The girl and the two women led them into the cabin.

In the middle of the floor sat a boy clutching a grimy white hen. Feathers littered the hearth. The cabin had some plain furniture, Barrett saw, and windows, though some of the panes were cracked. Barrett smelled something savory. The old woman offered fried squirrel to him and his father. Barrett ate a piece: delicious. They offered coffee, too, but it was so bitter that Barrett couldn't drink it. One of the children brought a dipper of water. Barrett did drink that.

The laughter had died down like leaves settling on the ground after a breeze. The boy bent his head over his crossed arms as if protecting the chicken. Barrett saw that the boy was older than he had thought at first, almost a man.

"Philip didn't like what we did," the old woman said, "using Emmy that way."

Philip, the young man, raised his head, a grin flickering over his lips. "She did right well," he said.

Barrett's father looked around and asked, "How is Robert? Did the doctor visit him?"

"Here he is," the old woman said, gesturing to a pile of bedding in a corner. Barrett realized that the old woman was probably Robert's mother, and Philip was Robert's son.

The other woman spoke up. Barrett guessed she was Robert's wife and Philip's mother. "He was bit by a spider, the bad kind," she said. "That's what the doctor said."

Barrett's father made his way to the corner. The women lifted the covers from the man's legs. Barrett glimpsed a bare, bloated knee with a crater-like sore in the middle. A scary, rotten smell reached Barrett's nose.

"Robert, can you stand up? Can you walk?" Barrett's father asked.

"No," the man said, his voice hoarse, his pupils glittering, and Barrett remembered how hot and dry his own eyes had felt when he was sick.

"Did the doctor leave this?" Barrett's father said, picking up a jar of medicine.

"It don't seem to help," said Robert.

Barrett's father said to Robert's wife, "Put him in the wagon tomorrow morning and bring him to the road. I'll be waiting in the car, about eight o'clock. I'll take him to the hospital."

She nodded.

Robert said, "Philip goes back with y'all, Mr. Fenton. He knows that."

"Philip, does that sound all right to you?" Barrett's father asked.

Philip agreed. His mother ran outside and tore something off a clothesline: his other shirt, she said. Philip kept the white chicken in his arms, and Barrett realized the chicken would go with them. Philip's grandmother tied up the chicken's feet with string. "So Emmy can't fly away," she said. Barrett's father put Barrett on Hurricane with him, and Philip rode Skedaddle, holding the chicken in one arm. His long legs almost trailed the ground. The younger children followed at a distance through the woods. Barrett kept looking back until they were gone.

Nehemiah trained Philip for a few days at the Fenton household, and then Nehemiah was gone. Philip was born to cook, Barrett's mother declared. He learned how to fix roasts, game, vegetables, and sweets. Breads too, batter bread and rolls. Barrett's mother had cookbooks, and Nehemiah used to look up recipes, but Philip couldn't read, Barrett realized.

The stable boy, Stanton, had the room above the stable, so Philip slept in the tack room, on a cot. The stable had an oil stove, a flush toilet, and a sink with a single tap for cold water. Philip would let himself into the house through the back porch early every morning. Every night, he let himself out and made his way back to the stable. Barrett sometimes heard the soft sweep of the door. Philip had every other weekend off, and he would go home to his family. Barrett pictured him walking through the woods. It had taken a long time to reach the cabin on horseback. How long would it take to walk?

Philip never married. There was a man who visited him, a black man older than he was, who would come over in a mule-drawn cart, and he and Philip would go off together in the part of the afternoon when Barrett's mother was napping or riding. Barrett's brothers said bad words about Philip and his friend, and Barrett said them, too, trying out the words. There were questions Barrett wanted to ask, but he didn't know how to ask them. Philip and his visitor went clattering off in the cart, and where they went and what they did were mysteries to Barrett, despite his brothers' jokes. When Philip returned, he never looked or acted any different. He'd be humming as he washed dishes.

Philip stayed slim. His face had a reddish tint, like Nehemiah's. Barrett would have sworn Philip was Nehemiah's grandson, but his father said no, they were from different families. Barrett admired the way his father could keep entire Orange County genealogies in his head. He knew the names and the kinships from all the years people came up onto his porch and asked for advice. He loved them, Barrett realized, as if having seven sons only made it easier for him to love the people of the entire county.

Barrett and his brothers grew up and went to war, all seven, deployed to the Pacific or to Europe. Even the oldest brothers went. John, at thirty-two, was divorced and had no children, and Alex, age thirty, was married and had a son born while he was overseas. They kept in touch through letters and the prized occasional visit home. Barrett saved the letters his parents wrote during his tour, letters about sausage-making and new foals. Aunt Iris wrote, too. Barrett's father had suffered a heart attack, Aunt Iris said, and the doctor insisted he had to rest. Philip helped him up and down the steps. A photograph Aunt Iris sent surprised Barrett: A tired old farm couple, his mother and father, squinted into the sun, their shoulders sagging. Where were the vigorous, dashing parents of his childhood? On the deck of his merchant marine ship, in the brilliant oceanic light, Barrett held the picture close. Nearsightedness and flat feet had ended his time in the army, but he liked the merchant marines better, because he traveled more. He bought a small portable motorcycle, and during shore leave in Italy, Belgium, and Poland, he explored the cities and the countryside, often with some pretty local girl along to guide him.

With great good fortune, Barrett and all of his brothers survived the war. Barrett had been home for only two weeks when his father had a second heart attack, which killed him. And then it seemed to Barrett that although his own life picked up its pace, his mother's life and Philip's continued almost unchanged. Philip worked for Barrett's mother during her long widowhood, fixing three meals a day and party food when she wanted to entertain. Barrett and his brothers, married now, with careers—Barrett was a civil engineer—gave Philip extra money when they were home. They were afraid their mother wasn't keeping up with his pay. Barrett's Aunt Iris died, and Barrett had the feeling that his mother didn't miss her, though Philip did. His face looked heavy and sorrowful, and suddenly his hair was gray.

Whenever Barrett's brothers' wives tried to chat with Philip, he was pleasant with them. He knew which one was married to which son, and which children belonged to whom. But he wasn't much for conversation, as Barrett explained to his wife, Patsy. Patsy was shy and gentle, the daughter of a Richmond doctor who had died about the same time Barrett's own father had. Barrett was glad Patsy didn't badger Philip the way the louder, wilder wives did, teasing him and drinking whiskey in the kitchen. Barrett sensed Philip would have preferred to be left alone to do his work, and imagined he was grateful to Patsy for the respectful distance she kept. Besides, Patsy didn't enjoy the other wives very much. "Showoffs," she complained to Barrett. "There's a lot of one-upmanship. Women are worse than men, that way."

For decades, Philip appeared in holiday photographs, wearing a white jacket, serving at the dining room table. Barrett was the first Fenton to get a Polaroid camera. It pleased him that his brothers got so excited, wanting Polaroids too. He told Patsy, "It's the only thing I've ever had that they didn't."

"And me," Patsy said.

"And you," said Barrett.

Finally, Barrett's mother, nearing ninety, pensioned Philip off like she'd done with Nehemiah. "He cried," she told Barrett on the phone. "He didn't want to go home." Barrett and Patsy were living up North by then, in Pennsylvania, with three daughters. His mother was scared of somebody dying at her house, she admitted, afraid of authorities coming. It was one of the few fears Barrett ever knew her to have.

"He went on home," she said, and Barrett pictured the cabin, deep in the woods. The darkness and remoteness came back to him. What condition was it in, he wondered, and what had become of Philip's family? Was the cabin deserted, with branches poking through the windows, or was it shipshape, with somebody baking bread inside to welcome Philip home?

"I think it's a mistake to let him go, Mother," Barrett said. "It's not too late to change your mind. Ask him to come back"

His mother grew angry and hung up the phone. She hated to be contradicted. She was never easy to get along with, Barrett fumed to Patsy, and was only getting worse with age.

Barrett had trouble remembering the names of the cooks and companions that followed. None stayed for long. Philip didn't live more than a year or two after he retired. The news traveled the circuit of Barrett and his brothers. Barrett felt his mother's own time was coming to an end. His brothers and their wives talked about it, asking, How long can she go on?

She died in August 1976, at ninety-three.

One of the seven sons, Gordon, had died in '58, at forty-four, but he'd lived hard, drinking and gambling. Their mother willed her property equally to the others. Barrett borrowed money and bought out his brothers' portions. It was what he wanted more than anything: to own the family home and live there again, though he would have to work hard to pay it off. He knew he could do it. His three daughters were grown and living elsewhere.

Patsy objected. She didn't want so much debt or such a big house. She wanted nothing to do with farming. They quarreled sharply, and Barrett felt their marriage wobbling toward divorce. At last, Patsy relented, but she extracted from him two promises: They would not raise horses, and they, or at least she, "wouldn't have to go to funerals all the time."

Barrett was surprised she didn't make more demands. He agreed readily to her terms. His boyhood friends were starting to die, and funerals always upset him, to the point where he could have cried at a stranger's. He would go to those that mattered most, but he'd go alone. As for horses—he'd never felt about them the way his mother had, so he suggested to Patsy that they rent out the stable and pastures, and the horses that lived there would belong to other people. That was fine with Patsy, and they packed their belongings in the Pennsylvania house and moved.

Barrett easily found horse people to rent the barn and the fields, and Patsy would occasionally stroll out to chat while they saddled up. But when Barrett suggested they invite their tenants in for coffee, she said, "The four-legged ones would be okay, but not the two-legged ones."

Barrett laughed, though he sometimes wished Patsy were more sociable. He had told her how his father warned his mother about horse people, and she repeated the admonition so often that for Barrett it wore a little thin. Through the family grapevine, she'd learned of the affair between his mother and Ben Burleigh. "With all those children," she marveled, "how did she have time?" Barrett would say, "Aw, it was so long ago." Patsy mused, "How much was physical, do you think? Or was it more of an emotional involvement?" And Barrett would change the subject. Didn't she understand it was hurtful, even now?

When Barrett's brothers brought their wives back to the old place, Patsy served simple meals and adeptly discouraged overnight visits. Barrett's brothers lived out their span of days, and some grew old and older still. Barrett outlived them all. He was the last one.

Halfway home, that October day in 1927, Philip's chicken, Emmy, broke free from his grasp. She shook the binding from her feet and flew up toward a pine tree. Philip called after her, lunging from the saddle. As the white hen settled in the pine, with the sun streaming behind her, Barrett realized it was late in the day. In the woods around Philip's cabin, it might already be dark.

"Well, look at that," Barrett's father said. He took off his hat and waved it toward Emmy's perch, but the chicken stayed where she was.

Philip slid off the pony and ran toward the tree. He angled his thin body into the limbs, but he fell, tearing his pant leg, and his face showed fear. Barrett felt suddenly as if he and his father had kidnapped Philip. What he was seeing was homesickness and sorrow. Emmy was still in sight, but it would be hard to get her back.

Barrett's father dismounted, went to the base of the tree, and called, "Birdy, birdy, come on down here."

"I'll get her," Barrett said and eased his legs over the saddle. Seventeen hands high, Hurricane was. Barrett fell, knocking the wind out of his lungs, but he stood up again. The tree was so tall that he thought of Jack and the beanstalk in the story his Aunt Iris had read to him.

This was Barrett's beanstalk. Up and up he climbed. Sap stuck to his hands. He was hungry and thirsty. At home, his mother and brothers and Aunt Iris might have eaten supper long ago. Above him, the chicken was a rustling white blur. Despite being tired, Barrett knew he was well again, that the doctor was satisfied when he listened to his heart. Barrett's thoughts moved back and forth. A spider bite could lame a man, even kill him. How could he have forgotten about Philip's father, the man in the corner, for even a little while? What if his father forgot about the man?

No, his father would be waiting on the road in the morning as he'd promised. Yet maybe that was too long to wait.

The chicken sailed out of the tree.

She flew higher than Barrett knew a chicken could go, to the very top of the pine, where she disappeared. Barrett balanced himself and looked down. It was the highest he'd ever been. His father looked up, and their eyes met. His father's face was serious and attentive, the way it was when he sat on the porch with people who were troubled about legal matters. Most other men would be laughing about Philip and Emmy, laughing so hard their shoulders would shake. Other men would tell the story at the table and laugh all over again, but not his father.

Barrett himself would tell this story, he thought, though he didn't know what words he would use. And who would listen? Dudley would, and Aunt Iris. And Barrett felt there were future people he would tell, people waiting for him when he was grown.

For an instant, while his father's gray eyes held his, Barrett saw right through his father's life. His father must be feeling old. He was in his middle fifties, yet he had been a boy once, bareheaded and free. You were young for a while, Barrett saw, and then, if you lived, youth was gone. He had a chill, and he couldn't tell if it was a last wave of sickness or something else. One day his father would be gone, and his mother, and his brothers.

Philip kept his hand over his mouth, staring up at the tree. At last, he sobbed. The sound carried on the still, chilly air.

"Come on down, Barrett," his father said. Barrett did, and they got back on the horses.

"I'll come back and look for her," Barrett told Philip.

He did. For days after that, Barrett and his brothers packed their pockets with dried corn, took Philip with them, and hiked back into the field. There was never any sign of Emmy.

Late in life, when Barrett was so old that people saw him as a person from another time, he lived alone in the house where he'd grown up. Patsy had died, and their daughters and grandchildren lived in other places. Still there were beauteous days, with warm afternoons and nights as crisp as apples. Barrett loved coming back to his wide porch after a game of golf, a meeting of his grief support group, or a date with a girlfriend. He gave parties, and afterward he loved the silence. It held so much. No brothers hunted in the fields, no Fentons other than himself clambered up the steps, but the stillness was cheerful. He had a long run of good days, good years, doing things just the way he wanted to.

One Thanksgiving, when his daughters visited with their families, the memory of that day in 1927 came back to him. His daughters had known Philip as their grandmother's cook, when they were children. Barrett began, "My father took me with him when he went to get Philip. That family lived way far back in the woods."

He paused, and his oldest daughter said sharply, "Daddy, you're too thin. Here, have some more cake."

"I don't want any more," he said, but she pushed another slice onto his plate.

The middle girl, the fidgety one, bit her lip, but she was paying attention. Of the three, she was the most likely to ask him about his early life, and to listen. The youngest one's phone rang, and she glided away. Outside, Barrett's grandsons shouted, throwing a Frisbee.

Barrett's train of thought deserted him. "It's getting hard for me to hang a story together," he said, lifting his hands as if trying to pack the story between them, feeling how impossible it was to tell the truth of an event, to know the truth of another person's life. His mother's, for instance: She was a mystery, yet the older Barrett grew, the more his father seemed a mystery, too, putting up with Ben Burleigh and being dignified about it. Why hadn't he sought a divorce? Maybe he thought it would be too painful for his sons.

And what had happened to the red horse with the black mane? Plain as day, Barrett saw his mother struggling to mount the animal. The horse propped, sticking out his front legs and lowering his head, so she slid right down his neck. That enraged her. Was he sold? Was he buried in the red clay somewhere on these hundred acres? And Ben Burleigh: He had fallen off his horse during a hunt, dead. Barrett's mother, a widow by then, grieved so hard she took to her bed.

Barrett's daughters cleared the table. Barrett went into the living room and sat in his favorite chair, feeling tired, the meal he'd eaten settling heavily in his stomach. A grandson burst into the room waving a skinned palm. Then they gathered around Barrett again, daughters, sons-in-law, grandchildren.

The middle daughter said, "Daddy, finish telling about Philip."

Barrett took a breath and found that it was there after all, in his mind: the taste of fried squirrel, the big family, and, in a corner of the cabin, Philip's father, Robert, so desperately sick.

Barrett said, "Philip's father wanted him to have the job," and then he was silent. His daughters exchanged glances: He saw that. The long ride to the cabin and back, on the horses—he wanted to describe that journey, but he found himself leaping ahead. "When we got back, Dudley ran out to meet us. He'd been sick with that bad thing." *Scarlet fever* was on the tip of his tongue. "He was a whole lot better," he said, "almost well again."

His daughters nodded. Dudley, their favorite uncle, had died the previous year.

"Father picked Dudley up," Barrett said, "and swung him around, just laughing."

His father's laughter was a deep, wonderful *ho-ho!* He could remember his mother saying, "See, the roses are back in his cheeks," and hugging Dudley. She hugged Barrett too, and he thought, *it'll be all right now.* He hoped the hug meant Ben Burleigh would go away. Nehemiah brought out a cold supper for Barrett and his father. Then Nehemiah took Philip back into the kitchen and fed him, too. By then, it was dark outside, and the house felt warm and safe.

Amazing, to reach back eighty years and find all that. His parents' happiness had delighted him that day; he felt it all over again. But back at the cabin, back at the cabin: Something tugged at Barrett.

"And then what, Daddy?" asked the youngest daughter, tucking her phone into her pocket. Barrett felt the sadness on his face before he knew the reason for it. His daughter asked, "Did something bad happen?"

"His father," he said.

"Whose father?" rattled his oldest daughter, and Barrett shook his head, searching through her impatience to find quiet again.

"Philip's father," the middle daughter murmured. "Just let him talk at his own pace."

Yes: It was Philip's father, Robert, who filled Barrett's mind. Barrett was struck with concern, a useless emotion now that so much time had passed. Hadn't he thought even once of Robert in all these years? He felt as worried as if Robert were still waiting in that cabin with his ruined leg and bright, dry eyes.

Barrett's daughters gazed at him expectantly. He wanted to finish the story, but he didn't know if he could.

There'd been talk of the hospital, of poisonous spiders, of the fact that lying on a cold floor wouldn't help a man get better. Barrett remembered that. But he couldn't remember if Philip's father had lived or died.

Cary Holladay is the author of five volumes of fiction, most recently *A Fight in the Doctor's Office.* She has received fellowships from the National Endowment for the Arts and the Tennessee Arts Commission and an O. Henry Prize. A native of Virginia, she frequently uses history in her stories. With her husband, poet and fiction writer John Bensko, she teaches at the University of Memphis.

JOHN BENSKO

*T**his story is based on an experience that my father told me about. When he was very young, his own father took him to fetch a cook for the family. They went on horseback deep into the woods of Orange County, Virginia, in the 1920s.*

Over and over, I imagined what that day might have been like for my father, his father, and the man who was hired. At first, the story seemed straightforward, but the more I worked on it, the more the complexities of race relations, family dynamics, and memory demanded my attention. I also put into the story a lot of things I love about that part of Virginia, such as black walnut trees.

My father died a couple of years ago. His own father and the cook had been dead for many years. Ben George, editor of Ecotone, *where this story first appeared, pointed out, "It's the stories that survive."*

Wendell Berry

FLY AWAY, BREATH

(from *The Threepenny Review*)

A ndy Catlett keeps in his mind a map of the country around Port William as he has known it all his life and as he has been told about it all his life from times and lives before his. There are moments, now that he is getting old, when he seems to reside in that country in his mind even as his mind still resides in the country.

This country mapped in his mind cannot be presumed to be the actual country, which nobody ever will fully know; it is the country of his own life and history, fragmentary as they necessarily have been; it is his known country. And perhaps it differs also from the actual, momentary country insofar as time is one of its dimensions, as reckonable in thought as length and breadth, as air and light. His thought can travel like a breeze over water back and forth upon the face of it, and also back and forth in time along its streams and roads.

As in thought he passes backward into time, the country becomes quieter, and it seems to grow larger. The sounds of engines become less frequent and farther apart until finally they cease altogether. As the roads get poorer or disappear, the distances between places seem to grow longer. Distances that he can now travel in minutes in an automobile once would have taken hours and much effort.

But it is possible, even so, to look back with a certain fondness to a time when the sounds of engines were not almost constant in the sky over us or on the roads and in the fields around us. Our descendants may know such a time again when the petroleum all is burnt. How they will fare then will depend on the neighborly wisdom and the skills that they may manage to revive between now and then.

The country in Andy Catlett's mind has assuredly a past, which exists in relics and scraps of memory more or less subject to proof. It has presumably a future that will verify itself only by becoming the past. Its present is somewhat conjectural, for old Andy Catlett, like everybody else, cannot be conscious of it while he is thinking of the past. And most of us, most of the time, think mostly of the past. Even when we say, "We are living now," we can mean only that we were living a moment ago.

Nevertheless, in this sometimes horrifying, sometimes satisfying, never sufficiently noticed present, between a past mostly forgotten and a future that we deserve to fear but cannot predict, some few things can be recalled. Listen.

In all the country from Port William to the river, only one light shines. It is from a flame on the wick of an oil lamp, turned low, on a little stand table at the bedside of Maximilla Dawe in a large unpainted house facing the river in Glenn's Bottom below the mouth of Bird's Branch. The old lady lies somewhat formally upon the bed, seemingly asleep, in a long-sleeved flannel nightgown, clean but not new, the covers laid neatly over her. Her arms lie at her sides, the veined and gnarled old hands at rest. She is propped, in the appearance at least of comfort, on several pillows, for she is so bent by age and work that she could not lie flat.

She has been old a long time. Though "Maximilla" was inscribed in her father's will, by which he left her the family of "the slave woman known as Cat" and his stopped gold watch, and though it was signed in her own hand at the end of two or three legal documents, she was never well-known to herself by that name. Once upon a time she was "Maxie." For at least as long, to herself as to all the neighborhood of Port William, she has been "Aunt Maxie." To her granddaughter, who was Andy Catlett's grandmother, she had always been "Granny Dawe," as to Andy she still is known.

Andy's grandmother, born Margaret Finley, now Margaret Feltner, sits by the bedside of Granny Dawe in that room in the dim lamplight in the broad darkness of the river valley in the fall of 1907. Margaret Feltner is a pretty woman—or girl, as the older women would still have called her—with a peculiar air of modesty, for she knows she is pretty but would prefer not to be caught knowing it. She is slenderly formed and neatly dressed, even prettily dressed, for her modesty must contend also with her knowledge that her looks are pleasing to her young husband, Mat Feltner.

With her are three other young women, also granddaughters of the old woman on the bed. They are Bernice Gibbs, and Oma and Callie Knole. Kinswomen who know one another well, they sit close together, leaving a sort of aisle between their chairs and the bed.

Their voices are low, and their conversation has become more and more intermittent as the night has gone on. The ancient woman on the bed breathes audibly, but slowly too and tentatively, so that they who listen even as they talk are aware that at any moment there may be one more breath, and then no more.

But she is dying in no haste, this Aunt Maxie, this Granny Dawe, who lived and worked so long before she began to die that she was the only one alive who still knew what she had known. She was born in 1814 in the log house that long ago was replaced by the one in which she now is dying. At the time of her birth, the Port William neighborhood was still in its dream of itself as a frontier, "the West," a new land. The chief artery of trade and transportation for that part of the country then was the river, as it would be for most of the next hundred years. When the time came, she bestowed her slaves and herself upon a man named James John Dawe, owner of a sizeable farm in the river bottom but whose knack was for the store and landing, the port of Port William, known as Dawe's Landing, and this left the care of the land to her. With the strength and the will and the determined good sense that have kept the farm and household in her own hands until now, she ruled and she served through times that were mostly hard.

The Civil War had its official realization in movements of armies and great battles in some places, but in places such as Port William it released and licensed an unofficial violence also terrible, and more lasting. At its outset, Galen Dawe, on his way to join the Confederate army, was shot from his horse and left dead in the road, no farther on his way than Port William, by a neighbor, a Union sympathizer, with whom he had quarreled. And Maxie Dawe, with the help of a slave man named Punkin, loaded the dead boy onto a sled drawn by a team of mules. Looking neither right nor left at those who watched, she brought home the mortal body of her one son, which she washed and dressed herself, and herself read the great psalm over him as he lay in his grave.

The rest of her children were daughters, four of them. Her grief and her bearing in her grief gave her a sort of headship over daughters and husband that they granted without her ever requiring it. When a certain superiority to suffering, a certain indomitability, was required, she simply was the one who had it. Later, when a band of "Rebel" cavalry hung about the neighborhood, she saved her husband, the capable merchant James John, from forcible recruitment or murder, they never knew which, by hiding him three weeks in a corn shock, carrying food and water to him after dark. By her cunning and sometimes her desperate bravery, she brought her surviving family, her slaves, and even a few head of livestock through the official and the unofficial wars, only to bury her husband, dead of a fever, at the end of the official one.

When the slaves were freed in Kentucky, when at last she had heard, she gathered those who had been her own into the kitchen. She told them: "Slavery is no more, and you are free. If you wish to stay and share our fate, you are free to stay, and I will divide with you as I can. If you wish to go, you are free to go."

There were six of them, the remaining family of the woman known as Cat, and they left the next morning, taking, each of them, what could be carried bundled in one hand, all of them invested with an official permission that had made them strange to everything that had gone before. They left, perhaps, from no antipathy to staying, for they arrived in Hargrave and lived there under the name of Dawe—but how could they have known they were free to go if they had not left? Or so, later, Maxie Dawe would explain it, and she would add, "And so would I have, had it been me."

She and her place never recovered from the war. Unable to manage it herself, and needing money, she sold the landing. She hired what help she could afford. She rented her croplands on the shares. After her daughters married and went away, she stayed on alone. To her young granddaughters, and probably to herself as well, the world of the first half of her life was another world.

No more would she be "Maxie" to anybody. Beyond her own descendants and their in-laws, she was "Miss Maxie." Increasingly she would be "Aunt Maxie." She was respected. By those who lacked the sense to respect her she was feared. She held herself strictly answerable to her necessities. She worked in the fields as in the house. Strange and doubtful things were told about her. She was said to have shot off a man's ear, not that she had missed, but so he would live to tell it.

And now her long life, so strongly determined or so determinedly accepted by her, has at last submitted. It is declining gently, perhaps willingly, toward its end. It has been nearly a day and now most of a night since she uttered a word or opened her eyes. A younger person so suddenly moribund as she would have been dead long ago. But she seems only deeply asleep, her aspect that of a dreamer enthralled. The two vertical creases between her brows suggest that she is raptly attentive to her dream.

That she is dying, she herself knows, or knew, for early in the morning of the previous day, not long before she fell into her present sleep, her voice, to those who bent to listen, seeming to float above the absolute stillness of her body, and with the tone perhaps of a small exasperation, she said, "Well, if this is dying, I've seen living that was worse."

The night began cloudy, and the clouds have deepened over the valley and the old house with its one light. The first frosts have come, hushing the crickets and the katydids. The country seems to be waiting. At about dawn a season-changing rain will begin so quietly that at first nobody will notice, and it will fall without letup for two days.

When midnight passes through the room, nobody knows, neither the old woman on the bed nor the young ones who watch beside it. The room would seem poor, so meager and worn are its furnishings, except that its high ceiling and fine proportions give it a dignity that in the circumstances is austere. Though the night is not quite chilly, the sternness of the room and the presence of death in it seemed to call for additional warmth, and the young wives have kindled a little fire. From time to time, one or another has risen to take from the stone hearth a stick of wood and lay it on the coals. From time to time, one or another has risen to smooth the bedclothes that need no smoothing, or to lay a hand upon the old woman's forehead, or to touch lightly the pulse fluttering at her wrists.

After midnight, stillness grows upon them all. The talk has stopped, the fire subsided to a glow, when Bernice Gibbs raises her hand and the others look at her. Bernice is the oldest of the four. The others have granted her an authority which, like their grandmother perhaps, she has accepted merely because she has it and the others don't. She looks at each of them and looks away, listening.

They listen, and they hear not a sound. They hear instead a silence that reaches into every room and into the expectant night beyond. They rise from their chairs, first Bernice, and then, hesitantly, the others. They tiptoe to the bed, two to a side, and lean, listening, at that edge which they and all their children too have now passed beyond. The silence grows palpable around them, a weight.

Now, as Andy Catlett imagines his way into this memory that is his own only because he has imagined it, he is never quite prepared for what he knows to have happened next. Always it comes to him somewhat by surprise, as it came to those who remembered it from the actual room and the actual night.

In silence that seems to them utterly conclusive, the young women lean above the body of the old woman, the mold, or one of them, in which their own flesh was cast, and they listen. And then, just when one of them might have been ready to say, "She's gone," the old woman releases with a sigh her held breath: "Hooo!"

They startle backward from the bedside, each seeing in the wide-opened mouths and eyes of the others her own fright. Oma Knole, who is clumsy, strikes the lamp and it totters until Bernice catches and steadies it.

They stand now and look at one another. The silence has changed. The dying woman's utterance, brief as it was, spoke of a great weariness. It was the sigh of one who has been kept waiting. The sound hangs in the air as if visible, as if the lamp flame had flown upward from the wick. It stays, nothing moves, until some lattice of the air lets pass the single distant cry of an owl— "Hoo!"—as if in answer.

Callie Knole turns away, bends forward, and emits what, so hard suppressed, might have been a sob, but it is a laugh.

And then they all laugh, at themselves, at one another, and they cannot stop. Their sense of the impropriety of their laughter renews their laughter. Looking at each other, flushed and wet-eyed with laughter, makes them laugh. They laugh because they are young and they are alive, and life has revealed itself to them, as it often had and often would, by surprise.

Margaret Feltner, when she had become an old woman, "Granny" in her turn, told Andy of this a long time ago. "Oh, it was awful!" she said, again laughing. "But the harder we tried to stop, the funnier it was."

And Andy, a hundred years later, can hear their laughter. He hears also the silence in which they laugh: the ancient silence filling the dark river valley on that night, uninterrupted in his imagination still by the noise of engines, the great quiet into which they all have gone.

The laughter, which threatened to be endless, finally ends and is gathered into the darkness, into the past. The night resumes its solemn immensity, and again in the silence the old woman audibly breathes. But now her breaths come at longer intervals, until the definitive quiet settles upon her at last. They who have watched all night then fold her hands. Her mouth has fallen open, and Bernice thinks to bind it shut. They draw the counterpane over her face. Day whitens again over the old house and its clutch of old buildings. As they sit on in determined noiselessness, it comes to the young women that for some time they have been hearing the rain.

Wendell Berry was born in 1934. An essayist, novelist, and poet, he has been honored with the T. S. Eliot Award, the Aiken Taylor Award for poetry, and the John Hay Award of the Orion Society. He is a native of the small Kentucky community where he lives and works with his wife, Tanya, and their children and grandchildren.

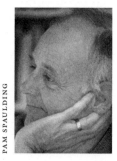

PAM SPAULDING

To say how a story I wrote "came to be written" would be harder and less possible than to write the story. To begin with, there is not a lot that can be said about inspiration, but without it I wouldn't amount to much as a writer. I have been writing mostly in, and in one way or another about, the same place all my life. Some things I learned fifty or sixty or more years ago I unaccountably become able to imagine. I imagine some things I never experienced and was never told, though what I imagine seems to illuminate what I know. I know some local history and geography, which seems to influence the history and geography that I imagine. By now I have learned some, not all, of the art of writing, and that is a help.

Juyanne James

THE ELDERBERRIES

(from *The Louisville Review*)

They seemed the blackest of all our black people. We used to
say of them, *their boat just arrived from Africa,* meaning that
their blackness had not had a chance to be diluted yet. Most of us
looked upon them as being special, and by this, we didn't necessarily mean that they were ill or lacking in any way, but that they had
qualities all people wished for, prayed for, would have done just
about anything, even die, for: they knew how to survive. It came
as no surprise then, when some of the less qualified souls of the
neighborhood saw the Elderberries wading through the bilious
flood waters on that second day after the storm had passed. These
lesser folk thought erroneously that the Elderberry family had lost
its sense of reasoning. This was after the levees had given way and
allowed whatever waters that would to enter our community and
lap and tear away at our houses and even carry some of our people
away. The Elderberries were the first to gather themselves and head
for safer, less callous surroundings.

They moved in a cluster, just as they had lived their lives; but
here, on this day when the flood waters were rising, they waded
out in obvious bunches, as though they would willingly be taken
up by the swirling enemy in these small, tightly drawn entities,
but they would not allow even one of them to be caught alone and
taken up and dragged away by the stale and impertinent water.

We had watched them gather empty plastic water jugs—those five-gallon types, which most of us simply threw away after we'd emptied them of their wholesomely good water, but which this family had begun saving, for some mysterious reason, over the past months. Those of us who had been invited into their home had actually seen their collection of empty jugs, piled up in a corner off from the laundry room, or stored in large garbage bags in the garage. Now, on the day of the storm, they tied these water jugs together, in large bunches like blue balloons. They began to attach these to the children's arms. We then saw even the littlest of the grandbabies' heads and chests bobbing above the water, with their arms stretched out at their sides; and though we could not see that it was so, we knew that their small feet kicked beneath them like tiny propellers and pushed them along this new waterway that had become our street.

The Elderberries had always been strong people, but we didn't think they knew this—it was as though their strength had been an outer coating that protected them in the world, but because they were looking from the inside, they could not see it. At one time, there had been five generations of them living in that house on the corner. The house had taken on the mythological impression of having reared, or stored, equal degrees of greatness and sadness. The great-grandmother, for instance, had been perhaps a hundred years old when she died and had often recounted stories of her people having gone around the parishes and lived among the native tribes of Louisiana. She herself had a whole lot of Indian blood, as we always say, and was dark in a red-skinned way. Somehow, down through the years, the subsequent generations had married darker persons, as though they were trying to wash out all the natives' blood and get back to their original blackness. The grandmother had married a man who had worked the old sugarcane plantations in Terrebonne Parish. He was a tall and thin-skinned man, prone to arguments with even the most amiable persons he met. He was the first real Elderberry, we figured, but their name could have come down in some other way entirely. They never talked openly about their business; those of us who were interested simply had to gather many of these truths on our own time.

The mother was the only child of that union, but she made up for all the meagerness of her father's genes: altogether, she had sixteen children, most of them by the same man, but we couldn't be certain about that. The children all pretty much looked like brothers and sisters, but every once in a while a brighter-skinned berry would appear amongst them, as though the mother had gone off and slept with a white man, or one of those new breed of South Americans that were slowly making their way to the city. For some reason, those men loved themselves some black, black women. When the child turned out to have straight, pretty hair, we deduced that we had been right in assuming the mother let herself get around with a gaggle of men, or at least with whomever she pleased. There had never been a husband, not a legal one. One old Johnny had pretty much achieved common-law status as the husband—he had lived with the family for a good ten or twelve years—when he came up missing one day, as though he had stumbled into one of the canals on his way from drinking late one night. That was actually the story that went around among us. Some said they even saw him take the tumble in—everybody knew that those canals were more mysterious than not: sometimes foolish children swam in the waters, using ropes to pull themselves out, and sometimes grown men fell in, sank to the bottom, and were never seen again. We always thought the water was deeper in some places. In some of the canals the water was dank and insufferable, and during the hard summers, an alligator could be seen gliding along the concrete walls, looking for whatever food it could find.

The children Elderberries, if and when we allowed ourselves to talk openly about them, were simply the joys of our lives. They were mostly daughters, with a few sons thrown in, as if for effect. These girls weren't like other young women. Most all of them followed in their mother's vein and slept around from an early age.

We always suspected that even the mother's boyfriends had sexual access to these girls. Every so often one of them would come up pregnant in a mysterious way, which meant that none of us had seen them on a date or even had a young man over for dinner or tea, or just to sit around and look at each other from across the room. Those of us who attended the same church as these young women would then have to sit through a special prayer service—the pastor of our small church would stand with them at the front of the sanctuary and ask them how they had sinned. They would inevitably say that they had fornicated before the Lord and were now with child and needed the prayers and forgiveness of the church family. We would all sit there and cross our arms and raise our temperatures and put away our smiles and begin to store up unjust feelings about the girls' mother because above all, we blamed her for not taking better care of these beautiful young women. As these girls stood there at the front of the church, we would pray with them, and while we were praying, we would ask God to watch over them a little closer because in our hearts we didn't believe the mother had been doing such a spectacular job.

So, the girls had produced their own little cache of children over the years. It seemed that once the girls had fallen into this habit of birthing babies out of wedlock, they could not break themselves. They could not find an alternative means of conducting their private lives. We knew the girls essentially had self-esteem problems. We had seen them as children, sitting attentively on the knees of the men in their lives, or standing between the men's knees with their elbows planted on their thighs, or sitting on the floor at the men's feet, obviously adoring these men, wanting, as all young girls want, consideration and notice from a male figure. It was never their fault that these less than conscientious, these profligate men, then took advantage of the young girls' need of a father in their lives. So, the years passed, and as we often said, the girls became younger versions of their mother, and the Elderberry clan grew disproportionately to all the families in our neighborhood.

They stored themselves up in that large house on the corner, and we believed they would always be there, like a reminder of nature's nerve and cheeky willingness to disrupt and overtake us.

The mothers of the newest breed of Elderberries flanked their children as they waded through the flood waters. The male members of the family pushed at old tires or oil buckets—some of them had very little life support other than their strong arms beating fiercely against this watery foe. The mothers stretched out their bodies, their backs just above the water, their feet gliding like swimmers at a resting pace, their arms straight, their hands holding on to the leftover water jug bundles, or their children's blow-up toys, or whatever items they could find that would float and carry them to safety. The mother of this great procession that had begun to wind its way down the street—now looking like a worn-out madam from way back—lay on her stomach on a floating mattress, with her mother, who was now old and who spent most of her days in silence looking out her bedroom window, as though she were waiting for some such catastrophic thing as this flood to come along and carry away her body from this very place. Like a parade of floating flowers, the convoy appeared to us, as if in dreams, as we looked upon them—we, still caught in our basements and on our rooftops, peering down on what could have appeared to be the only survivors in this new game of nature's making.

It must have been those brave souls—the mother, her mother, all the children Elderberries, and all their children—that awakened in us our own need to persevere. Many of us gathered ourselves like newly trained soldiers, now ready for whatever battles would come. We began by emptying the water jugs we had brought with us into the attic, although the water had been bought and paid for, and too precious to be emptying into this new water-sogged earth. We took large swigs of it, doused ourselves in it. The water gushed down our chins in clear, cool waves, soaking into our dirtied clothes. After our bellies were filled, we upturned the jugs and allowed the remaining water to go flying like drying sheets flap-

ping in the air. Drops of it landed at our feet, and we noticed the
irony of our situation at once: even now, we regretted letting even
a drop of the water go free.

The bunches of Elderberries floated well before us, but we could
still see them, for there were so many. The moment our bodies
sank into the brownish-gray water, we knew there was no way to
turn back. It was the smell of the water that disturbed us mostly. It
seemed to carry the highest rank of lingering death. Instinctively,
we kept our mouths closed, for sometimes as we floated along,
our bodies dipped below the surface and temporarily buried us in
a type of horror that made us find instant strength. It was in those
brief moments of submersion that we found our greatest ally: our
own wills demanded that we survive. Sometimes, one of us would
begin to drift away from the crowd of floating people, and another
of us would reach out with an arm or a finger or our full open
hand and pull that person back into our watchful alliance.

After we had been in the water for an hour or so, we heard one
of the Elderberries cry out. Immediately, our hearts jumped—they
may as well have leapt from our bodies and bounced across the waters with us, the sound of the heartbeats thrumming new ripples
into the surface. We sent our eyes out before us to do our searching, for we needed to know what had happened. We could see that
the Elderberries were still floating along in their caravan, but that
they had dispersed somewhat. Instead of the circular roundness
of their large assemblage, they now resembled a crescent moon
in shape, as though their middle had been cut out or eaten by a
larger, hungrier being. We worried ourselves over what might have
happened to these leaders of our new existence. Still, we pushed
ourselves along in the foul-smelling water.

It was not long before we came upon the bodies of a man and
a young boy lying prostrate upon the water's surface, their two
heads bumped against the side of an old building along what we
assumed was Franklin Street. The two bodies were stuck together,
as though they had embraced each other and had perished in that
position. The bodies had begun to swell already and we could see

small swarms of flies making homes upon them. Even though the Elderberries had prepared most of us for our sighting of the bodies, there were still screams that rang out and frightened the gentler souls that inhabited our group. It was then that we noticed that these cries had been the only sounds that we had heard since we lowered ourselves into the stank waters, all along our journey to higher ground. None of us had dared speak, had dared open our mouths to whatever fear that now fed us and held us captive. The silence was of the type that we grown men and women had never known in our lives. We listened to our feet flap, or to our arms as they gobbled at the water. We listened to the weight of the other bodies near us as they pushed themselves along and sent small waves to beat against our own backs. We listened to the voices in our heads that every so often sought to defeat us and tell us that we were sure fools for having left the safety of our rooftops and attics. We listened to other people who yelled out to us from their rooftops or their balconies or the tops of their cars and trucks and buses and just about every stationary object that they had found to rest and find shelter. *Come and help us,* they said. *Wait for us,* they said. *When you get downtown, tell them we're here waiting,* they said. None of them asked us where we were going; the whole world seemed to know where our journey should end. We looked ahead again and felt assured, for we saw the Elderberries gliding along in the distance. We ignored all else we had heard and simply listened for whatever our leaders would tell us.

As the Elderberries neared the streets closing in on St. Claude, the water began to give way, and the taller members of the family seemed to be walking instead of swimming along. Their arms were held high and they reminded us of dancers balancing themselves in a routine. The sky was beginning to darken, this time not by the weight of storm clouds but by the natural darkness of evening pulling its shades. We began to push even harder, though our legs and arms had long lost the energy needed to keep moving. As the evening grew dimmer, we began to lose sight of the Elderberries—

their black skin seemingly disappearing, as if it were dissolving and becoming amassed with the night. Our souls wanted to cry out to them then, to say, *Wait for us,* or *Don't leave us out here alone.* Some of us began to panic, as though we thought the entire clan of Elderberries had suddenly given up, had stopped fighting to survive, and had allowed themselves to sink down into the water. Some of us did actually cry out to them, saying, *Where have you gone, Elderberries, where have you gone?* And because no immediate answer came from those who went before us, we collectively began to doubt that we would make it. Those who had been weak and were barely holding on to our group were now let go of and allowed to find their own way. Those who had clung to only the barest of life supports—three or four water jugs—and those now worn and beaten by the water and the weight of a body to carry began to flap around in the water, their arms like paddles coming down flatly upon the surface. Those of us with strength in reserve, though limited, feared for these individuals, but we did not attempt to assuage their weakening hearts; we simply turned our heads and let our feet kick in anger and disappointment. We sent our eyes out, like beacons this time, or high-flying sentries, in search of the remains of the Elderberries because, for all we knew, they had been taken up by the enemy waters and perished like refugees at sea for too long. Some one of us caught a small glimpse of our leaders—perhaps a glimmer of moonlight against one of the water jugs, or a lighter-skinned hand reaching high in the air—and we hoped that all of them were now out of the water, or mostly so, and would soon be walking on solid, dry ground.

There! someone shouted. *There they are, to the left.* And we realized that in minutes we had allowed ourselves to drift down the wrong street, a street that would have taken us away from our leaders and opened our way to new and possibly greater danger. We paddled our way back in the direction of the Elderberry bunches. We grabbed at those who had fallen loose from us as we had floated into disarray. We became strong again in our numbers and in our hearts. Our feet began to kick in vicious circles beneath the water.

Our eyes never left the direction of our leaders, and when they began to walk entirely on dry land, we saw the full lengths of their bodies appear to us in the moonlight. The rich blackness of their arms and legs glistened and made us think of the cave people who must have washed themselves in the lakes and rivers of so many thousands of years before us. These Elderberries, their legs were firm and bare, for their clothes had all but fallen off them or been torn away by the water. And yet, the strength in the pits of their backs was so obvious to us that even when their arms became filled with their children—for there was much hugging and holding on to each other after they left the water—we knew that if they had to turn around and swim another great distance to whatever safety they could find, they could and would do so, without once taking time to doubt it.

Before long, we too came upon the dryer land, and we too could walk upright instead of crawling on our bellies. We joined the Elderberries, and they celebrated with us as they had done among themselves. We hugged the young women and their children, and we latched our arms around the young men. They picked us up and twirled us in the air, as though they had the strength of several men in their shoulders. We laughed until the tears fell down from our eyes and dropped like we had buckets to be filled. Other people, those who had followed us as we had followed the Elderberries, came upon this happy congregation, and joined in our celebrating. The Elderberries then turned and began to make their way toward downtown. Without asking where they were going, the rest of us simply followed closely behind, for we knew that in this darkness, we would have to remain close to see them. Their skin was so black now, even blacker than we had ever seen it.

———————

Juyanne James was born and raised in Sunnyhill, Louisiana, but calls New Orleans home. Her collection of short stories, *The Elderberries and Other Stories*, is in its final revision. The collection draws heavily on the tragic events of Hurricane Katrina and its aftermath. Her short fiction appears in the *Louisville Review* and is forthcoming in the *Southern Review*. She has been nominated for a Pushcart Prize, and she is the fiction editor of *94 Creations*. She teaches creative writing and African American literature at Our Lady of Holy Cross College in New Orleans.

VENESTA JAMES

*T*he Elderberries" grew from the smaller concept of parabolic writing into a greater need to retell a people's story. Some years before, I had written a short piece of fiction where the heroine embodied the characteristics of her namesake, the scarlet genus Salvia. I received such good feedback that I vowed to write another. Later, as I read Toni Morrison's The Bluest Eye (yet again), I noticed her figurative use of the elderberry, which, as Morrison says, uses its "skin and flesh" to protect "its own seed." Although I noted in the margin that this would be a great title for that next allegorical story, as well as a perfect way to pay homage to Morrison, I had no idea what the story would be. That came later, after Hurricane Katrina, the failed levee system, and the flooded city of New Orleans.

I was thankful to escape the city but spent the next months cramped in a broken-down house about an hour north of New Orleans. We were able to listen to radio accounts of what was happening in the city, but we had no electricity and therefore no visuals. Perhaps this is why when, many weeks later, I saw news reports of those stranded individuals being plucked from rooftops and attics and bridges, the images resonated with me, and I could not forget them. Mostly the media portrayed these New Orleanians (the largest percentage of which were African American) as helpless and desperate people who needed someone, anyone, to save them. I knew in my heart that there were resilient people out there who were not waiting for help but were finding ways to save themselves. The New Orleanians I knew were more like Morrison's elder tree, with its rich dark berries, protecting "its own." This *is when the story began to form for me, for I wanted to reset those flawed images.*

Months later, when I was back in New Orleans and writing fiction again, the story poured out of me in one smooth draft. By that time, I had come to think of the Elderberry clan as an almost mythological representation of those resolute families of New Orleans—those that have been here for so many generations, through so many of life's storms, having waded through the worst of it over the years. In the end, "The Elderberries" is simply a story about the survival of the spirit of New Orleans.

APPENDIX

A list of the magazines currently consulted for *New Stories from the South: The Year's Best, 2009,* with addresses, subscription rates, and editors.

Agni
236 Bay State Road
Boston, MA 02215
Biannually, $20
Sven Birkerts

American Short Fiction
P.O. Box 301209
Austin, TX 78703
Quarterly, $30
Stacey Swann

The Antioch Review
P.O. Box 148
Yellow Springs, OH 45387-0148
Quarterly, $40
Robert S. Fogarty

Apalachee Review
P.O. Box 10469
Tallahassee, FL 32302
Semiannually, $15
Michael Trammell

Appalachian Heritage
CPO 2166
Berea, KY 40404
Quarterly, $20
George Brosi

Appalachian Journal
Belk Library
Appalachian State University
Boone, NC 28608
Quarterly, $24
Sandra L. Ballard

Arkansas Review
P.O. Box 1890
Arkansas State University
State University, AR 72467
Triannually, $20
Tom Williams

Arts & Letters
Campus Box 89
Georgia College & State University
Milledgeville, GA 31061-0490
Semiannually, $15
Martin Lammon

The Atlantic Monthly
600 New Hampshire Avenue NW
Washington, DC 20037
Monthly, $39.95
James Bennet

Bayou
Department of English
University of New Orleans
2000 Lakeshore Drive
New Orleans, LA 70148
Semiannually, $15
Joanna Leake

Bellevue Literary Review
Department of Medicine
New York University School of
  Medicine
550 1st Avenue, OBV-612
New York, NY 10016
Semiannually, $15
Ronna Weinberg

Black Warrior Review
University of Alabama
P.O. Box 862936
Tuscaloosa, AL 35486
Semiannually, $16
Lucas Southworth

Bomb
New Art Publications
80 Hansen Place #703
Brooklyn, NY 11217
Pentannually, $25
Mónica de la Torre

Boulevard
6614 Clayton Road, PMB 325
Richmond Heights, MO 63117
Triannually, $20
Richard Burgin

Callaloo
Department of English
Texas A&M University
4121 TAMU
College Station, TX 77843-4212
Quarterly, $48
Charles H. Rowell

The Carolina Quarterly
Greenlaw Hall CB# 3520
University of North Carolina
Chapel Hill, NC 27599-3520
Triannually, $18

The Chattahoochee Review
Georgia Perimeter College
2101 Womack Road
Dunwoody, GA 30338-4497
Quarterly, $20
Marc Fitten

Cimarron Review
205 Morrill Hall
Oklahoma State University
Stillwater, OK 74078-4069
Quarterly, $24
E. P. Walkiewicz

The Cincinnati Review
Department of English and
  Comparative Literature
McMicken Hall
Room 369
University of Cincinnati
P.O. Box 210069
Cincinnati, OH 45221-0069
Semiannually, $15
Brock Clarke

Colorado Review
Department of English
Colorado State University
9105 Campus Delivery
Fort Collins, CO 80523
Triannually, $24
Stephanie G'Schwind

Commentary
165 East 56th Street
New York, NY 10022
Monthly, $5.95; yearly, $45
Neal Kozodoy

Conjunctions
21 East 10th Street
New York, NY 10003
Semiannually, $18
Bradford Morrow

Crazyhorse
Department of English
College of Charleston
66 George Street
Charleston, SC 29424
Semiannually, $16
Anthony Varallo

Crossing Borders
University of Tulsa
Tulsa, OK
Semiannually
Geraldine McLoud

Denver Quarterly
University of Denver
Denver, CO 80208
Quarterly, $20
Bin Ramke

Ecotone
Department of Creative Writing
UNC Wilmington
601 South College Road
Wilmington, NC 28403-3297
Semiannually, $16.95
Nick Roberts

Epoch
251 Goldwin Smith Hall
Cornell University
Ithaca, NY 14853-3201
Triannually, $11
Michael Koch

Fiction
c/o Department of English
City College of New York
Convent Avenue at 138th Street
New York, NY 10031
Semiannually
Mark Jay Mirsky

Five Points
Georgia State University
P.O. Box 3999
Atlanta, GA 30302-3999
Triannually, $21
Megan Sexton

Fugue
English Department
University of Idaho
200 Brink Hall
Moscow, ID 83844-1102
Biannually, $14
Andrew Millar and Jeff Lepper

Gargoyle
3819 North 13th Street
Arlington, VA 22201
Biannually, $30
Lucinda Ebersole and Richard
   Peabody

The Georgia Review
Gilbert Hall
University of Georgia
Athens, GA 30602-9009
Quarterly, $30
Stephen Corey

The Gettysburg Review
Gettysburg College
300 N. Washington Street
Gettysburg, PA 17325-1491
Quarterly, $24
Peter Stitt

Glimmer Train Stories
1211 NW Glisan Street, Suite 207
Portland, OR 97209-3054
Quarterly, $36
Susan Burmeister-Brown
   and Linda B. Swanson-Davies

The Greensboro Review
MFA Writing Program
3302 Hall for Humanities and
    Research Administration
UNC Greensboro
Greensboro, NC 27402-6170
Semiannually, $10
Jim Clark

Grist
English Department
University of Tennessee
301 McClung Tower
Knoxville, TN 37996-0430
Annually, $11.95
Laura Koons

Gulf Coast
Department of English
University of Houston
Houston, TX 77204-3013
Semiannually, $16
Fiction Editor

Harper's Magazine
666 Broadway, 11th Floor
New York, NY 10012
Monthly, $21
Ben Metcalf

Harpur Palate
English Department
Binghamton University
P.O. Box 6000
Binghamton, NY 13902-6000
Semiannually, $16
Fiction Editor

The Hudson Review
684 Park Avenue
New York, NY 10065
Quarterly, $36
Paula Deitz

The Idaho Review
Boise State University
Department of English
1910 University Drive
Boise, ID 83725
Annually, $10
Mitch Wieland

Image
3307 Third Avenue, W.
Seattle, WA 98119
Quarterly, $39.95
Gregory Wolfe

In Character
John Templeton Foundation
Attn: In Character
300 Conshohocken State Road,
    Suite 500
West Conshohocken, PA 19428
Triannually, $18
Charlotte Hays

Indiana Review
Ballantine Hall 465
Indiana University
1020 E. Kirkwood Drive
Bloomington, IN 47405-7103
Semiannually, $17
Danny Thanh Nguyen

The Iowa Review
308 EPB
University of Iowa
Iowa City, IA 52242-1408
Triannually, $25
David Hamilton

Iron Horse Literary Review
Department of English
Texas Tech University
Mail Stop 43091
Lubbock, TX 79409-3091
Semiannually, $15
Stephen Graham Jones

The Jabberwock Review
Department of English
Mississippi State University
Drawer E
Mississippi State, MS 39762
Semiannually, $20
David Johnson

The Journal
Ohio State University
Department of English
164 W. 17th Avenue
Columbus, OH 43210
Semiannually, $12
Kathy Fagan and Michelle Herman

The Kenyon Review
www.kenyonreview.org
Quarterly, $30
David H. Lynn

The Literary Review
Fairleigh Dickinson University
285 Madison Avenue
Madison, NJ 07940
Quarterly, $18
René Steinke

Long Story
18 Eaton Street
Lawrence, MA 01843
Annually, $7
R. P. Burnham

Louisiana Literature
SLU-10792
Southeastern Louisiana University
Hammond, LA 70402
Semiannually, $12
Jack Bedell

The Louisville Review
Spalding University
851 South 4th Street
Louisville, KY 40203
Semiannually, $14
Sena Jeter Naslund

McSweeney's
849 Valencia Street
San Francisco, CA 94110
Quarterly, $55
Dave Eggers

Meridian
University of Virginia
P.O. Box 400145
Charlottesville, VA 22904-4145
Semiannually, $12
Matt Supko

Mid-American Review
Department of English
Bowling Green State University
Bowling Green, OH 43403
Semiannually, $15
Karen Craigo and Michael
    Czyzniejewski

Mississippi Review
University of Southern Mississippi
Box 5144
Hattiesburg, MS 39406
Semiannually, $15
Frederick Barthelme

The Missouri Review
357 McReynolds Hall
University of Missouri
Columbia, MO 65211
Quarterly, $24
Speer Morgan

Narrative
narrativemagazine.com
Triannually, $57
Carol Edgarian and Tom Jenks

Natural Bridge
Department of English
University of Missouri-St. Louis
One University Boulevard
St. Louis, MO 63121
Semiannually, $15
Steven Schreiner

New England Review
Middlebury College
Middlebury, VT 05753
Quarterly, $25
Stephen Donadio

New Letters
University of Missouri at Kansas
  City
5101 Rockhill Road
Kansas City, MO 64110
Quarterly, $22
Robert Stewart

New Orleans Review
P.O. Box 195
Loyola University
New Orleans, LA 70118
Semiannually, $14
Christopher Chambers

Nimrod
University of Tulsa
600 South College
Tulsa, OK 74104
Semiannually, $17.50
Francine Ringold

Ninth Letter
Department of English
University of Illinois
608 South Wright Street
Urbana, IL 61801
Biannually, $21.95
Jodee Stanley

North Carolina Literary Review
English Department
2201 Bate Building
East Carolina University
Greenville, NC 27858-4353
Annually, $10
Biannually, $20
Margaret Bauer

Northwest Review
1286 University of Oregon
Eugene, OR 97403
Triannually, $22
John Witte

One Story
www.one-story.com
Monthly, $21
Hannah Tinti

Ontario Review
9 Honey Brook Drive
Princeton, NJ 08540
Semiannually, $16
Raymond J. Smith

Open City
270 Lafayette Street
Suite 1412
New York, NY 10012
Triannually, $30
Thomas Beller, Joanna Yas

The Oxford American
201 Donaghey Avenue, Main 107
Conway, AR 72035
Quarterly, $24.95
Marc Smirnoff

Peeks & Valleys
editor@peeksandvalleys.com
Quarterly, $15.95
Mary Anne DeYoung

Pembroke Magazine
UNC-P, Box 1510
Pembroke, NC 28372-1510
Annually, $10
Shelby Stephenson

The Pinch
Department of English
University of Memphis
Memphis, TN 38152-6176
Semiannually, $18
Corey Clairday

Pleiades
Department of English and
  Philosophy
Central Missouri State University
Warrensburg, MO 64093
Semiannually, $12
G. B. Crump and Matthew Eck

Ploughshares
Emerson College
120 Boylston Street
Boston, MA 02116-4624
Triannually, $24
Margot Livesey

poemmemoirstory
University of Alabama at
  Birmingham
Department of English
HB 217
1530 3rd Avenue, S.
Birmingham, AL 35294-1260
Annually, $7
Linda Frost

Post Road Magazine
www.postroadmag.com
Semiannually, $18
Rebecca Boyd

Potomac Review
Montgomery College
51 Mannakee Street
Rockville, MD 20850
Biannually, $20
Julie Wakeman-Linn

Prairie Schooner
201 Andrews Hall
University of Nebraska
Lincoln, NE 68588-0334
Quarterly, $28
Hilda Raz

Quarterly West
University of Utah
255 S. Central Campus Drive
Department of English
LNCO 3500
Salt Lake City, UT 84112-0494
Semiannually, $14
Pam J. Balluck

The Rambler
P.O. Box 5070
Chapel Hill, NC 27515
Semiannually, $24
Dave Korzon

River Styx
3547 Olive Street, Suite 107
St. Louis, MO 63103
Triannually, $20
Richard Newman

Salamander
Suffolk University
English Department
41 Temple Street
Boston, MA 02114
2 years, 4 issues, $23
Jennifer Barber

Salt Hill
English Department
Syracuse University
Syracuse, NY 13244
Semiannually, $20
Daniel Torday and Tara Warman

Santa Monica Review
Santa Monica College
1900 Pico Boulevard
Santa Monica, CA 90405
Semiannually, $12
Andrew Tonkovich

The Sewanee Review
735 University Avenue
Sewanee, TN 37383-1000
Quarterly, $25
George Core

Shenandoah
Washington and Lee University
Mattingly House
Lexington, VA 24450
Triannually, $25
R. T. Smith

Short Story
P.O. Box 50567
Columbia, SC 29250
Biannually, $12
Caroline Lord

The South Carolina Review
Center for Electronic and Digital
   Publishing
Clemson University
Strode Tower, Box 340522
Clemson, SC 29634
Semiannually, $28
Wayne Chapman

South Dakota Review
Department of English
414 Clark Street
University of South Dakota
Vermillion, SD 57069
Quarterly, $30
John R. Milton

Southern Humanities Review
9088 Haley Center
Auburn University
Auburn, AL 36849
Quarterly, $15
Dan R. Latimer and Virginia M.
   Kouidis

The Southern Review
Old President's House
Louisiana State University
Baton Rouge, LA 70803
Quarterly, $25
Jeanne M. Leiby

Southwest Review
307 Fondren Library West
Box 750374
Southern Methodist University
Dallas, TX 75275
Quarterly, $24
Willard Spiegelman

Sou'wester
Department of English
Southern Illinois University at
   Edwardsville
Edwardsville, IL 62026-1438
Semiannually, $15
Allison Funk and Valerie Vogrin

Subtropics
Department of English
University of Florida
P.O. Box 112075
Gainesville, FL 32611
Triannually, $26
David Leavitt

Tampa Review
University of Tampa
401 W. Kennedy Boulevard
Tampa, FL 33606-1490
Biannually, $22
Richard Mathews

The Threepenny Review
P.O. Box 9131
Berkeley, CA 94709
Quarterly, $25
Wendy Lesser

Timber Creek Review
P.O. Box 16542
Greensboro, NC 27416
Quarterly, $17
John M. Freiermuth

Tin House
P.O. Box 10500
Portland, OR 97296-0500
Quarterly, $29.90
Rob Spillman

TriQuarterly
Northwestern University
629 Noyes Street
Evanston, IL 60208
Triannually, $24
Susan Firestone Hahn

The Virginia Quarterly Review
One West Range
P.O. Box 400223
Charlottesville, VA 22904-4223
Quarterly, $32
Ted Genoways

Wasatch Journal
Wasatch Journal Media
357 South 200 East
Salt Lake City, UT 84111-2866
Quarterly, $20
William A. Kerig

West Branch
Bucknell Hall
Bucknell University
Lewisburg, PA 17837
Semiannually, $10
Paula Closson Buck

Yemassee
Department of English
University of South Carolina
Columbia, SC 29208
Semiannually, $15
Darien Cavanaugh

Zoetrope: All-Story
The Sentinel Building
916 Kearny Street
San Francisco, CA 94133
Quarterly, $24
Michael Ray

Zone 3
P.O. Box 4565
Austin Peay State University
Clarksville, TN 37044
Biannually, $10
Blas Falconer, Barry Kitterman,
    and Amy Wright

PREVIOUS VOLUMES

Copies of previous volumes of *New Stories from the South* can be ordered through your local bookstore or by calling the Sales Department at Algonquin Books of Chapel Hill. Multiple copies for classroom adoptions are available at a special discount. For information, please call 919-967-0108.

New Stories from the South: The Year's Best, 1986

Max Apple, BRIDGING

Madison Smartt Bell, TRIPTYCH 2

Mary Ward Brown, TONGUES OF FLAME

Suzanne Brown, COMMUNION

James Lee Burke, THE CONVICT

Ron Carlson, AIR

Doug Crowell, SAYS VELMA

Leon V. Driskell, MARTHA JEAN

Elizabeth Harris, THE WORLD RECORD HOLDER

Mary Hood, SOMETHING GOOD FOR GINNIE

David Huddle, SUMMER OF THE MAGIC SHOW

Gloria Norris, HOLDING ON

Kurt Rheinheimer, UMPIRE

W. A. Smith, DELIVERY

Wallace Whatley, SOMETHING TO LOSE

Luke Whisnant, WALLWORK

Sylvia Wilkinson, CHICKEN SIMON

New Stories from the South: The Year's Best, 1987

James Gordon Bennett, DEPENDENTS

Robert Boswell, EDWARD AND JILL

Rosanne Caggeshall, PETER THE ROCK

John William Corrington, HEROIC MEASURES/VITAL SIGNS

Vicki Covington, MAGNOLIA

Andre Dubus, DRESSED LIKE SUMMER LEAVES

Mary Hood, AFTER MOORE

Trudy Lewis, VINCRISTINE

Lewis Nordan, SUGAR, THE EUNUCHS, AND BIG G. B.

Peggy Payne, THE PURE IN HEART

Bob Shacochis, WHERE PELHAM FELL

Lee Smith, LIFE ON THE MOON

Marly Swick, HEART

Robert Love Taylor, LADY OF SPAIN

Luke Whisnant, ACROSS FROM THE MOTOHEADS

New Stories from the South: The Year's Best, 1988

Ellen Akins, GEORGE BAILEY FISHING

Rick Bass, THE WATCH

Richard Bausch, THE MAN WHO KNEW BELLE STAR

Larry Brown, FACING THE MUSIC

Pam Durban, BELONGING

John Rolfe Gardiner, GAME FARM

Jim Hall, GAS

Charlotte Holmes, METROPOLITAN

Nanci Kincaid, LIKE THE OLD WOLF IN ALL THOSE WOLF STORIES

Barbara Kingsolver, ROSE-JOHNNY

Trudy Lewis, HALF MEASURES

Jill McCorkle, FIRST UNION BLUES

Mark Richard, HAPPINESS OF THE GARDEN VARIETY

Sunny Rogers, THE CRUMB

Annette Sanford, LIMITED ACCESS

Eve Shelnutt, VOICE

New Stories from the South: The Year's Best, 1989

Rick Bass, WILD HORSES

Madison Smartt Bell, CUSTOMS OF THE COUNTRY

James Gordon Bennett, PACIFIC THEATER

Larry Brown, SAMARITANS

Mary Ward Brown, IT WASN'T ALL DANCING

Kelly Cherry, WHERE SHE WAS

David Huddle, PLAYING

Sandy Huss, COUPON FOR BLOOD

Frank Manley, THE RAIN OF TERROR

Bobbie Ann Mason, WISH

Lewis Nordan, A HANK OF HAIR, A PIECE OF BONE

Kurt Rheinheimer, HOMES

Mark Richard, STRAYS

Annette Sanford, SIX WHITE HORSES

Paula Sharp, HOT SPRINGS

New Stories from the South: The Year's Best, 1990

Tom Bailey, CROW MAN

Rick Bass, THE HISTORY OF RODNEY

Richard Bausch, LETTER TO THE LADY OF THE HOUSE

Larry Brown, SLEEP

Moira Crone, JUST OUTSIDE THE B.T.

Clyde Edgerton, CHANGING NAMES

Greg Johnson, THE BOARDER

Nanci Kincaid, SPITTIN' IMAGE OF A BAPTIST BOY

Reginald McKnight, THE KIND OF LIGHT THAT SHINES ON TEXAS

Lewis Nordan, THE CELLAR OF RUNT CONROY

Lance Olsen, FAMILY

Mark Richard, FEAST OF THE EARTH, RANSOM OF THE CLAY

Ron Robinson, WHERE WE LAND

Bob Shacochis, LES FEMMES CREOLES

NEW STORIES FROM THE SOUTH: THE YEAR'S BEST, 1993

NEW STORIES FROM THE SOUTH: THE YEAR'S BEST, 1994

Pamela Erbe, SWEET TOOTH

Barry Hannah, NICODEMUS BLUFF

Nanci Kincaid, PRETENDING THE BED WAS A RAFT

Nancy Krusoe, LANDSCAPE AND DREAM

Robert Morgan, DARK CORNER

Reynolds Price, DEEDS OF LIGHT

Leon Rooke, THE HEART MUST FROM ITS BREAKING

John Sayles, PEELING

George Singleton, OUTLAW HEAD & TAIL

Melanie Sumner, MY OTHER LIFE

Robert Love Taylor, MY MOTHER'S SHOES

NEW STORIES FROM THE SOUTH: THE YEAR'S BEST, 1995

R. Sebastian Bennett, RIDING WITH THE DOCTOR

Wendy Brenner, I AM THE BEAR

James Lee Burke, WATER PEOPLE

Robert Olen Butler, BOY BORN WITH TATTOO OF ELVIS

Ken Craven, PAYING ATTENTION

Tim Gautreaux, THE BUG MAN

Ellen Gilchrist, THE STUCCO HOUSE

Scott Gould, BASES

Barry Hannah, DRUMMER DOWN

MMM Hayes, FIXING LU

Hillary Hebert, LADIES OF THE MARBLE HEARTH

Jesse Lee Kercheval, GRAVITY

Caroline A. Langston, IN THE DISTANCE

Lynn Marie, TEAMS

Susan Perabo, GRAVITY

Dale Ray Phillips, EVERYTHING QUIET LIKE CHURCH

Elizabeth Spencer, THE RUNAWAYS

New Stories from the South: The Year's Best, 1996

New Stories from the South: The Year's Best, 1997

Dale Ray Phillips, CORPORAL LOVE
Patricia Elam Ruff, THE TAXI RIDE
Lee Smith, NATIVE DAUGHTER
Judy Troy, RAMONE
Marc Vassallo, AFTER THE OPERA
Brad Vice, MOJO FARMER

NEW STORIES FROM THE SOUTH: THE YEAR'S BEST, 1998

PREFACE *by Padgett Powell*
Frederick Barthelme, THE LESSON
Wendy Brenner, NIPPLE
Stephen Dixon, THE POET
Tony Earley, BRIDGE
Scott Ely, TALK RADIO
Tim Gautreaux, SORRY BLOOD
Michael Gills, WHERE WORDS GO
John Holman, RITA'S MYSTERY
Stephen Marion, NAKED AS TANYA
Jennifer Moses, GIRLS LIKE YOU
Padgett Powell, ALIENS OF AFFECTION
Sara Powers, THE BAKER'S WIFE
Mark Richard, MEMORIAL DAY
Nancy Richard, THE ORDER OF THINGS
Josh Russell, YELLOW JACK
Annette Sanford, IN THE LITTLE HUNKY RIVER
Enid Shomer, THE OTHER MOTHER
George Singleton, THESE PEOPLE ARE US
Molly Best Tinsley, THE ONLY WAY TO RIDE

NEW STORIES FROM THE SOUTH: THE YEAR'S BEST, 1999

PREFACE *by Tony Earley*
Andrew Alexander, LITTLE BITTY PRETTY ONE
Richard Bausch, MISSY

New Stories from the South: The Year's Best, 2000

John Holman, WAVE

Romulus Linney, THE WIDOW

Thomas McNeely, SHEEP

Christopher Miner, RHONDA AND HER CHILDREN

Chris Offutt, THE BEST FRIEND

Margo Rabb, HOW TO TELL A STORY

Karen Sagstetter, THE THING WITH WILLIE

Mary Helen Stefaniak, A NOTE TO BIOGRAPHERS REGARDING FAMOUS
AUTHOR FLANNERY O'CONNOR

Melanie Sumner, GOOD-HEARTED WOMAN

NEW STORIES FROM THE SOUTH: THE YEAR'S BEST, 2001

PREFACE *by Lee Smith*

John Barth, THE REST OF YOUR LIFE

Madison Smartt Bell, TWO LIVES

Marshall Boswell, IN BETWEEN THINGS

Carrie Brown, FATHER JUDGE RUN

Stephen Coyne, HUNTING COUNTRY

Moira Crone, WHERE WHAT GETS INTO PEOPLE COMES FROM

William Gay, THE PAPERHANGER

Jim Grimsley, JESUS IS SENDING YOU THIS MESSAGE

Ingrid Hill, JOLIE-GRAY

Christie Hodgen, THE HERO OF LONELINESS

Nicola Mason, THE WHIMSIED WORLD

Edith Pearlman, SKIN DEEP

Kurt Rheinheimer, SHOES

Jane R. Shippen, I AM NOT LIKE NUÑEZ

George Singleton, PUBLIC RELATIONS

Robert Love Taylor, PINK MIRACLE IN EAST TENNESSEE

James Ellis Thomas, THE SATURDAY MORNING CAR WASH CLUB

Elizabeth Tippens, MAKE A WISH

Linda Wendling, INAPPROPRIATE BABIES

New Stories from the South: The Year's Best, 2002

PREFACE *by Larry Brown*

Dwight Allen, END OF THE STEAM AGE

Russell Banks, THE OUTER BANKS

Brad Barkley, BENEATH THE DEEP, SLOW MOTION

Doris Betts, ABOVEGROUND

William Gay, CHARTING THE TERRITORIES OF THE RED

Aaron Gwyn, OF FALLING

Ingrid Hill, THE MORE THEY STAY THE SAME

David Koon, THE BONE DIVERS

Andrea Lee, ANTHROPOLOGY

Romulus Linney, TENNESSEE

Corey Mesler, THE GROWTH AND DEATH OF BUDDY GARDNER

Lucia Nevai, FAITH HEALER

Julie Orringer, PILGRIMS

Dulane Upshaw Ponder, THE RAT SPOON

Bill Roorbach, BIG BEND

George Singleton, SHOW-AND-TELL

Kate Small, MAXIMUM SUNLIGHT

R. T. Smith, I HAVE LOST MY RIGHT

Max Steele, THE UNRIPE HEART

New Stories from the South: The Year's Best, 2003

PREFACE *by Roy Blount Jr.*

Dorothy Allison, COMPASSION

Steve Almond, THE SOUL MOLECULE

Brock Clarke, FOR THOSE OF US WHO NEED SUCH THINGS

Lucy Corin, RICH PEOPLE

John Dufresne, JOHNNY TOO BAD

Donald Hays, DYING LIGHT

Ingrid Hill, THE BALLAD OF RAPPY VALCOUR

Bret Anthony Johnston, CORPUS

Michael Knight, ELLEN'S BOOK

New Stories from the South: The Year's Best, 2004

NEW STORIES FROM THE SOUTH: THE YEAR'S BEST, 2007

Guest edited by Edward P. Jones

New Stories from the South: The Year's Best, 2008

Guest edited by ZZ Packer

Karen E. Bender, CANDIDATE

Pinckney Benedict, BRIDGE OF SIGHS

Kevin Brockmeier, ANDREA IS CHANGING HER NAME

Stephanie Dickinson, LUCKY 7 & DALLOWAY

Robert Drummond, THE UNNECESSARY MAN

Clyde Edgerton, THE GREAT SPECKLED BIRD

Amina Gautier, THE EASE OF LIVING

Bret Anthony Johnston, REPUBLICAN

Holly Goddard Jones, THEORY OF REALTY

Mary Miller, LEAK

Kevin Moffett, FIRST MARRIAGE

Jennifer Moses, CHILD OF GOD

David James Poissant, LIZARD MAN

Ron Rash, BACK OF BEYOND

Charlie Smith, ALBEMARLE

R.T. Smith, WRETCH LIKE ME

Stephanie Soileau, SO THIS IS PERMANENCE

Merritt Tierce, SUCK IT

Jim Tomlinson, FIRST HUSBAND, FIRST WIFE

Daniel Wallace, THE GIRLS